# Been Had Paper

## The Rise of Tha Fam

### RAFAEL SANCHEZ

Been Had Paper

The Rise of Tha Fam

©2021 Rafael Sanchez

print ISBN: 978-1-09839-428-8

ebook ISBN: 978-1-09839-429-5

# CONTENTS

# CHAPTER 1

# BEAST MODE, YOUNG N THUGGIN IN DA 941

As soon as my alarm clock rang! I got up and out of bed so I could take my morning piss, just as I was brushing my teeth, I saw a huge hickey on my neck that was not there the night before. I heard movement in the kitchen and was met by Tee-Baby, a five foot, three inches tall, light skinned woman with freckles that decorated her soft and fat cheeks....braids that stopped at the top of her ass.

She was dressed in a yellow negligee that barely covered her thick thighs. Her breasts were about a strong B cup, her stomach flat and behind her was an ass so fat that it made you just want to lay on it like a pillow. She was built like a true Southern Belle and no man could deny that.

"Oyah, you are up early! I was just about to make you breakfast and bring it to you in bed."

"Nah ma, you good, I gots to make a few runs, but come here and give me a kiss, and please explain why you did this to my neck, You know Roxanna is going to be pissed if she sees me like this".

1

"Fuck that Chico hoe, I'm all the woman you need."

"Tee-Baby you a real tripp, you know I won't leave Roxanna, we been through a-lot together. But come bathe me before I hit the block."

After my shower, I got dressed in a Jordan shirt with the matching shorts and socks. I put on my Retro Bred 13's and my 400 Gram Cuban Link Chain and 250Gram Bracelet. I grabbed my four Churp phones and my LV backpack with my dope and rubber bands.

"Tee-Baby, hit my line tonight and I'll tell you when to pull up."

"So you want to see me again tonight?"

"Yes Mami. I do, shit you know I can't get enough of that pussy, plus I can't go around my bih with this shit on my neck, so all this ass is mine until this fades off my neck"

I left the house with $80 for food, gas and gars, but $7,500(seventy five hundred) worth of heroin and a zip of gas just to smoke on....

On my way to the lean man, I had to make a few plays at Burger King on 57th street in Oneco. While waiting, the car starts to overheat, so I shut the ignition and gave this 88 Box Chevy a chance to cool down before I jumped back on the road to chase a check....Once I got the car cooled down and caught up to all my buddies,I left so I could get a 6oz drank from the lean man, at his trap, Nelly was there with a friend getting ready to pour up. I was in and out because I had seven more buddies waiting on me at my trap across the bridge on 60th. Bradenton, Florida is a gold mine in the drug trade. The Heroin Epidemic is at an All Time High....

On my way back to my car, I noticed Nelly was standing by my passenger door.

"What's up Lil Mama, what you got running?"

"I'm sliding with you Oyah! That's if it's cool with you."

"Shit I have to bend a few corners but if you sliding, you going to eat this dick, I don't know what you think this is, you won't be smoking none of my Gas for free, so what it's going to be?"

"Bae you ain't saying shit, pull that dick out and let me show you why you should choose me to wife up."

"Look Nelly, you already know this dick belongs to Roxanna, so let that shit go before you get canceled."

"Damn nigga, what that Bih got that I don't?"

"She doesn't question me and speaks when spoken to, that's something you need to learn Lil Mama because you bad as shit and I would hate to have to cancel you..."

On my way to the trap, Nelly ate this dick like it was her last meal, she breathed on the head then sucked me into her mouth and licked the head as if it was a Blow Pop, then she swallowed me whole and started sucking loudly, moaning all around him. I swerved a lil because she had my eyes rolling in the back of my head. I was thankful that my Box had 5% tint on it. The heat from her mouth had my toes curling, I reached over her shoulders and cupped her big soft booty. As I was squeezing it, I pulled up her Burberry skirt to expose her bare ass and pussy. I slid 2 fingers into her wet and warm pussy and fingered her, the fast and faster I went, the faster she sucked me. I closed my eyes at the red light because it was feeling so good. When I opened my eyes, her tits were bouncing in one another. That sight caused me to mash the gas and pull off from the light burning rubber as I turned up my flip out touchscreen radio listening to "Plies -Ride wit-cha Fire" I started humping into her mouth hitting the back of her throat. When she pulled me out of her mouth, she licked the head and rubbed it all over her face before deep throating it over and over again. That was all it took before I felt my seeds rising in my sack. My stomach tightened and that's when I let her have it. I was letting it fly into her mouth. Mmmm. Mmmm, Mmmm. was all she said as she milked me with her eyes closed and a smile on her face. She got done right on time as I was pulling up in the driveway of the Trap.

As we made our way to the house door, you could smell a mixture of weed and cooked coke in the air. I knew Moon, Big-B or Nando had to be here but there were no cars in the driveway. Once inside, I saw Big-B and two other young-in's from the hood playing Call of Duty on the Playstation3, smoking Fat Gars. I dapped them up and told Nelly to go into my room and wait on me while I handled something real fast. I gave her my zip so she can roll up. Then I went to the kitchen so I can sit all the dope on the counter next to the bucket of acid just in case Bradenton Police hit, we can get rid of all the dope.

Moon and Nando walk in the back door of the trap. They were feeding our pits and getting "King Tut" condition for his next fight. I hustle on all levels, there is no such thing as enough money.

"Whats good bruh? Did you move all that food yet? I'm about to re-up, Nando already gave me the loot he owed me and Piloto on his way. I'm trying to go all in, I need 50 Bands put up by the end of the month."

"I got you Big Bruh, Nando already gave me the rundown on everything. You are trying to lock the 941down. First it was just 60th, then Oneco, and now you want the entire area code."

"Moon, if we are going to be out here taking Penitentiary chances, we need to do it big and make it worth it...I'm not trying to be one of them niggas doing a Bid all miserable and broke. If I ever go to prison, Ima have plenty of stories to tell....Plus I'm Fed Bound, I ain't ever trying to do state time. So with that being said, is my niggas with me or not? I'm tired of eating from the dollar menu,I want to eat steak and shrimp."

"Oyah, we riden with you my nigga."

"Bet!" So Nando, set up your crew and Moon you do the same. I'm going to give y'all a Trap and some phones to work off and I want y'all to set them up from Palmetto, Bradenton to Sarasota. I have a few contacts out in Sota to get y'all set up out there.

 Hold up, let me take this call, its Piloto"

"Yoooooo! What's good, talk to me."

"Oyah, my driver will be there soon. I gave him a nice package for you, just give him what you got on hand and pay me on the next re-up."

"Okay bet, I got you and good looking out, you won't ever regret your choice of helping me. My loyalty to you is in Blood."

"Okay Oyah, I'll see you next week around the same time."

"Bet! Yo, we about to turn shit up in these streets, hit the Big homie, "City" up and tell him we need some artillery just in case we have to make an example out some of these niggas."

"Yo Oyah, who that with you in the room?"

"Bruh, you real nosey my nigga, but what makes you think there is anyone in my room?"

"Because your door is closed and that's the only time you close your door."

"Big-B, this nigga, Moon, swear he knows me lol, so who is she because I know you ain't ever going to bring Roxanna on this side of town."

"Hell Fuck No. Bae, bring your fine ass out that room when you get done rolling up."

The door opens and out comes Nelly with the Gar lit and passes it to me.

"Yes Daddy, are we about to leave?"

"Nah not yet. Tell my brothers Hello and you can chill in the living room if you want."

"Big-B, I need y'all niggas to hold my phones down for the rest of the night. Y'all can keep $5 off every bag you sell and put up the other $15 for me. I'll catch up with y'all niggas tomorrow, be safe. Moon, meet me at my spot around 9, I'm about to drop her off and bend a few corners before Piloto's people pull up."

"But Babe, I'm not ready to go home yet!"

"Shit, so what you want to do because you can't go where I'm about to go."

"Can I just stay here until you get done, then you can come pick me up later so we can fuck, I want some of that dick. I'm horny and my pussy is still wet from sucking your dick on the way over here."

"Well that's up to Nando and Big-B, so you need to ask them."

"Nando and Big-B, do you mind if I chill here with y'all boys? I don't want to go home and be bored all alone, Please."

"Fuck yea you can stay." Big-B said.

"Okay bet, I'll see y'all niggas later, holla at me if you need me and Nelly make yourself at home, these niggas Fam."

On my way to my mom's house, Roxanna hits my line.

"Bae, where are you? I'm missing you and I'm hungry."

"Mami, I'm out of town on a business trip. Go in the closet and grab some loot out of that Jordan box, you know which one and go out to dinner with one of your friends, I'll be home in a few days. I love you and keep me in your prayers."

"Okay bae I will, I love you too."

"Hello, anyone home?"

"In the kitchen baby." My mom answered.

"Hey mom, how are you doing? I was in the area so I wanted to see my queen for alil, plus I'm hungry and I can't go home."

"Why the hell not? You and that girl fighting again?"

"No mom, I can't go home because I got this hickey on my neck and I don't feel like fighting with her S.M.H."

"Oyah, when are you going to learn to treat that girl right? She doesn't deserve the shit you keep putting her through."

"I know mom, but I just can't help it, but anyways I need a favor from you. Ima have Roxanna bring you 10 Bands for a downpayment on one of them new Chargers. I want it Black on Black and it has to be a HEMI."

"Okay, tell her I want to get my nails done and go shopping, so to bring $11,500(Eleven Thousand Five Hundred)"

"That's a bet mom, take her with you and tell her I'm out of town so she won't be bothering me ,I don't want her to see me with this on my neck. But serve me a ToGo plate because I'm waiting on someone from Orlando and they should be here soon."

"Okay baby be safe out there please."

"I got you mom, I promise."

At my duck off spot, my phones started to ring but they were in the room while I came out to the dining room table so I can put something in my stomach. My Nextel went off and I knew it was Piloto calling to let me know his dude was close by. When I answered the phone a white Honda Civic pulled up and Piloto told me that his dude was outside. I opened the door and in came dude with a duffle bag, we exchanged bags and he left before I could even get his name. Once the door was locked, I went over to the duffle bag and opened it up to see what this package looked like and to my surprise, it was a Brick of Heroin and 2 Bricks of Clean. My eyes got big and many thoughts went on in my head. My mind was clouded with thoughts of Cars, Houses, Hoes, Clothes, Rings, Chains and bracelets... My team is about to chew....

My Nokia SideKick rings, when I look at the caller I.D. I see that its Moon and I answered.

"Yoooo, whats good my nigga."

"Where you at?"

"I need you to pull up A.S.A.P."

"Okay give me about 30minutes and I'll be there."

Bet! Let me call Tee-Baby. Damn! This Bih trying me. She knows I hate getting sent to voicemail, dialing back if this bih don't answer this time, her ass will get canceled...Ring, Ring, Ring,

"Hello Oyah."

"why the Fuck I had to call back to back."

"I was in the shower Daddy, I just got done cooking. You are still coming over tonight right?"

"Yea, yea, yea, that's why I was calling you for."

"Are you ready for me now?"

"Yea come on, but do me a favor, stop by Walmart and grab me 2 boxes of ziploc and 4 boxes of sandwich bags."

"Okay daddy, see you in a few."

As I was sitting down in deep thoughts, I heard knocking at my door and when I looked at my 20 inch monitor, I saw it was Moon and his girl La-La. I let them in the house, dapped my nigga up and gave La-La a half hug and she gave me a kiss on my cheek but real close to the corner of my lip, too close for comfort, but maybe I was tripping or we was just moving real fast, so I brushed it under the rug and left it at that.

"So what's good bruh, that package landed?"

"Yea it's in that bag in the dining room. I need you to call up a meeting, it's time we have a Seat at the Round Table and Set Rules and a Foundation."

Seven knocks at the door, lets me know that it's Tee-Baby, so I tell La-La to let her in. When Tee-Baby walks in, she half hugs La-La and gives her a kiss on the cheek, when she gets to Moon, she did the same and hands him the Walmart bag, then comes over to me and wraps her arms around my neck and kisses me using a lot of tongue while grinding her pussy into my dick making me hard. I happened to look over her shoulder and locked eyes with La-La and if looks could kill, I would have been a dead man.

"Bae you and La-La go in the kitchen and make some snacks and put some soda and bottle water to chill. We're having a very important meeting."

"Yoo bruh, I made the calls everyone was instructed to be here at 12:30a.m. if they wanted to be a part of the team."

"Okay then bet, let's break this work down and get it ready to hit the streets. I have the Re-Rock Press in the hallway closet and all the cut is in a shoe box on the top shelf."

12:00 AM and all the work has been broken down into zips, and all the chairs have been set up around the pool table in the back room. Everyone showed up 15 minutes early. That's a sign that my team is hungry and ready to eat. I let Nando and Moon run the show and set the law because these are their men.

So that night, we set the Laws and came up with who is over what territory, I blessed the team with there Sacks and at the end of the night we came up with the name to our crew, "THA FAM" and went to the "Paper Moon" to see some Hoes pop pussy and shake ass...because in the morning, it's time to get to the bag and claim the streets that we run.

At the club I told Tee-Baby to find us a Bad Bitch to bring home with us and she was already two steps ahead of me. She got us a Thick RedBone hoe from Tampa that was down for whatever. I gave her $250 so she can pay the D.J., house and security and told her to meet us at the Brown Box Chevy with the 22's on it parked on the side of the club.

While waiting on the stripper hoe to come out, Tee-Baby started kissing on my neck and rubbing on my stomach with half her hand in my boxers. Then when I didn't stop her, she slid her hand all the way in and squeezed him and stroked him alil. She undid my Coogi jeans and pulled him out my boxer hole, rubbed him all over her face and popped him into her mouth. She started sucking this dick like she was trying to get me to marry her. Tee-Baby was sucking my dick like a Porn Star. She licked all under my dick and sucked each ball. She nipped at my dick head and made me tense up. Her head was so fire that I had tears in my eyes.

"Damn, Tee-Baby" That shit feels so good."

Then I heard a knock on my driver's window, I cracked my door open alil and told the stripper to hop in the back. All the while Tee-Baby kept sucking like no one else was around. The stripper leaned over the seat and kissed me on the neck. I put the car in Drive and went to Motel 6 off S.R.64 because I ain't want the bih from Tampa knowing where my spot is.

I got the room in my name and we made it upstairs. Once the door locked, the stripper and Tee-Baby started making out while taking off each other's clothes. I cut the lights on in the restroom and left the door cracked just enough to get a lil light, so I can see what's taking place with these two beautiful horny women. The stripper had Tee-Baby on the bed with her head hanging off the edge while she made love to her pussy with her tongue. I was rolling my Gar and all that could be heard was Tee-Baby moaning and that shit was making my dick hard. I lit the Gar, took a few pulls before I walked up on them and undid my jeans and dropped them around my ankles with my boxers. I reached over and played with Tee-Baby's nipples while the stripper kept eating her pussy. I had enough, the mixture between the Gas and the moaning had me ready to fuck so I fed Tee-Baby my dick. She went crazy on the dick and I felt myself about to cum, so I fucked her throat and sent my seeds flying into her mouth and she swallowed every drop of it.

Then I told them to get in the 69 position and eat each other out. I stuck my thumb in the stripper's ass while sliding my dick into her pussy and the warmness and wetness made me grow an extra inch. I got to sliding in and out of it with a nice rhythm. The stripper started moaning and calling my name

"Hmma, Hmmm-Hmmm-a you driving me crazy. Oyah! Oyah! Oyah! Uhhhhhh! Sheeitt! What is y'all doing to me. Tee-Bae you sucking on my clit, while Oyah got all his dick in me, a thumb in my ass, he rubbing, twisting and pulling on my nipples. Unn. Unnn shit, I'm about to cum all over your face Tee-Bae."

Her hips started to work overtime, while her ass crashed into my stomach and her thighs clamped around Tee-Baby's head.

"Ahhhhhh! Oyaaah!"

Her pussy squirted all over Tee-Bae's face and mouth and she just kept eating and attacking her clit and swallowing her juices.

"Tee-Bae, tell me that you love me, that you love what we are doing. Tell me or you ain't getting no dick tonight."

I grabbed the stripper by her hair and was crashing this dick into her scorching hot, wet pussy until I filled her up with my seeds. I pulled out and made her suck off all her juices. When she had me all cleaned up, I went to pull my boxers and pants up but Tee-Bae stopped me. She moaned,

"I need you so bad."

She grabbed my head and rubbed it up and down her crease and said

"This pussy needs you"

While pressing my fingers into her sex lips. She sucked on her bottom lip and moaned deep within her throat, her pussy felt puffy. The lips were thick and the longer she rubbed my hand on her crease, the wetter she got.

"Mmm-A, Oyah, just fuck me baby."

She sounded so sexy that I just lost it. My dick sprung up and I took my dick head and rubbed it up and down her crease, then slowly guided him in while she bit on her bottom lip.

"Unnnnn. Mmmmm-A, I feel you baby. This dick is mine. Tell me it's mine bae. You know that Chico bitch pussy ain't got shit on mine."

"Yes bae, Yea this dick belongs to you."

I put her thighs on my shoulders and kept on going.

"Umm. Umm. Umm. Huh. mmm. Shit. I love you Tee-Bae. I'll do anything for you. Any. Mother. Fucking. Thing. Hear Me?"

Back and Forth, harder and harder, I sped up my pace. Her juices were oozing out of her. She closed her eyes and I could tell she was on Cloud-9 by the look on her face.

"Yes. Yes. Yes. Oyah keep fucking me. Harder, Oyah fuck me harder."

The stripper came over to the bed and put both of her thick thighs over Tee-Bae's face and lowered herself enough for her to eat that pussy and suck on that ass. That's exactly what she did, while I kept fucking her. The stripper leaned over and kissed me, catching me by surprise but fuck it, I'm already Raw Dawging her. We made out while she rode Tee-Bae's face, and I fucked her hot pussy...We all started to Cum at the same time. First Tee-Bae started to scream and moan, then the stripper followed because her clit was being attacked by Tee-Bae tongue, then I was cumming deep in her womb and loving it...

Afterwards, we laid in bed with them rubbing all over my chest, stomach, and dick. I kept taking turns kissing one and then the other. I truly felt like a KING. I was going beast mode.

"SweetHearts, let's get some rest because I have a long day ahead of me tomorrow."

# CHAPTER 2

# MILITANT GRINDING

Bzzz. Bzzz. Bzzz.

The alarm clock on my phone went off. I got up out of bed and took me a shower, brushed my teeth and got dressed. Damn I feel like a king. I got two bad bitches naked in my bed. Last night was one hell of a night but now it's back to reality...

Picking up my phone, I noticed eighteen missed calls from Nando, Moon and Big-B. I called Big-B back first.

"Yoooooo, what's good Fam?"

"Bruh I've been calling you all morning, I'm down and need more ASAP"

"Okay bet, Ima grab some more and pull up on you at the trap.... Damn, bruh ain't bullshittin."

Now let me call Moon,... On the 4th ring he answered.

"Where you at Nigga?"

"I'm at Motel 6 off S.R. 64. Come get me so we can get Big-B right and check on the rest of THA FAM."

"Okay Ima hit your line when I'm pulling up."

"yea bet, I'm by the pool in the back."

"Bet!"

Looking for Nando's number I came across Rue's number but Ima call him later, I have to call Nando first,

"Yoooooo bruh what's good my nigga?"

"Shit, them 4 zips you gave me are gone."

"Okay bet Ima have you pull up on me at the spot when I get there."

"Bae this room is paid up for a few days, Ima slide but Ima leave you with my box, stay out the hood in my shit and don't have no one in my car. I'll catch up with y'all later on".

My phone starts to ring and the caller I.D shows it's Moon so I didn't even answer. I just walked out and went downstairs... He pulls up on me.

"Nigga, Who truck is this?"

"It's a baser rental. I got it for a week. Okay talk to me, how's everything going?"

"Man, bruh, what your plug brought you is Gas, the Baser's loving it. This dope is about to take us to another level."

"Oh yea, we catching a lil heat out here in Sarasota, those Chico's ain't been able to make any type of loot today. I had my mans go to the shops off University and 301 to catch all the buddies, my other nigga got a room at the Flamingo off U.S 41 and Desoto. That motel jumping with Junkies and Hoes."

"Okay Bet, that's the type of shit I like to hear. So let's go by the spot so I can grab some more work."

Slidden down east, when we got to the light on 15th by the car wash, I saw my nigga Rue, so I told Moon to pull up on him so we can chop it up in person and it will save me a phone call. As we pulled up, he noticed it was me and made his way over to the passenger's window, I cracked the window and told him to hop in the back seat.

"What's good bruh, I was on my way to Oneco but seen you and wanted to offer you an opportunity to eat with me. I got the blocks of Sand going for 19 racks and I'm about to open up a new trap in Oneco off 12th St and 63rd in the horse shoe. You trying to get down with Tha Fam or what?"

"One thing about it, Two things for sure and, Three thing for certain, I fucks with you."

"So tell me what's good. I need you because I'm trying to lock shit down on all levels, from pieces to heavy weight if a bih ain't with "Tha Fam", then they don't eat."

"Man Oyah, you know I'm game, just hit my line when you ready."

"okay bet. Let me get out of here, I got some shit I need to do. Be safe and Ima hit you in a day or two."

Sliding down 16th going to Oneco, we was listening to "Jeezy-Bottom of the Map" rolling up a 3 gram Gar of that "Sha-Sha" when Moon pulled up into Mike's Mini market on 15th and 57th Avenue to grab 20 packs of 12x12 Skinnys to bag up a few zips. Leaving Mikes I told Moon to hit the back roads and take 12th all the way down to 60th then bust that right and go down to 7th street, bust another right until he reaches the foot bridge, then cross over. As we was pulling into the driveway of the spot, Mom called my phone to let me know my charger was ready to get picked up that afternoon.

"Okay mom, Thank you and I love you. I will do something special for you soon, call me when you got it."

Inside I grabbed the book bag with all the Mannitol and Quinine, my Shifter, Plates and Straws. We have all baggies in the car, so we are good to go.

"Let's slide to the trap now, oh but wait, go in the freezer and grab a zip of Gas."

"Are we going to hit the cut or drive to the trap?"

"I'm going to leave the baser rental here, we can just hit the cut."

"Okay bet, grab 9 zips out the safe and let's go."

The trap was jumping, Big-B had a yard full of people. There were kids in the middle of the road on bikes, skate boards and Razor Scooters enjoying the day. I acknowledged everyone and kept it moving with Moon on my heels.

"Yo Big-B, let me holla at you for a minute. I need you to bag up this dope for me."

"Moon, grab six zips out the book bag and give bruh the rest."

"Here, bruh there go the work and all the utensils you need to cut and bag up. Take 42 grams of Mannitol and 42 grams of Quinine drop it in the Shifter and mix until it all turns one color, then take the 3 zips and mix everything together. The cut and the food should all be one color when you get done. Bag up 150 baggies per 10 grams then burn the top of the baggies to seal them. In the bag, there is 20 packs of 12x12 skinnies, every 3 packs is 150 baggies, you got the baggies to sack up grams that I left here the last time right?"

"Yea, bruh, I got them in the kitchen."

"Okay so when you sack up all 29 packs, then do the rest of the work in grams, split everything up evenly between 4 groups. Ima shoot you $75 for every 10 grams you sack up so at the end there should be 168 grams all bagged up, here is $1250(twelve hundred fifty), let me know when it's done so I can have Tha Fam pull up. Just hold my loot when they pay what they owe. You should have $22,000(twenty two thousand)when it's all said and done.... I have to go bust a few licks for these 6 zips I got, then Ima have to hit Piloto up because I can't wait five more days to Re-up. Tha Fam almost ran through a whole block of food and I'm linking up with Rue for the Coke. Ima turn Tee-Bae's apartment into a trap and move her to a ducked off spot out west Bradenton by Ana Maria Island Beach. I need her ducked off where Roxanna won't be able to find me, plus I want to stash 2 safes over there."

"Bruh go get the baser rental and bring it around here so we can go pick up this loot. Big-B, hit Nando up and let him know to be here in an hour and just give him 300 baggies and 40 grams broken down, tell him he owes $3,000(three thousand) for the 300 baggies and $4,800(forty eight hundred) for the 40 grams."

On my way to Sarasota to meet Turd, so I can sell him 2 zips of food, I decided to stop by Uzi and Davi's spot off U.S 301 South. I wanted to get them on the team. Both of them are Hustlers at heart and they making moves. Pulling up to their spot, there was a Baser Coming, Going and Chilling doing yard work. I told one of them to go grab Uzi or Davi for me and to let them know it's Oyah looking for them. Both of them came out the spot looking crazy. I had to let them know I came in peace. I just want to show them this Raw Dope that I have to offer.

"Ain't no pressure with us bruh, I know y'all Boys making plays and y'all got peoples y'all fucking with. I just want y'all to check this out. The Dope is A-1 and my prices are cheaper than my competition. Here, have 5 of these, have the Junkies shoot some up so they can tell you what it is, better yet take these 2 zips and if you like them you just owe me $3000(three thousand) for each, that's less than $120 per gram."

"Okay that's a bet, give me your number and if it's good then I'll have your loot plus enough for 4 more."

"That's what's up, I look forward to doing business with y'all, here is my number, 941-447-2613 y'all can call anytime."

"Bruh you still trying to slide to Sota?"

"Yea, Turd waiting on us. Get on Lockwood Ridge and take it all the way to MLK in Sarasota."

"Bruh we going Beast Mode out here with this shit. We are creating a real epidemic. "Young and Thuggin in the 941" is what we doing. Let me call this nigga and tell him to come out the door."

"Yoo-Ooo, we are pulling up into your driveway now."

"I'm out back, come back here, it's just me and my brother, the dogs are on their chains."

"Okay Bet"

Exiting the car and walking into the back yard, I saw K. Cramer and waved Hello to her. In the backyard, I seen Turd and a bunch of dogs. For a split second I forgot what I was there for, but I snapped right out of it. Turd, brother, came out with a lil purple Crown Royal bag with cash in it and soon as it was in my hands, I could tell it was more than $6,000(six thousand)

"Bruh this shit a lil heavy, how much is in here? Or did you give me a bunch of 1's, 5's and 10 dollar bills!"

"Nah homie, that's 9 racks of 20's. Turd ain't tell you to bring a extra zip."

"Hell nah, but I have 2 extra anyways, so what Ima do is give y'all the 4 zips and you just owe me for one."

"Okay bet,"

"I'll have your loot next time we link."

"Okay, here you go and you can put a 2 on a 1 and that shit still be Gas. Ain't nobody got better Dope or prices right now. Fuck with me and I'll make you a very rich man. What's understood never has to be explained."

"Ima fuck with Tha Fam, I want a seat at the Round Table."

"Slow it down a lil, when the time is right my team will let you know... But I'm out, tell Turd to get at me and that I have some dogs for his ass when he's ready to lose some money."

"Ima tell him, but he got some real killers in that Kennel, tell him I got $15,000(fifteen thousand) on my weight class."

"Okay Bet, I'll holla at you later, Oyah"

"Aight Bet."

Back in the car,

"Bruh, let's go back to Oneco and check up on Big-B"

"Okay Bet. Shit, since there ain't no Dope in the car let's take U.S. 301 all the way back to the hood and on the way we can check out the shops on University and 301 just so you can see what's going on with your own eyes."

Pulling into the shops, first thing I noticed was the parking lot empty and I told Moon right then and there, we were about to make lots of enemies, but fuck'em.

"You either with us or against us."

"Yeah you right, let's go to the trap."

It was about 2:30 in the afternoon and 60th looked like there was a party going on with Zombies, as the attendees. Our trap was getting a lot of traffic. Junkies from all over was flocking to Oneco for bags and grams of that "MONO." Pulling up in the driveway was the real shocker and my blood pressure went up instantly.

I didn't even give the baser rental enough time to a complete stop when I had the door wide open and was hopping out making my way into the house. Soon as the door was open, Big-B was on the sofa watching SHOTTAS with Nelly sucking him up. Soon as she heard my voice, she froze up and looked at me with fear in her eyes. Anyone would have thought she was my bih and got caught cheating.

"Oh my bad bruh, finish up and come out back, Ima go check on King Tut."

"I'm coming now, go faster and make me Nut so I can go holla at my nigga"

Out back, King-Tut seemed happy to see me. I fed him and gave him water as well. Big-B came out with a huge smile on his face.

"You good nigga, You busted in here like something happened and where is Moon?"

"He's out front on his phone, everything good, we had to go bust a few plays."

"What's good with the hood, it's looking like the walking dead out there."

"Shit my nigga thats what the "MONO" doing to them."

"But it's dead here!"

"That's because I have my lil niggas on bikes, beating down the block. Trust me Fam, I got you, only sales coming to the spot is the ones on the phone and the ones that don't wanna stop for the Block Blazers."

"That's real, I like that! What's good with Nando?"

"He came by, dropped you off your bread and I gave him what you told me. I got $22,000(twenty two thousand) for you in the closet right now but by tonight, I'll have another 10 bands for you."

"Hold up bruh, Mom calling me. Hello Mother, tell me something good."

"Well, your charger is fast."

"Is that right? Are you home?"

"Yea, I'm here"

"Well I'll be there in a few."

"Bruh, I gotta slide and pick up my new car."

"What the fuck did you go buy?"

"A Black on Black Dodge Charger, it's a 2006 and we still in 05, First nigga in the city with one."

"You truly snapped with that one, so what you doing with the Box?"

"Ima drop a motor, lift it for 26's and spray and Gut it. But let me go, I hope this nigga off the phone."

"Bruh take me to my mom's house, I have to go pick some shit up, oh yea let me go grab my loot so I can put it up."

Walking back up to the door of the trap I get a MySpace message from K. Cramer asking what I'm doing tonight. I wrote back "YOU" if you want! I opened the door and Nelly was back sucking Big-B's dick.

"You wild my nigga, Ima grab that."

"Yea it's in the room."

"Why is she still here?" I asked

"This is why, she's like my Sex Slave."

Forty five minutes later, I turned on 17th off 14th St and my mom had the car sitting in the middle of her driveway looking sexy. Moon had a smile as big as mine on his face.

"Nigga I know your ass didn't buy that."

"Yea, I did and Ima bolt up my Chevy and get it sprayed."

"Oh yea, you trying to stunt now. Ima have to grab me something."

"Yea, you do, because I want us to hit the Easter Parade in Sota and to Miami for Memorial Weekend, I also wanna go to Orlando for Classic Weekend."

"Bruh, honk the horn."

Honk, Honk, Honk, my mom opens her front door and comes out with a huge smile and the keys. I run up to her, give her a big hug and a kiss on her cheek. I grabbed the keys and told her I will see her later. As I was getting ready to start my car, she stopped me and told me Roxanna opened up to her and said how she is stressed out, and she's been thinking of leaving me.

"Mom, to be honest, I don't care what she do, her leaving me will be better for me. That mean, I just won't have to do it. Plus I got me a new bih that's more fun than she is. And since we are being honest, Roxanna will always be my bih. I have to run to my spot and put some cash up, so I'll see you later and don't worry yourself, Ima be safe out here."

"Moon, Ima catch up with you later, we are going to slide to Salem's Gyros in St. Pete around 1:00A.M. and you driving, we taking the charger too."

"Okay Bet! Just hit my line when you are ready."

Let me check MySpace... Oh shit I forgot all about K. Cramer, she's really trying to get at me. Well I'm in the mood to give her what she's looking for.., Ring, Ring, Ring.

"YooOoo, who this?"

"Bruh this Uzi, what's good?"

"You tell me, you calling me. Do you remember what I said if that food was gas I would have what I owe you for the 2. Well I got $18,000(Eighteen Thousand) for you, I need 4 more zips. Davi is going to be mad because he ain't trying to fuck with you on that level because his loyalty is with Big Rob, but your Dope is Raw and we can eat more fucking with you, so Ima spend money with you."

"That's real and I appreciate that. I will make sure to take care of you and make sure your whole team eats. Let me go grab what you want and I'll be there around 45 minutes, I'll hit this line back when I'm pulling up."

"Yea and lock my number in."

"I got you, see you in a few."

Let me call this girl!

"Yooooo, Roxanna, what's up with you, everything good at the crib?"

"Yea, Oyah, everything good but what do you really care, you ain't been home in how long."

"Bitch you wanna talk shit about me not being there but when you spending my cash that I be out all day making. I don't hear you talking shit then, so miss me with the bullshit, I'll see you in a few days, I'll holla at you. I love you!"

"I love you too Oyah!"

On my way to my spot so I can grab some more work, Tee-Baby calls me.

"Yooooo, what's up babe?"

"Nothing, I was thinking about cooking, are you hungry?"

"Nah, don't cook tonight, but I need you to meet me at your duplex, we need to talk."

"Okay babe, but is everything alright, did I do something?"

"I don't know, did you? Man just meet me at your place in like one hour, bye!"

Damn shit moving faster than I thought. Pulling onto my block, I noticed a lot of cops. Fuck, I wonder where they at. As I rode past them, I see they are at my neighbors house. Old man Jack done beat his wife again, but shit how Ima pick this work up with the police, ambulance and fire department outside my shit.

Fuck it, they busy with Old Man Jack, Ima just grab what I need, put this loot up and slide. Walking in the crib, all I can focus on is the flashing lights. I pray these police don't fuck with me. I open my Money Safe, and damn at the rate I'm going Ima need a bigger safe. I don't even know the total amount that's in here, well fuck it. Ima drop this loot in there and have Tee-Bae count it up for me when I bring it over to the new house. Once I had my other safe open with the dope in it, I noticed there was only 13 zips. Ima have to call Piloto in the morning or maybe I'll just text him now. Yea the sooner the better...

TEXTING: PILOTO- Yooooo, call me, I need you! I grabbed 4 zips and tucked them into my Crown Royal Bag, then tucked it into my pants so the police won't see me with anything in my hand when I walk out...

Back in my new car, I had Lil Wayne's Carter 1-GODS playing when I reversed out the driveway and rode past all the flashing light, thinking to myself, that's seems like a lot for just a nigga bitch checking his hoe, but fuck it, better him then me. Ima just go down 63rd to U.S. 301, so I can duck the law, I have no tints on my car yet. 10 minutes later, I pulled into the driveway and Uzi and his brother Davi was outside smoking with some fine Puerto Rican girls, so I hopped out, to see what they was working with. Uzi was happy to see a nigga but I felt heat coming from his brother's way. But fuck him, as long as Uzi spends with me then we good, he will thank me later when he riden around in a Benz and has more money then he knows what to do with.

"Yoo, hop in the Charger, that's in the glove box."

"Damn this that new shit, I just seen in a commercial."

"Yea I just got it today. Ima take it to Madd Mark's to get some music and tints, nothing major."

"Okay here is the cash, I ain't have nothing big enough to put 18 bands in so I put it in a shopping bag."

"Well I put the work in that Crown Royal bag... I'm gone, hit my line whenever, oh and I also have Sand."

"Nah I really don't fuck with Sand but I'll let you know if I ever need some. Be safe out here my nigga."

On my way to Tee-Bae's duplex, I hit Rue up and told him to pull up on me out there. We was both about 10 minutes away. Soon as I got in the neighborhood where her apartment was, I bent a few corners just to see how things are at night out there and to my surprise it was live, so when we start to have traffic it will go unnoticed...By the time I pulled up Rue was already there but Tee-Baby still wasn't so I parked and got in the car with him. We came up with a mean Master Plan to Lock the County down, Best of both Worlds. Crack and Heroin under the same roof...

Tee-Baby pulled up and went to unlock the door.

"Bruh come outside so you can see how the spot looks and get a full layout of the place. I also wanna talk numbers with you about the bills. Ima just shoot you my half of everything,"

"That's what's up then bust everything down the middle. I'm not going to be in the trap all day, everyday. Ima have Moon in there trappin."

"Yea I'm not going to be in there either like that. Ima give you the Sand at $19,000(Nineteen thousand) and you can pay on the back end."

"For real nigga"

"Bet, we are going to eat...Ima have wipe and drop, Vicks, shorts and pants, so you can get pieces, 8-balls, 7 grams, 14 and 28 grams, I want all my money."

"Yea I feel you. I got $20 Sacks, half grams, whole grams, fingers/10 grams and zips. Then when you want weight, I got that as well."

"So, when we start?"

"Ima have my girl move out her clothes tonight so we can trap this bih out by noon tomorrow."

"Okay Ima call you around noon then, but Ima slide."

"Bet, see you tomorrow. Oh this your Charger?"

"Yea, I just grabbed it today."

"I'm thinking about getting me a new car, but I don't know what yet."

"Grab the 300C Hemi, so we can come thru back to back."

"Ima look into it, that car is nice as fuck"

# CHAPTER 3

# MONEY, CARS, JEWELRY AND HOES

"Babe if you turning my apartment into a trap, where will I be staying and what about my stuff?"

"Just get your clothes. Ima get you a room at the Ritz Carlton. But I need you to find a nice house at least a 3 bedroom, 2 bath with a 2 car garage out by the beach, down Cortez or Manatee Ave, the Palm Aire area."

"Okay Bae, but what about my living room and bedroom set?"

"Fuck all that, it's part of the trap now, I want all new shit!"

"Damn okay then, I'll get on that in the morning. Make sure you do and try to keep the rent in the $1200-$1500(twelve hundred-fifteen hundred) range."

"I got you babe"

My Nextel Churp phone is going off. It could only be one person, Piloto.

"What's good bruh? I'm just returning your call. I was out to dinner with my wife when you texted me, but I'm home now."

"I'm down on the food, my team ran through all of it and we need more."

"What about Clean?"

"I just put something in motion for that, so I'll be ready a lil later on in the week."

"Okay Oyah, Ima send my driver down to you. He will be there first thing in the morning."

"Just call my phone when he close by."

"I got you, be safe."

"Tee-Bae, where is our friend?"

"I left her in the room."

"Tell her to get ready we going out tonight. Frank Lini and Papa Duck at Club Heat and I got us a Table. Invite one of your friends or cousins because it's a table for 4 people. I got 2 tables, one for us and one for Moon, Nando, Big-B and Rue."

"Okay daddy, I was just talking with my cousin Tootie, Ima tell her to step out tonight."

"I know you ain't talking about short, cute Tootie with the Bow legs and curly hair."

"Yea her, she my cousin"

"Damn she got a fat ass, I been trying to fuck that"

"Well tonight might be your lucky night"

"Shit! I sure hope so. If that's the case we going to the Ritz Carlton and getting us a Presidential Suite with the hot tub"

"Ima make that happen for you daddy, but I better not hear about y'all fucking behind my back or Ima cut your Dick off and shove it down her throat"

"Lol, Nah, when I wanna fuck her, I'll make sure to go through you"

"What are you wearing tonight?"

"My Red Monkey Jeans with my Cool Gray and White Versace shirt. Ima wear all my jewelry too"

"What are you wearing out?"

"I have a red Gucci dress and some Gucci heels"

"Damn you sure is going to be bad"

"Nigga I'm always a bad bitch"

"Yea you are, lol, that's why you my bitch."

Bzzz, Bzz, Bzzz, Bzz,

"YooOoo, what's good bruh, I need you to pull up on me."

"Where you at?"

"In Sarasota?"

"Same Spot?"

"Because Ima have Nando pull up."

"Yea and tell him I want the same as last time."

"Okay bet I got you. Is you going to the Heat tonight?"

"Yea, it's a bunch of nigga coming from off 24th and some niggas out the projects."

"I'll link with you there, but Nando will pull up in a few, be safe my nigga."

Let me text Nando so he can catch Turd then get ready for the night.

Churp-Churp

"Yooo Moon, you ready to slide?"

Churp-Churp

"Yea, I'm on my way to pick up Nando and Big-B from the trap. Then meet Rue at the RaceTrac on 1st Street."

"Y'all niggas wait for me"

The Club was on Swoll tonight, people from all over Tampa, St Pete, Ft Myers and even LakeLand. My crew walked up to the entrance together by passing a line that wrapped around the corner. There was a lot of mumbling coming from the line and it caused me to smile at them. We paid the bouncer $50 each so they wouldn't search us. Once inside I gave the waitress my name and she took us to our tables. Sparkles could be seen coming our way, with women half naked holding buckets of ice with bottles of Henny and Goose in it, cups and Chasers.

I ordered a band in $1 bills, Moon and Rue did the same. Tonight is going to be a Photo Shoot. As the night got late me and my crew put down on a lot of hoes. I made it rain in my section.

I even had my three ladies making it rain, they each had $500(Five hundred dollars)in ones.

One of the bottle girls walked over to see if everything was good with us and I told her I need the microphone so I can make an announcement. She looked as if I had three heads on me, so I shot her a big face hundred, and with no further questions she walked over to the D.J. booth and said something to them and pointed my way. Then I seen her and a man dressed in all Black holding the Mic coming our way.

"Who asked for the Mic and what is it that you want to say? Because we can't have you interrupting the club, people paid big to enjoy the night."

"Hold up homie we paid big and spent lots of cash so we can enjoy the night. If what you want is some cash just say so and I'll bless you. I'm a real hustler, so I respect the hustle. Here go a Big Face for you and let me get that Mic, oh is there a way to put the spotlight on us while I make my announcement?"

"Yea bruh, just give me a minute, once the light shines on y'all sections and the music lowered a lil, you can say what you gotta say. I'll go handle that and I'll be right back."

Soon as the light shined on our section, I stood up and held my bottle in the air.

"I just want to take this moment to Thank Tha Fam, I have a team full of Loyal and Solid Niggas, without y'all none of this could be possible, we came a long way, in a short amount of time and there is still so much more to accomplish. Thank you all from the bottom of my heart. I love Y'all Niggas, Tha Fam!"

The entire club erupted in a uproar and applauded us. After my announcement, the owner to the club came over to shake my hand and meet me himself, with him was Frank Lini, we chopped it up and exchanged phone numbers.

I was ready to leave, I got Tee-Bae, Tootie and the Stripper Hoe from Tampa with me.

"I'm feeling nice bae, you ready to slide?"

"Yes babe and Tootie can't hang tonight because of her kids. She doesn't have a babysitter, but Ima set something up for us later on."

"Okay Bet, handle that A.S.A.P. but let's go, y'all meet me at the room. Ima holla at my brothers then I'll be there."

"Okay daddy, give me a kiss. Muahhh"

"I love you and be safe, I'll be waiting."

That Tee-Bae crazy, now she loves me. She's really trying to lock me in.

"Yoooooo, y'all Boys good, stay until it's over, Ima slide, I have a lot to do early in the morning."

"Bruh Ima be with Big-B tomorrow, I got all your loot from what you gave me, plus the 12 Bands from Turd. Big-B told me he also got your cash and he almost all out of work."

"Ima link with y'all in the A.M. Stay safe and make sure y'all answer the phones so I can tell y'all when to be on stand-by.... I'll bring you more work, because Ima open a new Trap off 12th Street and 63rd Ave at Tee-Baby old spot."

"Who working your new trap then? Because I know you ain't about to let some outsider come in on our movement. We have to keep a tight circle."

"Nando, you don't have to tell me how to run my Team, I got shit under control. I will choose what I feel is best for Tha Fam, one thing I won't do, is ever recruit someone who is not worthy of building this Empire and helping to take us to the next level. To be honest, I was going to give you the spot. Have you run the 12th Street and 63rd Spot, while Big-B keeps the 60th trap and Moon can handle Palmetto and Sarasota. That way everyone eats and gets to build their own teams."

"Okay bet, that sounds like a plan, so I'll just see you in the morning then, drive safe because the Gray shirts are out and you know they pulling shit left and right.

Ima hit all back roads, I got Tee-Bae and stripper hoe waiting on me at Motel 6, but I have to be up early waiting on the re-up, I'll hit your line in the morning."

The room was pitch black when I walked in. Tee-Bae was sleep with her head on the stripper hoes chest, both was naked and it smelled like sex in the air. I played with Tee-Bae's pussy from the back but she didn't wake up, all she did was moan and rolled over. Fuck it, Ima just get me some rest until it's time for me to meet up with the transporter..... I got in the bed in between both of my babies. It's just something about them that I love.

7:23A.M. The next morning, I hear my phone going off and I could hear PILOTO's voice.

Churp-Churp,

"Yoooooo, my nigga, the driver is like 30 minutes away. He said he's passing Apollo Beach on I-75, so wake your ass up."

Churp-Churp

"Damn my bad big homie, I was dead to the world, but I'm up now"

Churp

"Ok, I'll let you know when he pullin up, I sent you 2, this time"

Churp

"That's love bruh, Ima send him back with $96,000(Ninety six thousand), that's for the shit I owed you plus Ima pay you for one of those Blocks and just owe you for the other"

Churp

"Yea, bro, I'm just sending you two because you moved the one in 72 hours so two should hold you for about a week, that way I don't have to be sending my driver out there back to back."

"I respect that big bruh, shit doing it like that is helping me get my bread up, just know next time Ima have $140,000(One hundred, forty thousand) for you and that will be for the one that I owe and I'll be buying another."

Churp.

"Let me know when he is outside"

Churp

"Bae Ima slide to Oneco, so when you wake up find a place and make sure you get your shit out your old apartment because it's getting trapped out by 5p.m."

"Okay babe, be safe and call me if you need me, I'll take care of everything for you today daddy."

"Okay, call me if you find something and when the apartment is clear for me to send my peoples over."

"I will, Ima get up now, shower and get ready"

As I was pulling into the driveway of my duck off spot, I looked into my rear view mirror and saw a white Honda coming down the road. I knew it was the transporter, so I hurried, ran in the house opened my safe up and grabbed a brown paper bag from Save A Lot with the $96,000(Ninety Six Thousand) in it, came back out and handed dude the cash and he gave me a Nike backpack with my work in it, put his car in reverse and hit it without saying a word to me. S.M.H. I said to myself that Puerto Rican is weird.

Let me put one block away and bring the other to the trap. It's time to get in the Lab. I want Big-B to cut and re-rock it back and turn it into two blocks for me.

Churp, Churp,

"Yoooooo, Moon, wake your ass up it's time to get this bread nigga"

Churp

"What's good bruh, I been up waiting on you, I even checked on Sarasota, them Chicos are wilden out there, knocking basers out and all talking about what they going to do when they see anyone Repping Tha Fam."

Churp

"Oh yea, I knew a bih would start hating soon, but Ima get on MySpace and have City call me so we can grab some Sticks, Tec's and a few handguns at least like two for each of us. I also want the Traps to have a few Sticks each."

Churp.

"Yea, do that my nigga, grab me 2 Glock 40's, because Ima body me a nigga if he come at me sideways, these niggas think shit sweet"

Churp.

"Ima make a call to my niggas and have them slide through Sota and make an example out them niggas"

Churp

"YooOoo, Moon, slide by Luckies Smoke shop on your way over here, the one at the flea market across from Mikes in Oneco and grab 1000 Grams of Manitol and 1000 Grams of Quinine then meet me at the trap."

Churp.

"Bet, I'll see you there. Do you have Gars? If not, I'll grab some. I need to smoke before I eat."

Churp.

"Nah grab some. I only got half a Gar I was smoking on when I left my room in the morning."

Churp.

Back at the trap, Big-B was counting money on the kitchen, Jay-G and Dro was there on the PS3 playing Madden 06.

"Yoooooo, how's everything going out here?"

"Bruh, this shit is epic out here. Junkies are coming from all over to grab some "MONO" I got thirteen Bands saved up at my mom's house."

"That's what's up, where my money at that you had collected for me and from what you owe?"

"It's in my pillow case on the bed in the back room, I don't even know how much is in there. So make sure you count it, just in case it's short or something."

"Ima use your room to count up but keep your eyes out for Moon, he is about to pull up with the cut so you can turn this Block of Food into 2 blocks, so get everything ready. I got a brand new blender in the kitchen cabinet and the re-rock Machine is in the closet. Re-rock a Brick and a half for me and break the other half down to $20 baggies, then take half of the brick and sack it up in grams and half grams, then take the whole brick and sack it up in zips for me. Here go $4,500(Forty Five hundred) for your time and hard work."

"Thanks big bruh, you truly have made my life a lot better. Ima go shopping for some new Gear, I'm tired of wearing the same shit over and over."

"Don't trip, handle that with the work, let me put this loot up and get the Charger tinted, then we could slide to Tampa, I'm trying to get a new chain and rings."

Back at my duck off, I sat on my sofa with a pack of rubber bands and counted all my money and put it in $1000 stacks, all $20's together, $50's and $100's. I kept the $10's and $5's as pocket change. My total after my counting was $71,800(seventy one thousand, eight hundred) all profit. I'm sure glad about that because I was down to my last $5,000(five thousand)in my safe, plus I still have another 8zips left from the first batch. Damn my safe looking real good. I wanted $50,000(fifty thousand) by the end of the month, but here it is two and a half weeks left in this month and I already have $71,800(seventy one thousand, eight hundred) put up, plus a Brick paid for and 8 zips still at the trap and that's not even the other brick Piloto gave me on consignment.

I gotta holla at my niggas to see if they wanna go shopping today with me.

"YooOoo, Nando, what's good, you trying to slide to Tampa, I'm trying to hit the University Mall and The International Plaza."

"Hell yea I'm ready to go, Aight, so let me go get some bread then we can slide, Ima bring my lil bih with me."

"That's cool, Ima take two of my Hoes with me and let them grab a outfit, but let me call Moon so he can get ready, because I know he going to want to slide. Ima get my Charger tinted by Ray-Ray, then get it washed and have Tee-Bae drop my Box off to the Motor Shop

41

in Sarasota, I want to drop a 454 in it. So just be on standby in like two hours."

"Moon, get ready in two hours, we sliding to Tampa so we can ball outta control at their Malls. Ima bring Tee-Bae and the stripper, Nando going to bring Miranda, so you bring Lala."

Churp

"Okay bet, I have to go to Palmetto to catch my dawg in Up-Town then to New Town in Sarasota to meet a few niggas. I gotta get my bread up because I wanna snatch me up the New Monte Carlo and sit it on some 24"Floaters, DUB, before the Easter Day Parade"

Churp.

"Yea I'm dropping the Box off to get a 454 put in it, because I want it to smoke my 24's up when I get on the gas, then I'm taking it to Juan's at 941 Kustumz to get it sprayed, Gutted and Music and T.V.'s. I'm not sure if Ima go 24"s or 26"s yet."

Churp.

"Nigga go 6's on that bih, only other niggas on 6's are Haitian Bo and Dro, kill the Box Chevy game Nigga. Whatever we do, we do it big, so go big Nigga."

Churp.

"Yeah you right, Ima go Big, 26" DUB TRUMPS with the Gucci Background, Gucci Top and Insides Candy Red House of Color Paint. Ima even put the Swivel Boat seats in the driver and passenger side and Bucket seats in the back with the fiber glass center console."

Churp.

"Well Ima hit you and let you know when I'm ready then we can slide, do you want me to pick Big-B up when I go to Oneco?"

Churp

"Yea, you can, just make sure he gets done bagging up first because he doing two blocks and Tha Fam's New Trap about to open up with them Sho-off Niggas from Down East. We about to do a Collaboration, Tha-Fam and Sho-Off."

Churp

"Yea, Yea, Yea. Nando was saying something like that at the club last night, shit I like that, it's a good move on the Sand tip."

Churp

"So just let me know I gotta get the Charger Tinted. I hate driving with no tints, it feels like I'm being watched by everyone, I can't even smoke in peace. LOL."

Churp

## TWO HOURS LATER....

My car looking Sexy, 5% Tint all the way around, 30% on my front windshield, car washed, my bih looking good. Now a bih most definitely can't see shit in my car now. Let me call Tee-Bae to see if she's ready to drop the Box off.

Ring, Ring, Ring, Ring, Ring, Ring.

"Hey Daddy, are you ready for me to go to the shop? I was just dropping my stuff off to your storage."

"Yea, I'm headed there now, you know where it's at right? It's off U.S. 301 in-front of Metro PCS in Sarasota."

"Yea, we went there, that one day when you talked to dude about buying a new motor. I'll see you in about 20 minutes."

Before heading to the shop, I decided to slide by Roxanna's house and pick up my loot that I left over there. When I used my key to unlock the door, she was cleaning the bathroom, the house smelled like Bleach and felt fresh. When she heard me disarm the alarm, she came out to the living room in one of my tank tops, no bra on and thongs, just the sight of her made my dick jump a lil.

"Damn, so you remembered that you got a girl and a home!"

"Look Roxanna, I'm not even going to lie to you because you deserve better than that babe, I love you and will always make sure you are good, as long as you stay single. You just ain't cutting it for me."

"So you leaving me Oyah? Nigga I've been nothing but good to your dog ass and this is how you repay me, I love you for you, not for what you got, these hoes out here only fucking with you because you making major moves and they want you to take care of them."

"Look I'm not worried about no bitch right now, I'm just stacking these bands and to be honest if I do something for a bih, they would have to earn it, ain't no handouts with me, everyone around me serves a purpose."

"So what are you saying Oyah, that you just use people? That, if you can't use them, then you don't want them around?"

"Nah you saying all that, not me. What I said was if a bih thinks they are going to benefit off my hard work and didn't contribute in anything, then they got another thing coming."

"But Roxanna I gotta go, we will talk some more in a few days. Come here and give me a hug"

She felt so good in my arms that my hands slid down to her ass and I kissed her on the neck just like she always liked.

"Roxanna I love you"

"I love you babe, I need this body."

Roxanna lowered her head and then looked up into my eyes looking like she was ready to cry.

"Why are you doing me like this, Oyah, I thought I was all you needed, I thought you loved me"

Her voice started to break up and her eyes got watery and it made me feel some type of way. I held her in my arms and kissed her neck,

"I do love you, but what I'm trying to do is damn near Impossible because of your insecurity, I can't do all that nagging shit."

I kissed her lips and squeezed her ass, she shook her head

"No this shit ain't right Oyah, you can't be telling me you love me but drag me through the mud. I've been by your side since day#1, I gave you my Virginity, Oyah you said I was your Lil Mama forever"

"You are babe, I just need you to tighten up."

I rubbed all over her ass, then started to pull her thongs off and let them fall at her feet. I cupped her pussy and slid 2 fingers into her soaking wet pussy while biting her neck and sucking on it giving her hickies all over her neck. That drove her crazy, she fell to the sofa pulling me down on top of her.

"No Oyah this ain't right"

Babe, smell that pussy"

I ran my fingers by her nose and then put them in her mouth. She sucked on my fingers like they was my dick. I pulled my fingers out her mouth and started to finger her again, then I lowered my head to her pussy and sucked on her clit.

Every now and then I would lift my head to ask her if she loved me, but she would just moan and grind her pussy all into my face.

I stood up and got between her legs dropping my shorts along with my boxers, then I pushed her legs all the way by her shoulders and her pussy was out looking like a ripe mango.

"Tell me you love me Roxanna"

I put my dick head right at her warm opening. She reached between us and tried to force me to put it inside of her, but I pulled back.

"I need to hear you tell me that you love me and that I'm your King, tell me what I already know."

I ran the head all over her clit then put him into her hole. Teasing her, I pulled him back out. I needed to hear those words because I knew she still loved me.

"Tell me babe and Ima beat this pussy up like you been missing and wanting me to do."

I put the head back into her, stroked in and out two times, then just held him there, then pulled him back out and laid him on her wet sex lips.

She moaned

"Okay Oyah, you my king and I love you more than anything in this world."

"Now, please fuck your baby daddy."

"You are making me crazy, I need you so fucking bad."

She blinked her eyes and tears fell down her cheek. I leaned over and kissed each tear. I took my dick and slid it into her hot, wet and warm pussy. Her walls sucked at me immediately, I felt right at home with this Mexican pussy. I got to beating that pussy up.

"Harder, Oyah! Harder, baby! Please! Mmmm, Yes! I need it harder! Mmmm, Mmmmm."

My hips slammed into her again and again, I was trying to kill that pussy.

Then my sidekick started to ring and Roxanna saw it was Tee-Bae and started to snap out on me. I sent her to voicemail. Roxanna was an emotionally weak woman and right now I felt like I needed to give her some space.

"I'm gone bae"

I grabbed my shit and hit the shop, Tee-Baby must be waiting on me. Damn I ain't planned on staying that long over here.

Ring, Ring, Ring,

"What's up bae, Ima be pulling up in like 5 minutes, give Jay-Bird the car."

"Okay babe, do I have to say anything to him or do he know what to do because they just looking at the car."

"Nah, he knows just give him the keys, I'm pulling in now, you with the stripper?"

"Yes and she got a name"

"I never got her name. LOL, what is it?"

"PARADISE and that's sad you been fucking her but don't know her name."

"Sad for her, not me. But we going shopping in Tampa. Ima slide by my spot to pick up some loot and meet Tha Fam so we can all pull out at the same time. Bae grab my Gray 730 Nextel and send a text to Moon, Nando and Big-B saying to meet us at the duck off spot in 30 minutes."

I was doing 90 on U.S. 301 when the speed limit is only 50, it was perfect timing all the lights was green. I just wanted to open the Hemi up and see what it do. Once I got to the light on S.R. 70 and 301, I made that left and took it straight to 9th street, made another left and rode 9th street to 60th and made a right, I crossed the foot bridge and pulled up to my spot, we all exited the Charger and went inside. I gave Paradise and Tee-Bae the gars I had on the counter and told them to roll as many gars as they can and that the weed was in the freezer.

In my spare room I opened the money safe and pulled out $20,000 (twenty thousand) leaving $51,800 (fifty one thousand, eight hundred) behind but I got 8 free zips to put back those 20 Bands.. I want me a new chain and a ring and some new gear.

I heard car doors outside closing so I knew my team was here, I yelled out into the front room,

"Bae open the door, my brothers are here and give them some weed so they can roll up before we slide."

"Okay daddy I got you"

When I walked out of the room, the whole team and their women was here,

"Look! We going to Tampa but we have to be back by 5:30pm because our new trap is due to open and I have to get the work and let Rue and his people in, plus Nando you being promoted to operating your spot! Big-B, so are you, from this day forward across the footbridge is your territory and 12th is yours Nando. Moon you got Palmetto and Sarasota."

"Bruh I got a cousin who owes $4,800(forty eight hundred) for a bunch of traffic tickets out of Manatee County and he on probation, they talking about violating him if he don't start making payments. He a trapper and I could use him to help me make runs, because I be on my way to Palmetto and I get a call from Sarasota or North Port, then have to rush and catch them, and vise versa. So adding him to the team we can be running 2 cars at the same time, that way we won't miss any plays."

"Yea that's cool but since he working for you, then you have to pay him outta your pocket. But is y'all ready to slide, so we can get there and make it back in time for Oneco's newest Trap Grand Opening

Let's Slide Lala knows how to roll up in the car."

"Yea and so do Miranda."

On our way to Tampa, we rode 3 cars back to back, going over the Skyway, Tee-Bae reached in my lap and squeezed my dick through my shorts. When I ain't stopped her she went a step further and pulled my dick out and gave the head a passionate kiss before sucking him whole, at a real fast pace over and over. The Stripper said

"Damn Tee-Bae you greedy for the dick"

"Look babe there is enough for both of y'all. Tee-Bae rides Shotgun going to Tampa and you can ride Shotgun going back to Bradenton. We are about to ball."

The entire time I was talking to Paradise, Tee-Bae was putting those jaws to work. I felt myself about to cum so I guided Tee-Bae, even though I really didn't need to because she always going Beast Mode on the dick. I busted all in Tee-Bae's mouth and she swallowed every drop. Then she put my dick away turned around to Paradise and said

"Don't get beside yourself bitch, this dick is mine and I'm allowing you to get some. Now give me a kiss and make me feel better"

They started to kiss and moan, just the sound was getting me excited.

When we pulled into the International Plaza, they both stopped kissing and started laughing, why I don't know but I was ready to fuck up some Comma's. We all went inside and went straight to Neiman Marcus, none of the females knew how to shop in a high end store. They are used to Forever 21 and shit like that.

"Yooo Ma come here,"

I called out to one of the workers.

"Yes may I help you sir"

"You sure can, our lady friends need your help getting fly, if you was able to get whatever you wanted what would it be?"

"Sir are you saying they can have anything from in this store?"

"Yes they have earned this shopping spree."

"Okay ladies let's go have fun"

Damn she fine as fuck. She may not be all that cute in the face but she damn sure got Ass, Hips and Tits. Ima shoot her my number before we get up out of here.

"Hey ladies, take y'all time Ima go check out another store named "FLY" and hit "Gucci" up. Tee-Bae come here, I went in my pockets and pulled out a 10 Band Stack out and peeled off $5,000(five thousand) here bust this in half for you and Paradise."

The rest of the team blessed their women with loot and we all left to see what we could find. On my way to "FLY" I walked past a store named "Milano Exchange" that had some fire designer. As soon as I walked in, a Balmain outfit caught my attention, it was all white with gold. I didn't even ask the price, I just told the guy my size and he got it for me and took it to the fitting room. I tried it on and it fit right. I sent a picture of myself in the fitting room to Roxanna and Tee-Bae to see what they think, and they both loved the fit. I never heard of Balmain before today. At the register my bill came to $2,300(two thousand three hundred)for the entire fit. Now I had to find some shoes. Nando and Moon wanted to stop by Gucci so we all walked over there and first thing I seen was a pair of all Gold Glitter Gucci Shoes. A white lady followed me all over the store, so I put her ass to work since she was racial profiling,

"Excuse me Ma'am, can you please get me these in a size 43, that's Euro size for a 9"

"Okay Sir, I'll be right back with the shoes, is there anything else that you see?"

"Yea I see everything but nothing else is catching my attention. Is there a belt that's white and gold."

"I'll check and see"

"Okay"

When she walked off I went to look at what Nando and Moon was doing. These niggas was trying to buy up the entire store. Moon was getting a Gucci Candle and a Baby Bib, a diaper bag, shoes, belts and some shirts and even a hat. Nando just got a belt, some shoes and a shirt.

"Yoo where the fuck Big-B go?"

"I ain't seen that fat bih since we was in Neiman Marcus. He said he was going to "FLY" because these High End Stores don't got shit for a fat nigga" Moon said.

"Let's go by Fly and see what all they got when we get done in here. The lady came out with a white and black Gucci box carrying my sneakers and a all white leather belt with the Gold Double G's, I told her I want both, she said

"Excuse me sir, you want to know the price for each?"

I smiled and said,

"Baby if I have to ask the price that means I can't afford it, I got bread"

and I pulled out both stacks of Big faces and flashed her. The woman's eyes got huge then she had the nerve to offer me soda, water or champagne.

"Nah Ma'am just ring me up so I can go to another store and spend some more of these big faces. Y'all nigga done, let's go to Fly now."

Inside Fly, Big-B was there racking up on some fly gear. Nothing caught my attention so I was ready to link back with the women's and then go grab some food. I told Moon to text Lala and tell her to meet us at The Capital Grille, and to let everyone else know the same thing. Inside the restaurant I asked the waitress to get us a table that seats at least 16 people. I know my girls are going to have at least 2 bags each. Soon as they walked in we locked eyes and they made their way over to us and to my surprise I was wrong. Each one of them had at least 2 bags in each hand. We all ate, drank, laughed and talked about future goals and plans.

"Yooo I wanna slide down Fowler to the University Mall to check out the Arab Sean or Rick to get me a new Chain and Ring"

"Shit let's go"

Moon said,

"I want some shit as well"

Big-B picked up our check at The Capital Grille and paid it for us. Our total was $482.30, Big-B just gave the waitress $600 and told her to keep the change.

"Oh babe I have to get back to look at the house on Holmes Beach."

"Damn, okay this what we going to do, since Moon trying to get some jewelry and so am I, why don't you take my car and all 3 of y'all ride back and me and Moon can slide to the Mall then we will link with y'all later."

"Okay bae, see you back in the hood."

"Come on nigga, give your girl a kiss and let's slide. We have to make this fast because the new trap about to open, we got to be back by 5:00PM because 5:30PM Rue going to meet us at the spot"

"Lala, give me a kiss and hug, I don't know where the fuck your stupid ass think you going without saying bye, I should slap the shit out of you. Thank God I'm in a good mood and don't feel like embarrassing you in-front of Tha Fam."

"I'm sorry bae I just thought y'all was rushing to leave."

"I don't give a fuck if we was rushing, Bitch next time you size me Ima put my foot in your ass in front of everyone."

The entire time Moon was checking his bih she locked eyes with me, like she wanted me to save her, but I don't get into anyone else relationship problems, so I walked over to Tee-Bae and Paradise while they was putting the bags in the trunk and grabbed Paradise by her wide hip and pulled her towards me and kissed her neck then bit it and whispered in her ear that she my bih now and her and I was chilling alone once I get everything situated. She reached back and grabbed my dick and squeezed it, then turned around wrapped her arms around my neck and we made out, then I gave Tee-Bae a hug and kiss.

"Let's go Moon give that girl a break, we got shit to do and not much time to do it."

"So nigga what are you trying to grab?"

"I want one of them bracelet all V.V.S."

"Oh you about to snap."

"Ima get a Jesus piece flooded with yellow, blue and white diamonds on a white gold and a ring to match. I also want to get chains for all my girls. I want to grab them those big X and O chains with Oyah in the middle like a big name plate."

"Yea you wild Nigga"

"LOL They my bitches so everyone needs to know that, Ima even get Paradise a chain and she better wear it while she dances."

Pulling up to the mall I counted how much cash I had on hand left, while Moon looked for a parking as close to the door as he could get us. We parked and walked in, first jeweler we ran into was Rick but he ain't have what we was looking for so we walked down to Sean but I felt like he was taxing me so I told him I will be back. Around the corner was a Jeweler named Anul and he had what Moon and I was looking for, and he was going to custom make my bitches chains. The chain I wanted came out to $8,500(Eighty five hundred) and the ring was $1,800(Eighteen hundred). I had a total of $12,000(Twelve thousand) to spend here. It was a lil more than 12 bands but I had to keep something for the ride back. So I gave Anul the entire $12,000(Twelve thousand)and told him put the rest towards the Three X and O's chains I'm having him make for me.

"I got you Oyah, give me about 3 weeks and I'll have them all done for you."

"Okay Bet so you ready to slide bruh?"

"Yea I got what I came for, I'm just thinking about getting me a chain made of a Moon, or the letter "M.""

"If I was you I'd get them both."

"Yea Anul here go $5,000(five thousand) make both, I want the "M" in white diamonds and the Moon in yellow, make sure they a nice size and flooded, I'll bring you another $5,000(five thousand) later on in the week"

"Okay Moon I got you, trust me you will be happy with my work and when y'all come to pick up the chains I'll have a gift for the both of y'all."

"Okay bet just call me when it's all done and we will slide back up here."

"Bruh let's get back to the hood, it's time to make this loot back."

"Yea let's slide..."

## CHAPTER 4

# *THAT CHECK CALLING...*

Back in Oneco I had baser Tammy cleaning out the New Trap, getting things ready for the Grand opening. I got a text and thought it was Tee-Baby. When I read it, the text was from Rue asking if I was at the New Spot.

"Yea bruh pull up, we here now just doing a lil last minute cleaning before we open up for business."

BLING, he texted back

"Okay I'm on my way now."

"Yooo Moon, call Nando and tell him pull up so I can give him the keys. Ima slide to the duck off and grab some work for Davi and Uzi. Also hit Big-B and tell him to bring Nando 300 Baggies and 50 Grams bagged up individually, that will put him in the Red $11,100(Eleven thousand, one hundred). I also gots to go by the duck off and grab a 1-2-5 for Rue, that will put him in the Red $2,500(twenty five hundred). And just from this one house I'll be getting $13,600(thirteen thousand, six hundred)every week."

I could hear music coming from at least one block over and my gut was telling me that was Nando in his 4 door Acura. The music got louder and I could hear his racing exhaust pipe getting close. By the time I made it to the front door, he was pulling into the yard. I had to give him a hand signal so he could lower his music. We don't even know our neighbors yet and he already making a scene out here.

"Yoo what's good big bruh. I'm ready to make them Stacks and move into my own spot. I want to buy me a Cutlass."

"Nigga worry about making this bread, then all that will come, trust me. I got you bruh, you is Tha Fam and we make sure Tha Fam is good."

Where is this Nigga Rue at, he should have been here by now. My time is Money, I got Turd waiting on me trying to grab 5 zips of food and a 1-2-5 of Sand and I also gotta meet them crazy Puerto Rican brothers Davi and Uzi.

"Well Ima Slide bruh, I have to go pick up my cousin Punkin so we can make a few plays. Ima start in Palmetto and work my way into Sarasota, then once he knows all the routes Ima let him work Palmetto and the beach area, while I work Sarasota, North Port and Bradenton."

Speaking of the devil, here comes Rue pulling up in his Cadillac.

"Okay Moon go handle your business, I'll link with you later."

 Rue hops out the car with another guy.

"What's good Oyah, this my Main Man "Bullet"

"What's good bruh"

we dap up.

"Bruh this is who Ima have in place for me at the Spot, he good people and he about his issue."

58

"That's what's up, let me introduce you to my man who will hold shit down for me!"

"Yoo Nando when you get done come check it out"

"What's up, I was just returning some calls telling my people where to pull up at now."

"Nando this is Rue and his mans Bullet, these Boys from East Bradenton but they trying to expand their wings. Rue a Beast in the kitchen with that Sand, so we doing a Collaboration SHO-OFF and THA FAM. Bullets will be in the trap with you, all the Stones are his and all the food is yours. Big-B about to drop off the Sack for you."

"Yoo Rue I gotta Slide. I left you a 1-2-5 in the back room in the Orange Nike Shoe Box, don't wait until you run all the way out before you call me to Re-Up."

"Nigga Ima hustler, I got this. Just let me do me and we going to be Booming in no time"

"That's what I love to hear, call me if you need me, I'm out."

Sliding down 63rd on my way to link with Uzi and his brother, one of my hoes from Sarasota texted me and told me to call her, I found that kind of off. So I just texted her

"What's up lil Mama."

Pulling up to the brothers Spot Uzi was out there with a baser working on his KTM 400. I hopped out and dapped him up,

"That's on my passenger seat, grab it and leave the money on there."

"Bruh your name is ringing out here and it's pissing a lot of people off. That ain't good my Nigga, People talking about getting at you."

"It's crazy that People mad about how I move out here. I'm not doing shit the next man can't do. But Tata always told me, If I don't Got'Em hating then I must not be doing something right. So having haters let me know I'm doing what I'm supposed to be doing. I'm making sure Tha Fam eats. A Real Boss guarantees the whole team eats."

"Yea you doing that because I'm eating harder then when we was fucking with Big Rob. Your prices could be a lot better but the work is good as fuck. I can play with the work and do what I want with it and the shit still be Gas."

"I could make the zips cheaper but the quality won't be as good"

"Nah I'll keep paying the $120 a Gram."

"Yoo Uzi, where is the hate coming from? Because I'm not trying to get caught Slippin out here."

"Bruh I fucks with you so Ima keep it G with you. It's those Dominicans Niggas from Sarasota, Bella and Tapia. They mad because their pockets are starting to hurt."

"It's enough money out here for all of us to eat. Ima pull up on them, I know they go out to Latin Quarters every Saturday. Don't worry your name will never come up in any of this. But let me slide. I have to go serve my nigga in Sota now."

Headed down U.S.301 listening to "Plies- I am The Club" smoking me a gargoyle that Hatchet from Sha-Sha all I could think about is these Dominican bastards. We are going to have to get some type of understanding. Pulling into Turds Spot I see K. Cramer smoking on his front porch. I grabbed the work out the glove box, tucked it into my pants and got out the car and walked past her while she just looked at me with a smile as she continued to smoke. I knocked on the door and a white Junky lady answered the door.

"How may I help you?"

"Tell Turd, Oyah is outside"

Then I turned around and went back to my car, all the while I felt K. Cramer's eyes on me. Once inside of my car she could no longer see me, because my front windshield was tinted but I could see her trying to strain her eyes. Turd walked out the house with a Olive Garden brown paper bag and got into my passenger seat and handed me $15,000(fifteen thousand). Here, this for the 5 zips. I reached into my pants and pulled out the work. It was in a Walmart bag.

"Do you still want the 1-2-5 of Sand?"

"Yea my brother getting the money together now"

"You see there he go"

"what's good my nigga what makes you wanna sell Sand?"

"I like to have more than one income"

"Respect fool, I like that on some real nigga shit. Ima slide back to my side of town."

"Hold up, have you heard anything about me or Tha Fam because I heard those Dominicans are keeping my name in their mouth and hating on Tha Fam. They just don't know who the fuck they fucking with."

"Nah bruh I ain't hear shit but if I do, best believe Ima let you know, and if you need me for anything just holla at me, if it's a problem that I can't handle on my own then I have some Hittas in Puerto Rico that will come clean shit up then be gone in the wind."

"Ima keep that in mind and let you know, but let me slide bruh be safe and keep your head up."

"Yooo who that white girl is up there?"

"Oh that's my home girl, she be coming over to grab some smoke from me, why what's up?"

"Shit that bih stay trying to give a nigga some pussy but if she fucking with you then I was going to spare her."

"Nah bruh, do you. Ain't none of us fuck her"

"K. Cramer, come here Lil-Mama."

"Oh so now you know me, because a few minutes ago you walked past me like you don't know who the fuck I was."

"It ain't that so calm down, I was just being respectful to my nigga's Spot. I ain't know if you was fucking one of my dawgs."

"So now that you know I ain't, what you going to do with me?"

"Get in, we going to get a room and I'll show you better then I can tell you."

She licked her lips and got right in.

"What room is we going to?"

"The Sleep Inn, right by the Sarasota airport, is that good enough for you?"

"Anywhere babe I would have fucked you right here in the car. I just wanna put this pussy on you and show you what you been missing out on."

"Keep that same energy, Hold up lil mama my nigga calling me. Yoo what's good Nando?"

"Purp over here and he wanna link with you."

"Tell him to hold up, I'm on my way. I'm on 301 by Desoto, so I'll be there in about 10 minutes."

"You got somewhere to be at anytime soon because if so I'll just drop you off and get up with you later."

"Nah I'm with you for as long you want me daddy."

"Okay Bet, we going by my trap, I have some business to take care of then we can slide to the room."

On my way to the trap, we was smoken a fat Gar of that gas and "Plies Smell Like Water" came on, I passed K.Cramer the Gar and reached over and rubbed her thigh. She opened her legs and gave me full access to that pretty pink pussy. It was already Hot and Wet. I rubbed on her clit then slid 2 fingers into her pussy and moved them in and out at a fast pace until she Nutted all over my hand, then I smelled it.

"Why the fuck did you just smell your fingers, you act like you was expecting me to be Stank!"

"Chill lil Mama, if you was stink I would have been putting your ass out as we speak. Plus you may never know, it be the pretty ones who don't be keeping up with their hygiene or doing so much fucking that their PH Balance be off, but then they wanna call themselves Bad Bitches."

Pulling up on the block, I grabbed a napkin and wiped my hands clean of her nut. I pulled in the driveway and hopped out, Purp and his man J.Gangsta was out front smoking a Newport. I dapped them up and looked back at my car to see what K. Cramer was doing but I couldn't see shit.

"What's good bruh, talk to me?"

"I'm just chillin, I was looking to get into the dope game. I hit a nigga for $27,000 (twenty seven thousand) but I'm trying to flip like $15,000(fifteen thousand) and use the rest to snatch up some wheels."

"How did you know to holla at me?"

"Rue told me about you, he said to link with you, that you putting together a Team."

"Bruh you know how J. Gangsta and I get down. Put it in my life and you can use us at your disposal. Like B.I.G said, More Money More Problems. You about to make a lot of Haters."

"Man they already started with the bullshit, I'm waiting on City to get back at me now, I put in a order for Some Heavy Artillery. Ima pull up to the club they be at every Saturday and see what's really good with them niggas."

"Look Oyah, we grew up together my nigga, we go back to Harllee days, 6th Grade, I wasn't going to speak on anything because Purp got shit under control but who got a problem with your movement, let us take care of that for you so we can show you our work."

"Nah J.Gangsta I know how y'all get down let me handle it first and if shit gets outta control then I'll get at y'all. But Ima give you 5 Zips for the $15,000(fifteen thousand) y'all got."

"If it's gas, Ima re-up with you at least 2x a week."

"That's what's up, I stay on deck."

"Let me slide, I have a few things to handle but come out Saturday."

"Okay bet, we about to go buy a Slider and let a few people know we good and to holla at us. But we will link Saturday around 9. Ima tell you now, if the nigga gets Slick, I'm knocking his ass out and if anyone gets stupid Ima burn one of they ass."

"Fuck'Em Ima pop off first, but we will link Saturday."

"Yooo Nando how shit going?"

"It's slow but we just opened up, Shit going to start picking up"

"Okay bet Ima go by the trap on 60th and pick up the work and put it up with this cash I picked up today. Where is Bullet?"

"He in the back room cutting up some Stones, he beaming, at the rate he going, he will be done in the next day or 2."

"Okay, when I come this way tomorrow I'll bring another 1-2-5."

Back in the car I handed K. Cramer a Brown paper bag with the $15,000(fifteen thousand)in it and told her to put it up in her purse. She did as she was told no questions asked.

"Damn I like that, I might just have to keep her around. We have to go by one more of my Traps."

"Damn how many Traps do you have?"

"Only 2 at this moment but I also have road runners. Let me text my nigga and tell him to be ready, I'm almost there and gots to be in and out...."

He texted back, I got everything ready for you."

Pulling up to the Trap on 60th, I saw Big-B had King-Tut chained to the tree, he must have been conditioning him for the next fight in 3 months. I beeped my horn, got out and played with my Grand Champ, he was so excited to see me. Big-B walked out with my LV backpack.

"Bruh sit that in the back seat for me."

"Okay bet"

He opens the door and sits the backpack on the ground behind the driver's seat,

Oh shit, what's up with your big head ass."

"Hey Big-B, I ain't seen you in a minute."

"Bih what you doing in Bruh's car?"

"Nothing yet but if he don't hurry up Ima suck his dick then fuck him right in this driveway. He wanna get a room, but I told him we can set this seat back and I'll ride his dick and let him nutt all over me."

"You get down like that?"

"No but I will for him."

"You just trying to secure a spot in my niggas kennel."

"Bitch don't try me, I ain't no dog"

"But he is and that's how he is going to treat you."

"Big-B, you just mad because I won't fuck you but I'll let Oyah have his way with me LOL"

"Bruh be careful with that hoe, she will try to trap you and those ain't the types of headaches you want...."

"I got this, none of my nutt will go in her unless she swallow. But Ima slide and put that up, I'll catch up with you in the morning."

"Love Bruh, be safe out here."

I told her, we going to slide to one of my spots and just chill there for a lil.

"Are you going to be alone?" She asked

"Yes we are, so make yourself at home if you want."

Pulling up out front. I reversed my car on the side of the house.

"We're here!"

I cut my engine off and she got out, her skirt was sitting above her ass and you could see her black thongs separating her pale white ass cheeks. She didn't even rush to fix it, like she was almost doing it on purpose.

I grabbed the backpack out the back seat, opened the glove box and pulled all the rest of the loot and put it in the backpack, zipped it up and got out. We walked into the backyard to use the back door. It was closer to my room than the front door. I unlocked the door, opened it and let her walk in first. Soon as I closed the door, locked it and turned around, she was kissing me and grinding her pussy all into my dick. I dropped the backpack, grabbed her, and she wrapped her legs around my waist and we crashed into the wall, making out, kissing all sloppy. I had one hand on that ass and the other wrapped in her hair pulling her head back so I can kiss and suck on her neck. By the time I sat her back down on her feet, she had a Hickey on both sides of her neck.

I stood looking at her because she wasn't as thick as any of my other chicks but she was pretty and her body had enough meat on it for me to have fun with her. She sat on the sofa in the front room and took off her shoes then she stood up and pulled down her skirt and took off her shirt. K. Cramer was now in-front of me in a matching Black bra and Thong set. Something about the way that black looked on her pale skin made my dick sprung up in my shorts.

She saw how excited I was, she grabbed me around the waist and pulled me in-front of her, then pulled my Jordan's Shorts down to my knees taking my Polo boxers with them. My dick stuck out almost poking her on the lips and she moaned. I could feel the warmness of her mouth on the tip of the head.

I wrapped my hand in her blonde hair and fed her my dick.

"Damn I ain't know white girls could suck dick so good. If I knew this, I would have been gave you your issue."

I'm not sure if it was just how she got down or was it me giving her compliments but she was eating this dick up like a Slut on a Porno Video. Her head game was real nasty and sloppy but very good.

K. Cramer would suck hard and fast using no hands making my dick hit the back of her throat, gagging and choking on the dick, making her nose run and her tears fall, while she massaged my balls. I couldn't take much of that. My Seeds Shot into her mouth, she swallowed some of my cum then let the rest drip out of her mouth down her lips and onto her chest. She unhooked her bra and let it fall at her feet and massaged my cum into her tits.. I stood her up, turned her around, smacked her hard on first the right ass cheek. She jumped and screamed out loud, then I did the same to the other cheek. Leaving a red hand print on each cheek. Then I ripped her thongs off her and bent her over the armrest of the sofa.

"Damn, Lil Mama, you is literally dripping wet right now."

I lined the tip of my dick with her hole and stuffed it in that lil tight, warm and wet pussy. She bit on her bottom lip and moaned real sexy,

"Mmm, Mmm, damn you in me, I've been waiting on this moment for a long time."

"Shut up and take this dick."

I grabbed her by the neck and used it to pull her into me and I rammed this dick into her with so much aggression.

"Hmm-a, Hmm-a. I can't, I can't take it Oyah, you beating my pussy up. Daammn, Daddy, Sheeiitttt! I'm cumming on this dick, your lil mama is cumming all over that dick."

Then she screamed "AHHHH! Oyaaah!"

I could feel her pussy clamping on my Dick as she squirted all over my sofa. Damn that's going to leave a mess.

I then pulled out, sat on the sofa and told her to ride this dick until I cum. She walked over to me, turned around, grabbed a hold of him and slid me into her hot pussy and rode me up and down, squeezing her pussy muscles on my dick as I massaged and rubbed on her red ass cheeks with my thumb in her asshole. I could feel my nut sacks getting tight and that's when I pushed my Dick all the way up in her and let my seeds spill into that pussy.

"Let's go get in the shower and get cleaned up, we got real sweaty and nasty fucking around with you LOL."

"Don't try and put all the blame on me, you played a big part in that session."

In the shower I watched the water beat down on her tits, her pink nipples looking like pencil erasers. I got to feeling my dick get hard again but I had to shower real fast and handle somethings so I left her in the shower to handle her business. I dried off, put on my boxer and shorts then went and grabbed the backpack from off the floor, so I could put away my loot and dope. When I put in my code and my safe flashed green and popped open I texted Roxanna,

"Baby I need you to order me a Shotgun Safe, I'm running out of room in the safe that I have now."

"She text right back, okay my love, where do you want me to ship it to?"

"Ship it to your house then I'll get Dinky to pick it up in his truck. Order 2 Safes so I can leave one over there as well."

I dumped everything out the backpack on the floor and separated all the dope from the money. I had a Brick of Heroin that was uncut, another brick broke down into zips and a lil over a half brick bagged up in $20 baggies and grams. Plus I still had the Coke that was just starting to move. I put up the dope and had to count up the loot.

In my money safe I had $51,800(Fifty One Thousand, eight hundred). I pulled out the $1,800(Eighteen hundred)

"K. Cramer, come in here please."

When she walked in her eyes got huge, damn near like a Cartoon when their eyes pop out their head. I couldn't do shit but laugh.

"Oyah, what the fuck man,"

"What's wrong Lil Mama?"

"Oyah, you putting my life in danger. Where did you get all that money from? Is there anyone looking for it? Will anyone try? Take it from you?"

"Look Ma just calm down, this loot is mine and I earned it. I need you to grab me something to eat from Perkins. I'm starving, you hungry Lil Mama? Here is $100. Get me a T-Bone Steak, Hash Brown, 4 Scrambled Eggs with Cheese, Cheese Grits, Bacon and a large Pepsi. Get you whatever you want. My keys are on the coffee table and be careful with my shit."

"Okay bae, I'll be back in a few, do you need any gars?"

"Yea get me a double pack of Swisher Kings, Oh and get the Steak cooked medium well, Thank You!"

As soon as she walked out I locked the door, opened the drawer to my night stand and got a brand new pack of rubber bands and broke all my stacks down so I can count them and wrap each stack up individually. By the time I got done counting I had $50,000(fifty thousand) in the safe, and another stack with $55,600(fifty five thousand, six hundred). I kept that $600 as pocket change and put up the rest, bringing my total to $105,000(One hundred five thousand)

I gots to get City to come through for me, let me text this nigga and see what's up.

"Yoooo big bruh, this is Oyah, I need you bad as fuck. I'm willing to shoot you an extra few dollars just for making that happen."

SENT, He texted right back,

"My bad bruh but I can meet up with you in about 2 hours. I got your whole order, plus some more."

"What do you want for everything?"

"Give me $3,500(thirty five hundred)and Ima bless you with bullets for all the Stick and 100 Round Clips, Ima also give you 32 round clips for the glocks ."

"Okay bet, Ima be at the trap in 2 hours with your Loot, there's a Pond out back that we can use to test them out, see you in a few."

There was knocking at the door when I looked through the window I saw K. Cramer with a brown paper bag from Perkins and drinks. I opened the door and grabbed the food out of her hand. She walked in and took a seat on the same sofa she just fucked on. I sat the food on the coffee table and she went through the bag and handed me my food and got ready to eat hers.

In the middle of me eating my food, my sidekick started to ring and Tee-Baby's name was on the caller I.D. Damn, what should I do! Fuck it, Ima answer it, ain't none of them my woman, we are just kicking it.

"Hello!"

"Oyah I found a 3 bedroom, 2 bath not so far out there on the beach, it's better than the last because it's got a nice backyard for your dogs."

"If you like it, get it and just text me the address so I can pull up."

"Okay, I will do that"

"Babe I have to Slide back by the Trap, what you trying to do?"

"Just drop me off at my moms house but I hope you don't play games with me, now that you got the pussy."

"I got you lil Mama, I got a lot going on and no time to play games. I will link with you when I get a lil down time."

After dropping K. Cramer off, I shot back to my duck off and grabbed the $3,500(thirty five hundred)for City and an extra $2,500(twenty five hundred) for the new spot, then let my Red Nose Pit loose so she can watch over my spot while I'm gone. I left my car parked at my Spot and just hit the cut, to get to the trap.

Big-B had this bih swinging over here. I'm really proud of my nigga and how far he has come. He had the Grill out with Hotdogs and Hamburgers on there for the kids. Ribs, Steaks and Chicken for the adults. Three 50 gallon coolers. One with Capri-Sun and water for the kids, the other with soda and water for the adults and the other with beers. The man across the street had his music playing and the entire block was just enjoying the day. I guess this was Big-B's way of giving back to the hood.

"What's good homie, you hungry?"

"Nah, I just ate about an hour ago. I wish I would have known you had the grill out, I would have come over here to eat."

"I'll save you a plate with a lil of everything."

"Bruh, who's all in the Spot because I have City about to pull up in like 45 minutes?"

"Nobody inside but Baser Cory out back feeding the dogs and cleaning their Kennel. Moon just left here dropping off $12,000(twelve thousand) for you and he picked up 4 zips. He was with his cousin Punkin."

"City about to bring us some Heat, just in case a nigga gets brave and wants to try his hand. I ordered enough Sticks for every Trap and then some and enough Hand guns for every member in Tha Fam."

Finally after an hour and a half, City pulls up. He hopped out of the car and went to the trunk and pulled out 2 huge duffle bags.

"Go in the house, the front door is open".

I walked in and locked the door behind us, then made sure the back door was locked as well. We went into the bedroom so we can use the Queen size bed as a table to hold all the guns on. He bust the first bag open and pulled out 5-AK-47's, 3-SKS and 2-Mini AR-15's.

"You have 10 Sticks here, everything comes with a 100 round drum except the AR's. Here go 40 Boxes Shells for the AK's and SK's and 5 boxes for the AR's.

Now in this other bag is all type of shit, here I bought you, 2-.40 Glocks, 4-.45 COLT 1911, 2-Smith and Wesson .357, 4-9MM GLOCKS and 5-.22 Keltec. I'm also waiting on some Uzis to come in, if you want those let me know."

"Bruh I need everything you got, I'll take them all off your hands, just put together a package for me and let me know your price."

"I got you my nigga."

He grabbed his money, counted it then left.

I sent a text out to Moon and Nando so they can get their Heats. I need to make sure Tha Fam is good at all times. We got enough shit to set this city on fire.

Let me slide to Roxanna house in Palmetto to see if she placed my order. As I was turning right by RaceTrac and Lincoln Park, I saw Carl on his dirt bike. I pulled over so he could pull up beside me. Once he did, I told him to lock my number in his phone (941)447-2613 and he did.

"I got the zips going for $3,000(three thousand) uncut. Pure as it gets."

"Ima hit your line in a few hours. I've been meaning to get up with you for the longest because my trap ain't been getting any traffic and the lil traffic that is coming all they talking about is Tha Fam boys got some real gas."

"Yea bruh you can put a 2 on a 1 and it still be some Gas. Fuck with me and I can guarantee you will eat. I also got Sand, the 1-2-5, it's going for $2,500(twenty five hundred)"

"Oh yea! I've been trying to find some fire Coke. Shit fucked up out here in Palmetto."

"Just hit my line and Ima bless you, so you can have shit on lock out here."

"I got you, soon as I put my bike up, I will be calling."

With that being said, he pulled off popping a wheely down the block. I pulled off and drove up to Roxanna house.

I used my key to get in, locked the door behind me and walked to the bedroom. She was blow drying her hair, so I gave her a kiss on the lips Hello, then sat on the bed. Pulled out some money, then getting ready to count. Looking over at her, she had on a yellow Bra and Thong set that was laced. I could see her brown pretty nipples through the fabric.

"Damn, you are beautiful Roxanna!"

"Thank you Baby, but you are only saying that because I'm almost Naked. No other time you say I'm beautiful. You make me feel like I'm just ugly, Oyah!"

"Please don't start babe, I was just giving you a Compliment. You looking like a Young "JESSICA ALBA" to me right now, and best believe I wouldn't be fucking with you if you was ugly."

"I came over to hit your hand with some loot so you can pay some bills and go shopping. Then later Ima do something for you and my mom. Here goes $2,000(two thousand), babe did you order the safes for me?"

"Yes babe you know I always listen and do whatever you ask me to do."

"That's one of the reasons why I love you Mami. But when they get here, have them bolt one up in the walk-in closet to the wall and floor and they can leave the other in the box in the hallway and I'll have Dinky come get it in his truck. So where are you getting ready to go, wearing sexy bras and Panties like that?"

"Well now Ima go pay the water and light bill then hit the International Plaza and do a lil shopping, then go and get my nails and feet done."

"Okay babe, I just wanted to drop you off some loot and see you for a lil bit because you was on my mind and I was missing you."

I stood up, "I love you Roxanna."

I gave her a real passionate kiss while squeezing that ass.

"Don't start shit you ain't going to finish."

"LOL, I see you got jokes."

I slapped her on the ass and walked out. Before I can even get my car started my phone Buzzz indicating that I have a Text Message. I slide my Sidekick open and the message is from Tee-Baby with the address of the new house I'm putting her in. I didn't even text back, I just drove over there. I drove down Manatee Ave going west at the light on 75th, I turned right then made another right onto Riverview Rd and our house was the 4th driveway on the right. You couldn't see the house from the road, then when I pulled all the way down the driveway and past all the trees, I seen a huge Spanish Style House, with a 3 car garage and lots of Landscape. There is no fucking way this house is in the budget I gave her. I pulled my Charger right beside her Old Mazda, cut it off and got out. The front door was wide open so I walked in and called out to the Ladies. The first to come out was Paradise.

"Hey daddy, do you like?"

"Yes this is a Bad Ass House, it's on some Scarface shit, where is Tee-Baby at?"

"She out back, the house came with 2 Sheds so she checking them out to see if there is anything in them."

"Let's go out back so I can see how the backyard looks."

Before I could even take a step, she pushed me against the wall putting both her hands on my chest and looking deep into my eyes before kissing me passionately.

"Thank you Oyah, I really appreciate everything you do for me, for saving me and treating me as a person. I love you for that."

Damn she caught me by surprise, I never knew she was feeling like that. But you can say, I love her too!

Outside was nice, lots of land, lots of trees and a 8 foot Privacy fence all the way around. In the corner was the 2 Sheds and Tee-Baby all sweaty. Her leggings had a sweat mark soaked with sweat.

"What's up lil Mama, you out here working hard I see."

"Yea it's a lot of boxes with tiles in there."

"Leave that shit and call your aunty and tell her I got $300 if she come and do a deep clean on this house and get her to put all that on the side of the road so the trash man can pick it up when he comes by. I was going to have Baser Cory come by but I don't want anyone at this spot unless it's Family."

"Okay daddy, Ima call her in a few, but what is the budget for the furniture?"

"Ima give you no more than $10,000(Ten thousand) and talking about budgets, how much is this house going to cost me every month?"

"Well it's only going to cost you $1,000 and we will pay the other $800, lights and water."

"Oh for real, that's what's up."

"Yea nigga that's the least we can do, you always looking out for us."

My Nextel went off.

"Oyah! What it do my nigga."

Churp!

"What's good, Purp?"

Churp!

"We need to link up."

Churp!

"You trying to grab?"

Churp!

"Yea the same shit bruh, that's some real gas you got, my phone Booming hard."

Churp!

"Okay, meet me at the trap in like an hour."

Churp!

"I'm on my way, I'm coming from Tampa."

Churp.

"Y'all come give me a kiss and I'll see y'all later, we still got the room paid up for 6 more days, so y'all have 6 days to make this house a home because I'm not paying for that room. Ima Slide to the hood. I have a few plays to catch.

## CHAPTER 5

# MO MONEY, MO PROBLEMS

At the Trap, Purp and J. Gangsta pulled up in a black Monte Carlo SS, wrapped in 5% tint. Both of them hopped out looking crazy hyped, they both gave me a hug instead of just dapping me up.

"Oyah we appreciate what you doing for us. On some real Nigga Shit, let us know if you need us to put down on a bih out here. We are part of Tha Fam now so if a bih try anyone in Tha Fam, then they trying all of us."

"Talking about that, I'm trying to pull up to the Club Latin Quarters where the Dominicans be posted up at every Saturday."

"Yea we pulling up with you, but we coming either after you get in or before."

"Come inside, I got something that I wanna show y'all. It just came in today. I'm waiting for the next shipment."

I led them to the room. J. Gangsta was like a kid at the Candy Store.

"Bruh, who all this for?"

"It's for all the members of Tha Fam. I got Tec 9's, Uzis, Street Sweepers and even Vests coming. We going to have enough fire power to go to war with anyone. Y'all boys grab some shit to keep on y'all."

"I want a .45 Colt 1911, fuck that J.Gangsta I want the 357."

"Y'all go ahead and grab it. I'm waiting on Moon and Nando to pull up so they can grab what they want and need."

"Yoo Big-B come in the back room."

"What's good bruh."

"I need you to Grab a AK-47 and a SKS and put them up around the trap, also grab 2 9MM's and 2 Kel Tec.22. That's just to hold down this house. I want you to give Nando a call, so he can come pick up his fire for his Trap, but give him the same package you got also tell Moon to come grab 2 COLT . 45 1911's. Pack up the rest of those guns, just leave one of the AR-15 out.

Ima duck that bih off at the duck off, and have Tee-Baby come and get the duffle bag with the rest of them.

Purp you said you wanted the same shit like last time right?"

"Yea bruh, here go $17,500,(seventeen thousand five hundred) that's for the 5 Zips and the 1-2-5."

"Okay Bet, Yoo Big-B, give bruh 5 Zips of food and a 1-2-5 of Sand. I got some shit I have to go handle, so Ima slide but y'all niggas be ready by 11pm tomorrow so we can pull out. I wanna get us a table and all."

"Bet Bruh, we will be here by 10:45 the latest."

"Big-B, give me a backpack so I can put the loot up that Moon brought and this loot from Purp and J. Gangsta. Also put the Mini AR-15 in the backpack for me, so I can put it away as well. Let me call Tee-Bae before I get caught up doing something else and it slips my mind."

Ring-Ring-Ring. On the 3rd ring she answered.

"Yes, bae"

"I need you to pull up on Big-B at the spot on 60th. He is going to give you a duffle bag. I need you to take it to the new spot and put it up for me"

"Okay, then me and Paradise going to the Paper Moon so she can dance."

"Okay babe, keep an eye on her, don't let anyone disrespect her, if they do make sure you hit my line. She is our bitch. Then when y'all get done, go straight to the room."

"I got you babe."

Walking through the cut to the duck off, my Nextel goes off.

"YooOoo, Oyah."

Churp!

It was Moon.

"What's good with you my nigga?"

Churp!

"I just ran into Haitian BO and he needs some Sand, I told him you got some of that Pink Shit, so he asked for your number."

Churp!

"Give it to him."

Churp!

By the time I made it in my duck off, my Nextel was sounding off again, this had to be Haitian BO because I ain't recognize his voice and didn't have him saved into my contacts.

"Yoo Oyah. You there?"

Churp!

"Yea. What's good?"

Churp!

"Moon just gave me your number. I need to link up with you A.S.A.P"

Churp!

"He told me what you looking for. I want $20,000(twenty thousand) for a block. It's gas and it do what it's suppose to do when you put it in water."

Churp!

"Give me 2 blocks then."

Churp!

"I only have 1 block left and a 1-2-5."

Churp!

"Okay I'll take that."

Churp!

"Pull up to my spot across the footbridge on 60th, the house number is 708.B"

Churp!

"Give me 45 minutes, then I'll be over there."

Churp!

Shit is really starting to pick up on both ends. Ima have to get a hold of Piloto so he can get me right on both ends. I opened the money safe and sat the loot I just picked up on the side, so I can count later when I get the money from Haitian BO. I locked the safe then placed the A.R.15 on the coffee table in the front room. My baby was always on guard mode, protecting me. She sat at the door and didn't move. If you didn't know I already had a dog, you will never know. She was a silent killer, she wanted to get her mark by surprise. I then went to the safe with all the dope and put my code in it. The keypad lit up green and the door popped open. I grabbed the bag with all the sand in it and placed it in the LV backpack that was sitting beside the safe. Then I pulled out 10 Zips, 600 Baggies and 75 Grams of food and put them in the book bag. I locked up everything, let the dog out the back door so she can use the bathroom while I put more dog food in her bowl and filled up her water bowl. Once she was done, I let her in, locked the back door and I headed out the front with all the work. I hit the cut and came out on 60th. Walking up to the trap, Haitian BO was pulling in behind me in his Duly Dodge Ram.

He hopped out and we dapped up.

"What's good bruh, I like this truck, I've been thinking about getting me one."

"Well if you like this one, you can buy it. It's a 2005 with only 19,000 miles on it."

"Damn that's still brand new. What do you want for it?"

"Shit, since it's for you, give me a brick and $15,000(fifteen thousand). Ima flip that shit and grab me the F-250 King Ranch."

"Let me re-up and I got you, but come inside so we can handle business."

In the house, I sat the backpack down on the kitchen table. Pulled the food out the backpack and Haitian BO reached over and grabbed a Zip.

"How much for a Zip of this? Some of my basers been asking about it, Saying Oneco got some of the best food out there."

"That's what you got in your hand is what the entire 941 area code is going crazy over. I'm letting the Zips go for $3,000 (three thousand) each."

"Oyah let me do some homework and I'll get back at you on this."

"Here go the Sand. If you wanna drop it, everything you need is in the kitchen."

"Nah bruh I trust that everything is everything and if it ain't I'm sure you will do right and fix it."

"Bruh my product is A-1 and I do very good business."

"Here is $22,500(twenty two thousand, five hundred), but Ima need more, I have 8 Traps just in Oneco, plus I serve Niggas double up. So Ima run through this work like in 2 days."

"I will be back in the hood by then. It's just one call and 4 hours away."

"Let me know when you get back right and I'll take 2 Bricks."

"Okay bet, be safe out there, you know them Crackers are deep out here."

"I got a Stash Spot in the truck, so I'm not worried about the police."

"Yooo Big-B, Ima go lay down, I'm tired as fuck and don't feel being bothered."

"Where you going?"

"Ima go stay with Roxanna, but first Ima put the rest of this loot up then shoot to Palmetto. I ain't been giving her no time."

"Bruh, in this bag is 10 Zips, 600 Baggies and 75 Grams of food, that should hold y'all over for 2-3 days. Ima slide but make sure you are ready, we going out tomorrow. But Ima go shoppin in the morning for them new Retro 10's that are dropping."

"Grab me a pair bih!"

"I got you, a size 9 right?"

"You know it."

On my way to the duck off, I texted Roxanna.

"Bae, come get me from my duck off spot."

"Where am I taking you, Oyah?"

"To your house and I'm staying the night so tell your other nigga don't even bother coming over."

"Oyah! Shut the fuck up, ain't no other nigga coming to my house. I go to his house."

"Don't get fucked up now!"

"Boy please you ain't worried about me."

"Roxanna you my bitch, that pussy is mine until I say otherwise. Now hurry and come get me. I need a shower then go to sleep."

"Okay I'm on my way."

At my duck off Stomi was waiting for me at the door. Soon as I walked in, she jumped on me, happy to see me back. I moved her then went to the safe room. Put my code in and pulled out the Money from earlier so I can count it all, and rubber band them up separately in stacks of $1,000. In the end, my total came up to $52,000(fifty two thousand) plus the $100,000(one hundred thousand) I already got put up in the safe.

I took $2,000(two thousand) from the money I just counted and put the rest up, making my total in the safe $150,000(One hundred fifty thousand) Another $20,000(twenty thousand) and I'll pay Piloto for the Sand, the Brick of food I owe him and pay him for another one. Right when I had all the Loot counted, put up and the safe locked, I heard knocking at my front door. Stormi walked by the door, sniffed and walked away, letting me know it was someone she knew. It couldn't be anybody else but Roxanna. So I made sure everything was locked up and let Stormi run out the front door to use the bathroom and to show Roxanna some love. Once she went to the bathroom, I called her back in and locked up the house.

I got in the car and gave Roxanna a kiss.

"Let's go bae, are you hungry?"

"Nah, I cooked, there is food at the house."

"Oh so let's go home then. What did you cook?"

"Fried Pork Chops, Yellow Rice and Black Beans and a Salad"

"You must have known I was coming over tonight."

"LOL! You is funny. I cooked because I was hungry and because that's what I wanted to eat, you wasn't even on my mind while I was cooking."

"Damn that hurts Mami, I'm not even gonna lie."

Pulling into her driveway, she parked, cut her head lights off then turned in her seat and looked in my eyes.

"Oyah, I love you, Lord knows I do, but I don't deserve the way you are treating me. I'm too good and way too loyal to be treated the way you treat me"

"I'm sorry lil Mama, just please don't give up on me. I'm out here grinding, taking Penitentiary chances to make a better way, so we can have the funds to do what we want. I don't wanna be in these streets forever. Let's go inside Mami."

I got out of the car and used my key to unlock the door. Bae keeps the house feeling and smelling fresh. She walked in behind me and locked the door.

"Mami Ima shower real fast, can you warm me up some food."

After my shower, I sat on the bed, ate my food and watched "The Wire" on BET, until I fell asleep holding Roxanna close to me. She had her bare ass pressed on my dick, but I was so tired that I didn't even try to get me some pussy. Roxanna was just happy to have me in bed beside her.

My phone started to ring at 9:33AM. When I answered, it was Carl.

"Yoo what's good Fam, you mobile right now? I need you but my car is getting a Tuneup."

"Yea but I'm in Palmetto right now, I have to slide to Oneco then come back. Where you at?"

"I'm on Canal Road behind the Car Wash in those Shops."

"Okay I'll call you when I'm pulling in. What was it that you wanted?"

"Bring me 3 Zips of food and a 1-2-5."

"I'm down on the Sand right now but I'll be back good by tonight or tomorrow."

"Well fuck it, bring me 4 Zips then and just let me know when you get right, I may need some more."

"I got you bruh, you will be my first call once it's in my hands."

Roxanna's side of the bed was cool, meaning she been out of bed for a while. I got dressed and counted my loot real fast. I came up with a total of $5,300(five thousand three hundred). I took $2,300(twenty three hundred) out and left it on her night stand. I walked out into the kitchen, Roxanna was dressed in only a Tank Top cooking breakfast.

"Damn it smells good in here. Ima brush my teeth and wash my face. After we eat, drop me off in Oneco. I have a few plays to bust then we going shopping. Ima hit the club and you coming with me."

"Okay so Ima need my hair done."

"Just get it blown out, straighten. I left you some loot on the nightstand."

My Nextel kept Churping, while I was brushing my teeth, but it was on the charger in the room so I couldn't get it right then and there. Whoever it was, I'll just hit'Em back later after I'm done eating. Roxanna knew me well, she made me Bacon with eggs, fried sunny side up, on a bagel with butter and cheese, and a glass of iced cold orange juice. While I ate, she got dressed in one of my boxers and T-shirt.

"Where the hell you going dressed like that?"

"Ima just drop you off then hurry on back home, shower and go get my hair done by the Dominicans on 41st and 63rd in that Plaza."

"Fuck a Dominican, I hate them bitches, hatin for no damn reason."

My phone goes off this time, the person speaks,

"YooOoo, Oyah! You ain't wake up yet, Shit is crazy out here. The Dominicans just came by and told me, if I keep pushing your dope that they will get my trap hot, to the point where Ima have to just move."

"Ima holla at them tonight and put a stop to the bullshit."

"Yea bruh, do that because I don't need any drama right now. Shit going good and I'm eating. I need 4 zips as we speak."

"Okay, can you meet me at my trap in Oneco across the foot-bridge on 60th?"

"Yea Ima head that way now."

"Okay bet, I'm on my way too."

"You ready bae? Let's Slide! Take 1st Street to U.S. 301 South then go all the way to SR70 and make that right. Go all the way down to 9th street and make a left and take 9th until you reach 60th make a right then go over the footbridge, the house sits on the left side of the road."

"That's your spot?"

"Yes it is. That's one of my traps, I just ain't never bring you here. Big-B works this house."

"Babe your mom texted me saying she is worried about you because she has been calling you but you ain't been answering."

"Damn, I've been meaning to call her back, she just be calling at bad times."

"I at least feel better knowing I'm not the only one who can't get a hold of you when I want"

"Did she say what she wanted when you spoke with her?"

"Yea, her roof on the house needs to be replaced and it cost $8,200(eight thousand two hundred) for her size house."

"So she want me to pay that for her? SMH, what makes her think I can afford it?"

"Oyah, Moms ain't stupid, she knows what it is with you."

"Ima shoot her the loot tomorrow, let her know she can tell the roofer that they can come through."

Pulling into the driveway of the trap, Roxanna put the car in Park and just sat there zoned out.

"What's wrong babe?"

"Oyah! Why can't you just do right by me!"

"Bae I'm trying but it's just hard, I can't really explain why because truth be told I don't know why. Just Stay Strong and it will all work out for the best. I love you and will see you in a few."

I walked in the trap and Nelly was cleaning up wearing nothing but Booty Shorts and a matching Bra. She looked my way and licked her lips. All I could do was smile at her and shake my head. She done put that pussy on my Dawg and got his mind gone. I kept it moving into Big-B's room.

"Wake ya fat ass up!"

"I'm up just laying here waiting to get my day started, what's good bruh?"

"I need 8 Zips, Turd is on his way for 4 zips then I gotta go back to Palmetto to serve Carl, he wanted 3 Zips and a 1-2-5 but I'm down on the Sand so he wants 4 Zips of food as well."

I could hear music coming from outside.

"Nelly, who that out there?"

"I don't know, some guy with a mouth full of golds in a White Magnum."

"Oh that's my nigga Turd, let him in."

The door opens and I could hear Turd say,

"Damn you fine."

"Bruh come back here."

Soon as he came in the room, he gave me a $10,000(Ten thousand) Stack all hundreds and a $2,000(two thousand) Stack with $5's, 10's and $20's in it.

"There you go bruh on the dresser, grab any 4 zips."

"Okay I'm out, make sure you hit my line when you get right with the Sand."

"I got you my nigga, drive back safe."

"Yea you do the same."

"Bruh Ima slide back to Palmetto then Ima hit the mall and get ready for tonight. That nigga Carl want 4 Zips too but something just don't feel right with him."

"Have him meet you in person at a store or something."

"Yea Ima have him pull up to Lincoln Park. You know all the Chico's are out playing soccer right now."

On my way to Palmetto, I sent Piloto a text.

"YooOoo! Fam, The Sun Don't Shine Forever!"

It was a nice calm sunny day but something just didn't feel right to me. When I pulled up I saw Carl in a 98 BMW 325i with a white girl in his passenger seat. I backed into the spot right beside him, and waited for him to come over. My phone started to ring, it was Piloto.

"YooOoo! Talk to me bruh."

"You tell me, I got a text from you like 15 minutes ago."

"I got all your loot for the food and Sand. Ima need more then 2 Blocks of Sand this time."

Carl tried to open my door but it was locked.

"Okay bruh, my driver will be there in a few hours, be on standby."

"Tell him go to Roxanna house in Palmetto that's where Ima be."

"Okay he knows where that's at"

"I'll let him know."

"Okay bet, I'll holla at you later on then...One"

I hung up and unlocked the door so Carl can come in.

"My bad bruh, I had to take that call real fast.

"You good bruh, but check this out, I got 2 spots out here that Ima put this in, but doing that it's going to make some people mad."

"Fuck who ever don't like what you are doing, don't ever let the next man stop you from eating out here."

"Here you go bruh, that's $12,000,(twelve thousand) but Ima need some Sand."

"That will be on deck tomorrow afternoon. This is 4 Zips, you have to cut it or you will kill off your Junkies."

"I got this bruh, my Mexican partner is going to help me out with all that."

"So Ima just holla at you tomorrow when I get right."

Carl got out my car and went to his. We pulled out the park with me following behind him. He turned left headed to up-town and I turned right headed to Roxanna house.

Pulling into her driveway, I saw her walking out the front door. I parked, left my car on and hopped out.

"Bae, where are you going?"

"To get my Hair, Nails and Toes done."

"Well go do you some shopping. Ima need your house for a few hours."

"You ain't going shopping with me?"

"Nah bae, I have a few new outfits in the closet, I'll just wear one of those. I have some important business to handle."

"Yea whatever, I'll just see you later."

"I love your big head ass too."

"I was going to say I love you, after I got my kiss, you know I wasn't going to leave your side without getting a kiss and telling you I love you."

"You better not ever dare try a real nigga like that. I'm leaving when you leave, so hold up I gotta put this loot up real fast. I have to run to Oneco and pick up some more loot."

"Hurry up before you make me late to my hair appointment."

"Let's go, I just put that in your Panty draw."

I walked out her house, got in my car and headed towards Oneco. My Sidekick started to ring and it was the Machine Shop calling so I answered.

"Yoo, what's good"

"Bring me $10,500(ten thousand five hundred) Your motor is done, the A/C works great and this Box Chevy is a Beast."

"I'm out of Town but I'll come through first thing when I get back."

"Just pull up when you get back."

I stopped at Mike's to grab some Swisher Kings and when I got out the car, there was a Beautiful, Dark Skinned woman, with dreads and a Chubby face. She was skinny with a booty that fit her body structure. I walked up on her and asked what her name was, she told me she went by Fat Face.

"I'm Oyah!"

"Boy I know who you is, everyone in this City know who you is, your name is being thrown around. Not too many people like you."

"I don't give a fuck who don't like me as long as you do."

"Boy you crazy on some real shit."

"What's your phone number?"

"Give me your phone so I can lock my number in your phone."

"Here and Ima text you later so I hope to hear something back."

"If you wasn't, I wouldn't be giving you my number."

"That's real, I gots to run in this store and grab some things then hit the road."

"Okay, Oyah! Talk to you later"

Back at the duck off spot, I opened the Money Safe and put all the cash into a Gucci duffle bag, then put all the dope I had laying around in a Nike backpack. I opened the Dope Safe and took out the uncut brick of food, the 26 Zips and the baggies and grams, put all that with the rest of the dope in the Nike backpack and got ready to leave. Damn I forgot. I put the Mini AR-15 in the duffle bag with the $150,000(one hundred fifty thousand).

I locked up the Spot, popped my trunk open, dropped the Gucci duffle in there, closed the trunk and hit the cut. 60th was in full swing with Big-B's workers on bikes. I walked in the trap and handed bruh the backpack with all the dope.

"Sit this up for me bruh, Ima move it later, I'm just waiting on my new safes to get here."

He grabbed it and walked out back with it and I walked out the front door, hit the cut and hopped in my car. I drove careful doing the speed limit all the way back to Roxanna house.

My Nextel go off, when I looked it was Rue.

"YooOoo, what's good my nigga?"

"I got your bread but Ima need a half because I wanna put some dope in my other trap on 10th Ave down East."

"I got you, I'm on my way from out of town. I'll hit your line soon as I touchdown. I got a Churp now from Moon.

"Yoo bruh, where you at?"

"I need you!"

Churp!

"Go holla at Big-B, he got you."

Churp!

"A'ight bet."

Churp!

Then as soon as I was done with Moon, Tee-Baby calls my Sidekick, I slide the phone up and put her on speaker.

"What's good babe?"

"Daddy, I need some Loot for the furniture."

"How much do you need?"

"Well I'm buying everything that will make a house a Home from IKEA in Tampa."

"You still ain't say how much you need."

I pulled into Roxanna driveway, cut my car off, popped the trunk and grabbed the Gucci duffle and made my way to the front door.

"Just give me like $10,000(Ten thousand) and that should be enough."

"Okay give me some time, I'm a lil busy right now. I'll call you later" then I hung up.

Damn, Shit Crazy as fuck right how, everybody needs Money right now. Mo Money, Mo Problems. I walked inside the house, sat the Gucci duffle on the coffee table and just fell back on the sofa. Trying to figure out how to balance everything out in my life right now.

My Nextel Churp goes off again. I just wanna cut all my phones off, fire me up a 7gram Gar and just face it, so I can calm my nerves.

"YooOoo

Churp! It was Piloto.

"Talk to me bruh"

Churp!

"The driver about to pull up, he at the light by RaceTrac."

Churp!

"Aight!"

Churp!

I watched out the window until he pulled up, this time he was in a mini-van. I walked out, he slid the back door open and gave me a black duffle bag and I gave him the Gucci duffle bag, we both went our separate ways.

Inside the house my heart was beating fast because I was excited. The bag felt really heavy. I opened the bag and couldn't believe my eyes, so many Bricks was stuffed into one lil duffle bag. I ended up pulling out 5 Kilos of Coke and 3 Kilos of Food. This Nigga Blessed the Situation. I'm going to really Power Up. The entire Team will Power Up. I put everything away except for the 3 Bricks of Sand.

I took the 3 Bricks out then in a shopping bag from Save-A-Lot. I put the AR-15 up in the hallway closet and texted Haitian BO.

"Bruh I'm back on the Sand."

Then I text Carl,

"Come to Burger King in Oneco."

He texted right back,

"I'm on my way, I'll be there in about 30 minutes."

"Aight!"

I had to bust one of the Blocks down the middle. I put 504 Grams in each Zip lock bag. Then headed out the door, on my way to Oneco.

My Sidekick buzzed. What the fuck do Tee-Baby want now! When I answered, It was Anel letting me know my 3 chains are done and Moon's chains will be done in 2 more days. I told him,

"I'll just pull up Tuesday with Moon to get everything at once."

"Okay Oyah, see you then"

Let me send a text to Piloto.

"Bruh, thank you! I truly appreciate everything you doing for Tha Fam, so I owe you $215,000(Two hundred fifteen thousand) now!"

He texted right back.

"Yea we on the same page, just be safe out there and let me know when you need me again."

"Aight, I'll hit you in like a week because I only have 2 Blocks of Sand left."

"Damn, you moving through that shit fast."

"We got money down here, niggas playing with Stacks out here."

Pulling up to Burger King, I didn't see Carl anywhere so I went to the drive thru and got me a whopper meal with a milkshake, then pulled around the building, parked and waited on him to pull up while I ate my food. He pulled up with a different female. When he got in my car, we dapped up and he pulled out $2,500(twenty five hundred)

"Here bruh this is a half block, you owe me $7,500(seventy five hundred) for this."

"Fuck whoever don't like how you moving, let them know you part of Tha Fam and we got Power to terminate a bih contract."

"That's what's up, with a solid team behind me I can really turn shit up out here."

"Aight, just holla at me if you need me."

I headed straight to my Trap off 12th and 63rd to see Nando and Rue.

"Yooo Nando, how things going?"

"Shit starting to pick up. I got your Loot from that last batch."

"Let me get it. How is Bullet doing?"

"He Booming hard as fuck right now."

"Follow me to my car, I got a bag for you to hold down until Rue gets here. He is going to give you $12,500(twelve thousand, five hundred) and I'll just get it from you tonight at the club. Oh do me a favor and text Rue and tell him you are ready for him."

"Aight, I got you bruh. Where you going at now?"

"Ima go to the Trap across the footbridge."

On my way to 60th, Haitian BO texted me.

"Bruh, what's good, I need 2 of them, please tell me you got me."

"I'm in Oneco leaving 12th, you wanna pull up on me or you want me to come to you?"

"Shit come to 58th on the left side, you will see my Cutlass outside."

"Give me about 5-10 minutes and I'll be there."

"Aight bet...."

On 58th, Haitian BO had this block looking like the CourtYard of the Carter in New Jack City, Basers everywhere. I pulled into his driveway and he was outside with a baser washing his car. Haitian BO had one of the Rawest Cars in the City. Lambo Doors, 26 "Rims, Candy Paint and a whole lot of music.I can't wait to finish my Box

Chevy. He walked over to the car and invited me in, so I grabbed both bricks off the passenger side floor and stuffed them into my pants, cut my car off and got out. I followed him inside his spot to the kitchen. He already had his pots and baking soda out and ready.

"Here you go bruh."

"Oyah you don't mind if I drop a few grand just to check it out do you?"

"Nah go ahead, it's the same shit you got the first time."

"Oh, Okay! Fuck it I'll just do it later, I have to watch this baser with my car because if he scratch my shit, I will cut him up with a machete and use him as Chum to fish for Shark off the skyway bridge."

"Bruh you is Ruthless."

"LOL, only if you knew the half, you will look at me as a Maniac, a Lunatic."

"Well I'm glad I don't but let me get going."

"Your money is in the bag inside of the microwave."

"Aight bruh, I'm gone"

I hopped in my car and went to the trap on 60th, it's always booming out here, I'm proud of Big-B. I backed up on the side of the house and cut my car off. I looked at all my phones before getting out and noticed a text from Piloto, saying the bag was short $20,000(twenty thousand) I called him instead of texting him. Ring-Ring-Ring-Ring!

"Yoooo, Oyah, What's going on? There was only $150,000(One hundred fifty thousand) in that bag."

"My bad bruh, I was rushing and forgot the rest of your loot in Roxanna's house."

It's all good just have it the next time we link."

"Nah Ima have Roxanna drop it off first thing tomorrow, I don't need to think I'm trying to be slick."

"I never got that impression from you, but just let me know when she's on her way."

"Okay Bet, I'll call you when she is on her way."

"No problem, take it easy."

I got out my car with all the money and walked in the trap.

"Where you at Fat bih?"

"I'm on the back porch fucking around with King Tut. We got a fight lined up for $8,000(eight thousand)plus a few Side Bets."

"Okay and where is that loot Moon dropped off?"

"It's in the closet in that Footlocker bag. I also put $6,000(six thousand) in there, from baggies and Grams. We running kinda low on the baggies."

"Okay bet, tomorrow break that other brick down, cut and bag it up."

"I got you."

"Ima Slide to the duck off and put all this loot up..."

# CHAPTER 6

# PAINTING THE CITY RED

I left the trap and hit the cut going to my duck off spot. As I walked up the driveway, I noticed my front door was open and the door frame was all broken. I posted up in the cut and called Big-B, he answered on the 2nd ring.

"Yoo what's good bruh?"

"Bruh bring me a Stick around here, somebody broke into the duck off."

"Aight, I'm on my way."

I hung up the phone and put all the money in my neighbors trash can just in case the intruders were still in the house and shit get crazy.

Big-B hit the cut faster than I thought his big ass could move. I snatched the A.K.47 out of his hands and sprinted towards the trap. The sun was shining extra hard and the neighborhood was very quiet. Big-B was right behind me with 2 hand guns. I motioned for him to go around back while I go in through the front. I pushed the front door open and stood to the side to see if any movement could be seen or heard. I didn't hear any movement coming from in the house but when I looked in, I noticed Stormi laying in a pool of blood. Damn these heartless bastards killed my dog. I walked with murder on my mind. I walked in and opened the back door and let Big-B in. We cleared the entire house and nobody was here. I looked around and the entire house was flipped. This shit had me mad. I looked at Stormi and her skull was smashed.

"Bruh, who all knew about your spot."

"Nobody but Tha Fam. I never had anyone come over."

"Bruh you had to get followed here or something, this spot ducked off. A bih was looking for something."

The sofas were cut open, whoever did this took their time and was looking for something specific. Something told me to move all the cash and dope somewhere else and Thank God for that.

"The safes were open?" Big B asked

"Nah, but you can tell they was trying to get in them. You know I got the safes bolted down to the beams in the wall and floors, so those ain't moving."

"Big-B! Do me a favor and call up baser Cory so he can clean this spot up and go by Home Depot, so he can grab what he needs to fix the front door."

"I'm on it now, but what are you going to do about this spot now?"

"Ima use it to fuck hoes and for us to just chill in. I have a new spot I just grabbed, but Ima slide outside and holla at my neighbors to see if they seen anything that wasn't of normal routine."

Ten minutes later I walked back up to my spot with no information. Someone will answer for this, I'm not mad about the break-in, but killing my baby is something different. Stormi was the sweetest dog I ever came across.

"Oyah, you have to think who all could have known you stay here? Did you ever bring any of your hoes here?"

"Fuck! Fuck! Fuck! I had that white hoe K. Cramer here the other day. I fucked her then while she was in the shower, I started to count the loot from all the drops that day. The bitch even started to panic when she saw a few bands and asking all kinds of questions."

"Bruh, this bitch going to make me kill her."

"So what are you going to do?"

"Ima get Purp and J. Gangsta to lay on her, because she ain't do this, she may have gave them the run down, but this here is a niggas work."

"Aight, Ima get on baser Cory so he can get this shit fixed and Ima have Nelly come over and put shit back in order and clean up."

" We still going out tonight?"

"Hell yea, I can't have a nigga beefin with me and not do anything about it."

"So we pulling out in about three hours then?"

"Yea at 11:00PM, so hit Nando and Moon up and let them know we going to meet at Sonic on U.S. 41 so we can pull out together from there."

I went to my neighbors house and got my loot out the trash and hit the cut. At my car I put the bag in the trunk, hopped in then started up my car and drove to my new spot. My mind was on GO, I had all kinds of thoughts going on in my head and none of them was good. "ITS TIME I PAINTED THE CITY RED," make an example out of a few niggas so they know Tha Fam ain't to be fucked with, plus this City needs a make over.

I pulled up to the spot and parked my car in the garage. I popped the trunk, got my money then went inside. Nobody was home, so I counted out all the money I had collected today, my total was $70,500(seventy thousand, five hundred). I grabbed $10,000(ten thousand) and put it in the medicine cabinet in the master bedroom.

I then sent Tee-Baby a text letting her know where I left it. I took out $8,200(eighty two hundred) out for my mom's roof so I could take to her on my way to Roxanna house, then I left the rest up in the attic. I walked out, locked the door. Tee-Baby texted back,

"Okay bae, sorry I wasn't there, Paradise and I are getting our hair done because they are having some big event at the Paper Moon tonight."

I got in my car, started it up and made my way towards my mom's house. As I was riding down 14th St, I pulled up to the light on 21St Ave. In the Bravo parking lot was a Buick Park Avenue-2001 for sale so I got the number off the side window and when the light turned green, I drove up to the next light on 17th Avenue and made a right then my first left onto 13th Street and pulled into my mom's driveway. I parked, cut the car off and walked up to the front door, using my key to get in.

The entire house smelled like some Loud. Mom was sitting at the kitchen table with, "Anet" her childhood friend smoking and taking shots of Patron.

"I see you ladies started early."

I gave my mom a hug and kiss on the cheek, then walked over to Anet and did the same but I could have sworn I heard her moan in my ear. Anet was a short woman under 5'5 about 140lbs, Puerto Rican with long curly hair. An ass so fat makes you just wanna bite it then kiss it.

"Mom, can I get a minute of your time?"

"Yea anytime"

We walked into the front room and I pulled out the $8,200(eighty two hundred) for her roof.

"Here you go, Roxanna told me you needed money for your roof, so this is $8,200(eighty two hundred) I still ain't forget that I owe you a date or something special for getting me the Charger."

"Baby you ain't gotta do anything crazy, just get me something good to smoke on."

"Mom you smoke what I smoke, so you always smoke the best weed around."

"Well get me some more lol."

"Go out to my car and grab what's in my cup holder."

Soon as my mom was out the door, I looked at Anet.

"What was all that moaning about?"

"When you hugged me, my pussy throbbed and got wet."

"Is that right, you must want some of this young dick?"

"I do but Tata is my friend."

"You let me worry about my mom. Ima take y'all on a trip to Miami soon, everything will be on me, so just be ready when she tells you."

"Okay baby."

She walked up to me, grabbed a handful of dick and kissed me in the mouth and sucked on my lips. Right when she backed up, my mom came back in the house.

"You need to air that car out, it smells like pure gas in there. L.O.L!"

"Talking about a car, there is a car in the parking lot of Bravo that I want if it's good. They are asking for $7,000(seven thousand) see if you can get him down some and I'll bring you back whatever you spend out that loot I just gave you."

"Okay, I'll call you later"

She gave me a hug goodbye and a kiss on the cheek. Then I gave Anet a hug goodbye but I let my hands slide down to her ass and I squeezed them cheeks. She moaned again and grind her hip into me, making my dick throb a lil. Mom noticed and said,

"Anet you better be careful with my son, before he have you around here acting like a mad woman following his every move."

"Tata you a trip, ain't nobody worried about Oyah, he is like a nephew to me, I've watched him grow into a man."

"I'm gone, y'all ladies enjoy the night, love y'all! Mom, go check on that car for me please. I need me a Slider."

"Oyah, you know when you ask me to do something for you, I do it so please just chill."

"I love you mom, call my phone later."

I left and was on my way to Palmetto when Purp hit my line.

"What's good bruh, we still going out tonight?"

"Yea, you know I need to eradicate this problem before it becomes a bigger problem and it starts to cost me money. We going to meet at Sonic at 11:00P.M, the one on U.S. 41."

"Aight bet bruh, see you then."

Coming over the bridge by the Manatee Civic Center, Roxanna called me.

"Babe, where you at?"

"I'll be there in 5 minutes."

"Okay, I'm almost home as well."

"Aight, see you soon."

"Oh babe, I don't feel like stopping, grab me some more Swisher Kings and 4 Pepsi in a can."

"Okay, love you."

I pulled up out front of the house and reversed in the driveway, cut the car off and popped the trunk. I unlocked the door, ran inside and grabbed the mini A.R.15 and brought it outside and put the gun in my trunk. I had to move fast because I didn't want Roxanna to ask any questions. The less she knows, the better.

I locked up the car just as she was pulling into the driveway. Damn that was close, a few seconds longer and she would have seen me in action. I walked over to her car and opened the back door and grabbed her bags out the back.

"Damn girl, I thought you was only getting one outfit?"

"I only got one for tonight but I bought some for other nights as well. I even went to Vickies Secret and got some things I want to wear for you."

"Is that right? Well tonight I want you naked under your dress."

"I got you babe, but you have to give me some dick tonight before we go out because I'm horny and this pussy wet and wanting daddy."

"Ima break you off then we have to shower and get ready because we have to link with the guys at Sonic at 11:00PM."

"Well let's hurry up then."

We rushed into the house and locked the door. I couldn't even make it in the room before Roxanna was on her knees pulling my shorts down until my dick popped out like a magna flashlight. Roxanna was on her knees just looking at the dick as if it was her first time seeing it. She pulled me towards her and popped my dick right into her mouth without using her hands. She swallowed the dick whole, making the bottom lip kiss my balls. She was spearing her head into me over and over, all the while she locked eyes with me. Roxanna was moaning on the dick. Mmm-a, MmmM-a, Mmmm-a! She pulled me out her mouth then stuffed one of my balls into her mouth and hummed on them and rubbed my dick all over her face. Then she licked on my balls, all under my dick until she reached the head and then she popped me back into her mouth and started to Jack my dick while she sucked until her lips hollowed.

"Damn Roxanna! I'm about to nut bae"

She sucked harder and faster. I busted all down her throat. I tried to grab her by the back of the head and she stopped sucking and told me not to touch her, but the whole time she was jacking my dick, moving her hand back and forth milking every last drop out of me.

Roxanna pushed me down on the floor, good thing she has O.C.D and cleans her house all day long and plus she had carpet. I rubbed all over that ass with one hand while I stuffed my dick into her lil hole. I could feel her pussy oozed all down my dick and it made squishy noises. That pussy was hot, she rose all the way up then back down while she dug her nails into my chest.

"Ummm Oyah,"

She was riding me in a steady motion.

"Damn this pussy feels extra good."

"Hmmm. Hmmm. Hmm. Oyah, Ohhh yes baby, Cum in this pussy."

She bounced up and down on me while I held her ass and sucked on her pretty pink nipples. I sucked all over them, trapping her nipples with my lips and pulling on them. She pulled on my dreads then bit down on my shoulder. I gave her just what she wanted and filled her up with my cum. She felt me shooting off in her and she started to cum at the same time.

As soon as she was done, she hopped off me and just walked away without saying anything to me. Roxanna made me feel used, but for some reason that turned me on. I let her shower while I looked through the closet to see what I wanted to wear. I came out with a LRG fit and I matched them with some white , blue and black Retro 6's. When she got out the shower, I got in and just let the hot water beat on my back. It was relaxing to the point that I stayed in there longer than I thought. I hurried up and finished up, got out and dried myself off, put on my Polo boxers and walked into the room. I applied deodorant and put on my Dolce and Gabbana Light Blue Cologne then got dressed. I looked at myself in the mirror and thought, I am a fly young nigga. Roxanna had on a skin tight Black Bebe dress with some Versace heels and a matching Versace clutch. I got me a bad foreign bih. I grabbed my loot and put it in my pocket, put on my Cuban link chain and bracelet and my Iced out pinky ring, and headed out the door.

"Make sure you set the ADT alarm on the house."

"I always do daddy."

"Cut the lies, I've been over here a few times and never had to disarm the house."

.Okay babe, I'll make sure I do it now, Damn!"

"Here you go, you gotta drive so I can roll up."

I gave her the car keys and walked over to the passenger door. We got in and she started the car. Plies- Got'EM Hatin came on the radio.

"Turn that shit up bae."

We pulled out heading to Oneco. I had a Circle K bag in my back seat with gars in it from earlier. I have to keep packs on deck at all times. I had a half zip in my glove box.

"Bae go to the Sonic on U.S.41."

"Boy, you hungry?"

"Nah ma we meeting Tha Fam there, you forgot?"

"Oh yea I did. All I can think about is what we did back at the house, your dick game is good. I just wish you would eat my pussy."

"Maybe I will do that for you when we get back home"

By the time we pulled up to Sonic, I had 6 gars rolled up. Moon and Big-B was already there. Moon had Lala in the car with him. Big-B was alone in a Rental. I texted Nando and Purp.

"Where y'all boys at?"

Soon as I hit send, Purp and J. Gangsta pulled up in another Rental and parked beside me. We all got out the car at the same time and dapped each other up.

Purp pulled his shirt up to show me he was strapped, then Moon, J.Gangsta and Big-B patted his waist, letting me know they was all packing heat. Nando pulled up in his Acura with a Stick on his passenger seat and 2 Pistols on his lap.

"Y'all ready or what?"

"Bih, we was waiting on you, but let's roll out."

We all pulled out back to back. I was leading the Convey. We rode down U.S. 41 towards Sarasota until we reached the light on U.S.41 and Whitfield Ave. I turned right at that light then made an immediate left onto the plaza where Latin Quarters is at. The parking lot was filled with cars and the line was all the way down to the end of the Plaza. It was more women than men from what I can see. I'm here on business but if I wasn't I would be mad that I had Roxanna with me. We all pulled up in-front and paid to park our cars right at the front door.

The people in line was looking at us because we all walked up to the front door of the club. Roxanna and LaLa walked in front of us and the bouncer blocked our way so I spoke up.

"I got $500 for you if you let us skip the line, I'm not trying to wait in no long ass line, plus I want a section for my crew with 4 bottles."

"That's going to be separate from the $500 you gave me."

"I know that, you saying that like we don't got money. Better yet, call the owner Rafie and tell him Oyah demands for him to come see him."

The bouncer got on the radio and said something into it but I couldn't hear and not even one minute later, Rafie was coming towards me with a huge smile on his face.

"Oyah! How are you doing?"

"We would be better if we could be seated in a section with 2 bottles of Remy and 2 bottles of Goose. I also need $5,000(five thousand) in $1 bills and nothing but Exotic and foreign bitches in our section."

I peeled off $6,000(six thousand)and gave it to Rafie

"This should be enough."

"Yes Oyah, I'm so sorry for the inconvenience. I'll make sure that never happens again."

In the club the vibe was lit, we had all kinds of foreign females in our section. Puerto Rican and Black, Asian and Black, Cubans, Dominicans, there was even a Arabian woman in our section. You can see our bottles being brought out to us from across the club. It was a train of 6 bottle girls. There was one bottle on a tray with sparkles that each female had. The other 2 Bottle girls each had a tray. One with a huge bucket of ice, cups and chasers and the other with a tray with 5 $1000 Stacks.

As the night went on, my team was enjoying themselves, everyone had them a new foreign bitch. Everyone except Moon and I because we had Lala and Roxanna there with us. I kept feeling like Heat was coming towards us from the other side of the club and when I would look, it was those damn Dominicans "Bello and Tapia" they wasn't even enjoying the night because they was busy watching our every move. I pulled up on Purp

"Bruh, get her number and let her go about her business. I need y'all to play the parking lot and follow them Dominicans so we can know where they stay at. If the situation looks sweet, go for what you know."

"Bruh let's handle that, we got all that under control."

Purp and J.Gangsta walked out the club. I gave them about 5 minutes to get in position. Then I told Moon to give Lala his car keys and I sent Lala and Roxanna to Moon house. Once they was gone, me, Big-B, Moon and Nando walked over to Bello and Tapia and I took a seat in between both of them while my team surrounded us just in case things got out of control we can be able to get shit in line.

"What's good with y'all boys? Hope y'all was able to enjoy the night because Tha Fam sure did. We even added some Dominican Hoes to our flock. But Ima cut the small talk, I'm the head of Tha Fam. We are not a gang, we are family, so when I'm hearing that people are sending threats towards anyone in my family, I get worried. I hate to worry about anything."

"Look, we know exactly who you are Oyah! And who Tha Fam is. But when it comes to Heroin, this is our city. That market belongs to us."

"Says who? Because as far as I'm concerned, you flew here and I grew up here, so you have no fucking business saying anything around here is yours."

"Oyah, Oyah, Oyah, no need for hostility. We can work this out and come to a mutual agreement that will work for the both of us."

"Let me hear what you got in mind because you already pissing me off!"

115

"Let me supply you with your dope. Doing it that way, you can sell anywhere you want because we will both be eating."

"What if I refuse your offer and just keep doing me, the way that I have been."

Bello is the bigger outta the two. I looked around because I felt myself getting madder by the seconds. On the table in-front of us was a bottle of Moët Rose. Big-B gave me the look like he was ready to move. I stood up, looked down at the bottle of Moët and told both of these plantain eating bitches

"No Deal, Tha Fam runs Manatee and Sarasota County. We move our dope anywhere we feel like and fuck whoever don't like how we move."

Before anyone could even speak up and say something about what I just said, I blanked out and all I could see was Red. I snatched the bottle of Moët up and in one swift move, I smashed Bello with the bottle on his head. Big-B knocked out Tapia with a one- hitter quitter. Then he slammed his other man that tried to steal. Everyone in the club started to disperse. While I was beating Bello ass to a pulp. Moon and Nando was beating the other Dominicans that was with them. Big-B cleared a path knocking everyone out in his way until we made it out of the club.

Outside, Moon and I hopped in my car and Big-B and Nando each got in theirs and we pulled off headed to Manatee Woods to Moon's crib so we could figure out our next move.

When we walked in the apartment, Roxanna ran up to me,

"Are you okay babe? Are you hurt, do you need my help with something?"

"Nah Ma! What makes you think I'm hurt?"

"Shit all that blood on your shirt and face."

"Oh this ain't my blood. Moon come out front with me so I can holla at you."

Big-B and Nando was out front already smoking and making sure ain't nobody followed us and is trying to sneak up on us.

I gotta call Purp to see what he doing. Ring! On the first ring, he picked up.

"Yoo what's good bruh? Y'all boys safe?"

"Yea we at Moon spot, but what's good with you and J. Gangsta?"

"We parked down the block from what looks like could be a stash spot or something, because the house right on the Bay on Pearl St."

"Bruh how many cars are at that spot? Ima come that way now"

"Nah bruh, we got this under control, just be on standby just in case we need you."

"What y'all boys going to do?"

"We about to run off in their spot, let me holla at you later."

"Aight bruh be safe."

Purp had 2 Glock .45 with extended clips on each and J.Gangsta had an AK-47 with a 100 round drum. They drove the rental Damn near to the front door. They parked in the driveway, left the car running and hopped out, and the doors opened. They stood on both sides of the door and J. Gangsta counted to three. 1,2,3.....and Purp booted the door flying open. J.Gangsta stepped through the door first then Purp followed right behind him. Tapia was sitting on the sofa talking on the phone, when the door went crashing open, he dropped the phone and tripped over his own feet trying to get to his fire on the kitchen counter. Bad move, J.Gangsta let the stick bark and Tapia caught 6 bullets to his upper body and his lifeless body crashed into the wall painting it red. Purp did a quick sweep of the house looking for Bello. He was hiding in the Master bedroom in the walk-in closet. Purp smashed him so hard with the .45 that blood splashed everywhere and it knocked him out. He kicked him in the ribs as hard as he could trying to get him back up. J.Gangsta walked in and busted out laughing.

"Look at this soft ass Dominican, you don't look so powerful now."

He woke up begging for them not to kill him.

"Get your bitch ass up and where's all the money at Big Timer? You better start talking and I'll spare your life or you can be tough and I'll splash your ass the way my brother did your boy in the front room. I'm ready to kill so give me a reason why I shouldn't do you right now!"

"Please don't kill me! I have $200,000(two hundred thousand) stashed in the mattress of the spare bedroom and the garage. I have a lil over 3 keys of Mexican Tar. Just take it and leave my house."

"Purp watch this nigga while I go check out what he saying. If he sending me on a funny mission, hit that bitch with all 64 rounds."

"No! No! Please! I'm telling you the truth. I don't want to die. I know y'all coming about what happened at the club. I want no problems with Tha Fam. I promise to let shit go, I won't retaliate or get cops involved in anything, just let me live."

"Look bitch ass nigga, shut the fuck up before I pop your ass."

"Bruh I found the work and a bunch of cut."

"Bag all of it up and go find the cash. I know someone heard something, it's been too many shots fired."

"BINGO, I hit the jackpot bruh."

When I seen J. Gangsta come around the corner, back into the room with a black trash bag and his A.K. in one hand and a pillow case in the other, I smiled and looked down at Bello who had fear in his eyes.

"Purp, kill that bitch ass nigga and let's go."

I hit him 5 times to the face and 3 times to his chest, just to make sure he was dead. We headed out the door. Things look normal outside so we just headed down east.

Ring! Ring! Ring!

"Yoo Oyah! We about to pull up in a few minutes so have the door open."

"Aight Nando and Big-B out there already. Is everything good with y'all?"

"Yea bruh, we good. I'll holla at y'all when I get there."

"Aight bet!"

I walked out the front door and told Big-B to keep an eye out for Purp and J.Gangsta. Soon as I said that, the car hit the corner fast as if they were running from the law or something. Soon as they got in a parking spot, J.Gangsta called for Big-B and gave him the 2 pistols and the stick.

"Bruh get rid of these and make sure they can never be found."

"I got you bruh, Ima have Joey cut them up into lil pieces, then Ima dump them in different parts of the Gulf of Mexico."

"Big-B go handle that now then come straight back over here soon as you get done. Y'all niggas take a shower and give Nando y'all clothes so he can burn them. Ima have Ray-Ray come clean y'all car out."

"Hold up bruh, go grab the bag and pillow case that's in the back seat."

"I got you, just wash up so y'all can tell me what's going on."

"Babe you and Lala go to your spot and we will link with y'all later on, Tha Fam and I have business to take care of."

"Okay babe, be safe and call me if you need anything, I LOVE YOU!"

"I love you too babe and I will, I promise."

"Moon get these niggas some basketball shorts a T-shirts with Jordan slides because everything they just had on is going to the Grill, so it can get burned."

While Purp was in the shower, I went to the car and in the back seat was a pillowcase and a trash bag, both had some weight to it. So I grabbed them up and hurried up in the apartment and locked the door. I sat both of them on the sofa, then sat down on the recliner and rolled the gars while Moon get shit situated for Purp and J. Gangsta. When I got done rolling, Moon came out the room, then Purp came out the bathroom in the master bedroom. I fired up a Gar and we waited on J. Gangsta to get done.

Between me, Nando, Moon and Purp we burned both gars before J. Gangsta made it out the shower and joined us, so we each rolled up one. I felt like one Gar each wasn't going to be enough to ease our minds after these 2 wild niggas broke the news. They ran down everything that took place, by the end I smoked my whole Gar and was so hyped that I was ready to celebrate.

"That's what I'm talking about, fuck them Dominicans. We about to catch heat because everyone saw us beefing tonight at the club, but that won't amount to anything. Now bitches are going to think twice before they try to come at Tha Fam."

"Bruh, we need to get low for a lil just in case a bih seen us following them fools."

"Yea that's a good idea, y'all can take my Charger and go to Orlando for a few days or at least until I can figure out what's-what. Also take some hoes with y'all so they can get the rooms in their names."

"Hell yea that's a good idea, Purp, let's get them foreign hoes from the club. I want some new pussy."

"Yea Ima hit the bih I was kicking it with all night."

"Let's count up what's in the bag and split it between all of us."

"Nah no need for all that, y'all 2 niggas earned whatever is in that bag."

"Well at least keep all the dope then, plus they say it's Tar and I don't know how to turn Tar into Powder. My people like powder.

"How much dope y'all hit for?"

"Bello said it was a lil over 3 bricks."

"I know just what to do with the Tar, leave it up to me, I got this."

"So here are the car keys. Let me know when y'all make it to Orlando and get situated. Ima hit the streets when I wake up, just to see what the hood is talking."

"Okay bet that up bruh, hold our loot for us until we come back, I don't wanna travel with all that. We going to take $20,000(twenty thousand) and just make way with that. Give our phones to Big-B so he can catch our people while we gone."

"Y'all good, we a family and we got y'all back. Make this trip like a mini vacation and enjoy y'all selves."

"Aight bet, we finna slide, and get at you once we are situated."

"Moon, take me to Palmetto. I'm tired as fuck and I have to be up in a few hours. Nando, grab all that work and give it to Big-B. Tell him to turn those 3 bricks into 6 then to mix all of it with the work from Piloto. I'll link with y'all when I wake up."

# CHAPTER 7

# BREAKING NEWS

Sunday morning at 10:30, my alarm clock on all my phones went off at the same time. When I opened my eyes and tried to reach for my phones on the nightstand, but couldn't move because Roxanna was laying on my chest with her leg over my waist. I moved her just a lil so I can reach over to turn the alarms off on the phones. I grabbed the remote and turned on the tv so I could watch the news and get the weather for the day.

First thing Bay News 9 showed was a mugshot picture of Bello and Tapia, two Bradenton residents found shot to death. These men was head of a drug trafficking ring that imported their own Heroin into the United States. As of this moment, we have no leads on the suspects. Anyone with any information please contact crime stoppers.

That's a good thing that the News Station ain't saying too much about what happened. Ima have to hit a few corners and see what the hood is talking about.

"Roxanna, I need you to go get $20,000(twenty thousand) out your draw with your thongs and boy shorts in it, then run it to Piloto in Orlando, so he won't think I'm trying to play any games with his money."

"Okay daddy, let me shower real fast, then I'll go."

"And, I need you to get a rental because I let my boys hold my car for a few days."

"Let me call them so I can make reservation to pickup a truck." Roxanna said

"You do that real fast while I shower then."

When I got out, she already had the car reserved for me and bacon, egg and cheese on a bagel with some apple juice waiting on me.

"Eat babe while I shower then we can slide."

"What type of car did you get?"

"They didn't have any trucks ready for pickup so I got a S-Type Jag for you."

"Aight bet!"

One hour later I was pulling out the Budget Car Rental with a Pepsi Blue S-Type heading to Oneco while Roxanna went to handle that with Piloto for me. I text Piloto to let him know that I was sending Roxanna, so he can be expecting her.

I was feeling myself sliding in this S-Type listening to Young Jeezy-Soul Survivor. I pulled up to the Trap on 60th and Big-B was already outside getting the Dirt Bikes ready for Chunky Sunday. Big-B loves to gamble and today he had 3 races lined up. I got out the car and dapped him up.

"What's good bruh, when did you buy that Jag?"

"I didn't buy it, I rented it because I let Purp and J.Gangsta take my Charger to Orlando for a few days."

"Nando told me what took place, you don't think that was a bad move, that's going to bring heat our way?"

"Fuck no, it had to go down that way to avoid a war that would've brought a lot of heat on Tha Fam and cost us a lot of money. Plus that's one less group we have to worry about competing with. That's more money for you, me and Tha Fam."

"What did you do with the Heats?"

"Joey cut them up, then I took him over the bridge by Manatee Memorial Hospital and we threw a few pieces into the water, then we did the same going North on the Skyway and coming back South on the Skyway. Those bangers will never be found."

"Aight bet! Did you break that other brick down yet?"

"Nah Ima get on that now."

"Okay, did Nando bring you those other 3 bricks of Tar?"

"Nah, but why you got Tar this time? We have a lot of people who sniff. That's going to fuck up our flow."

"Big-B, do you believe I would do something to fuck up our flow of money? Because slowing things down on the trap is slowing down the money that comes into my pockets and safes. I'm trying to get Rich not stay broke. I want you to take the brick you have now and turn it into 2, then the 3 bricks of Tar Nando got, turn those into 6. After you blend all that up, mix the 2 bricks with the 6 and blend it all together and make 8 Bricks. Ima flood the streets and drop the price on the dope so Tha Fam can have a wiggle room to eat more.

Start on that, Ima have Nando swing on by with that so he can help you and I need the rest of those zips that I brought over here."

"It's all in the room inside of the night stand."

"Okay bet, Ima go make some plays, then meet up with you at the park down East because I need to make some of that free money on those races."

"I hit Uzi up, bruh, I'm on my way to you now."

"Aight, I'm gonna just knock on the door."

"Okay bet."

On my way to Uzi spot, I texted Fat Face to see how she was doing, but she ain't never text back, so I hit K. Cramer up and she answered on the 7th ring.

"Hello babe, how are you?"

"I'm good Mami, just taking things one day at a time. But I'm missing you and would like to see you again."

"I miss you as well Oyah, but I'm out of town to my house in Boston. We had a death in the family so Ima be up here for a few days. I'll just get back at you when I'm back in town."

"Aight, don't forget about me."

"Never that babe, see you soon."

That Hoe left town just in case I would start looking for her, she would be far away.

This car is catching everyone's attention and I have no tint on it. Ima have to get someone to pull up at the park and get my rental tinted. At Uzi spot, it was dead, that ain't seen right to me because the trap was booming. So I stepped out the car with the Louis Vuitton bag and let it hang over one shoulder. I rang the bell and a cute Puerto Rican girl answered the door wearing a Purple La-Pearla Bra and Thong set.

"Uzi is in the back room." She said in horrible English.

"What's good Fam, how are you living?"

"Bruh, I'm living like a King as you can see, " he pointed towards the woman, who let me in and twirled his finger in the air."

She stood in front of me with a Kool-Aid smile while I looked her up and down and licked my lips. Then she slowly spun around so I could see her ass and how it swallowed her G-String.

"Yea you living good bruh and who is this Red head you got sitting with you rolling up?"

"Oh this is a friend, her name Jenny, but I call her Jenny from the block."

"Where do you wanna handle this business at?"

"Excuse me ladies, can y'all go out into the front room while I take care of business."

Jenny from the block stood up and she also had on a La-Pearla Bra and Thong set but hers was Red and she was like 5'1 with nice tits and ass on her.

"Damn Uzi, you have 2 bad Hoes here with you, where is Davi?"

"He went out with his baby mamma Bridget."

"So, how much you trying to grab?"

"I need 10 Zips if you can fill that order."

"Uzi you fucking with the connect, I can fill any order you wanna place."

I unzipped my Louis Vuitton backpack and pulled out the 10 zips. Uzi's eyes got huge.

"How much dope you got in there?"

"After the 10 you just grabbed, I have 16 more Zips."

"Damn bruh, you wild for riding around with all that work on you."

"Do you know what I could do if I had all that work!"

"Can you handle a whole brick if I was to front it to you?"

"Yea it will take me a few days to get your money back but you will get all your loot."

"Look, flip these 10 Zips and save as much as you can and I will bless you on the next Re-Up with the remaining 36 Zips."

"Aight bet that up bruh."

"Bruh, why is it so dead around here? I have never seen this block so dead."

"Here go $30,000(thirty thousand) he pulled it from under the couch he was sitting on, wrapped in a brown paper bag. The block is dead today because it's Sunday and I don't work on Sundays. Today is my day to relax and enjoy myself."

"What's so special about Sunday's?"

"I was raised a Catholic."

"Oh okay then."

My phone rang and it was Roxanna.

"Yoo what's up babe, hit Piloto up and tell him I'm coming down his street now."

"Okay hold on, Ima Churp him."

"YooOoo Piloto!"

"Churp!"

"Talk to me."

"Churp!"

"My girl about to pull up."

"Churp!"

"Okay, I'm going downstairs to open the door now."

"Churp!"

"He coming down now babe, what you doing when you leave from there?"

"Ima go by the Orlando Premium Outlets and see what I can find."

"Aight, let me know when you get back. I love you."

"I love you too, bye."

"Uzi, I gots to go bruh, just let me know when you ready."

I put all the loot in the backpack, zipped it up and headed towards the door. Jenny from the block was sitting in the front room, when she saw us, she asked if she could ride with me. She was looking so cute, I told her Yea.

"Okay hold on let me put on my shirt and pants real fast."

"I'll be outside in the car waiting."

Uzi walked me to the door

"When you get done with her, drop her off at her spot. Ima layup with Jessica and I don't wanna be bothered."

When the door opened and he saw the S-Type, he got hyped.

"You fucking Snapping bruh, this bih clean."

"It's a rental, I'm broke nigga, I don't got the funds to pay for a car like this."

"Yea! Fucking! Right! Nigga this me, I know what you doing out here."

"Oh yea Oyah, did you hear about what happened last night?"

"Nah, what happened bruh."

"The Streets saying Bello and Tapia got killed by their Dominican connect, because he found out that one of them was working with the Feds. It's Breaking News right now. Tapia got hit with a stick and Bello got hit almost 100 times all over his upper body. Those Dominicans ain't playing around."

"Fuck then bitches, they got what they was looking for."

Jenny from the block came out of Uzi's spot wearing some really short jeans shorts and a crop top wife beater. Damn, this Redhead is Sexy. She got into the car smelling like strawberries.

"You ready to slide?"

"I'm with you, so I'm on your time babe."

"Aight, let me text my nigga from Sota and let him know that I'm on my way."

Sliding down U.S. 301 going to Sarasota, I was listening to "Lil' Wayne Fire Man,"

"Ma roll up, I'm trying to get high."

"You Smoke in this expensive car?"

"Yea it's just a car."

I turned down 21St, then made a right onto Maple Avenue and pulled up on Turd. Before I could even come outside Turd was walking out his spot. I hopped out with my backpack.

"What you trying to grab bruh?"

"The same thing, 6 Zips. Let me run inside so I can grab the loot."

When he came back out, I was sitting in the driver's seat with the door open and the backpack on the ground. Jenny just passed me the Gar and Turd handed me 2 stacks of bills.

"That's $18,000(eighteen thousand)bruh. Who this? The white girl K. Cramer I keep hearing about because if so, you better be careful with her."

"Nah bruh, this ain't that bih, but what about her because she fucking with someone out Tha Fam."

"She was cool with my brother, the nigga had her around her a few times until she took some loot from him."

"Yea I got her from over here one day, you remember I asked you about her and you said you wasn't fucking her."

"Yea, Yea, Yea, I remember that but I ain't know who the bitch was at the time. I just wanted her away from here because she was trying to smoke up all my weed. It be so many hoes coming through that it is hard to keep up with them."

"Yea I bet L.O.L! But Ima slide we are going to be riding the Dirt Bikes and 4 Wheelers at the East Bradenton Park later on around 1:00P.M., Ima slide through, I got me a brand new KX-450."

"Aight bet, I'll see you then."

When we left the spot, Jenny told me she knew K.Cramer. I instantly got pissed but I ain't show her any signs.

"How do you know her?"

"We went to school together and we was real cool until she started fucking my brother and set him up to get robbed by another guy she fucks with from Palmetto."

"Do you know who this nigga is?"

"Nah, all I know he from Jackson Park in Palmetto, that's where she always be at."

"Do you know where she stay at?"

"Yea she stay right behind Harllee Middle school with her mom, dad, sister and they have a bunch of pets, but the dogs are mean, they will bite the shit out of you."

"We going to drive by there and point out the house for me."

"Aight bet, I got you daddy."

Is it all white hoes ain't shit or is she just reacting because of what happened to her brother. Whatever it is, Ima keep a close eye on her and won't let her too close to the circle. We pulled up to a nice house on Magellan Drive.

"That's it right there babe, the green house with that old car in the garage."

"2308?"

"Yea that's it, they been living here for some years mow."

"Aight, bet that up Mami."

We drove to the old duck off spot, so I can check on Big-B to see if he was able to handle all of that for me.

When we got to the old duck off spot, you couldn't even tell my door was ever kicked in. We walked in then I sat on the sofa, kicked my Jordan's off and turned on the news. Jenny sat down beside me and crossed her legs in a Indian style position. I looked her way and she had one of the fattest pussy I have ever seen. Her pussy sat in those Jean shorts looking like a Mango. But what I heard on the news caught my attention. It flashed on the top of the hour....

Live Coverage from the scene where two men were murdered in cold blood at Bradenton residence. The two deceased are connected to a organization based out of NYC called Trinitario, who are responsible for 90% of the murder rate in the Tri-State. Officials believe the murders happened because the Trinitarios found out about Jose Gonzalez aka Tapia cooperation with the D.E.A.

I had a huge smile on my face. Jenny asked

"Babe what do you find so amusing about what you just seen."

I didn't even answer her, I just stood up from the sofa looked down at her, I have some weed in the freezer and gars in the kitchen draw

"Roll up so we can slide to the park."

I walked out the house, headed towards the trap. I pulled my phone out and looked at my text messages. J. Gangsta had texted me saying they was staying at the "W" in downtown Orlando. I called them and Purp picked up on the first ring.

"Yoo what's good Fam?"

"Everything is good, y'all in the clear."

"Aight bet, we will be back tomorrow then, because J. Gangsta wanna do a lil shopping."

"Just hit my line when you get back."

"Aight bet."

Dinky was at the trap strapping down the bikes and getting them ready to go down East to the park.

"Bruh, I was just about to call you, Ima need to use your truck for like 2 hours sometime this week. Ima shoot you $200 and fill your tank up."

"You ain't got to do all that bruh, but just let me know when you need it and you can come pick it up from my house."

"Aight Thanks."

I walked in the spot and Big-B was cleaning up, and putting all the Keys in a beach cooler.

"Nando dropped off some loot for you and grabbed 1200(twelve hundred)baggies so he in the Red $24,000(twenty four thousand) plus he got 100 grams so that's another $12,000(twelve thousand)he owes. Nando also said Bullet is going to need a Re-up by the morning. 12th street is doing numbers over there."

"Ima head to the Park but Ima leave my young-in's here making money while we are gone. Let me call Tee-Baby, so she can come grab the cooler and put it away at our new spot."

When I called her, she sounded out of breath.

"What the fuck is you doing?"

"Nothing babe, Paradise and I are cleaning up the house. I'm waiting for the store to deliver all the items I bought."

"Come by the trap and pick up this Cooler and put it away some place that's cool at the new spot."

"I'll be there in an hour."

"Aight, bruh is going to have one of his people give it to you because none of us are going to be here."

"Okay then be safe out there Oyah. People are getting killed in those streets."

"Always Mami."

At the park, there was over 30 dirt bikes and 4Wheelers. Hank had the big Grill going with Ribs and Chicken. The girls was dressed in the smallest piece of clothes they could find, all the Trick outs was lined up on the side of the field where we were going to be riding at. D.J.-Big Dawg was out there with huge concert speakers.

The niggas outta Red Quarters were there as well and R-2 wanted to holla at me, so we walked to the Jag. Jenny was in the driver seat, so I got in the passenger seat and R-2 hopped in the back seat.

"Take this for bruh because the first race is about to start."

"Oyah! Your name is making noise out here and Rue said you the man I need to holla at, I'm looking for some good Sand."

"Yea, I got the whole thing going for $20,000(twenty thousand)."

"When can I see one?"

"Whenever you are ready to cop."

"You know where my trap is at, next door to Rue's mom's house."

"Yea I know."

"Well come by tomorrow, the earlier the better."

"Say less, we'll just link then."

By nightfall, I done made $17,000(seventeen thousand) just side betting with Tha Fam.

"Ima go get my Box Chevy tomorrow and shoot to Tampa to grab my chains for my 3 women."

I would have made more but we lost 3 out of 10 races, but $17,000(seventeen thousand)was good money and it came right on time for me to get my shit out the shop.

"Yoo Big-B, How much did you make out here tonight?"

"I made around $15,000(fifteen thousand). I ain't really count it yet."

"Well check it out, Ima get me some BBQ, then Ima drop Ol-Girl off, then go rest up because I'm fucking tired and have a long day tomorrow."

"Lil-Mama, where you going? because I'm dead tired and I'm ready to go home and rest up."

"One of them foam trays of food is yours."

"Take me home, I stay in Sarasota off Lockwood Ridge."

"Aight let's slide."

"When will we chill again?"

"Maybe tomorrow, I have a few things to do, then I'll be free after."

I dropped Jenny off at her house, then jumped on I75 going North. I got off on the Palmetto exit and drove to New Town where Roxanna stayed at. I pulled up and she still wasn't home. So I parked the car then went inside with my Louis Vuitton bag filled with cash and 10 Zips of food. I threw the bag in the closet, took my clothes off and got in the shower. The hot water was relaxing once I was done, I dried off then laid in the bed naked with the ceiling fan on full blast and before I knew it, I had dozed off. When I woke up, Roxanna and I was spooning in the bed together. We were both naked and she had her ass pressed on my dick. Her warm skin made me get hard instantly and when she felt that dick poking her pussy, she moaned and grabbed my dick and guided me into her hot, wet, tight hole. I lifted her leg until it was almost pointed directly to the ceiling fan.

I long stroked her pussy from the side and she moaned so sexy like. Roxanna's pussy was oozing her juices. I moved in and out of her pussy at a steady pace, hitting every wall in that tight pussy. I grab onto her tits

"I love you Mami"

"I love you more daddy. Mmm-a!"

She bounced back into me harder, while I plowed in and out of her pussy, harder and harder. She grabbed the pillow and bit into the corner of it and screamed as loud as she could. Her ass was slapping my stomach making loud clapping sounds.

"I'm cumming Roxanna"

"I'm cumming too daddy, let's cum together. Uhhh!"

"This pussy feels so goooood. So, So fucking good!"

I slammed forward and she smashed her ass back into me meeting every single stroke and we both nutted at the same time. She felt so good that I didn't even pull out. I kept my dick in her while she worked her pussy muscles, squeezing my dick keeping me hard.

"If you ever leave me or fuck another nigga, I will kill you a slow death."

"Stop talking so crazy, this body is yours, I ain't going anywhere."

My phone went off and it was Purp.

"What's good bruh?"

"We are on our way down there now."

"Okay just swing by Manatee Woods when you get down here."

"Aight bet, see you soon."

"Babe let's shower real fast because I need you to take me to Sarasota to pick up my Chevy so I can drop it off at your brother's shop."

"What are you going to do to it?"

"Everything! Paint, Music, Guts, 26'DUB Floaters. I wanna pull it out for the Easter Parade. Go get your ass in the shower while I count up this loot. When are those safes getting here?"

"It's scheduled to get here Thursday."

"Aight bet."

I got up, went to the closet and grabbed the Louis Vuitton backpack. I dumped everything onto the bed. I put the 10 Zips back away and sat the backpack on the floor beside the bed. I counted up and separated all the money rubber banding them up individually in stacks of $1,000. I have $108,500(one hundred eight thousand, five hundred) in the safe and I'm about to add another $59,100 (fifty nine thousand, one hundred) bringing my total amount in the safe to $167,600(one hundred sixty seven thousand, six hundred).

When Roxanna was done in the shower, she got out and started to get ready while I hopped in the shower. She was in the mirror of the bathroom doing her hair when I got out the shower. I dried off, brushed my teeth, put on my deodorant and my boxers. I got dressed in some basketball shorts, tank top, black socks and Jordan Slides.

"You ready Ma?"

"Yea, I've been waiting on you."

"Let's slide."

I picked up all the money, put it in the bag and drove to the Motor Shop to get my Chevy.

When I pulled up, my Chevy was sitting out front looking so old and ran down. I walked in and Gator was just coming out with papers and my car keys.

"I saw that Jag pulled up and was wondering who it was but when I noticed it was you, I started to get your paperwork on the motor. This 454 Big Block has 1275 HorsePower. You will be able to hit 360 burns outs on 26' rims like it ain't nothing, if you ever have to get on the gas, this motor will get you outta a Jam."

I went into my backpack and pulled out the loot that I owed Gator and gave it to him.

"Oyah, you can drive this car anywhere, but please don't let anyone else ever work on this motor but me."

"I got you bruh, Ima take this bih to Tampa right now to go grab some chains."

"Yea that's good, open this bih up so you can see what this motor all about. I put bigger gears in your rear end, drop a 700-R Transmission and did your exhaust. You are good to go and your A/C works better than that Jag you are in."

"Well I'm gone, I'll call you if anything."

I started the Chevy and it had so much compression that the motor felt like it wanted to jump out the car.

"Roxanna, Ima call you a lil later, I have a few runs to make. Keep the Jag, I'll get it from you later."

"Okay daddy, just call me a lil later, Ima go see your mom."

"Aight babe."

I headed down East, when I pulled up in Manatee Woods, I saw my Charger parked out front. These niggas said they was going shopping and then coming out here. It has been just a lil over two hours since we last spoke. I knocked on the door and J. Gangsta answered.

"We was just texting you to let you know we was back."

"Y'all can hold the Charger down for a lil. I got a rental and Ima test drive my new motor in the Box."

"Yea I heard that bih from when you was at the light."

"I got something I need y'all to handle for me. That hoe K.Cramer had someone break into my duck off, good thing wasn't anyone home and I moved all the dope and loot. She stays right behind Harllee Middle School. The house is the only greenhouse on Magellin Drive, and the house number is 2308. Don't harm anyone that's in the house, just tie them up and kill all the animals. I want the Dogs and Cats dead, The Fish and Birds. All Pets must go and make it a horrible death, cut the cats and dogs up or better yet break the birds wings, then let the cats and dogs eat them while making the parents watch. Then make her dad eat the fish while it's still alive. I want this to be Breaking News on Bay News 9."

"Aight bruh, we going to handle that right now, so we can make the 10 O'clock Top of the hour news."

"I got 10 Zips in this book bag, Ima give all 10 for $2,000(two thousand) each. Y'all look out for me and Ima make sure y'all eat. That bitch got my dog killed, so now I want her family to suffer how I did. If you can get her to talk and tell you who it was that had the balls to break into my spot, then do that because I want that nigga dead, and his body never to be found."

"Aight bruh! We got you, that type of shit gets me excited. But we got your $15,000(fifteen thousand) we owe you for the last 5 Zips and the $20,000(twenty thousand) for the 10 Zips. I need to go handle that for you then, link with Nando to get my phones back."

"Aight bet, Ima slide to Tampa then Ima drop my Chevy off to 941 Kustumz because I wanna pull it out for Easter. To be honest we all need to be out there putting on for Tha Fam."

"Moon you coming with me, your chains are done."

"Hell yea I'm coming, let me go grab some loot then we can slide."

I picked up the $35,000(thirty five thousand)I just made and put it in my Louis Vuitton bag with the rest of the loot.

"Let's roll out Moon!"

Me, Purp and J. Gangsta walked out the apartment. They went to get in my Charger and I yelled out.

"Don't go handle that business in the Charger, take the Slider, then sell your Slider and buy y'all something else, unless y'all put it up and only use it when y'all go slide something."

"We going to see how things go because I wanna buy me a new car, I'm not sure if I want to get a BMW or a Cadillac and Purp wants a Maxima."

"Get them all L.O.L but Ima link with y'all later. There go Moon coming now."

Moon and I took the Chevy on a test drive to Tampa. I raced a 2003 Mustang GT and smoked that bitch by at least 5-6 car lengths. We made it to University Mall in less than 20 minutes.

"Damn bruh, you got one of the fastest Chevy in the game, it makes me wanna get me a old school car."

"Get you one so we can pull out back to back."

I parked and we got out the car. I grabbed the backpack, put it on and locked up the Chevy. Once inside the mall we went directly to Aneels shop. When he saw me, he had a big smile on his face, then we shook hands and he opened the safe and pulled out my chains and Moon's.

The Yellow Canary Diamond Chain was hitting. You could cut the lights off and still see it shine.

"Bruh, you about to make me go back in the Lab, you killing shit out here."

"Yea you better, I can't be out shining you.

"It's okay, you my brother, anyone else I would be up here dropping them bands off. But let's get back to Bradenton so I can drop my car off to get tricked out."

"Aight."

We both paid Aneel what was owed to him then slid.

I went west on Fowler until I reached I-275, then I got on the interstate headed back towards Bradenton. When I got on the Howard Franklin Bridge, I dropped the transmission into overdrive and mashed the gas. Moon and I was pinned to our seats. I looked at the dash and it read, I was doing 120MPH, but that's because that's all it had, the car was increasing its speed. I know I was going every bit 160MPH. I was on the Skyway in no time at all. We didn't even get halfway through the Gar by the time I got to the toll plaza.

I texted Roxanna and told her to meet me at her brother's shop. She texted back right away.

"I'm already here daddy."

"Okay just wait there I'm coming off the Skyway now."

Moon passed me the Gar and I took a big hit. I was starting to make good money and was feeling like I was on top of the World. When I pulled into 941 Kustumz, everyone looked my way. My Chevy is not even done yet and it's already demanding attention. I hopped out and Abel walked up to me and ask.

"Brother-In-Law, what do you want done?"

"All I know for sure is, I want them 26' DUB Trump Floaters and you can do you, just make sure my shit looks good when you get done. I want everything done, music, paint, interior, lift all that shit and I need it done by Easter"

"Oyah, I got you but what is your spending limit on everything so I can know what I'm playing with?"

"Try and keep it around $20,000(twenty thousand) for everything. I'll bring you half on Friday and the other half when it's done."

"Okay, give me the keys so I can start stripping it."

"They in the car, let me grab my book bag and weed then I'm gone."

"Okay I'll see you on Friday."

"Babe, let's go to your house so I can drop you off with this loot, then I can go handle some business."

"Okay, are you coming back over tonight?"

"I should be but if I don't then that means I got busy at the traps."

As soon as I said that, she got really sad, looking like she was about to cry.

Moon said, "Sis don't start that shit now bruh has a huge responsibility between all these traps he is in control over a lot . You ain't fucking with a average Oneco Nigga. Oyah is the last of a dying breed and because of him, we all going to be good Sis."

She responded saying ,"Moon I understand all that, I just need him to treat me like I deserve to be treated, for him to let these hoes know I'm his woman."

While Roxanna and Moon was talking, I went into my bag and pulled out the $35,000(thirty five thousand) that I got from Purp and J. Gangsta. I grabbed Roxanna's purse and put a few stacks into it but between her driving and Moon talking, I slipped the Gold box holding her Chain into her bag, then covered it with the rest of the cash.

"Umm babe, I put $35,000(thirty five thousand) in your purse please make sure you put that up for me."

We pulled up to her house and we all got out, Moon got in the passenger side seat, I gave her a kiss and hopped in the driver side and we pulled out.

"Bruh, how your cuzzo Punkin doing with the phones? I ain't seen or heard about him since that one day."

"He good bruh, my cousin is a Hustler for real, that nigga all over. I'm thinking of just letting him run the phones for me."

"That's your call just make sure when he pumps up that he keeps the same energy."

"I got him bruh."

"Aight, well I gots to go by the trap on 60th, you going with me or do you want me to drop you off at your house?"

"Nah, I'm sliding with you, Ima have LaLa meet us over there with the Re-Up money because my cousin is running low."

"Bruh tell her to pull up at the old duck off spot. That's where I'll park the Jag and hit the cut to get to the trap."

"Yea, Ima text her now and let her know."

We pulled in the driveway of the duck off spot and parked. I grabbed my backpack and we both went into the house. Moon went into the back room and got on the XBox playing Madden 06, it had just came out.

I called Tee-Baby, she answered on the first ring.

"Hello my love, what's good?"

"What you and Paradise doing?"

"Nothing, she fixing up the front room while I do the kitchen."

"Did you get all the furniture for the house?"

"Yea, I'm still waiting on the dining room set, but everything else is here and in the morning we going to Bed, Bath and Beyond to get bedding and curtains."

"Okay, well I need you to hurry up and do what you do, then both y'all come over here to the duck off."

"I'll be over there in no more than an hour, do you need anything before I get there?"

"Nah Mami, Im good, just hurry up."

"Ima walk over to the Trap bruh."

"Aight, bring me 8 Zips when your come back."

"I got you!"

I hit the cut and I could tell there was something going on out here. I could feel the tension in the air. I used my key to get in the trap and the tension seemed like it got even more intense.

"What's good with y'all?"

"Shit, y'all niggas looking like y'all ready to murder somebody."

"Bruh some Mexican or Puerto Ricans moved in across the street and it's slowing shit down for us here. They short stopping the basers."

"They got good dope, because if not then all the basers will come right back to us the next time."

"One of the basers said they have some good shit over there, it's that gray dope."

"We going to have to run down on them Chico's, because if they wanna sell dope on this block then they have to shop with Tha Fam and sell our dope or move someplace else."

"Let me get all that dope! Ima move it to my new stash house. Keep a brick and give me all the rest. Take the brick I leave here and bag up 504 grams into baggies and make the baggies extra fat."

"Okay bet"

Big-B walked into his room and came out with a duffle bag and handed it to me and I left back to my spot. I got a call from J.Gangsta

"Where you at?"

"I'm at the spot behind the trap on 60th."

"Okay who all there?"

"Moon and LaLa and my other bitches Tee-Baby and Paradise are coming over."

"Well order a few boxes of pizza and hot wings at 10PM, a good tv show is going to be on."

"Is that right, well say less!"

As I was walking up the driveway with the duffle bag, LaLa pulled in behind me. I waited on her to park and get out, she looked me up and down with an attitude for no damn reason.

"You are a real trip sis, what have I ever done to you?"

"To me, shit! But you are a real Hoe, you wanna fuck anything with a fat ass."

"So is that why you hate me, because I swing this Dick like a chopper?"

"Don't worry about it nigga just know I don't fuck with you coming or going."

I walked in and told Moon that Tha Fam was on their way so order some pizza and wings. LaLa sat on the sofa but for whatever reason kept looking my way. She was acting like she had a attitude but her eyes and demeanor said something else. I took my seat at the recliner and rolled me up a Gar before dumping all the dope outta the duffle bag.

"We have a minor problem right now, that Ima have to take care of and put a stop to it before it becomes a major problem."

"Nigga that don't seem like a problem to me, all I see in-front of you is Stacks and a whole lot of opportunity to make a bad situation good."

"How much dope do you have in front of you?"

"This here is 7 kilos of Some fine China white mixed with some Mexican Tar. But dope could never be a problem unless it's just some real trash dope. The problem is the Chico's moved onto 60th and they are short stopping the trap. If they wanna make money on that block, they will have to get down with Tha Fam."

There was a knock on the door but since there was over a half a million dollars in dope I ain't take no chances, I had my Glock 40 and I walked up to the door as quietly as possible and looked through the peephole. It was Tee-Baby and Paradise. I opened the door with my 40 Caliber in my hand to let them in. Once they walked in I peaked out the door and saw my Charger coming down the block so I waited for them, that way I ain't have to get up again. When they pulled in and got out the car, I looked at J. Gangsta and he had a menacing look in his eyes and I would soon be finding out why.

Inside the door we was all smoking and viben when the pizza guy knocked on the door.

"Your bill is $80."

I cut him off

"Here is $100, keep the change."

I grabbed the food from him and locked the door. I hated having my front door with work all over just laying around and even more with this much work out.

We had it on Bay News 9, it was 9:56PM. Tha Fam was all sitting around the front room eating, smoking, talking and making future plans, just waiting for 10PM. So we can watch the top of the hour. Soon as it hit 10PM. We was all locked in, no one knew what to look for except for me, Purp and J.Gangsta.

Everyone else, even the females, was wondering what it was I was trying to see. Tee-Baby thought I was trying to see the weather because I was trying to do something for all of us.

Breaking News: Reporting Live from Bradenton, Florida, this is Amanda Seal, here live at the scene of a gruesome home invasion. Two men dressed in all black wearing black ski masks, home invaded this family home. Nothing was taken from the residence. Mr and Mrs Cramer were home, luckily the suspects didn't harm them. It seemed more like a hate crime or like someone was trying to send a message. We have never witnessed anything like this in Manatee County. The home invaders came in and tied the victims up, sat them in the front room on the sofa and made them watch as they cut, stabbed, burned, beaten with a bat and even drowned their dog in the fish tank. Every living creature, animal wise, died a gruesome death. Then one of the suspects stood in front of Mr Cramer and said

"He better Thank God that my order was to spare human lives and make all animals share the same fate his Bosses Dog did."

If anyone has any information leading to an arrest please call our crime stopper hotline. There is a $1,000 reward if your information leads to an arrest. I looked at J.Gangsta and now I know why he had that menacing look in his eyes....

# CHAPTER 8

# YOU GET DOWN OR LAY DOWN

Paradise was the first to voice her opinion.

"What type of sick fuck would have people, home invade a bih to kill all their animals, like that's some MOB type shit."

"Come over here baby and sit on my lap"

And she did. I told Moon to pass me the Louis Vuitton backpack on the floor by the loveseat. When he did, I opened it and gave her the Gold box and looked over to Tee-Baby. She had a look on her face that if looks could kill, Paradise and I both would be dead right now. Paradise opened the box, looked in and screamed and gave me a big hug and one of the most passionate kiss ever. Then I put the chain on for her. She had a Kool-Aid smile. I then smacked her on the ass and told her to get up.

"Tee-Bae! Bring that ass here, you know daddy loves you."

She came over with a stink attitude and sat down on my lap extra hard. I went back in the bag and pulled out another Gold box, she hurried and opened the box and her eyes lit up like a kid on Christmas morning.

"I know your crazy ass ain't think I got Paradise a chain and didn't get you one."

I helped her put on the chain and she was all smiles as well.

"So to answer your question Paradise, the sick ma'fucker who ordered that was me, the same niggas lap you was just sitting on."

"Why would you do that to those animals when they ain't do shit to you, Oyah you probably don't even know those people."

"You are correct babe, I don't know those people nor do I care about them, fuck'em, they better be lucky I didn't make them pay for their daughter's sins. Their bitch ass daughter had my spot robbed and had my dog killed for no reason at all."

Stormi was a sweet dog, just thinking about how they did my dog makes me want to kill her mom the same way so that hoe K. Cramer can feel my pain. That shit got me mad all over again.

"Oyah give me the word and I'll go beat that old bitches head in with a hammer."

"Purp you need to chill bruh and Oyah you have caused enough havoc behind Stormi's death, let's focus on getting these bands up." Moon said.

"Moon you dead right! Ima just wait because the nigga who disrespected me and thought shit was sweet will pay for breaking into my house, and killing my dog....What if I hadn't moved the Dope or money, they would have hit a nice lick on me. Better yet, I got an idea! Babe grab that duffle bag and take it home and put it up for me, and

Paradise, I need you to grab my backpack with the loot and take it with y'all. The team and I got to go handle some business."

"Moon, you and Lala can go do what y'all do, Ima take Purp and J.Gangsta with me to go take care of this situation on 60th."

"Aight just holla at me later then bruh."

"Oyah, what situation on 60th are you talking about, because you ain't mentioned anything about that to me. We could have been went and seen about a situation?"

"Let's go by the trap so I can grab some fire just in case shit gets out of hand."

"Okay, but how you wanna handle this problem once we get there?"

"We are going to give them a chance to Get down with Tha Fam or Lay Down Forever."

Coming through the cut, the first thing we saw was the Chico's across the street from the trap. I guess our presence and demeanor made them feel some type of way because everyone in their yard stopped what they were doing and watched us as we walked up the driveway of the trap. They must have relaxed when they saw where we was going because the conversations started back up and everyone got back to doing what they was doing. I walked in the trap followed by Purp and J.Gangsta and we went to the back room, lifted the mattress and grabbed 2 Colt.45's, tucked one away on my back and the other went on my side.

Big-B came in the room,

"What's going on Fam?"

"Shit, us three about to go holla at these Chico's and see what's up with them."

"I'm coming with y'all."

"No you ain't, I need you to keep an eye out if you see we out numbered or out gunned then come through with the Stick and let them have the entire 100 rounds."

"Aight I got y'all."

Everyone checked their guns and took them off safety. We walked across the street and Four of the Chico's stood up. When we got like 6 feet away from them, I stopped and so did Purp and J.Gangsta. I introduced us all and let them know we are Tha Fam. Two of the Chico's, I guess the ones who run the show introduced themselves as Gordo and Chilly.

"We come to you with an opportunity to make some real money with a solid Team. This block here was established by Tha Fam, before us, there was only Crack, Sand and Weed sold on this block. So with that being said, all these junkies belong to that trap across the street. If you wanna continue making money on this block, off my Blood, Sweat and Tears, then you are going to have to push work for Tha Fam, simple as that. There is no negotiation. We supply you with the work, pure, so you can cut it however you want and push it how you want. But if you ain't trying to take that route then you can always move on your own."

"Oyah Right?"

"Yea that's me!"

"Well let me say this, I truly appreciate your offer but truth be told, this city don't belong to anyone and I personally don't like the vibes I'm getting from you. It almost feels like you trying to put down on us like we some bitches or something. Who do you think you are dude?"

"That was the first thing I said to you when I walked up, did you forget that fast!"

"Fuck this shit"

Purp said right before he stole Chilly and dropped him with one punch. Then he whipped out his 44 BullDog and pointed it at his head. J.Gangsta and I pulled out our heat and pointed it at Gordo and the rest of his goons.

"Let's not turn this into a massacre out here because it won't end well for y'all."

Gordo had his hands up looking scared, while Chilly was trying to be a tough guy. He told Purp to suck his dick. Purp blanked out and slapped the shit outta Chilly in the mouth with that .44 Bulldog knocking every tooth out in the front of his mouth....

"Now I told y'all, don't make me turn this into a a massacre because I will and nobody on this block will know what's going on. These are my people. They see and hear everything but when it comes to the Police about Tha Fam, nobody hears or sees anything. I take care of my hood."

"Oyah, we want no problem bruh. There has to be a way we can figure this out without all the violence."

"Gordo, shut the fuck up before you find yourself in a problem with me."

"You see, you ain't smart at all, that's why your bitch ass is on the dirt with more than half your teeth missing. Fat Boy, you need to teach this stupid bitch how to shut his mouth before this becomes a messy situation for all you Chico's."

Chilly looked up from the ground and spit blood at Purp. Bang! Bang! Bang! Purp shot the bitch twice in the leg and once in his stomach.

"Ahhh-Fuck Man, you ain't have to shoot me!"

Big-B ran up on us with the Stick and hit two of Gordo's men that tried to make a run for their lives. Boom! Boom! Boom! Boom! Boom! Boom! Boom! Fire spit out the barrel of the Stick causing pure Pandemonium, killing both men right in their tracks.

Purp looked down on Chilly. Arrrrgh! Arrrgh! He hollered while loading his stomach and blood pooled through his fingers.

"Aight bruh! We'll do whatever you want us to do. Just please don't kill me!"

"Too late for all that crying Nigga. Kill that bitch Purp!"

Bang! Purp hit him right in between the eyes. Making his head explode like a watermelon.

"Now Gordo! What it's going to be with you, are you getting down or are you laying down?"

"Ima ride with y'all niggas, I just don't wanna die."

"Oyah, this nigga going to be a real problem for us later on in the future."

"Nah, J.Gangsta, he ain't, are you Gordo?"

"Nah bruh, I just wanna eat, fuck them niggas."

Bang! My bullet ripped through his shoulder.

"Arrgh! Man that hurts! You shot me, why did you do that?"

"You are a real shit eater, I could never have someone on my team that has the potential to switch up on us for a chance to make money. You see my niggas are my brothers and I'll die for anyone of my brothers."

"But I....."

Bang! Bang! Bang! Gordo took 3 Hollow tips to the head. He was dead after the first shot, the other 2 was because it felt powerful to take his life.I could hear the sirens getting closer so we locked up the trap and hit the cut to the old duck off. The girls was still there when we got back and I snapped.

"Didn't I tell y'all to fucking leave? Get y'all stupid asses out of here right fucking now. Put all the guns away in the attic, let's shower and get the fuck away from this side of town. 60th is about to be on the news. So Big-B, go help Nando on 12th and when the smoke clears up, I want y'all two to open up a spot and put one of y'all dawgs to run it. Maybe down east, so the junkies don't have to travel all the way to Oneco to get their fix."

"Okay then but Ima want to get money on all levels if we are going to take that route."

"Ima slide and handle some shit then go home. I'll catch up with y'all tomorrow."

"Aight bet, be safe and call us if you need us."

I hopped in the S-Type and rode to my New spot to get some understanding with these girls. I was sliding and listening to Plies while smoking me a Gar of that Sha-Sha, with deep thoughts running through my head. It's time to expand Tha Fam and take over Manatee County, Nah fuck that, I want Sarasota County as well. I pulled up to my spot, hopped out and walked in. This girl didn't even lock the door, SMFH!

"Yoo Tee-Baby, bring your ass out here."

She came out the laundry room with a basket full of sheets and blankets.

"Why you ain't got the front door locked? You are making it way too easy for a nigga or Police to run off in here and catch you slipping."

"I'm sorry babe, I won't let that happen again."

"I hope not because shit about to get real crazy out here in these streets, in the next six months. I'm going to buy you a new car because I need you to be able to move under the radar."

"Ok okay babe, is there anything I should be worried about."

"Yes you need to worry about a bih trying to snatch you up, so stay on them mirrors while driving and when you come home bend a few corners just to make sure you are not being followed."

"I got you daddy, I promise to be on point."

"Let me get that Louis Vuitton backpack."

"It's in the room, in your closet,"

"Damn I got my own closet?"

"Yes there is a walk-in one in the room and a walk-in in the closet. Yours is in the room. I got one in the restroom so I can go from my closet to the mirror. L.O.L"

"Yea whatever. I like the bedroom set and the living room set. You spending my money well!"

"You said make it a home, I just want you to be comfortable."

"Yea, keep that up bae you're going to have me not wanting to ever leave."

"That would be ideal, Oyah I'm selfish when it comes to you, if it ain't Paradise I don't wanna share you. I want you to just be our man. You don't feel like with us two that's enough for you?"

"Look Tee-Baby I fucks with you, but I'm out here in the streets getting this money so please don't act surprised because you know what all comes with fucking with a Dope Boy. But I have to slide and take care of some shit so I'll link with you later."

I gave her a kiss and left before giving her a chance to respond back to me. I headed straight to Roxanna house. I was missing my bae and I wanted some of that good pussy. I texted letting her know I was on my way, so that she can be awake and ready. I got a text from Uzi telling me that he was ready to link with me. At first I thought it was my bae texting back, but it was one of my work phones. I wrote him back letting him know I was out of the way and that I'll link with him in the morning when I get back on that side of town....

I pulled up in-front of Roxanna house and got pissed off immediately. Her car wasn't in the driveway. I looked down to the sidekick and it was 1:34AM and she still hasn't texted back. Where the fuck is she at this time of night, the club ain't open. I parked and then went in the house, dropped my backpack off in the closet and got myself ready for a shower. In the shower all types of wild thoughts ran through my mind about what this woman could be doing. So I finished up, put on my boxers and shorts, took care of my hygiene, then went to check on my loot. This bitch starting to make me not even trust her.

All my money was where I had left it and it didn't seem to be touched. Thank God for that because I would hate to kill her and waste all that good pussy. Then my mind got to wonder. Is she giving my good pussy away to someone else because if I find out that she is, someone is going to have to die.

Fuck that Ima take my money and go to my house where I have two bitches there who want and need me. I grabbed the duffle bag out of the closet and the backpack, walked outside and put them into my trunk then I went back in the house to get all my jewelry. Roxanna had a wooden box on her dresser that held all our jewelry. And the first thing I saw when I opened it was her new chain that I just got her. Seeing that pissed me off even more because wherever she was at or whoever she was with, she didn't wanna be seen with a chain that said "OYAH" on it..... so fuck that hoe, then she wants me to do better. I grabbed all my jewelry and I took her new chain, fuck it, she don't deserve it anyways.

I hopped off in the S-Type and slid to my spot, I had this spot for a few days and I haven't even stayed there yet, it's time that I get acquainted with it.

Fifteen minutes later I tried to walk in the house, but the front door was locked. So, she listened to what I said, I liked that. I didn't have keys to the front door so I walked back to my car, started it up, clicked the garage opener and drove in and parked my car. I closed the garage door, popped my trunk, grabbed both bags and entered the house through the laundry room. I didn't know my way around the house yet with the lights off, so I had to use the walls to help guide me to the master bedroom.

Soon as I walked in the master bedroom, I couldn't do anything but smile at the sight in-front of me. The T.V. was on and Tee-Bae was laying on her stomach and that ass was looking so good. She had on a Tank Top with some light blue Thongs. Paradise was laying on her side, naked with a pillow in between her legs, both sleeping. I put the bags in the closet and took my shorts off then climbed into bed in between both of them and dozed off. I woke up hours later feeling brand new. When I looked at my phone it was 1P.M. Damn, I slept in. I don't even remember falling asleep. I know I ain't put my phones on the nightstand. I was alone in the bed and I looked over towards the closet and the duffle bag and backpack was on the top shelf of the closet and my shorts was gone.

I got up, took my morning piss, washed my face, brushed my teeth and went looking for Tee-Bae and Paradise. I found Paradise doing some laundry and asked her where Tee-Bae at!

"She went to the Dollar Store to grab a few things." Paradise said.

"You got your phone, if so text her and tell her I said to grab me some ziplock bags and sandwich bags."

"Okay baby"

I couldn't help but grab on her ass, she was still naked. Her ass was really soft. Paradise sent the text and we started to kiss and I sat her on top of the washing machine and put my fingers in her pussy while I sucked on her pretty brown nipples. I could feel her juices seeping past my fingers. The scent of her pussy drove me crazy. I put her thighs on my shoulder and pulled her pussy to my mouth. I peeled her brown lips apart, exposing her clit so I could suck it into my mouth. I was making loud slurping sounds while I gripped her ass and slid a finger into her ass...

"Huhhh, Oyah, Damn you eating my pussy daddy, it feels so fucking good. "Ummm, shit!"

I was fingering her ass hard forcing her to hump into my face, while I sucked on that clit and licked up and down her crease. I tongue fucked her tight sweet tasting pussy and sucking all over her pussy lips. Paradise sat up on my shoulders and got to rocking back and forth with her hand wrapped in my dreads.

"Umm! Ummm! Ummmm! Damn I'm about to cum all over your face."

I gripped her ass even more and slurped and sucked faster and harder until she creamed my face. Soon as she climaxed, we heard the garage door opening up. We kissed then she got back to doing laundry while I went to wash my face and rinsed my mouth out.

Tee-Bae came into the kitchen and was unpacking the bags. I went and got the duffle bag with all the work in it and pulled out the 7 Bricks of Heroin and bust 3 bricks down into zips and kept 4 bricks whole. I ended up with 108 zips. Once I sell all these zips, I'll have $342,000(three hundred, forty two thousand) just off that, plus I still have to collect from Tha Fam.I sent out a multi text to Tha Fam letting them know to pull up on the duck off behind the trap on 60th with the address 2055 61St Ter. West Bradenton, Florida. Everyone texted back right away letting me know they was about to pull up within the next hour. I packed the 4 bricks of Heroin and the 108 zips into the Gucci duffle bag then went to my pantry, opened up the ice cooler and pulled out the 2 bricks of Sand, so I can pack up into my duffle bag as well. I left the other duffle in the closet with $237,600(Two hundred, thirty seven thousand, six hundred). On my way out the door with the Gucci duffle, I gave Paradise and Tee-Bae both a kiss.

"Ma, there is some loot in that duffle with a odd $7,600(seventy six hundred)take the odd loot out, give Paradise $3,000, you keep

$3,000(three thousand)and use the $1300(thirteen hundred) to get me a rental, pickup truck for at least a month and also go by Walmart and buy me a Blue Tarpaulin with some rope."

"Okay daddy, Ima handle that now, thank you"

Paradise said thanks as well.

On my way to my old duck off, I stopped by Peaches to grab me something to eat. I bought myself some bacon, eggs with cheese, cheese grits, toast and home fries with a large orange juice. I took it to go and I called Big-B,

"Bruh, bring all the work to the duck off behind your spot. We are going to have a meeting with the entire Fam, so we can come up with a strategic way to take over the city."

"Okay, I'll be there in like 30 minutes."

When I passed 60th, I saw yellow tape everywhere, the block was still roped off. I just hurried and got to the duck off and parked the S-Type in my next door neighbor's yard and walked up to the spot with just my food in my hands. I left all the dope in the car.Moon pulled up right behind me as I was walking into the house, so I left the front door open while I sat down to eat. He came in smoking on a fat Gar that smelled so good.

"Pass that shit nigga and locked that door"

"Hold up my cousin Punkin coming in."

"Oh okay then I finally get to meet him."

I could hear multiple car doors closing outside. I got up to see who it was and in Punkin, Nando, Turd and Uzi came.

"Yoo what's good with y'all niggas, I'm waiting on a few more people to pull up. I want to speak with the whole team so we can have an understanding as to what needs to take place from now on. I need some Dro while we wait, go in the kitchen, I have a few pounds in the freezer and the gars are in the cabinet next to it."

Thirty minutes later, the entire team was here.

"Yoo Big-B, go next door and grab that duffle bag out the trunk of the S-Type. Here are the keys and make sure you lock my shit up."

"Aight bet."

Big-B was out and back before I could even pass my gar to the next man. I got the duffle bag and dumped it on the floor.

"All this work is paid for. I have a connect that will never run out of work. Tha Fam will never know what's a drought and that's a promise. I'm tired of living in the moment, eating Chinese takeout and Pizza. I want everyone in this house today to figure out who is in their way and try to make them an offer to get some real money with us. If they don't want to bite the bait then let me know and I'll pull up on them with my people and make one more attempt to get them on the team. Then if they still ain't talking right Ima handle the situation how I feel is best. So all you put y'all loot on the coffee table and Ima give y'all enough work to get things started. They either getting down with Tha Fam's movement or we going to lay them down forever."

"Purp, we need some more Shooters on the team. I want them to work under you, because I have a feeling lots of people are about to die. Tha Fam is taking over."

# CHAPTER 9

# *THE TAKE OVER...*

I ended up with $193,500(one hundred ninety three thousand, five hundred) I texted Piloto

"Yooo, I need you to call me!"

My team was on a mission, each and everyone has a job to do. It's time we apply pressure to the streets. Everyone went their own ways.

My phone started to ring and it could only be one person, Piloto!

"YooOoo, talk to me bruh! Everything good on your end?"

"This shit a Epidemic in my hood. I got all your loot already and need more on both ends."

"So you got the loot on everything?"

"Yea, $215,000(two hundred fifteen thousand)."

"Okay, that's amazing how fast you moving the work."

"Can you send Roxanna to come drop off the money because my runner is a lil tied up right now."

"Piloto, I'm not trying to have her all in my business."

"So, what are you trying to do then?"

"I'll just hold off until your dude gets right. I still have some food to hold me over, I'm just down on the Sand!"

"Oyah, tell me! Why wait, when you can send Roxanna!"

"I'll just link with you in a few, let me holla at her and see if she is up to it."

"Okay let me know."

I rode to my new spot so I can get my money situated. I called Roxanna and she answered on the first ring.

"My bad daddy, I was with my mom last night."

"Can you slide to Orlando to meet up with Piloto for me?"

"Damn, no, I love you or miss you, just asking for a favor!"

"Are you going or should I find someone else?"

"I'll go damn."

"I'll be to your house in like a hour to bring you some loot."

I hung-up with her and headed to my house to get the rest of the loot before I headed out to Palmetto. Forty Five minutes later, I was pulling up at Roxanna's house. I beeped my horn so she could come out and grab this grocery bag with the $215,000(two hundred fifteen thousand). When she was walking towards the car, she had an attitude,

"Where is my Chain?"

"It's with my jewelry. You wasn't worried about it last night when I was trying to call you and you wasn't answering my calls!"

"Oyah, please don't start, I told you what it was."

"The money is in the trunk in that Gray grocery bag. Text me and let me know you made it up there safe."

"Yea!"

And she walked away, that gap she had was looking so right. I got a beep on my Nextel from J. Gangsta.

"Bruh meet me at my cousin's house down east in Wood Winds."

"Churp!"

"Is you talking about Ling-Ling's crib?"

"Churp!"

"Yea, I'm about to pull up. I want to introduce you to our new Shooters."

"Churp!"

"Aight bet, I'll be there in like fifteen minutes."

"Churp!"

Oh shit! I didn't even notice that Turd texted me. Let me just call him back.

"Yooooo what's good Fam?"

"Churp!"

"I stepped to 2 Sets and we 1 for 1. Them niggas from off osprey about to be a problem and then niggas from cross the track fucking with the work. I gave them a sample and tomorrow they want 20 zips."

"Churp!"

"I need you to find a spot on those niggas block, next door, across the street. It don't matter to me, just find a spot and someone to work it and I'll handle the rest."

"Churp!"

"Aight bruh, Ima get on that now."

"Churp!"

Pulling into Woodwinds Projects was like Harlem in the 80's. Basers and Junkies everywhere. I was being flagged down by everyone I passed, just because of the car I was in. When I got in front of Ling-Lings apartment, there was no parking so I just parked in the street. Purp was the first to come to my car and told me to come inside.

J. Gangsta introduced me to a few niggas, "Poe-Poe" was 16 years old, "Mike-O and Mike-E" then you had a short stocky nigga wearing a Mo-Hawk and his name was "Mo-Hawk Dirty Red."

"Bruh these all the Shooters you need to make happen, whatever it is you got in mind."

Mo-Hawk Dirty Red spoke up, "Bruh I have a cousin named "BOO" who is nice with his hands. The nigga got a mean knock out punch. I will like to have him on the team as well."

"Purp and J.Gangsta, both y'all in charge of the Enforcing and Security Pack, so it's your call on bringing in BOO. I have a situation in Sarasota that I have to go handle with some niggas from Off Osprey. They are causing a problem. I don't even wanna talk with them, we are beyond that point now, it's time to make an example In Sota, letting them know that Tha Fam is playing for keeps."

"When you ready to slide Bruh? We got a Slider and all to pull up on them."

"Let me hit City up so I can get us some more fire then we can slide tonight."

"Aight bet, but check this I have a spot right down from them. Big Bully niggas trap, they already booming over there. Ima have my Dawg Suave in that spot and he has some Soulja's who follow him as well."

"Yea I like that move, fuck them niggas, either you with us or against us."

"Yoo City! You in town?"

"Churp!"

"Yea, I'm in Oneco on 58th."

"Churp!"

"I need some more heat, whatever you got bruh, you know what type of shit I like."

"Churp!"

"I got you, where do you want me to pull up on you at?"

"Churp!"

"I'm in Woodwinds Projects down east Bradenton, you will see my charger and a Blue S-Type Jag all the way to the back."

"Churp!"

"Give me like thirty minutes and I'll be there, just have $5,000(five thousand) for me and Ima hook you up."

"Churp!"

"Aight I got that on me, I'll see you in a few then. One!"

"Churp!"

"I just put in a order for all new throw away heat for all of y'all. Purp, go get your Slider. We don't all need to slide. It's going to be me, Poe-Poe and J. Gangsta. I want you to see how Strategic and Swift Poe-Poe is. He is a fool when it comes to this."

"Mike-O and Mike-E, I want y'all to put something together out there in Palmetto off Canal Road. Make it happen by any means."

"Shit, we been waiting on that, it's a Mexican named "Chino" who got shit on lock out there. He part of some Mexican Cartel. We going to set him up then rob him and kill him so we can take over all his spots on Canal Road."

"Aight bet, let me know when y'all get it set up and we can knock off, all his spots at the same time."

"Aight Ima go handle that now, then link back up with you." Mike-O said.

I walked into Ling-Ling's room. She was a short 5'Red chick about 100 pounds soaking wet. Slim thick, no tits but she had a lil booty that fit her slim frame and a cute face.

"What's good Lil mama?"

"Nothing Oyah! What you doing at my apartment?"

"Well me and J. Gangsta is doing business together, so you will be seeing me around a lot. Plus I've been waiting to run into you but I don't ever see you out anywhere. God is good, because he put me in the position so I can always see you."

Ling-Ling had a pretty smile.

"Is that right and what you looking for me for?"

"Because you are sexy as hell and I wanna get to know you on a more personal Level. Do you fuck with any of these niggas here?"

"If I did, that shit ain't matter to you. Nigga you in my room with the door closed."

"Yea I guess you right. So is you going to answer my question?"

"No Oyah! I don't fuck with anyone at all."

"Good keep it that way. Oh and I'm hungry, I want some yellow rice and chicken. Make sure you make enough to feed the whole Fam. Here is $500, go grocery shopping."

"You think you run shit don't you?"

"Don't worry lil Mama, I'll make you a believer"

And with that I turned and walked out of the apartment. Right as I walked out, City was pulling up and hitting my Nextel line.

"Yoo I see you bruh."

"Churp!"

"Oh okay I see you too!"

"Churp!"

City pulled up and parked. Ling-Ling walked out the house and with an attitude she said.

"How do you want me to go buy groceries but you got my car blocked in."

"Come on lil mama, take my car."

I popped the trunk and took out my backpack with the work and cash in it.

"Aight you good to go now."

Soon as she pulled off, I told City to come on inside so we could handle business.

"J.Gangsta make sure nobody comes in this apartment until City is gone."

"I got you bruh, go handle your business."

Inside City just kept pulling Heat out nonstop.

"That must be a deep duffle bag you got there. LOL."

"Nah, I just had it stuffed. I got 20 Sticks and 20 Handguns. I'm still waiting on that special order you asked for, it should be here in a few days with some more Sticks and Hand guns."

"I want them all. I need some vest too"

"Aight I got you."

"Here is your loot."

He took it and without counting we dapped up and he left. I walked him to the door and once he pulled off, I told all the fellas to come in and see what I had got them. Everyone ran to the guns and picked them up like kids on Christmas morning. Everyone get a Stick and hand gun, the rest stays here, just in case we need more. City blessed us with enough Ammo to go to war with the army.

"Somebody please get to rolling, I'm trying to get high!"

I heard "Plies-Pussy Smells like Water" playing outside.

"Someone get that door, lil mama is out there and help her with them bag, she's cooking for us."

Ling-Ling came in the house with a lot of Winn Dixie bags.

"Damn lil mama, how much groceries did you buy?"

"Well you gave me $500 so I bought a bunch of food to cook all week long."

My phone buzzed. It was Roxanna letting me know she made it and dropped the money off, so now she going to the mall until he calls her to pull up. I didn't even text back.

"J. Gangsta passed me the gar."

I took a big pull and he asked me,

"What's my cousin and you got going?"

"Nothing bruh, she's just cool peoples."

"Yea she is, and she need a man that's going to treat her right. I thought that man could be you."

"We will see what's up in the future. Right now my focus is on this take over."

Speaking about that, let me hit Turd and let him know that I'm ready.

"Yoo my nigga, what it do?"

"Churp!"

"I'm chillin just got two more Chico's on the team. They both said they been trying to holla at me but could never link up with me."

"Churp!"

"That's what's up, but how many spots do you think we need to hit so we can get off on them Osprey niggas."

" I want us to have control of that whole block. They have 3 traps on Osprey and like 2-3 people working each."

"Churp!"

"Okay Ima pull up on you around 2A.M."

"Churp!"

"Aight bet, Ima have my people in line for when you get here."

"Churp!"

"Aight bet."

"Churp!"

"Lil Mama, how long before the food is ready?"

"Give me no more than a hour."

"Okay because I'm starving."

"Y'all niggas come outside, I wanna holla at y'all."

Outside I sat on the trunk of the S-Type.

"We are going to need 3 cars with 3 people in each. There is 3 different traps we are going to hit. I want them shut down and when the heat dies down, we going to open a new trap and I want y'all to send 2 workers over there so they can work the trap side by side with Turd's people's."

Purp spoke up,

"Them niggas in Villa Park trying to get down with us. You know Lil'Head doing his thing on the Sand tip."

"If we going to fuck with anyone out Villa Park, I want it to be MADD BALL."

"Yea he would be a good move."

"Ima pull up on him in the morning so I can put him up on game. Well let's go in here, smoke and then eat because my stomach is touching my back."

"Aight!"

Four hours later, I was laying in Ling-ling's bed feeling sick because I ate so much. She was in the bed beside me talking on her phone. When I heard her say the name Tee-Baby. I sat up and asked her,

"How you know her?"

and she said, "Nigga that's my cousin"

"Why, you talk to her?"

"Yeah she's cool, we real good friends."

"Is that right! I bet y'all fucking, ain't y'all?"

"Listen we are just friends, now let me sleep for a lil because I have a real busy night and more than likely I won't get no rest."

"Whatever Oyah, you ain't shit but a Hoe!"

"Come here let's cuddle, at least until I fall asleep and please keep that door closed."

I kicked my sneakers off and got under the covers and pulled her towards me. She felt so good in my arms but too small at the same time.

I heard knocking on the door and Ling-Ling opened it,

"Cuzzo, tell Oyah it's about that time."

"I'm getting up now. I'll be out there in about ten minutes."

"Aight bruh, we got three Sliders out here, we just waiting on you."

"Lil Mama, pass me my phones!"

"Whatever y'all going to do, please be safe and make sure J.Gangsta makes it back home safe."

"We good lil Mama, it's nothing like what you think."

I looked at my phones to see what time Roxanna got back, but

The only person who hit my phone was Tee-Bae letting me know she got a "XLT-EXCURSION." So I texted Roxanna

"Where are you?"

She hit right back,

"I'm home Oyah."

"Why the fuck you ain't been hit me up when you got there?"

"Because I just got here."

"Aight I'll be there in a few."

"Ima be sleep Oyah."

"I don't give a fuck, I can let myself in like I always do. I'll see you in a few."

Then I cut that phone off so she can't bother me for the rest of the night.

"Y'all ready, we have to go to Sarasota on 24th so we can link with Turd, he going to point out all the spots for us, then post up on the corner of Osprey just in case shit don't go as planned, him and his people can come in and clean house. Let's roll then because I'm ready to let them niggas have it."

On our way to Sarasota, we rode three cars deep with four niggas in each car. The driver and three niggas ready to lay some shit down. I was making sure my stick was fully loaded and I had my .45 1911 sitting on my lap. We pulled up onto Turds block.

"What's good Fam, we doing this like this!"

"We following you, and every time we pass a trap house, hit your brakes and hit your blinker pointing to the house, then the car that is directly behind you will fall off and get into position. Once we all ready you send a text to everyone at the same time giving us the green light. We need to be in and out, ten minutes tops. Anyone ain't out in ten minutes, Turd I need you to send some people in to assist with the situation. Try not to kill anyone until you hit for all the dope, guns and cash"

"Aight big homie, but after we hit, you want us to kill anything with a heart beat right?"

"That's correct, let's slide because I have some shit I need to go handle in Palmetto."

As we rode down Osprey, we all got into position. It was me, Poe-Poe and J. Gangsta riding together on this lick. The driver reversed in the driveway and we hopped out. I ran around the house to the back door while Poe-Poe and J.Gangsta hit the front. Soon as I heard the front door being kicked in, I booted the back door right by the lock sending it flying open. When I got in, these niggas had everything under control. In the front room was two guys and one girl that J.Gangsta had face down on the ground while Poe-Poe backed another guy and a naked chick that looked to be Mexican and white out of a room.

"Tie them up and search this shit and if anyone screams or tries to run Ima splash their brains all over this carpet, y'all understand me!"

The naked girl started to beg for her life.

"Please don't hurt me, I really don't even know these guys, but I do know in the dresser behind the first drawer is a bunch of money."

"Shut the fuck up, you stupid bitch, before I kill you when they let us go.!"

"Fat boy, is that anyway to speak to a lady who is trying to give us what she thinks we are here for in hopes that we don't kill y'all."

"She don't know what she's talking about, all the money is in the dirty laundry in the master bedroom."

"Y'all niggas check everything."

"BOMBA!" Poe-Poe yelled out.

"I found 3 kilos with a "F-50" stamp on it."

"Do y'all know who the fuck y'all robbing?"

"Nah fat boy, why don't you tell me and just maybe I'll change my mind."

"This Latin King Tito's spot and he will murder each and every-one of you guys but if you don't steal anything and just leave he will never have to know about this."

"Who the other 2 spots down the block belong to?"

"Other members of the Latin King."

Poe-Poe and J. Gangsta came back each with a pillow case.

"Y'all got everything?"

"If we didn't then they got it put up real good, but there was about $20,000(Twenty thousand) and 3 Blocks."

"This how this going to work, fuck the Latin Kings, we Tha Fam and we keeping this block. All three Traps are being hit as we speak and y'all all share the same fate, DEATH!"

"Lil bruh, kill everyone except him. I want him to watch since he thinks we should be shook about a bitch name Tito or the Latin Kings. After you splash them, use their blood to put a L.K. on the walk with a X over it."

"No please don't kill me" one of the guys said

"Nigga, this is what you signed up for, Poe-Poe kill his bitch ass first."

Lil bruh stood over him and gave him four shots, Bang! Bang! Bang! Bang! to the back of his head. I pulled out my .45 and hit the other nigga Bang! Once in the back of the head.

"Poe-Poe get to writing, I wanna leave a message that we know who they are."

The naked chick started to cry

"Please don't shoot me. I don't wanna die. I'll do anything. I'll suck all y'all dicks, y'all can even run the train on me, just please spare my life. I won't ever say anything to anyone, y'all don't ever even see me again, I promise."

I popped her twice Bang! Bang! in the Back of her head.

"You stupid bitch, what made you think I even want you touching me! J. Gangsta air that bitch nigga out and let's go, we been in here 9 minutes now."

With that I turned to head out the door with Poe-Poe on my heels holding both pillow cases, when the door opened, all I heard was gun fire nonstop.

Bang!Bang! Bang! Bang! Bang! Bang! Bang! Bang! Bang! Bang!

Right as we made it to the front porch Turd was pulling in. When he saw us and heard the gunfire he hopped out ready for war. I waved him off. We all got back in the whip and drove off back to 24th. In front of Turds trap, we talked about future plans for Osprey and we all got an understanding for what's to take place so I called Tee-Baby , she was sleep when she answered

"Babe I need you and Paradise to meet me but come in two cars because Ima need the Excursion."

"Right now Oyah?"

"If I ain't need you right now I wouldn't have called you this late. Meet me at the field behind Waste Management on 63rd."

"Okay babe Ima wake her up now and we will be on our way."

"Let's go to the field behind Waste Management on 63rd so we can burn these cars."

"Yoo Turd, we going to link up when the heat dies down, call me if anything."

We put all the dope, cash and guns from the lick in one car and we rode Coyote Style all the way to the field. As we was pulling in, so were the ladies. I pulled up on the empty field and told Tee-Bae and Paradise to slide back to the house and I'll link with them when I get done.

"Yoo Purp, have one of the men load up all the stuff we got in the truck so we can burn these cars up."

"Aight, Ima handle that now."

Once the Excursion was loaded up, the driver of each car stuffed a shirt in the gas tank, then pushed it as far down as they could get it and set fire. They hopped in the Excursion and as we was pulling out, I heard a large explosion BOOOOM! All that could be seen was a huge black smoke cloud and flames. I drove to Wood Winds so we could go over our lick and see what all we got.

At Ling-Ling house we moved the coffee table and dumped all the stuff on the floor. We ended up hitting a nice lick in the process of taking over Osprey. Between all three houses, we got 5 bricks of coke, 1 brick of Heroin, 2 bricks of Meth, and a lil over 10 pounds of some Dro. There was also $72,400(Seventy two thousand, four hundred) in cash between all 3 houses not including the Jewelry.

"Y'all keep all the dope, tomorrow I want 3 more men on 60th where Big-B at, give it about 5 days then I want 9 men on Osprey, all 3 of them traps get opened back up. I'm waiting to hear back from Mike-O and Mike-E to see what they about to do on Canal Road. I know they have their lil brother that hustle by any means and they don't mind getting their hands dirty when needed, plus I fucks with

Keybo, the second to the youngest of Mike-O's brothers, the long way. We been getting money since early high school years, 9th grade, moving pounds of weed by bus. The school bus that is, so I have to put my dawg on as well.By the end of the week, I want Canal Road, Osprey, 12th Street, 60th Ave and I'm thinking about doing something Out West. Purp, I want you and J.Gangsta over the Osprey movement. Big-B, can have 60th, Nando 12th, Moon and his cousin can Road Run. Ima set Keybo up with Canal Road. Y'all take Madd-Ball with y'all to Sarasota, give him the game and when he is ready we will set him up in Villa Park with his own trap.Y'all niggas is all straight on the work right? Plus y'all got everything from the lick. That's all y'all, Ima just grab the cash and y'all can split the work the way you see fits best."

"Aight, bet Oyah, we about to eat for real now. We're going to put shit in motion then let you know what's good."

"Ima slide, I have to pick some shit up from Roxanna house, but do me a favor, can you drop the Jag off for me at her spot when you get some time and then take the Charger to 941 Kustumz for me and drop it off as well and tell bruh I want some floaters, a touch screen and 4 Dimes in the trunk, nothing major."

"You already got a touch screen."

"I want them to have a 9' double deck Pioneer touch screen. Here's $22,000(Twenty two thousand), tell him that's for my Box and I need it before Easter."

"I got you bruh, holla at you tomorrow."

"Aight, Ima go dump these guns in the water on my way to Palmetto. Y'all niggas got Heat?"

I reached into the closet and grabbed the duffle bag with the rest of the guns.

"Yooo, J. Gangsta go grab the sticks out my truck and leave what's dirty and put the sticks up. Ima take this .45 with me."

"Yea we got our personal heat, you know we stay strapped."

I went to the docks at the waterfront and dumped all the burners into the Manatee river, then went to Roxanna house, it was almost 6A.M. The sky was starting to lighten up. I pulled up to her house and hopped out without even cutting the truck off. I unlocked her door and walked into her room and woke her ass up.

"Where that's at?"

"You walked right past it, it's on the sofa in the front room."

"Okay and what the fuck took you so long?"

"Shit, ask Piloto that."

"What you did while you waited on him?"

"I went shopping, out to eat, then I went to his spot where he be having me pull up and just chilled there until he gave me the bag."

"So why the fuck you ain't answer your phone or hit me up so I could know what's going on."

"I was busy, damn, let me sleep."

"You dead sleep right, I'm gone."

I grabbed the duffle bag and slide. On my way to my spot. I stopped at the RaceTrac to grab me some Gars and a drink. On my way inside the store, a white Camry stopped in the middle of the street and let off like 30 rounds but I ducked behind a Lincoln Navigator. Right when I was pulling my burner out getting ready to shoot back, the car drove off. I had to get the fuck out of there before Palmetto Police pulled up. I got a truck full of dope and I refuse to get caught with this shit. I hopped back in the Excursion and hit it over the bridge, headed home so I can get all this dope off me. I took all back roads home trying to avoid cops and anyone following me. After making sure I wasn't followed, I pulled into my driveway and got out, then put in my 6 digit code in the keypad and opened the garage. I parked the Excursion inside and locked the door. I got the duffle bag with all the loot and dope and went inside. Tee-Bae and Paradise was spooning on the bed naked and dead to the world. I went into the spare room and dumped the bag and was surprised.

Piloto sent me five keys of food and ten keys of Sand. Yea, Tha Fam truly about to eat, especially with all the new traps that we just took over. It's either you roll with us or get rolled over. I put everything away then got in the shower. As the water ran down my shoulders, all I kept wondering was who the fuck could it have been that was trying to take my life. It could have been someone that was haten on me or even someone trying to retaliate for something I had done. Damn I thought I had all my loose ends tied up. Somebody is going to pay for what happened. I washed up and got out, dried off, put on my dove deodorant and got in bed behind Tee-Bae, she ain't even move. I dozed off into a coma like sleep. I woke up to all my phones going crazy and Tee-Bae or Paradise wasn't in the bed. I looked at my phone and the time read 2:17P.M. Damn, I slept late.

I replied back to all my people's who texted me.

"Yoo what's good, I just got back in town."

Mike-O had texted telling me he got something setup for a Take Over Of Canal Road. I texted him back saying we will link a lil later and put things into motion.

I turned on Bay News 9 to see what the weather was like for today. I sat up in the bed and text everyone back telling them to meet me at my old duck off spot. What I heard next got my attention. This is "David Clark," Reporting Live from Sarasota, Florida, where it has been multiple murders. Behind me is just one of three houses on the same street where over Ten people was murdered in cold blood. Detectives with the Sarasota county sheriff's believe these murders are acts of drug deals gone bad. There are no suspects at this time, but if you know anything relating to these murders, please call 941-999-8675, you will be kept anonymous. These crackers should thank us for cleaning up their City. I'm about to build a System that's going to help the people in the Community and keep kids safe and in school.

I got up and rolled me a Gar and lit it before walking out the room looking for the ladies. Tee-Bae was on the phone crying. So I walked up beside her and asked what was going on, then I passed her the Gar so she could smoke and get her mind right.

"My cousin got shot to death last night in Sota. She was visiting a friend of hers and I guess they was beefing with another gang. Their trap got robbed and anything with a Heart Beat got flat lined. The police told my mom that it was a Gang hit because the dude she was with, was Latin King and they are beefing with the MS-13 Gang."

"Look, we going to take a trip so you can ease your mind because I need you to be strong and keep your head on the swivel."

I felt bad not because her lil cousin was dead but because my baby was hurting. I went back into the room, showered and got ready to leave. I grabbed the last brick and the 58 Zips, stuffed them all into my backpack and was on my way out the house. Tee-Bae was looking so sad. I went into the book bag and got $10,000(ten thousand) out and handed it to her. She looked up into my eyes and asked

"What is all this for?"

"Send your cousin away in style, pay for her funeral."

"Thank you babe, I love you."

"I love you too babe. I'll catch up with you later on."

"Okay be safe out there."

"I will"

Then I walked out into the garage and got in the Excursion and left. Twenty minutes later, I was pulling up to my old duck off spot and there was a suspicious looking car parked a few houses down so I ain't pull into my driveway. I just rode past them trying to get a better view and I saw two guys just sitting in there. I gotta call someone to check on these niggas. I got on my Nextel and hit Purp.

"Bruh, where you at?"

"Churp!"

"On the east side, why what's good?"

"Churp!"

"I was pulling up to my spot in Oneco but there's a car on the block. I thought it was Troll but it ain't, it's some niggas. Ima park around the corner then walk up on them and see what's good, but I feel like it's someone we got because I got shot at last night when I left my bitch house in Palmetto."

"Where you was at when it happened?"

"I was at the RaceTrac. A bih shot at me damn near 30 times, they were in a Toyota Camry. But let me get back at you. I'm parking on the next block then Ima slide up on these niggas. It's too much shit going on for them to just be out here."

"Aight bet, hit me up after and let me know how shit went or if you are going to need me."

"Yea, I'll holla at you bruh."

I parked the truck, grabbed the .45 and hit the cut but the car was gone when I got back on the block. Fuck I wanna know who it is because Ima body me a bitch for fucking with my sanity. I went back and got the truck, spin the block a few times to see if I can see the car but it wasn't anywhere to be found. So I pulled up to the duck off, reversed and parked. Then I went inside, grabbed the rest of the work out the attic and called Moon.

"Yoo, Yoo!"

"Churp!"

"What's good Fam?"

"Churp!"

"I need you to swing by, Ima bless you with some shit then I'm gone for a minute."

"Churp!"

"I'm on my way, are you at the duck off?"

"Yea I'm here now."

"Aight bruh, I'll be there in like 30 minutes."

I sent out a Multi Text to everyone in Tha Fam to get here and even to Tee-Bae letting her know to go in my duffle bag and bring me Three Bricks of Coke. No later than an hour later it was looking like a block party, the entire Fam was here.

"I'm glad everyone was able to make it on such short notice. The reason for this meeting is so I can stock all y'all up on some work and to let y'all know Ima be out of town for two weeks. It's a war about to start up. I'm going to put in a order for some more artillery so that won't be an issue. Purp and J.Gangsta, I need y'all to watch over the traps on 12th Street and 60th Avenue, also open up all the other traps that we have been taking over, just make sure you have some niggas that's with the shits at all the spots because there is someone who wants me dead. Last night a bih got off on me and caught me slippen at the RaceTrac, then today there were two guys in a car parked a few houses away."

"Look bruh, we going to get everything up and going, don't stress yourself out. We got shit under control."

"I want someone to stay here at this house as well. Mike-O! Tell Keybo I need him on my team, to come post up here at this spot then when I get back, him and I will chop it up."

"Okay Ima get on that now then and we about to just start up a Trap on Canal Road and just say fuck them Mexicans and just handle whatever comes with it."

"Okay bet Ima be gone for two weeks, please have all the Traps up and running. Also please be careful out here because ain't no telling who it could be getting at me. I thought we tied all loose ends by killing everyone."

"Nigga we going to get to the bottom of all that while you're gone."

"Moon take my keys Ima text you the address to my spot when you need Re-Up and here go my work phones.

Ima bless all y'all with the last of the work that I have, and when y'all need to Re-Up Moon will get y'all right. I'm leaving him my phones. The money from the last batch, hold onto it until I get back and I'll just collect everything from y'all at once.

"Purp, did you go see Abel at Kustumz about my Box?"

"You know I took care of that for you already and I dropped off the Charger as well."

"Okay cool, bet that up. Tell that nigga to have my shit done by Easter."

"Aight, Ima pull up on him tomorrow."

Let me call City so I can handle that with some more artillery for all Tha Fam members.

"Yoo City! I need you again as many as you can get me. Ima leave the loot with my Dawg. He will be at that same spot in Wood Winds."

"Aight bet! I'll be around there in a few days."

"Y'all, I'm gone! Just holla at me if anything comes up. We got you my nigga, trust me. Tha Fam going to hold shit down and get to the bottom of who's disrespecting the team."

I pulled all the dope out the backpack and gave it to Moon.

"Tee-Bae, hand bruh those blocks, then head to my mom's house so we can figure out where we going and what we doing."

"Okay baby, Ima stop by my aunty house and give her that money for my lil cousin funeral, then I'll be over there."

Everyone left their separate ways, I truly hope the team can hold up while I'm gone.

# CHAPTER 10

# RED EYE FLIGHT

Pulled up out front of my moms house and put the biggest smile on my face when I saw Anet's Expedition parked in the driveway. Damn I came right on time, just the person I want to see. If I didn't have so much going on, I would have been got some of that pussy. Anet and my mom have been friends for a very long time. I grew up looking at Anet as an Aunt. I parked and grabbed my Louis Vuitton backpack with the $40,000(forty thousand) in it, got out and let myself into my mom's house. The house smelt so good from whatever it was that she was cooking. My lil brother Joe was playing the PlayStation in the living room. I dapped lil bruh up and kept it moving into the kitchen.

"Hello mom"

I went and gave her a hug

"You are always in this kitchen when I come over here."

"Shit, you just always come over at the right time."

"Hello Anet! How you been?"

I gave her a hug and she wrapped her arms around me and gave me a hug like she just been missing me. I squeezed that fat ass with both hands then licked on her neck before kissing it.

"I've been fine, just ready to get away from my bitch ass husband."

"Damn if you think of him like that then you should get a divorce from him."

"It ain't that easy, the nigga will act tough with me but a whole bitch when a nigga steps to him."

"Today might be your lucky day because I came over here to holla at my mom about taking a trip."

"Ma, you know I owe you for getting me my Charger. I truly appreciate everything you do for me. I'm taking you to Miami, so we can go shopping, then we going to Puerto Rico, so we can just chill and relax. Ima have two friends come with us, female friends of mine, so please treat them good. I want this to be a nice vacation for us all. Anet can come with us so you can have someone to vibe with and since she wanna get away from her dude, then this trip is right on time."

"I'm good Oyah! You can go enjoy your vacation with your mom and hoes. I don't got money to do all that."

"Anet, who said anything about money? I got plenty loot. This trip on me."

"No I can't let you spend all that money, I'm good, I'll just see y'all when the trip is over."

"Man, you coming with us, Anet! So cut the bullshit out. For real, before you piss me off."

I unzipped my backpack and dumped all the loot in it out on the floor in the kitchen. My mom and Anet's eyes got huge.

"Oyah how much is all that?"

"It's $40,000(forty thousand)mom, we about to hangout, all this money unaccounted for."

There was a knock at the front door. I walked to the door and saw that it was the ladies. I unlocked the door and let them in.

"Lock the door behind y'all and come to the kitchen."

When I went to head back, my baby sister T-Jay ran up to me and I scooped her up, gave her a hug and a bunch of kisses. I sat her back down and she ran back to her room. I went into the kitchen and Anet was picking up the money, putting it back in the backpack.

"Ladies this my mom, "Maria" and aunty "Anet" and mom this is "Terica" but I call her "Tee-Baby" and this is "Paradise.""

"Hello ladies, have a seat, are you hungry?"

"Yes Ma'am, I am!" Paradise said.

"It smells so good. Mom, what are you cooking?"

"White Rice, red beans and potatoes with fried pork chops."

"Damn I'm hungry now. I hope you have some Pepsi in here."

"Oyah, you know I keep a few cases in here for you, they are just hot."

"It's all good, Mom you got ice, Ima roll up so we can smoke before we eat."

"When are we leaving?" my mom asked.

"Well, we can leave right after dinner"

"Oyah, we have to pack up and get ready, we can't just leave like that."

"Pack for what?"

I grabbed the backpack and pulled all the money out.

"Mom, I got bands to blow. Here go $2,500(Twenty five hundred) for each of y'all to go shopping with, buy everything brand new. Shit I know that's what Ima do."

"Okay since you put it that way."

"We taking my Rental truck. Tell your husband to watch over Joe and T-Jay, that's the least he can do is watch his kids, while you go on this trip. Shit he don't contribute to anything else around here."

After dinner Mom and Tee-Bae cleaned up the kitchen and we got ready to leave.

"I'm not driving. Ima get in the back on the third row seat."

"I'll drive daddy, Paradise said."

"Okay Mami, you and Tee-Bae can sit upfront, Mom and Anet can sit behind y'all while I get all the way in the back. Bae, we going to Miami, South Beach. There is a 5 Star hotel named Sagamore on Ocean Drive that I wanna go stay at."

"Okay I'll get us there babe."

Four hours later, we was pulling up to the Sagamore and checked into our rooms. Mom and Anet got a room together, while me, Tee-Baby and Paradise got us a room.

"Look, let's go get some rest and first thing in the morning we can go hit the Aventura Mall."

We all went our separate ways to our rooms. The next morning we got up and got ready to go hit the Streets of Miami. I was starving so we went to KeKe's for breakfast to kill time until the Mall opened up. We had all eyes on us all day, during breakfast and now at the mall. We was one of the first people in the mall besides the workers. We hit every major Designer Store. The ladies had so many bags, they had to make a special trip to the Excursion to put them up and then come back to finish shopping.

Tee-Bae talked me into going to Victoria Secret with them to get underwear. She tried on at least twenty pairs of bras and panties and kept coming out the dressing room to get my opinion on how I thought it looked. Then Paradise came out and showed me what she had on as well. I don't know why y'all ask me if I like what y'all have on knowing damn well Ima like it and keep it up, Ima come off in there and get me some of that pussy right in these peoples store.

Right when they went back in so they can change back Into their clothes, my mom came out dressed and headed to the cash register so she can pay for her stuff. Then the dressing room Anet was in opened.

Fuck! I had to adjust my dick because it got semi hard instantly. Anet was standing in the dressing room in a Olive green lace bra and thong set. Her pussy was so fat you could see her print clear as day. Anet looked like she had a ripe mango sitting in between her legs. Then she turned around so I can see that ass out them jeans. She had a flawless body. Anet was built like a Stripper.

I stood up and went over to her, snatching her up in my arms. I gripped all that ass and whispered in her ear how good she looked in her bra and panty but I wanna see her out of it. She told me,

"You will tonight, come to the room. Me and your moms hotel room is a three bedroom. I even have a Hot Tub and Mirrors all around in my room."

"Oh I'll be there tonight baby."

Everyone paid for their stuff in Victoria Secrets, then we all drove back to our rooms so we could shower and get into our swimsuits. We all went down stairs to the pool. It was right on the beach. Mom was tanning while Tee-Baby, Paradise and Anet and I was in the pool.

Tee-Baby and Paradise was playing volleyball in the water, while I was just chilling on the side. Anet swam up on me and reached straight for my dick. Just by her touch my dick got hard. She pulled the dick out my trunks, turned around and moved her thong bikini out the way and backed her ass up and slid my dick right into her warm tight pussy.

"Damn Ma, this pussy feeling real good, I want you out the pool."

She was moving back and forth making waves all around us. Anet gripped my arms and used them to pull herself back into me.

"Ummm, this Dick good Oyah. I don't know why I waited so long to get some."

I moved in and out of her pussy. We was fucking like nobody was around us and nobody was paying us any mind.

"Uhhh!"

She bounced that fat ass into me harder.

"I love this dick, please don't ever keep it from me. I need this Dick, I need you. My husband makes me feel ugly."

"Fuck that nigga ma, you are beautiful and you're built like a Stripper, his bitch ass don't know what he got. Huh. Huh. Huh. Huh!"

I sped up my pace, squeezed onto her ass cheeks and just plowed in and out of her pussy harder and harder. Our skins slapped together and sounded like people was clapping. Thank God it was loud out here because the music was on and people was screaming and having a good time.

"I'm cumming, baby. I'm cumming on this big dick. Ummm, Uhhh, it feels so fucking good. Damn this Dick is so, so, so gooood. "Uhhhh!"

She screamed and smashed her ass into me as we both Nutted at the same time. I pulled out of her and put my dick away and she turned around with the biggest smile.

"I never did anything that spontaneous before."

"Yea, that was some wild shit we just did with all these people all around us. But I want some more of that pussy, so I can fuck on you like how I

want to. I wanna see all that ass crashing into my stomach."

"You will baby, what I just did was give you a sample of what you've been missing out on."

"Is that right, I can't wait for you to suck on this dick while I eat that pussy."

"Damn daddy, you about to make me say fuck this pool and we just go upstairs and get our fuck on."

"Let's go Shit!"

"Nah Ima go chill and have some drinks with your mom."

Then she swam off to the other side of the pool and got out. Anet had a ass that demanded attention from everyone at the pool. Men and women had to take a look at how big, juicy and soft her ass looked.

We got ready to head upstairs to my room so we could smoke while my mom and Anet stayed chilling poolside.

"Is y'all ladies enjoying this vacation so far?"

"Yes babe, we are. Thank you so much for bringing me out here and helping ease my mind from my cousin's death."

"Don't even stress, y'all my ladies and both y'all deserve this trip. Everyone deserves this trip. We going out tonight to Club Rolex, it's a strip club. I'm not sure if my mom and Anet going to want to come, but if not, we will just go and they can find something to get themselves into. Someone roll up, I'm trying to get high when I get out the shower, also y'all get ready so we can hit the Strip for a lil and enjoy the Miami vibes. Then later on around 12AM. we can hit the Club."

I got in the shower as I was washing up, I felt a breeze on my back, when I turned around it was Paradise. She came into the shower with me. Her body was perfect. If I didn't know any better I would have thought she paid for her body.

"What are you doing in here when you should be in the other bathroom getting ready?"

"I came to thank you for this trip and for eating my pussy the way you did yesterday."

Paradise dropped to her knees in the shower and took my Dick into her hands. She pumped it twice then kissed the head and licked it until it was fully erect. She kept sucking and licking my dick while she played with my balls.

"Ummm, baby suck that dick Ma, get nasty with that shit."

Paradise spit was oozing out of the side of her mouth as she kept circling her head into my lap sucking hard and fast.

"Mmmm-a! Mmmm-a!"

She pulled my dick in between her tits and squeezed them. She used her tits to Jack my dick while she licked on the head with the tip of her tongue.

"Damn! Paradise! Fuck! This shit feels good, I'm about to cum baby. "Ummm," I'm Cummmmmming babe."

I nutted all over her face and tits. We both washed up then got out, dried off and got dressed while Tee-Bae went and got ready. We smoked two gars then left the room to hit the strip. Once we reached the lobby, I saw my mom and Anet talking to the clerk about getting massages at the spa. The lady told my mom she had to make a reservation in order to get a slot on the Spa schedule for that day. So I walked up behind them and turned to Tee-Baby and told her to get the truck from the valet while I handled something with my mom.

"Excuse me, Ma'am, what's the problem here, this is my mom and my aunty. If they want a massage you need to do whatever it is to get them back there."

"But sir, it's in our policy."

I cut her off.

"Fuck! That policy, we got money too. What it is because we ain't White?"

I pulled out $10,000(Ten thousand) in all $100 bills.

"Mom, how much is the package you trying to get?"

"It's $200 for each of us, we trying to get a deep tissue massage and use the steam room."

"Here is $400 for both of them and $200 for your pockets."

I threw the money on the counter and gave my mom $200 and Anet the other $200 and I kept an even $9,000(Nine thousand) in my pocket.

"Enjoy y'all evening, Ima hit the Strip then we going to the Rolex tonight."

"Okay be safe and have fun."

"I will Mom"

Then I walked out the hotel and hopped in the back seat behind the passenger side.

"Let's bend a few corners, then park on the strip so we can walk and have some drinks and get some food in our stomachs."

We rode all over, we even went to Liberty City just to see how they living down here. We smoked Six Gars. I was high as fuck when we made it back to Ocean Drive.

"Oh! Park up here, I wanna go check out "Mango's" they have a valet there, let them park this bih."

"Okay and I wanna take pictures in front of the Versace Mansion."

"I'll take them for y'all, but then we going for food and drinks."

We sat outside of Mango's at a table for four but it was only three of us. I ordered fried chicken with rice, beans and plantains. The ladies ordered skirt steaks with yuca and a chef salad. I ordered me a "Incredible Hulk" and Tee-Bae and Paradise got, "Sex on the Beach."

I decided to hit Moon up just to see how things going with Tha Fam.

"Bruh we good out here, enjoy yourself. I'll call you if anything comes up."

"Okay bet, be safe."

I hung up and then hit Purp up.

"What's good Fam, how shit going?"

"Everything is going good. The Trap on 60th opened up today and tomorrow we about to open up Shop on Canal Road in Palmetto and Osprey in Sarasota. We about to have the City in a headlock. I'm also working on finding out who it was that shot at you and who was parked by your duck off. Just enjoy yourself and when you get back shit will be on the up and up."

"Yeah! I'm glad to hear that bruh. Once everything falls into play, Ima take the entire Fam on a trip. But let me get off this phone so I can eat my food."

"Aight bet, relax and enjoy yourself."

I was feeling so good that as soon as I got my cup, I downed my drink then asked for another.

"Damn! Daddy you must have been thirsty."

"Nah, I just got good news and we out here enjoying the Miami nightlife. I'm just feeling myself. Let's eat up so we can head to Club Rolex, it's on the other side of town in Opalocka."

"Okay daddy."

We each had one more drink and finished our food. Back in the truck, I rolled up while we drove to Opalocka from South Beach. Sliding down I-75, I fired up and took a big pull of the Gar then passed it to Tee-Bae while I rolled up another Gar. I fired up that Gar then lowered the music from the controls in the back.

I called Nando. "Yoo! What's good bruh?"

"Shit, my nigga, Life is good right now."

"How is everything going?"

"We booming over here bruh. Me, Rue and Bullet just went and bought us some cars. Ima get my shit tinted, then drop some 24' DUB floaters."

"Are you going to be done before Easter?"

"Hell yeah, Ima be done before you get back from your trip."

"We about to shut shit down for the parade this year."

"Moon needs to get right and grab him some wheels."

"He will once he sees us Sliding."

"Ima holla at you later nigga, we on our way to the club."

"Aight be safe out there bruh."

Club Rolex was on swoll. The line to get in was wrapped around the building. We ain't waiting in this long ass line, let's walk to the front. The bouncer asked me how can he help me.

"I'm trying to get up in here with both my ladies, but your line is all the way around the building."

"If you buy a table with a bottle for each of y'all then you can get right in."

"Okay bet! Give me a bottle of Remy and for the ladies grab them a bottle of Moët Rose. How much is that going to run me?"

"$400, are you going to want any $1's?"

"Here go $2,000, give me $1,600 in $1 bills."

"A bottle girl will take you to your table. Enjoy your night."

A bottle girl who looked more like one of the Dancers came over and got us from the front door. At our table, we had a big bucket of ice, my bottle of Remy and two bottles of Rose and a silver platter with $1600(sixteen hundred) in ones. Before I sat down I told the bottle girl to get me three fine women and send them to my section. "Ace Hood" was on stage and had the club turnt. My dancer had so much ass on her that I couldn't keep my hands off her. I looked over and Paradise was beside me with her dress up over her ass dancing on Tee-Bae. I was starting to feel jealous because she had three bad bitches dancing on her when I only had one. Then she wanted to be greedy. She reached over and stuck her finger in my dancers pussy while she danced. The stripper went to moving real slow like she was riding a dick.

I was drinking my Remy out the bottle. I poured shots directly into the stripper's mouth. After a few hours the club started to die down.

"Y'all ready to leave, we still got to drive back forty minutes to the hotel?"

"Yea we can Slide."

Paradise turned the rest of her bottle upside down in the ice bucket, then did the same with Tee-Bae's bottle.

"Are you done drinking daddy?"

"Yea, but why is you turning then upside down in the bucket of ice for?"

"Because if you don't, they will re-sell some shit the next time the club opens up."

"Hell Nah, shit like that don't happen, for real."

"Bae I worked the club for a long fucking time. I know what goes on."

"Damn, I'm glad I always buy bottles, so I know my shit is sealed when I get it."

We jumped on the interstate and headed back to South Beach.

Back on Ocean Drive, the streets was still on Swoll. Bars and Restaurants was still open. People was walking back and forth on both sides of the strip.

"Daddy, I'm not even ready to turn it in yet."

"Well go hangout, this Trip was more for you ladies. Ima go up to the room and check on Tha Fam. I will see y'all later, you got the room key right?"

"Yea, it's in my purse babe and I got my .25 you gave me just in case one of these niggas get stupid."

"That's my girl, Paradise, when we get back to the hood, Ima give you one as well and Tee-Bae can take you to the gun range, so you can learn to shoot."

"Okay daddy, we will see you in a few."

"Aight!"

I entered the hotel, as I walked through the lobby, I pulled my wallet out and got the key to the room Anet and Mom was staying in. I got in the elevator and pushed three for the floor I was going to. I hope my mom is sleep, but if she ain't, fuck it, I'm grown.

I used my key to open the door. All the lights was on and Anet's bikini was on the floor by the balcony. She must have been enjoying the view of the ocean naked. I crept through the suite and the first door I opened was my Mom's room, she was in a deep sleep. I closed it then went to the other side of the suite and peeped my head into that room. Anet was laying face down on the bed, with her ass poking out looking so good.

I got an instant smile, walked in and locked the door behind me. I stripped all my clothes off, opened the curtains to the sliding glass doors that lead to the balcony. I slide the doors open to get that sea breeze in the room, I just pray Mom don't decide to wake up and come out to the balcony.

I climbed in the King sized bed in between Anet's legs. She had then spread just enough for me to have full access to her pretty pussy. Anet kept that pussy bald and it smelled like water. I sucked on the lips then kissed them as I spread her ass cheeks so I can eat that pussy how I really wanna eat it.

Anet didn't even move, so she was either really tired or she was just faking so I can keep doing what I was doing. I licked in her crease and sucked on her clit while I slid two fingers into that pussy. I was sucking on her clit so good that I was making loud slurping noises, and from her juices, you could hear splashing noises every time my fingers moved in and out of her.

Anet started to squirm and moan.

"Ummm-a! Papi! You making me so Horney."

Hearing her say that mixed with all the weed and Remy in my system did something to me. I spread her pussy lips open and licked all in her pussy while my nose was pressed on her ass hole. She had no smell whatsoever. I kept eating her pussy and rubbing on her ass.

"Hmmm-a! Hmmm-a! Mmmm-a! Don't do me like this Oyah, please don't Papi. You trying to have me around here crazy about you."

"My mom told you so, now it's too late for all that. We crossed those lines."

I kept fingering her pussy as I spoke with her and kissed her ass cheeks. Anet backed her ass up into my fingers. I spread her ass cheeks and licked the crease of her ass. Anet screamed,

"OH! FUCK! PAAAPI! You are driving me wild."

She gyrated her ass into my face. I got up and pulled her up on her hands and knees. Then she spread both of her cheeks and pressed my face into her crease and so I stuck my tongue into her ass.

"Feed me your dick Papi, I wanna swallow your cum."

I stopped eating her out and moved around the other side of the bed and guided my dick into her warm and wet mouth. Anet sucked me using no hands.

"OOOOH! FUCK! MAMI! You suck dick like a porn star."

I grabbed the back of her head and fucked her mouth. I moved in and out her mouth while she used her hand to rub and caress my balls.

I felt my balls swelling up and my stomach started to tighten up.

"I'm about to Cum Mami."

Anet sucked harder and faster at my words.

"DAAAMM! MAMIIII! You going to have me crazy about you. OOOHH! SHIT! I'm cummming! Bae!"

I filled her mouth up and Anet swallowed every single drop of cum I shot into her mouth.

Anet kept sucking while looking into my eyes in a deep trance, her cheeks hollowing out from her sucking. She cleaned my dick and sucked me back to life. Once my dick was stiff again, I pulled it out her mouth, Anet laid on her back and opened her legs so I can slide my hard dick into her pussy. Anet yelped as I pushed my dick into her juicy pussy. She was so tight that I just held my dick there and kissed her lips and sucked on her neck giving her a Hickey. She wrapped her legs around me and pulled me down closer to her. I kissed on her neck while she gyrated on my dick. I moved in and out of her while I sucked and licked on her brown gum drop nipples.

"Mmmm! Mmmm, Mmmm! Papi! This dick feels so good, don't you ever keep it from me."

I pushed her knees up to her chest and she put her feet on my chest while I dropped dick in her over and over.

"Papi, please cum with me!"

I could feel her pussy gripping onto my dick, stuck for dear life.

"I'm about to Cum Mami. Ohhh! Shit! "I'm about to Cum again."

"Oyah please cum in this pussy. Fill this pussy up so I can feel your hot Cum ooze out of me."

"Here it comes baby. I'm Cumming Mami."

"Ahhh! Shiiit! So am I Papi"

and her pussy clamped around my dick.

"Fuuuck! You feel so good Papi."

We both came at the same time.

I rolled off her and laid beside her in complete bliss. I can't believe my childhood dream done came true. I sucked and fucked Anet, a lady I looked at as my Aunty all my life, my Moms best friend. She put one leg and one arm over me and laid her head on my chest.

"Oyah, what do we do now that we have crossed that line?"

"We just going to take things day by day. There is no pressure Mami."

I must have dozed off because I woke up the next morning to my mothers voice.

"Anet! What the fuck are you doing in bed all cuddled up with my son and y'all both naked. I know y'all ain't been in here fucking."

"Mom it's not her fault, this was all my doing. I came over here on that high and drunk shit. I woke her up with head."

"What the fuck Oyah, I don't wanna hear that shit. Anet is like your aunt, she is family."

I put my head down feeling embarrassed and covered Anet and myself with a sheet.

"I hope both y'all know what y'all getting into."

"Mom, can you just please go so I can get dressed and leave. I have to shower and then we going to Miami international airport."

"For what, are we going to the airport?" Because our Trip is just getting started. We going to Puerto Rico."

"Oh okay! When are we leaving?"

"The first flight we can find. Now go so I can get dressed and let Tee-Bae and Paradise know to get ready."

Once my mom was gone, Anet wrapped her arms around me and rubbed her face on my dick.

"Let's not start anything that's going to get you fucked, we have a flight to catch."

"So can I have some of your time when we get to Puerto Rico, I'm not trying to be all clingy. I just want some more dick then you can go fuck on your ladies or whatever it is you do with them."

"You will, we are going to be out there for a week, so trust me, Ima give you all the dick you can handle before we get back to the hood because you know once we back, your husband is going to be all over you like stink on shit."

I started to get dressed, so I can go to my suite, shower and get ready to check out and leave. Anet got up and started for the bathroom. She was so fucking beautiful and her sex game is on point, just thinking about it made my dick get a lil hard.

I left the room and my mom was in the kitchen having some coffee. She looked at me and said

"Oyah, you know you are wrong."

"It's too late for all that mom."

"Well don't do shit to make me fuck her ass up, because about you, I'm going all out."

"I got you mom, LOL, you ass crazy, but Ima send my girls down here so y'all can start looking into flights. Make sure you're packed and ready because I'm trying to be on a flight by noon."

I went up to my suite and both my ladies was sleeping holding on to each other, naked. I woke them up by sucking on Tee-Bae's pussy while I stuck three fingers into Paradise fat pussy. They both woke up, but I didn't stop until I made both of them Cum.

"Now wake y'all asses up and get ready, we going to Puerto Rico and Tee-Bae make sure you leave your gun in the rental, put it up out of sight."

"Ima leave it in the airport parking lot and we will just get it when we fly back in."

"Then when y'all ready, go down to my moms suite and help her find us all tickets leaving ASAP. I wanna eat some Puerto Rican food for lunch."

It was 10:44AM and the plane was on the run strip. I'm not sure what my mom had planned but I know she was behind these seating arrangements. Anet and I was all the way to the back of the plane alone in a three seater. The middle seat was empty. Tee-Bae, Paradise and my Mom were in a row all together like ten rows ahead of mine. I wanted to get my dick sucked but there was a child in the row beside us with a lady who look like she could be her grandmother or something, so I just laid my head on Anet's lap while she rubbed on my head until I fell asleep. I woke up when Anet told me we were about to land. I'm always amazed at how beautiful this Island really is, I can't wait to get off this plane. We had a rental Escalade waiting for us.

"Mom, I'm hungry, check-in ain't until 4:00PM so we have about two hours to kill, let's go eat."

We was at the restaurant ordering our food. Tee-Bae and Paradise ain't know what to order so my mom ordered for them. It was 3:45PM by the time everyone got done eating. I was so fucking full that all I wanted to do was get to bed. I felt so fucking miserable. We rode to the hotel in complete silence. I was stretched out across the third row seat of the Escalade. We checked into the Hyatt Regency in Old San Juan. My suite had a Cali King bed so we could all sleep in one bed and my mom and Anet had their own room.

"Oyah, let's get some rest but tomorrow during the day, I want to go to El Yunque, it's a National Forest. They say it has a really beautiful waterfall."

"Mom, whatever you wanna do, we can do it. Let me go and rest up and tomorrow we can go as soon as the sun comes up."

"Okay go get you some rest."

Everyone said their goodbye and headed for the suites. I put my stuff down, took my clothes off and got right into bed, laying in the middle of this huge bed. I woke up to a call from Big-B. He sounded all out of breath.

"Bruh a bih just shot Moon and his cousin Punkin up. Word on the streets is that it was the Dominicans who are behind the bullshit. I'm trying to see how Moon is doing, they say he got hit in the neck and Punkin is dead."

"Let me hit you back, I'll be out there in a few hours."

I hung up and called Purp. He answered on my second ring.

"I'm on it Oyah, believe me, shit ain't staying like this. The murder rate about to go up in this city. It's War time now and I have a gang full of young wild niggas, ready for whatever."

"Okay but go get all the Hitters and meet me at my old duck off, so we can have a meeting before we start killing everything not relating to Tha Fam. Ima head to the airport now and catch the next "Red Eye Flight," back to Sarasota international.

I'll hit you when I land so someone can come and get me. Y'all be safe and try and have me some answers when I get there."

I explained to everyone that I had to leave, on the next thing smokin, but that they can stay. I even gave them $10,000(Ten thousand) spending money.

"Take me back to the airport so I can be on the next flight."

On the plane, I looked out the window in a daze and all I had on my mind was Murder. I will never let anyone disrespect Tha Fam and live to talk about it…

# CHAPTER 11

# *MY BROTHER'S KEEPER*

My plane landed at Sarasota International at 1:20AM. Purp and J. Gangsta was waiting for me. These niggas wild, here they are, in a Slider with more guns than we can each hold with both our hands, sitting curb side at the airport full of Security, Feds and Local Police. Fuck that shit, someone is going to have to pay for what they did to Moon and Punkin.

"What's good Fam, talk to me, let me know what all is going on."

"Damn, I don't even know where to start at. It's so much shit going on."

"Bruh! I thought y'all had shit under control when I spoke with y'all just few days ago."

"We do got shit under control but in the process of all that, we making lots of enemies."

"Fuck'Em all, so we know who shot bruh already?"

"Yes! It was some Dominicans from out West Bradenton. Tha Fam has a hit out on them, $10,000(Ten thousand) for each member and $30,000(Thirty thousand) for you."

"To be honest, I feel really insulted, but we have to do something about this. We on the come up. Tha Fam don't need no type of interruptions."

We pulled up down East to Wood Winds, all my Shooters was posted and ready to move. When I got out the Slider, Madd-Ball and Poe-Poe walked up on me and dapped me up.

"I wasn't expecting to see you back from your trip so soon big bruh"

"I had to catch a Red Eye Flight when I heard about what happened"

"Big bruh, I know Ima young nigga, but I feel like we have to find the bank."

"The nigga with the loot, who is paying for this so called hit on Tha Fam. We knock them niggas off, then can't nobody collect any loot."

"That's a good fucking point you making Poe-Poe. Let me make a few calls, I know a white bih who be around them Dominicans."

"Bruh, the nigga name is Chocolate, he's in charge of that gang called The Trinitario. He don't care that we killed his men. His problem is that those niggas had a Million Dollars of his Dope stashed and now they can't find it because the only two niggas who knew where it was are dead. So now, Chocolate wants us all dead."

I called Jenny from the block and she answered on the third ring.

"Hello Baby!"

"Where you at? I need to link with you."

"I'm at my girls house in Oneco."

"Come down East to Wood Winds."

"Okay I'm on my way."

"Purp, run me to Roxanna house so I can get the rental."

"Let's go now."

On my way to Roxanna house, we saw the Toyota that shot at me. It was at the gas pump at 7-Eleven, we pulled into the gas station and parked in the cut where we can keep an eye on the car. Kano and Glover walked out the store and got into the car, but never pulled off. Not even two minutes later, K. Cramer came out and got in the back seat of the Toyota.

"Bruh, now it all makes sense. The niggas was shooting at me because of her, either she fucking them and fed them some bullshit or they had something to do with Stormi getting killed. Follow them niggas, I wanna know where they're going. It's been a change of plans."

We pulled up into Jackson Park. They parked and went into an apartment.

"Bruh, fuck all that, let's run off in their spot and body these niggas and that bitch."

"Let's do it."

Purp reversed into the parking space beside the Toyota. We got out and walked up to the apartment. I couldn't see anything inside but I could tell that they were far from the front door. I pulled out a Glock 40 that was in the Slider when I got picked up from the airport. The car was left on with all the lights off. Jackson Park was dead, it was already 3:40 AM.

"Let's run off in there, save the white bitch for me. I want her to die at my hands."

I kicked in the door with one kick. It went crashing open then Purp ran in first and I was right behind him. The T.V. was so loud I don't even think they heard us hit the door because when we got to the room, she was getting the train ran on her. I stepped in the room and slapped Kano with my 40 so hard that I knocked him clean out. Then I kicked K.Cramer in her stomach.

"AHHH! Why is you kicking me for?"

Purp had Glover held at gunpoint.

"Bitch don't play stupid, you know why I'm here, all of you do. First y'all kill my dog, then y'all niggas wanna shoot at me. Yoo Purp! Splash his bitch ass."

"Man Oyah, I swear I ain't know it was you until after."

BANG! BANG! BANG! Purp splashed Glover's brains all over the carpet.

"Now bitch, what you thought shit was sweet?"

"Oyah, please don't kill me, I'm sorry."

"Yea! You most definitely is a sorry bitch! But guess what? The shit that happened at your parents house was me."

"Yoo Oyah, my nigga, we ain't know it was you that she was setting up, Real Talk."

"Fuck! Nigga! I don't give a fuck what you talking about so please spare me with the cries."

"But!"

BANG! BANG! BANG! BANG! I hit that nigga four times all in his stomach and chest area before he even got the chance to speak.

"Now get your bitch ass up and let's go!"

K. Cramer was crying and trying to get me to change my mind. But little do she know that she's about to share the same fate as Stormi.

"Bruh, search this apartment real fast, we have to go."

"Please Oyah! I'm sorry! Don't make me go with you, I don't wanna die."

"Let's go Hoe."

We walked out the apartment, everything still looked dead so I opened the front door and popped the trunk.

"Get your ass in there!"

She faked like she wasn't, so I slapped her with the Glock.40 and pushed her in the trunk all in one Swift motion. I slammed the trunk shut then went back in the house. Purp had a pillowcase with guns of all kinds and a huge safe. He struggled with it so I grabbed the pillow case and opened the back door for him so he could slide the safe in. Once everything was put up, we jumped in the car and pulled off.

"Go across the Skyway real fast and get off on the first exit."

"Aight bet! But where is the white bitch, You let her go? Don't tell me that you a tender dick about these Hoes."

"Man, don't size me like that bruh. I put that Hoe in the trunk. She wanted to kill a dog, an animal, well now an animal about to kill her."

We going to Lake Maggiore to feed the Gators.

"Damn that's going to be wild. You think they will be hungry enough to eat her entire body before someone finds her?"

"Just watch and see bruh."

We pulled up on a small footbridge and stopped the car. We was the only car that could be seen or humans in the area. I got out and popped the trunk, soon as I did, K. Cramer hopped out the trunk and took off running. Purp took off running behind her.

"Bruh don't chase that bitch!"

Purp stopped and looked at me like I was crazy.

"Watch out"

I pulled my gun out and sent three shots at her, Bang! Bang! Bang! Hitting her in the hip. K. Cramer damn near hit a front flip before crashing to the ground. My phone started to ring, it was Jenny.

"Yoo Purp, go get that bitch and bring her stupid ass over here."

K. Cramer's cries could be heard clearly. I answered the phone.

"Yoo talk to me!"

"I'm out here in Wood Winds, but I don't see you."

"Give me a minute and I'll be there."

"Is that someone crying? Are you okay?"

"I'm on the phone with you right, so yea I'm okay, but I'll see you in a few, don't go anywhere."

I hung up before she could even answer because Purp was dragging this Hoe by her hair to where I was at, while she kicked and cried pleading for her life.I found a branch on the ground, picked it up and threw it into the water.

"Why did you just do that?"

"I want to shake the water up so when I toss her ass in there, the gators can already be on point."

"Oyah! Please Don't kill me! I'll do anything, just don't kill me!"

"So you would do anything for me not to kill you?"

"Yes Oyah! Please just don't kill me."

"Get naked then so me and bruh can run the train on you."

"Yoo Oyah, I don't want none of that pussy, you shot the hoe, she has blood all over her."

"She said she'll do anything, so Ima get the pussy and you get the head."

"Yes! I'll do it, please just don't kill me."

K. Cramer started to get naked.

"Okay, now that you are naked, you leaving this world just how you came into it."

"But I thought once I let y'all run the train on me, that I could keep my life."

"Bitch we ain't pressed for pussy, only thing that's going to get this dick hard is watching you die by all them Gators."

I slapped her with my Glock and tossed her over the bridge. She screamed all the way until she hit the water. K. Cramer tried to swim to safety but found herself surrounded by gators. I screamed down on her.

"Nah! Bitch! You is breakfast"

And she vanished under the water. All that could be seen was bubbles and water splashing. The gators had pulled her under water and was fighting over her, tearing her, shredding her into pieces. Then out of nowhere like six gators popped out the water fighting over her head.

"Well that bitch is one less of a problem for us. Let's go back across the bridge so we can go handle that, then I wanna go see Moon at the hospital."

On our way over the Skyway I noticed Purp was in deep thought.

"Yoo Fam, is you good my nigga?"

"Yea, Yea, Yea! I'm just amazed at how fast those gators ate that bitch up."

"I'm about to make sure those gators never go hungry."

"L.O.L you wild bruh."

"Nah I'm loyal and can't nobody disrespect my Fam and live to talk about it."

"I know that's right. Let's make sure all loose ends are tied up so we can get back to this money. Can't no money be made if we out here at war with niggas, so let's clean up and get the gators nice and fat. LOL!"

When we pulled up to Roxanna house, her car was gone but the S-Type was sitting out there.

"Let me run inside real fast and see if this stupid bitch left the keys to the JAG."

I used my keys to let myself in. The first thing I saw was the keys on the Entertainment Center. I grabbed them and also seen my Safes in the hallway, I walked out the house and locked the door.

"I got the keys so I'll just meet you in WoodWinds."

On my way to East Bradenton my mind was clouded with many thoughts. My biggest was where the fuck could this bitch be at this time in the morning and the other is these fucking Dominicans and how the fuck did Glover and Kano even know I was in that Excursion, unless they just so happen to see me at RaceTrac and felt like it was their chance to get at me. But that's no longer a problem. Now we just have to take care of the other shit, A.S.A.P! I pulled up in Wood Winds, my whole team of Hitters was here. I walked over to Jenny and gave her $2,500(twenty five hundred).

"That's for you, but I need to know where all the Dominicans be in Sota."

"They all be to the Baseball field on FruitVille every Tuesday and Thursday after 3PM."

"So you don't know where they stay at?"

"My girl use to fuck with Junior and I've been to his house a few times. He stays in a huge house all the way in the back of Sarasota Lakes. It's the only Brick Red house on the last street and it's a dead end. He also has a Yellow, White and Green Speed Boat in his drive-way. You can't miss it."

"Thanks for that. Ima get up with you in the morning, I'm dead tired."

"Okay just call me whenever."

"Yoo Fam, tomorrow we need to put eyes on that house. I need to get some answers."

"Yoo Big bruh, I can slide out there now, just in case they wake up early."

"Okay bet! Just hit my line if anything."

Poe-Poe and Madd-Ball left to go put eyes on Junior's spot. Everyone else left for their house. I went to Ling-Ling's house, locked the door and went inside her room. She was sleeping so I took off my clothes, showered real fast, dried off, put on some deodorant J. Gangsta had piled up in the bathroom, from all the shit he gets from baser's. I put on my boxers and climbed right into bed with her. I pulled her towards me and she wiggled her ass so my dick rested directly in between the crease of her ass cheeks. I held her and fell asleep. The next morning, she woke me up wearing nothing but some thongs and a tank top. Her nipples was so hard they looked like they was about to bust holes in the shirt.

"Oyah! You hungry? I made pancakes and eggs with corn beef hash."

"Hell yea, I love corn beef hash."

I ate all my food and then I heard knocking so I grabbed my Glock.40 just in case. I always like to stay ready, so that way, I never have to get ready!

"J. Gangsta is outside waiting on you."

"Shit, why he ain't just come into the apartment?"

"Do you see what I have on right now?"

"Oh yea, you right."

I got up, brushed my teeth and got dressed.

"Damn my nigga, you fucking my cousin now?"

"Nah, we just cool and once everyone left I was so tired from everything that took place, I just stayed here and tapped out."

"Yea, whatever nigga, I know you."

"Let's go to the hospital. I wanna holla at Moon. He in Manatee Memorial right?"

"Yea, him and his cousin."

"Aight, let's go, we taking the Jag. Do me a favor and call Poe-Poe and Madd-Ball and see what's up with them?"

B.P.D (Bradenton Police Department) was all over the Hospital. We went to the I.C.U. floor and soon as we got off the elevator, I saw Lala

"What's up sis, how is Moon doing?"

"He good, he just had a flesh wound to his neck. It went in and out, but it had grazed over the main vein. The doctor said had it been a lil deeper, we would have been getting ready to plan his funeral."

Purp walked up on me and said we needed to get to Sarasota Lakes.

"Sis, tell Moon I got him. We have to Slide and take care of some things real fast, but I'll be back tonight so I can chop it up with you and him."

"Nah don't come here, just call my phone, he will be getting discharged as soon as the Detectives leave his room."

"Who is in there with him?"

"Detective Mike Skulmol with B.P.D. Violent Crime Unit."

"Oh damn, that Cracker is nasty. I'm glad he ain't see me. Have bruh hit my line when he get from around them."

"I will and you be safe out there Oyah!"

"I will sis!"

"Don't call me sis, just Lala."

I just turned and left the hospital, Lala is wild. She gives vibes like she wants me to dick her down. Ima keep my eye on her because if she playing it that close, then ain't no telling what else she doing.

Purp was curbside as soon as I walked out them doors. I got in the S-Type.

"Bruh let's go, that cracker Mike Skulmol up there questioning bruh about who shot him, I guess."

"We need to hurry up and get to Poe-Poe and Madd-Ball. Them niggas are in Junior's house. They got him, the wife and kids in that bitch tied up."

"Oh hurry up, I don't want them niggas to do anything to the kids."

We pulled into Sarasota Lakes and drove all the way to the back until I saw Madd-Ball's Lincoln Town Car. Soon as we pulled into the driveway, Poe-Poe opened the door and waved us in.

"Bruh, where is the wife and kids?"

"They in the kids room."

"Okay so what this nigga talking about?"

"Shit big bruh, the nigga acting like he don't speak English."

I kneeled down beside him and whispered into his ear so his wife wouldn't hear me. I didn't want to snitch on the man about cheating on his wife with a white bih.

"Look Junior, let's cut all the bullshit out. I know you speak perfect English. How you think I found you so easy. Don't ever trust a Pink bitch and don't ever show a bih where your family stay." I stood up

"Now tell me what's your problem with me and my family?"

"I don't even know you dude."

"Oh but I believe you do know me, just in case you don't, let me help you, I'm Oyah and your people shot one of my brother and his cousin."

"Hold up, you the head of Tha Fam?"

"Where you said his family is at?"

"They all the way in the back room."

"Did any of them see y'all face?"

"Nah, we was masked up."

"Can they hear us?"

"Nah I got them tied up with the TV on loud."

"That's perfect, so this how shit going to go. Do you love your family, Junior?"

"Yes please don't hurt them, my family has nothing to do with this lifestyle."

"Junior, your actions will assure your Family's safety. Now why I'm hearing that the Trinitarios got money put up to kill me and my brothers? We need answers or Ima bring the drama to your family."

"Look Bella and Tapia told us about the situation with the dope and then y'all got into a fight at the club. That same night both of them got killed. We don't give a fuck about them not being here anymore, but you killed them before we was able to collect our money. I was personally going to murder both them myself, but now shit is out of my control and my Capo wants you dead in exchange for the $2.6 Million debt that we can't collect anymore."

"I'm not going to lie, yes we killed both them bitch niggas and I would do it again given the chance. I don't do shit then regret it.

I heard they only owed one Million, so where does the other $1.6 Million come from?"

"Nobody but us knows how much work they truly have."

"Well fuck that work, it seems like y'all should be paying me because I did y'all a favor!"

"My Capo will murder you and your entire Team."

"Tell me Junior, who is Capo?"

"His name is Chocolate and he is like John Gotti, Untouchable! You will only see him when he wants you to."

"Nah, Ima see him when I wanna see him. I'll make him come see me. Y'all niggas take his bitch ass to St. Pete."

"Big Bruh why the fuck would we take him to Da Burg for?"

"Just put him in the trunk and do as I say. Call purp so he can Slide with y'all, he knows where I want y'all to take him."

"Okay big bruh"

"Madd-Ball is calling now but I still don't understand why I can't just body his ass here in Sofa."

"You will soon understand, trust me."

I left in my S-Type with J. Gangsta and Madd-Ball and Poe-Poe left with Junior in the trunk. We left the wife and kids tied up in the room.

"Bruh, we have to send the Hitters to the Baseball Park on FruitVille in Sarasota around 4:00PM!"

"Should we bring a Cooler with water and soda and some burgers to throw on the grill?"

"Nah nigga, I want y'all to bring some fire and set the whole park on fire!"

"OHHH! Okay! So it's that type of party."

"Who be over there? at a park!"

"You know Dominicans think they going to the M.L.B, but little do they know, a lot of their dreams are about to get cut short."

"Bruh, let's swing by the Trap's to make sure everything is good."

"Aight bet, we going to hit Nando's spot then Big-B spot. The traps on Osprey are just cranking up. I was there all last night until I came to my cousin's house this morning."

I called Roxanna. "Where the fuck you at?"

"I'm hanging with a friend of mine in Orlando, Why do it concern you for? We ain't in no relationship, so please miss me with all the extra shit."

"You know what, keep that same attitude Bitch."

I hung up and called Dinky.

"Yoo bruh, I need your truck for like two hours."

"Come get it, you know it's at my mom's house. Ima call her now so she can set the key in the truck for you."

"Aight, Ima leave $200 in the glove box when I drop it back off."

Damn 12th Street is on swole right now. Nando was chilling on the front porch getting his car cleaned. This type of shit gets me hyped, when I see my team eating and living life to the fullest.

"Yoo what's good Nando, I see you got the block on full swing."

"Hell yes bruh, I'm glad you back. I'm about to run outta work."

"Yea, I got you, we about to go check on Moon. He should be on his way home if he ain't already there."

"What's good with Bullet and Rue?"

"Shit bruh, everything is everything. Them niggas cooking the entire brick and busting them down into dimes. They not serving no niggas double-up or anything. Rock for Rock. I swear every baser in the 941 got this door Swinging."

"That's what I like to hear. Keep y'all foot on these niggas neck. Ima hit your line when I meet up with Moon so you can pull up on me and Re-up...But Ima slide so I can check on Big-B."

"Aight just hit my line when you ready for me to pull up."

"Bet, I got you my nigga."

60th was on full swing.

"How has everything been around here, has it been hot?"

"Nah everything been good, the police been busy with those Chico's on 64th. They done had a shoot out every night for the last four nights."

"Fuck'Em let them get the heat off us."

"How is the Trap doing?"

"We back chewing and Keybo and Dick got the spot across the street as well, so we got Oneco on smash right now."

"That's what's up, Keybo across the street now?"

"Nah but Dick is. Keybo should be at your old duck off spot. He whipping Heroin into his Coke and making some Exclusive Dope, once a baser smokes his dope, they are hooked and can't get high off anyone else dope."

"So across the street is just a hard trap?"

"Nah, Keybo just sell hard, but he got his Lil brother and step-brother Moody working beside him with the Heroin."

"I like that demo, he is putting down. Let me Slide, I wanna go holla at him then pull up on Moon."

"You good bruh, do you need some work?"

"Yea, I could use some more, I got your loot put up."

"Ima hit your line so you can pull up on me."

"Aight bet."

"Where this nigga J. Gangsta go?"

"He across the street at the other trap."

I got in the S-Type and pulled up in front of the other trap. I called Lala

"What's good Sis, is bruh out yet?"

"Yea, he in Circle -K getting some Swisher Kings."

"Okay Bet, I'll be in y'all's crib in like twenty minutes."

I hung up and bust me a gar down and rolled me a fat one.

"Let's Slide nigga, Moon about to pull up to his spot and there is money to be made and I wanna pull up at the Baseball Park."

"Aight, I'm ready to run down on these Chico's and pull their bitch card."

We drove to Manatee Woods, on our way, my phone rang, it was Purp. He must be at Lake Maggiore already.

"Yoo, what's good Fam!"

"Shit we here with this plantain eating bitch."

"What do you want us to do?"

"Find a stick and throw it in the water so you can get the Gators attention."

I could tell J. Gangsta was trying to figure out what I was up to because I could feel him staring at me, but I kept talking on the speaker phone and driving to Moon's spot.

"Once the water is shook up, pop that bih in both of his knees and have Poe-Poe and Madd-Ball toss his bitch ass in the water with our new friends."

"Aight bet, I got you."

My phone ran again soon as I ended the call with Purp.

"Fuck! Damn I know she about to talk shit. It's Mom. Hello mom, how is Puerto Rico?"

"You wouldn't have ask me if you was here."

"Mom I had to come back, did you get the money I left for all of y'all?"

"Yes Oyah, but why did you leave?"

"Because Moon got shot at and he got hit in the neck and his cousin got hit a few times as well."

My phone rang!

"Yoo, what's good Fam?"

"Mom, let me take this call on my other phone. I love you and will talk with you later."

"Yoo Fam, what's good! I need a Block of Sand. Big-B just told me you left from over here."

"I did, I had a few things to do but Ima call you when I'm ready to link and you can just pull up where I'm at."

"Aight just call."

I dropped J. Gangsta off at Dinky momma house, so he can take the truck and get both my safes from Roxanna house.

"Take this key, make sure you lock the door when you get done at her spot, and this the key for my spot. Ima pull up on Moon and see what's good with him then meet you back at Dinky momma house when you get done."

"Aight bet, see you in a minute."

We parted ways, J. Gangsta on his way to Palmetto and I went to Moon's spot. He was sitting outside on the steps texting on his phone and smoking a gar.

"What's good Fam, how you feeling?"

"I'm good bruh, just glad I'm out that stink ass hospital. Those Dominicans are going to pay for what they did to Punkin and me. My fucking cousin is still on life support and I just bought my car and now that bih is filled with holes and blood. We was at Club Atlanta in Tampa and we was on our way home on U.S. 41, when we came over the overpass by Rubonia and some old dark car pulled up beside us and Swiss cheesed the car. Punkin got hit 4-5 times and a bullet grazed me on the neck."

"Yea, ya shit looks like you got more than grazed, but I'm glad you are okay because I would have killed everyone with Dominican blood running through their veins if you would have lost your life behind that shit. "I AM MY BROTHERS KEEPER" This entire County will get burned down when it comes to Tha Fam."

"You good to move around or is your soft ass outta commission because there is money to be made, plus I found out where the head of the Trinitarios spend most of his evenings at."

"Oh nigga don't size me, Ima Soulja for real, let's get this money because I can't wait to catch up with dude. Ima hit that bitch with a 12-Gage buck shot to his neck from close range."

"Nigga you trying to knock his head off his shoulders! But let's slide, grab whatever loot you got as well so we can re-up."

"Aight, I got $120,000(One hundred, twenty thousand) for you and like 16 zips left."

"Okay bet, you sold the brick?"

"Nah, Big-B and Nando needed more work plus I had to get Keybo and Dick right, Mike-O and Mike-E, then the traps off Osprey opened up that same morning I got shot. The way shit going if you ain't Tha Fam, you don't eat."

"We are about to turn up and apply more pressure to these streets."

We rode to my spot so I can drop some money off and grab some Sand. As I was pulling into my house, so was J. Gangsta.

"Bruh, go help J. Gangsta put both them safe in the house for me, I have to get some shit together."

I put all the loot in my new safes, grabbed my last 3 Bricks of food and 3 Blocks of Sand. Damn Tha Fam moving this dope faster than I can count all this money. Moon walked in the room and saw all the money in my new safes and wanted to know where I got them.

"I ordered them online."

"Yea I need one of these for my spot. This bih heavy duty."

"You need to move into a house, then get you one of these."

We put all the dope in the backpack and got ready to leave. I called Big-B.

"Bruh, meet me in Wood Winds but bring the Re-rock machine, the shifter and blender and some sandwich baggies with the cut."

"Aight bet, Ima go get that and be on my way."

"Bruh, go back to Dinky's mom's house, we going to meet up there."

We all left at the same time. I called all my people's so they can meet me in two hours to re-up. That will be perfect timing to Slide by the park and check on those Dominican's, maybe we can catch them Slippen. Back at Ling-Ling's house, Big-B and I took over her kitchen and dining room area. I was trying to hurry up and cut all this dope up, so I can get it repressed and packaged.Right as I got done, Haitian Bo, Uzi and Davi came into the apartment.

"What's good with y'all boys."

"Shit I'm good my nigga, that Sand some real pressure."

"Yea it's pure, straight from Puerto Rico."

"Look, Ima grab two Bricks but in like a few days. Ima need anywhere between Three to Five Bricks so please try and be Strapped when I need you."

"I got Four Bricks left of this same shit here, but Ima call my plug and Re-up as soon as I get done here."

"Bruh, do me a solid and hold those Four Blocks because I don't want you to switch up and it don't be as good."

"Nigga, my shit is always good, but I got you."

There was a knock on the door.

"Big-B, see who it is and let them in."

I served Haitian Bo the Two Bricks and Uzi and Davi each got Twenty Zips. Nando, Keybo, Turd and Carl showed up at the same time. Everyone got served. I was just waiting on Bullet and Rue so I can get off this last Brick of Sand.I collected all the loot that was owed to me, plus I cashed in on all the work. Bullet pulled up and J. Gangsta let him in. He handed me a grocery bag with $40,000(Forty thousand)in it.

"Bruh, Rue had to handle something with his baby mama, so he sent me."

"I see you riding clean right now.!"

"Yeah, man thanks to you bruh. I want to get some rims and put some music in it."

"Let's slide down South and drop some 24' Floaters because I wanna bolt the Charger up too."

"Shit I'll be ready in another week or two, because I'm about to put my Mom and BabyMomma in new spots and I have to get them all new furniture."

"Aight bet, just holla at me and let me know what's up."

Everyone started to leave.

"Yoo, Keybo! Hold up, I want to holla at you. Do you got time to slide with me?"

"Nah I got my lil brother Dick in the car with me but I can drop him off then meet up with you in a few."

"Let him take your wheels and you slide with me then I'll drop you off wherever your car is."

"Okay, yea, we can do that, let me give him this work then we can slide."

When Keybo walked out, in came Moon, Purp, Poe-Poe and Madd-Ball. Madd-ball was crazy hype.

"Yoo, I never seen anything so gruesome in my life."

"L.O.L. I see you met our new pets!"

"What is y'all talking about?"

Moon said.

"Well we ran down on Dominican Junior and snatched his bitch ass up. He told me who paid for the hit on Tha Fam and why. We ended up snatching his bitch ass up and took him to St. Pete only Purp knew about the spot, so I had him go with these two wild niggas so they can toss him in the water and watch him be eaten alive."

"Here is a few pictures of the Gators ripping him apart."

"Man if you don't delete that stupid shit right now."

"Look, we all about to slide to Sarasota. Those Dominican's should be playing Baseball right now."

"Okay bet, let's load up then"

J. Gangsta said.

"Yoo Purp, what happened to that safe we had got the other night."

"I was just about to tell you that I got it in the back seat of my car still, but I can't find Joey to open it for us."

"Fuck it, just put it in Ling-Ling's house and we will come back later and find someone to open it for us."

Purp went out to get the safe while I went into the room and got a pillowcase. I had over $300,000(Three hundred thousand) here. I put it all in the pillow case and put it in the room with Ling-Ling.

"Lil Mama, we about to step out, don't open this door for anyone. I have enough loot in here to buy these apartments."

"Oyah, why would you leave all that money in here for, What if someone tries to come get it?"

"A bih ain't that stupid, but so you feel safe, Ima leave two of my men here. One in the house with you and the other outside."

"Okay then, y'all be careful."

"We will be, but cook some food for us."

I walked out, we had four niggas in each car and six cars deep. I am my brother's keeper and behind anyone of these guys, I'm going all out. We rode to FruitVille ready for war. Purp and J. Gangsta put together a Team full of Hitters that move at our Command.

## CHAPTER 12

# *THA EXTERMINATOR*

We pulled up to the baseball field and there was a lot of people out enjoying the day, bike riding, walking dogs, playing basketball and then there was a bunch of Dominican's around the baseball field. Purp looked over at me and said,

"Bruh, what you wanna do?"

"We are six cars deep, we can follow them and find out where they be."

The White Escalade is Chocolate's truck, the nigga we snatched up said he the head of the Trinitorio's and he is the one paying to get us hit.

"I want us to follow him and I want each and every car to follow the rest of his team."

Moon was in the back seat with Keybo and all they could think about is Murder. Both of them was on some fuck'it shit. They wanted to hop out and just hit everyone on the baseball field.

"Y'all niggas is really wildin out right now. My job is to make sure Tha Fam is good and letting y'all go out there with all these witnesses will be me failing Tha Fam. I want to catch him Slipping and burn his bitch ass without the police having to get on our trail."

Chocolate got ready to leave, as the baseball field started to get empty, my men started to follow certain cars. Only the ones of the men who did the Gang's hand shake. Chocolate pulled out in his truck with a fine ass, dark skinned woman at his side and a three series BMW tailing him. Keybo, Moon, Purp and I tailed the Escalade and BMW all the way to a house in North Port, Florida. This was a real suburban neighborhood, but the house they pulled up into was full of cars and street bikes. Chocolate and the Dark Skinned woman got out the truck and used a key to get inside of the house. Purp was the first to speak.

"This either her house and he just be here or that's his main bitch and they both live here."

"Either way now we have the up's on him."

"I'm with you when you are right, Oyah!"

I texted the address to this house to everyone in the car with me, so we can all have it in our phones. We left and headed back to the hood on I-75, Purp got a call letting him know that one of our men got shot and he is in really bad shape.

"Take him to Mattlean in Kingston Estate, to see if she can patch him up."

"Nah bruh, he gots to go to the hospital, he took five shots to the chest area."

"Okay bet, go on over there and keep me posted on what's going on. I'm not trying to pull up over there with B.P.D. all over. I got you my nigga, just get him some help."

"Yoo Purp, what's going on, who got hit up?"

"Man Romeo's lil bruh "Jon-Jon." He was in the car with "Tang and Boo!"

"Damn Fam, this shit is going to get crazy. Romeo is going to snap the fuck out."

"Yea, he is! I can feel his pain. Jon-Jon was a solid and loyal young nigga."

We pulled up to the Wood Winds, nobody had made it back yet. So I went inside and counted up the money in the pillow case.

"Yoo Purp, go and check on the rest of the team, then go holla at Romeo just to see where is mind at and if he trying to handle the situation. Even if he ain't, we will because he got hit up behind a situation dealing with Tha Fam."

After an hour or two, I counted up all the money and there was $434,000(Four hundred thirty four thousand) Damn I ain't ever think I would be playing with numbers like these. I still have a bunch of Heroin left. Let me call my plug.....

"Churp! Churp!"

"Yoo Piloto, what's good!"

"Churp!"

"Oyah my man! How is everything going out there with you?"

"Churp!"

"I got your money, the entire 500."

"Churp!"

"Okay I'll come out that way tonight."

"Churp!"

"You don't want me to just send Roxanna to meet up with you."

"Churp!"

"No, I think it's best if we keep her off the road."

"Churp!"

"Since when did you start caring about Roxanna and what she do?"

"Churp!"

"It's not about her, Oyah, look, I'll be out there to see you around nine tonight."

"Churp!"

"Aight, just holla at me."

"Churp!"

"Look Lil Mama, I'll be back in like an hour. I have to go pickup some more money. Did you cook?"

"Yea, I made smothered Turkey wings, Mac and Cheese, Rice and Blueberry cornbread."

"Shit! I need to hurry up."

Me, Keybo and Moon left. I dropped Moon off at his Spot and kept Keybo with me. We rode to my crib out West Bradenton and I picked up $66,000(Sixty six thousand) and my last four Bricks of Sand. I wanted to be ready for Haitian BO when he called. On our way back Down East to Wood Winds, I took my work to my old stash house. After putting up the Sand, we bent a few corners just to check on all of our Traps. Everything was looking good until we pulled onto 12th. I saw an old Blazer parked on the corner, with what looked like Four Dominicans in it. Keybo pointed it out first.

"Bruh, you see them, Four niggas in that Blazer back there!"

"Yea I peeped them, Ima circle around the block."

"Nah, just park. I'll run up on them."

"Hold up, I don't wanna bring any more heat to 12th street."

I hit Nando up.

"Yoo fool, you alright in there? it's a Blazer sitting a few houses down full of Dominicans in it."

"Churp!"

"We strapped in here waiting for whatever."

"Churp!"

"Bruh get out that house and let them know you see them, so they can pull off. I wanna see where they go. I want to exterminate the entire Dominican race from Manatee and Sarasota County."

"Churp!"

"Aight I'm coming out now."

"Churp!"

Nando came out the Trap and pointed an AK-47 at the Blazer, making it pull off. We followed the Blazer down 63rd and at the light on U.S.301 and 63rd. Someone in the back seat behind the passenger, let the window down and shot our way. They missed us and turned onto U.S. 301, Headed towards Sarasota. I pulled off behind them.

"Bruh, pull up beside them."

I swerved around the Blazer and pulled up on the side of it. Keybo snatched my .45 and pulled out his, then lowered his window and let them have it.

Bang! Bang! Bang! Bang! Bang!

The Blazer tried to get away but it was no match for the S-Type. I stayed right on their ass and Keybo kept the pressure on them.

Bang! Bang! Boom! Boom! Boom! Bang!

I slowed the car down letting the Blazer get away and I busted a U-Turn. It was 7'o'clock at night and U.S.301 was busy. We had to get out of this car ASAP. I hurried up to Wood Winds. I ran inside Ling-Ling's house.

"Lil Mama, I need you to drive this car to Palmetto when it gets dark for me. Better yet, go move it for me real fast, because it's right out front and park it on the other side of the projects. I had to make a few calls and line shit up because I can't keep having people take shots at me like we sweet."

"Yoo Fam, I need you to pull up DownEast."

Purp got excited!

"You good bruh, because I was just there and you called me back."

"Nah bruh I had to bend a few corners to handle some stuff and those Dominicans started to bustin at us. We chased them down U.S. 301 and Keybo let them have it. But it was a lot of people on the road so I turned the car around and came over here."

"You was in the S-Type while all this was going on?"

"Yea, but Ima send it back once my plug gets here with the work."

"Okay then Bet, Ima get us some cars so we can go handle those Dominicans later."

"Aight bet, I want to take at least Six people on this mission here."

I got the $434,000(four hundred thirty four thousand) out of Ling-Ling's room and put the $66,000(sixty six thousand) I just went to pick up with it, making the total $500,000(Five hundred thousand). I hit Piloto up.

"What's up Fool, where you at?"

"Churp!"

"I'm coming through Apollo Beach right now"

"Churp!"

"Meet me in Wood Winds projects on 15th and 13th East Bradenton."

"Churp!"

"Okay I'll be there soon."

"Churp!"

"Lil Mama, can you fix me a plate? Bruh do you want one as well?"

"Hell yea! I'm hungry as fuck. I was about to tell you to take me to Popeyes so I can get something to eat."

As we ate, I peeled off $3,000)three thousand) outta my pocket money and gave it to Ling-Ling.

"Lil Mama, go and buy a new bedroom set from Rooms To Go. Get a pillow Top, King Size Mattress."

"Okay and what should I do with my old bedroom set?"

"Give it to someone who will appreciate it."

My Nextel went off, Churp! Churp! Churp!

"Yoo, you're here already bruh?"

"Churp!"

"Yea, I just pulled in."

"Churp!"

"Come all the way to the last building on the left. I'll have my brother outside waiting. He is dressed in all black."

"Churp!"

"I see him!"

"Churp!"

Piloto came into the apartment with two duffle bags and sat them on the couch.

"Lil Mama, grab that loot for me and bring it out here for me please!"

She came out the room with nothing on but some Booty shorts and a tank top, Slim, Fine, Red Bih. Ling-Ling was struggling with all that loot.

"Damn Oyah, who is this Pretty lil thing you got here?"

"She Fam bruh. She's one of my brothers' lil cousin."

Piloto extended his hand to her.

"Hello my name is Piloto and yours is?"

"Ling-Ling! Nice to meet you Piloto."

She sat the money at my foot then went into the room. I got up, grabbed the bag of money and handed it to Piloto, then walked over to the couch and opened the first duffle bag. It was filled with Bricks of Sand, with the double G-Gucci stamp on it.

"These are different from the last. My people are in love with the work we've been having."

"Oyah, the work comes from the same place. You know I only deal with the best of the best."

"Yea, I know but that other Sand was pressure."

"Oyah to be honest, this coke here is better, it's 96% while the last batch was just only 93% pure."

I opened the second duffle bag and this one had Five Bricks of Heroin, China White.

"Piloto tell me what's the ticket for all this"

"You have 20 Bricks of Coke and 5 Bricks of Heroin, so that's $300,000(three hundred thousand) for the Coke and $350,000(three hundred fifty thousand) for the Heroin."

"Okay Bet! Yoo Piloto, I want to thank you my nigga, because of you I'm able to take care of my entire Family and Team. You can always count on me and my Team if you ever need us for anything. My loyalty to you is in blood."

"Vise Versa Oyah, I respect you as a Man, brother and a business partner."

"That's what's up, bruh after the next flip, Let's take a Big Ballin Trip, your Team and my Team. By the way, what made you take that ride all the way out here, strapped with all that work?"

"You are too Big of a Boss to be taking risks like that. I got Roxanna, her ass is expendable and I know you got your peoples."

"Nah, I had to take care of something with one of my good friends, so I just decided to kill Two birds with one stone."

"Oh you must be about to hang out, you got on your Rolex and your Chains."

"Yea, we going to just chill and fuck. Shawty loves to get dicked down and for me to bust a nut all over her face."

"Shit I know that's right, hang the fuck out then! Well I'm not going to hold you up any longer. I'll holla at you when I get your loot."

We dapped up and he walked out the apartment with all the loot. Piloto must have forgotten about Keybo standing outside on guard because he jumped when he saw bruh standing outside the door in the dark dressed in black. He got in his Jeep Wrangler and pulled off.

I grabbed both duffles and put them under all the dirty clothes in the closet.

"Keybo, go to the back room and grab all the Sticks, it's time for all the Exterminators to do their job. We are going to pay Chocolate a visit at that house in North Port."

I text Purp, "Where y'all at?"

"We are all about to pull up within the next ten minutes."

"Aight Bet, me and Keybo making sure all the Sticks are loaded up."

We pulled up Two cars deep to the house in North Port. They must have a lot of people who live here or these are all this niggas cars. J.Gangsta kicked the first door in while Boo kicked in the other. Keybo stepped in first with a pistol grip 12 Gage Pump. The first bitch to move he fired off, dropping him. He went to plead for his life in Spanish. I heard Keybo say,

"Shut the fuck up bitch ass Nigga."

He pulled out his Colt 45 and popped one into his head. I came in behind him and J. Gangsta came in behind me.Someone behind the wall in the other room started busting at me, so I returned fire.

Boom! Boom! Boom! Boom! Boom! Boom! Boom! Boom!

I could hear the Stick getting off in the back of the house, where Purp, Poe-Poe and MADD-Ball was. It sounded like they was handling business. No more shots was being fired my way, so I decided to go into the room and there it was, a Dominican holding two 9 mill's dead on the floor, but it wasn't Chocolate. We went room by room and in each we found Trinitarios or young women that looked to be under age. We pulled all the males out into the living room and tied them up with sheets. Then brought all the girls out. We cleared the house and while me and Keybo had all the women and Trinitarios in the front room, Purp, Madd-Ball, Poe-Poe and J. Gangsta searched the house.

"So is anyone of you niggas going to speak up and tell me where is this bitch ass nigga Chocolate at, because we came in search of him. You clowns are just collateral damage."

"So tell me where we can find him and I'll make this fast or piss me off and I'll make this shit long and painful. I also want to know what the fuck is y'all doing with these young girls in here, because I know they not family all naked and shit."

I asked but none of them answered me.

"So y'all just some mutes I see."

"Bruh, kill Three of them and leave Two of them alive."

Keybo got up close and personal with the Gage and put it to the first guy's head and without a second thought, he pulled the trigger. Boom! Blowing his brains all over the wall. It looked like Keybo spilled macaroni and red sauce everywhere. The girls started to scream and cry outta fear.

"If y'all Hoes don't shut the fuck up, I'll put a bullet in each one of y'all's head."

They stopped crying instantly. The second guy Keybo pressed his Gage into the guy's dick.

"Are you going to tell me what I wanna hear or are you still a mute?"

The Dominican laughed at Keybo and spit at him, but Keybo moved in time before it had a chance to land on him. That pissed Keybo off and he pulled out a butter knife and before I could even realize what was going on, Keybo was stabbing him over and over. Blood was splashing everywhere. Then he turned and hit the guy on top of his head two fast times sending blood flying all over him. Keybo had a crazy look in his eyes and was covered in dudes blood from head to toe.

"Y'all Two niggas better start telling me where I can find Chocolate at and what are these young girls doing here."

Jackpot! I heard J. Gangsta say. I pulled my .45 out and filled up the Fourth Dominican with hollow tips. Poe-Poe came around the corner with a bunch of Chains, Rings and Watches.

"Lil Bruh, take these Hoes to put on some clothes. They're looking scared."

"Look, y'all okay, we are not going to hurt y'all, but can you tell me what's going on here!"

"Chocolate is a monster, he told us all the same lie. That he will bring us to America and give us a job at his bar and he will charge us 15% of our checks until we pay him back, but as soon as we got here, Chocolate and a few more guys forced us to use drugs and let all these random people have their way with us."

"Look, do y'all want to be free from all this mess, if so, I would rid you of this bullshit, give y'all enough money to get back to the Dominican Republic."

"No, I don't want to go there, we would like to stay out here in the States."

"Look Ima have y'all go stay with me at my house until my girlfriends get back from their Trip, then they will set y'all up. How old are y'all anyways?"

"They are all under Eighteen. She is the youngest and I'm the oldest, I'm 23 years old. We will work to survive, we just don't want any drugs and to be having men take advantage of us anymore."

"Y'all don't have shit to worry about, y'all will have the house to y'all self until my girls get back, but the only way this will work, y'all need to stab this bitch ass nigga up so I can be sure that what has taken place here will never be spoke about again."

These Dominicans are some real Gangsta's, almost like Monk's. They ain't saying shit not even a plea for help, but I'm the real Gangsta.

"Ladies go into the kitchen and get knives. I want y'all to carve a message into his chest. I want it to say, "T.F" as big as y'all can get it and cut his Dick off and shove it down his throat."

"Fuck y'all Niggas, The Trinitario's will kill all you American Bastards."

"Nah homeboy we are Exterminators, I won't stop until I know ain't no more Trinitarios left in my City. Y'all have fun with him."

The girls latched on dude like a hungry pack of Hyenas. Damn they must have had a lot of anger built up because they hit him so many times, in the face, stomach, chest, neck, arms and thighs. He hollered like a real bitch. The oldest out the pack was so mad that she yelled,

"NO GRITES CABROM." That's "DON'T SCREAM BITCH."

"Damn Mami! You is a real bad bitch for real"

She over killed him, the rest of the pack had already pulled off him, while she kept on stabbing him OVER and OVER until I wrapped my arms around her waist and pulled her back so she could stop. She dropped the knife and turned around and wrapped her arms around me. She buried her face into my chest. I didn't know what to do so I held her in my arms. She cried and thanked me at the same time, telling me how good it felt to kill.

My Team all was looking surprised at how Gangsta these girls was getting down. Without telling them what to do, off his dick went down his throat, while one of the girls carved a huge T.F. on his chest.

"Let's get the fuck up outta here and get back on our side."

Purp and Poe-Poe had pillow cases and duffle bags in their hands while the rest of us helped the girls to the cars. We rode back to Oneco to my old duck off spot, so the girls could get showered up while we counted up what we had hit for. Keybo came up with a great idea of forming Two groups that operate under one umbrella, Tha Fam's! That night is when we formed Tha Hyena's. A hit squad of Male and Female Hitters that belonged to Tha Fam. We counted $800,300(Eight hundred thousand, three hundred)in cash, Eight Bricks of some Gray Heroin and a few Rose Gold Chains, Bracelets, and Rings. Madd-Ball, Poe-Poe, Keybo, Purp, J. Gangsta and I all got 100K each while our females to Tha Fam split the other $200K between them. Each one of the guys got a brick a piece while I kept the remaining Three Bricks and the jewelry. Everyone was happy with the bust down of the lick.

"Ladies, what do y'all wanna go buy?"

The oldest spoke up first.

"My name is Julissa, the others are Desiree, Amanda, Berlin, Scarlet and the youngest is Nadeen."

"Okay then, I have to slide, I will link with y'all tomorrow."

"Keybo, take them to the mall, so they can buy some clothes and whatever else they need. Ima go to Roxanna's house for the night."

I first rode to my spot and dropped off the Three Bricks and $58,000(fifty eight thousand) so I can have an even $200,500( Two hundred thousand, five hundred) put up. I kept $42,000(Forty two thousand) on me, so I can drop off some loot on my Chevy and Charger. Easter weekend is coming up in a few days. As I drove to Palmetto, I sent the big homie City a text letting him know,

"THA SUN DON'T SHINE FOREVER"

That was my way of letting him know that I needed his service and I told him to double up on me this time, because my Family just grew bigger. I was listening to "Plies Runnin My Momma Crazy" and decided to swing by Ling-Ling's house. I knocked on her door and she must've looked out the peephole because she opened up the door wearing nothing but a Tank Top and Thongs. She turned around and walked back to the room, her lil ass cheeks looked so good that I locked the door and followed her into the room. Right before she went to climb into bed, I grabbed her and spin her around so she can face me and with one swift move, I pulled her shirt over her head and kissed on her neck. Making her moan out loud.

"Mmmm! That feels good Oyah!"

I moved lower and started to suck on her chocolate drop nipples as I worked my hand into her Thongs. Then she pushed me off her and started to undo my belt and pants, once she got my dick out, it was hard as a MLB Baseball bat. Ling-Ling wrapped her little hand around my Dick and sucked as much of it as she could into her extra wet mouth.

"Oh my lord! This feels good lil mama, suck that Dick like a hoe for me, get nasty with it."

I wrapped my hands into her hair and moved back and forth fucking her throat. She has no gag reflex.

Ding, Dong, Ding, Dong! Someone was at the door but I didn't stop and she didn't either. Ling-Ling started to suck harder while she rubbed on my balls. I felt my stomach get tight and my feet started to tingle, while her lips and head went into overdrive with her putting on a show for me. I let loose into her hungry mouth.

"AAAHH! Fuck, Lil Mama!"

I filled her mouth up with Cum and she swallowed every drop. Ding Dong! Ding Dong! Ding Dong! I rushed to get my pants up, grabbed my fire and without looking through the peephole I snatched the door open and aimed my gun at head level but then I noticed it was J. Gangsta, so I lowered my Gun. He bust out laughing,

"Y'all must have been in here fucking!"

"Nah nigga but if we was, you would have really been cock-blocking."

"I thought you was going to Palmetto."

"I am but I stopped by here real fast so I can get me a new gun, that way I can throw away my used gun. But Ima slide now so I'll see you in the morning."

"Aight bet, Ima slide to one of my lil chicks house."

We both left at the same time, as I was going over the bridge by the hospital, I lowered my passenger window and tossed the used gun out into the Manatee River. A few minutes later I was pulling into Roxanna's driveway.

"What the fuck is going on here?"

Was my only thought. I got to be high or something because I know a bih ain't trying me like shit is sweet.

I got on the phone with Keybo

"Yoo bruh, grab the girls and swing by Ling-Ling's house and get them all strapped up. I got some work I want them to put in out here in Palmetto. Bring them to Roxanna's house."

## CHAPTER 13

# THA HYENA'S

Keybo pulled up with Tha Hyena's. Julissa was the first one out of the car.

"What's going on Papi, is there any trouble?"

"Not yet but there is about to be!"

Keybo, Desiree, Amanda, Berlin, Scarlet and Nadeen stepped out the car and surrounded me and Julissa, so they could hear what's going on.

"I want you ladies to go inside this house and don't kill any of them, just make them wish they was dead. Try not to speak so much and make sure you never mention Tha Fam or any of us. I want their minds to wonder. I also want you to act surprised when you notice the man ain't me. Ask the bitch who the nigga is and where is her man just to see what she say. Slap her ass up a lil."

"Okay Papi we got you, let's go ladies."

"Okay make sure you search the place, get them for all their Jewelry and cash, also find the keys to that vehicle and unlock the doors so I can search it and make sure we don't leave anything behind."

I watched as they made their way towards the house with Keybo leading the pack. At the front door, three girls stood to one side of the door while the other three stood to the other side. They had their guns out ready to run off in the spot. Keybo kicked in the door and my girls filled in one after another. I ran to the back of the house just to make sure dude ain't try to escape. Keybo came up behind me.

"Is everything back here good bruh?"

"Huh, Oh yea! I was just making sure ain't nobody try to come out the back."

I could hear Tha Hyenas putting in work. Nadeen was the loudest like she was the one in control of everything. Nadeen is like a small firecracker, small but a loud bang. She must have had the nigga pinned down because all I heard was

"Don't curl up like a lil bitch now, shit you wanted to be out here like a big boy. You wouldn't even be in this situation if you wasn't fucking with this nasty hoe, she has a man. We came in search of her man but we found you in here making love to her like she is your woman."

Pop! Pop! Pop! Nadeen was pistol-wiping him while the other girls was flipping the house. I heard Berlin yell at Roxanna,

"TU ERES UNA PUTA SUCIA!" YOU IS A NASTY HOE!"

Then it was followed by some hard slaps.

"Please don't hurt me, I'm pregnant, I don't want anything to happen to my baby."

"Damn I know I ain't just heard her say that she was pregnant. I wonder if she is claiming to be pregnant by me or by the fool in there."

Julissa kept asking where your car key was, Pop! She slapped him with the pistol.

"If you wanna keep being a lil pretty boy, you better tell me what I wanna hear or Ima keep fucking up your face."

Berlin said, "Where are his pants? check his pockets."

Nadeen found them and hit the unlock button, making the vehicle lights flash two times. Keybo and I walked up to the vehicle and opened the door and cut the inside lights on. I was looking for money and dope. Keybo was looking for anything of value. Under the back seat, I found a duffle bag. I snatched the duffle bag up and slammed the door shut. I sat the bag on the hood of the S-Type and opened it. Just what I wanted to find. Keybo found Two Nickel Plated LLama 45's.

"Look what I found, I got to have these."

"Yea those are nice, but I have enough money in this bag to buy 100,000(One hundred thousand) of those guns."

Tha Hyena's must have been having fun in there because I could still hear Berlin asking Roxanna

"Where all the money at?"

"He keeps it in the hallway closet in a small safe."

Amanda rushed to the closet and with Scarlet's help they carried the safe out to the car. When I saw them, all I could do was smile. I opened the back door so they can drop the safe off and told them to tell the girls to hurry up. Berlin slapped Roxanna on the head with the pistol, splitting her open until you could see the white meat.

"Please don't hurt me, I'm really pregnant."

Pop! Berlin slapped her again.

"PUTA CABRONA TU SAUES QUIEN ES EL PAPI." STUPID BITCH DO YOU KNOW WHO THE FATHER IS?"

"Yes and he will pay you whatever you want just please don't hurt me."

Amanda went back to the house with Scarlet. It's time to go. Scarlet unplugged the extension cord and used it to tie the dumb nigga up, while the other girls grabbed all his Jewelry and got ready to leave. Keybo went over to the vehicle and flattened all four tires with his knife. The front door opened and all the girls ran out the house one after the other with a huge smile on their faces. Julissa was the last to come out and she stopped at the door, looked back and said

"Consider this y'all's lucky day and Um Roxanna, tell Oyah next time he won't be so lucky, let him know Tha Hyena's are looking for him."

Everyone got in the car and we drove back to Oneco. In my car, Julissa was riding back to Oneco with me, while Keybo had the rest with him.

"I'm sorry Papi but there really wasn't much in that house to take except for a lot of Jewelry."

"Look Mami, you ladies did a great job tonight and we got a lot more than you think. Take a look in that duffle bag in the back seat."

I put on a song by "Plies-Just Hit Me A Lick." Julissa reached in the back seat and tried to grab the duffle bag with one hand but it was way too heavy for her, so she turned around in her seat and picked it up using both hands.

"Diablo Papi! This bag is heavy, what's in it?"

When Julissa got the bag in the front seat and opened it, her eyes looked like they were about to pop out of her head.

"Wow! This is a lot of money Papi, how much is it?"

"You will see when we get back to the Spot and count it all up."

We pulled up to the spot and Keybo pulled his car into the backyard and I followed him.

"Julissa, grab that bag for me while I get the safe out the back seat."

"No problem Papi."

In the house, we all sat in the front room on the sofa, the floor, we was all over. Everyone except for Berlin, she went to shower. Keybo rolled up a Gar, lit it and passed it to me while he started to roll another Gar.

"Mami, go to the closet in that first room and get me the money counter and rubber bands."

When Julissa got up off the floor, her ass was looking so good and fat in those jeans. Seven Gars later, we came up with a total of $500,000(Five hundred thousand). I kept $200,000(two hundred thousand) Keybo got $100,000(one hundred thousand) while Tha Hyenas split $200,000(two hundred thousand) between the six of them. Julissa was so happy that she said, "I ain't never seen this much money ever in my life, it got my pussy wet."

She was looking me dead in the eyes when she said that. Keybo started to grab the safe, but I stopped him.

"Nah bruh, all that in there is mine."

I put in my four digit code and opened the safe. There was $22,000(twenty two thousand) in it. I took that out and placed it in my backpack with the rest of the money, making the total $64,000(sixty four thousand), then I placed the $200,000(two hundred thousand) we just hit for in the safe and locked it.

"We're going shopping in the morning, so y'all get some rest."

I walked in the room and got ready for a shower. It's time for me to get a bigger place. This house is just way too small for Tha Fam and Tha Hyenas. I got in the shower and as I was washing up, the shower door opened up giving me goosebumps from the cold air hitting my body.

"What is you doing in here Julissa?"

"I want to thank you Papi. You have really saved our lives in more ways than you know."

"Ain't no need to thank me."

"But I want to"

And then she dropped to her knees right there in the shower taking my limp dick into her hand and kissing the head before taking as much as she could into her mouth.

"Ahhh! Fuck Mami! This shit feels good."

Julissa held onto my thighs and sucked my dick, spearing her head into me at a real fast pace. I put my hands on her shoulders and stopped her.

"I want some of that pussy."

She turned around so I can fuck her from the back, and held onto the towel rank and spread her legs. Her ass looked so right, Big and Soft with no dimples. Her hair got real curly from getting wet. I grabbed her waist with my left hand and my dick with my right hand and guided myself into her warm and tight lil hole.

"Mmm-a-Papi! Fuck this pussy and smack my ass real hard."

She had a sexy moan and I drilled her from the back making her ass wave up as it smashed into my stomach. It sounded like we was clapping our hands. Julissa really knew how to use her pussy muscle to make it feel like she was squeezing my dick with her hand. I couldn't take it anymore and tried to pull out, but she reached back and dug her nails into the side of my thigh and pulled me towards her. The flood gates opened up and I filled her pussy with my seeds. Julissa milked me with her pussy, squeezing then releasing over and over. Then when she felt my dick getting limp again, she stood up, grabbed a wash rag, applied body wash on it and bathed me, giving my dick and balls extra attention. We got out of the shower, dried off then got in bed naked. Julissa slept in the room with me that night. The next morning, I had to let her know that last night's activity could never happen again. I don't like to mix business with pleasure.

"Oyah I completely understand, I won't ever let anything come between what we have going with Tha Fam. I just wanted to show my appreciation for saving us and help give us a way to make ends meet, that's all."

"Thats real Mami, but next time just grab me some Jordan's or some jewelry. You don't have to give your body up to show a bih that you appreciate them. Save that for the person you love."

"If I wasn't so strong minded and would have been a tender dick, the way you worked that pussy would have had me around here ready to kill a bih about looking at you with lust in their eyes."

"You crazy Papi, but thank you for everything."

We got dressed and came out the room. Nadeen and Berlin was sleeping on the pullout sofa bed, Desiree was on the floor wrapped up in a blanket. I walked up to the back room and just cracked it open and Keybo was in bed hugged up on naked Scarlet and Amanda was naked in the bed as well. I know that's right, bruh flipped both of them last night. I pushed the door a lil more

"Wake ya ass up nigga, we got shit to do bruh."

I walked back out to the front room.

"What do you ladies want to get into today?"

"I don't know Papi, Julissa said."

"Well I have to make a payment on my car and make sure it's getting done, then I want to shoot to Tampa because it's time for some new jewelry and some clothes. Ima throw a Easter Bash at Club Heat on Friday Night, A Block Party on 11th and 59th in Oneco on Saturday morning, then slide by the beach early Sunday morning and Sunday evening the Easter parade in Sarasota."

Keybo walked out the room without a shirt,

"Shit, we about to turnup all weekend long."

" Let's swing by Yoder's Auto Sale, he got a few cars and trucks up there and it's time for a new car."

"Aight bet because I wanna buy myself a new car as well."

"Papi, we need to get us a SUV, something we can all fit in."

"Let's go there first then and see what he got."

My phone started to ring and when I looked, Roxanna's name came across the screen.

"Y'all hold up, it's Roxanna calling me."

I answered and put the phone on speaker so everyone could hear.

"Yoo, what's good!"

"Oyah, fuck you, while you out living your best life fucking only God knows who, I'm home with some Hoes that home invaded me looking for you to kill and rob you."

"Hold the fuck up, so you saying some hoes as in females came to your house looking for me to rob and kill me? That shit seems like some real bullshit, because if they came to kill me, why is you still alive then?"

"You think I'm lying about a bih coming into my house looking for you. I never lied to you before so why should I start now?"

"Look Roxanna, miss me with the bullshit because if what you're saying is true, you would be dead right now."

"Only reason why I'm not dead Oyah is because I begged them not to hurt me because I'm pregnant and I guess they felt my pain because they were females."

"Who all was you with when this home invasion happened?"

"I was alone Oyah! Who else will I be with? Anyways, what difference do it make if I was alone or not?"

"Look, it seems like you're okay so why are you calling me? Do you need me to pay for a window or door for you?"

"No asshole, I need you to pay for me to move somewhere else because I don't feel comfortable here anymore and since all this is behind you, then it's only right that you fix it."

"I'm not paying for you to move anywhere, tell your bitch ass baby daddy to pay for it."

"Nigga, I am telling him, don't try and play me like I'm the one out here fucking."

"I know you ain't putting that baby on me? Before I do anything I need a DNA test because I don't believe that's my baby. Now get your stupid ass off my phone"

CLICK! I hung up on her before she even got a chance to say anything back to me.

"Bruh, who the fuck was in her house anyways?"

"It was a Pretty Puerto Rican boy, he must have had a lot of Money because he had a Rolex on and all, Berlin said."

"Man, bruh, that was our connect, that's why I ain't want to go in there myself because I would have killed him and I want to make sure we have another connect before we do that."

"Bruh, that bitch ass nigga has to pay for crossing the line. Do you know where he live at because if so, we are paying him a visit."

"Yea, I know where he stays. Let me reach out to my cousin in the Bronx, he is hustling so I'm sure he can point me in the right direction."

"Aight bet, he ain't called you yet?"

"Hell nah and I don't think he is, because if so, what will he say, after he came to see me he went to fuck my bitch and got robbed because of me."

"Fuck'Em both, let's slide, I got shit to do."

We all hopped in the cars and drove to Sarasota. The lot was full of trucks and foreign cars. Keybo snatched up an Excursion like the rental I left at the airport in Miami. The girls all split the bill and got an Army Green Excursion and I ended up buying a Silver drop top BMW 645. Between all three vehicles, we dropped $80,000(eighty thousand)to move them off the lot, then in six months we come back to pay off the other half.

"Let's pull up to the RaceTrac in Palmetto, so I can return this rental to Roxanna."

We all rode down U.S. 301 to the RaceTrac.

"Keybo, I need you to follow me in your truck while the girls wait here in your other car, my car, and their truck."

I drove to Roxanna house and some Mexican guy was there working on the door. I parked the S-Type in her driveway and handed the keys to one of the workers and I left before she could see me. I ain't feel like seeing her at this moment. When we pulled back up to the RaceTrac, I got in the passenger side of my BMW while Julissa sat in the driver's seat. Nadeen and Berlin stayed in their new Excursion. Desiree and Amanda drove keybo's other car, while bruh drove the Excursion with Scarlet in his passenger seat. We all drove to Tampa with my BMW in the middle of both Excursions like I was the President. We pulled into the International Plaza and went directly to Neiman Marcus. I bought some Versace shades, while the girls went crazy.

"Look ladies, Ima run to the Gucci store and see if I can find some stuff in there. Y'all can finish doing what y'all do and we can all meet at the Capital Grille in let's say One Hour."

Keybo and I walked into the Gucci store and went crazy in there. I ended up with three big bags and Keybo had four then we went to get some food.

"This spot is nice bruh. Ima have to pull up with one of my girls."

"Yea this spot is a must for me every time I come to this mall."

The girls met us and we ate then we all slid to Gold N Diamond to see my Jeweler and to see what he had. I had all the jewelry from the licks in my backpack with all my loot. I pulled everything out and Aneel reached for the Rolex first,

"What you wanna do with this?"

"I want to trade it for another Rolex, a bigger one."

"I got all gold with 15 carats in 30 Pointer VVS Flawless Diamonds in the Bezel."

"What size and year is it?"

"It's a 41mm and it's 1999."

"Okay bet, let's do it, I also want a 500 Gram Cuban Link Flooded with VVS Flawless Diamonds."

"I got one right here for you, give me $15,000(fifteen thousand) for it."

I cashed him out while Keybo and the girls shopped. We all left out of there Icy. On our way back, I told Julissa how to get to 941 Kustumz so I could get a look at how my car was coming along. Soon as we pulled up, my Charger was sitting out front with 24' Drop Star Rims. Abel was inside the office. He took me to the back so I can see the Box Chevy and damn that bih clean.

"It's all done, we are just tuning it right now."

"Well let's go back to your office so I can give you some money."

I gave him $15,000(fifteen thousand).

"Ima take the Charger today and when I come get the Chevy, I'll bring you the other $12,000(twelve thousand)."

"Okay and your Charger sounds good and the navigation system works."

"Aight bet, give me the keys, oh and I want to order some 24' Asanti Rims for my BMW."

"Damn, that's yours? I thought it was a rental!"

"Hell fuck no, that's why I wanna put rims on it and a flip out touch screen."

"Just let me know what's up then."

"Aight."

As I was leaving, I saw Roxanna pulling in, I acted like I ain't even see her. We rode to the spot so we could come up with a game plan on our next move. We parked all the new cars in the backyard. Inside the house, I had to make a few calls so I can try and find a new connect.

"Yoo, Keybo, take this phone here and call Turd, Carl and Rue. Find out if they are ready to link up, while I make a few calls up North."

"Papi, do you need us to do anything?"

"Yea, take the Charger and go get some Wendy's and stop by Circle-K and get me some Gars."

I called my cousin Chewito in New York.

"Yoo, what it do my nigga, how is the family doing?"

"Everyone is good out here, you know grandma is going out to Florida to live and I got two kids on the way. So you know how that baby mama drama goes."

"Yea, I got a bih claiming to be pregnant by me as well but she also was fucking my connect, she just don't think I know."

"That's just crazy, make sure you get a DNA Test."

"Shit my nigga, you know that's mandatory, but I need to holla at you about finding me a new connect, because I don't know how long Ima be able to stay cool for. I'm ready to body him. The only reason why he still breathing is because I still need him."

"What are you trying to do?"

"Bruh, I need a connect who can fill my order of at least Five Kilos of Heroin and Twenty Kilos of Coke, every two weeks. I also need a good price because I'm coming with cash, no shortage."

"Give me a few days, I have to holla at my "O.G. Spyder," he in Washington Heights."

"Please make sure they got some good numbers."

"I got you lil cuz, you know I'm not going to let a bih get over on you."

"Aight just hit my line when you find something out."

"Bruh, I called the crew and most of them are ready to meet up so I told them to pull up on us at WoodWinds in like an hour."

"Have you heard from your brother Mike-O?"

"Yea, him and Mike-E on some hostile take over shit."

"I like to hear shit like that, we have to apply pressure!"

I got up and went out the door with a Gar. I wanted to check on my mom.

"Hey, how is Puerto Rico?"

"It's beautiful here, all your girls can't stop thinking about you, because everything is about Oyah. You even got Anet talking about you."

"What can I say mom, I am that Nigga!"

A Black Toyota Celica was driving real slow coming down the block, then it stopped right in-front of the spot. I pulled my .45 out, then the passenger window rolled down and the back door opened. It was a Spanish guy holding an AK-47, but before he was able to even raise the gun and point it my way, I dropped the phone and sent Seven shots towards the car. I heard glass shattering. I ducked behind Keybo's Cadillac and the gunman returned fire. Glass, parts of the tree and cement was flying everywhere. Then I saw Keybo and Tha Hyena's come from around the corner blasting at the car, creating a huge smoke cloud. The gunman that first got out, got hit and fell to the ground dead. I saw my Charger hit the corner and pull into a house across the street. Julissa hopped out with her gun blazing. Amanda got hit and when I heard her scream, I just snapped and came up from behind Keybo's car firing nonstop with Keybo and Tha Hyena's at my side.

Julissa crept up behind the driver right as he was getting ready to shoot our way and popped him twice in the back of the head. Killing him instantly. Keybo rushed to Amanda's side to check on her, she was hit three times. Once in the shoulder, her arm and her thigh.

Fuck, I can't see where the third gun man went. I kept trying to see him, but I just couldn't find him. Then the smoke cleared and I found my man slumped over the passenger window still with his gun in his hand. The car looked like a block of Swiss cheese. Julissa ran up to me.

"Papi, are you okay?"

"Yea I'm good Mami but Amanda is hit."

Berlin pulled the Excursion around the house and Keybo loaded her in the back. Then Nadeen and Scarlet hopped in with her and they sped away to the hospital. Keybo gave Desiree the keys to his Excursion and told her to follow him while he go duck the Cadillac off behind the new trap on 60th. I got in my BMW and Julissa ran in the house, grabbed my lil safe and all Tha Hyena's money and got in the Charger. We rode down East to Wood Winds. When we pulled into Wood Winds, Poe Poe and Madd-Ball was already on the scene with some Hoe. When they saw me, they came my way.

"Damn Big Bruh, this is your new wipe?"

"Yea but fuck all that, I got three dead Dominicans in-front of my spot."

"Yoo What! What the fuck is you talking about?"

"Man, it had to be the Trinitario's, nigga tried to hop out and all with a Stick. They even hit one of our girls three times."

"Who got hit?"

"Amanda, she just came on board. She's one of the six girls we had rescued from the Dominicans and you know we had them carve T.F. into one of their chests."

"Damn big bruh, we have to figure something out, because we can't keep letting niggas size us."

"I'm just trying to link up with a new plug and find Chocolate so we can take Tha Fam to a new level."

Haitian BO, Rue and Uzi pulled up at the same time. I served all of them and asked

"How is everything going with their operation?"

Rue spoke up and others shook their heads in agreement.

"Bruh we is eating on my end."

"That's what I like to hear, y'all be easy out there."

Just as soon as they left, Mike-O and Mike-E pulled up followed by Turd. I served them as well.

"Yoo bruh, shit kinda been a Lil weird lately since all that shit went down and we opened them traps."

"Like what type of weird, Police or Lurkers?"

"Nah it ain't the Police, it's the damn Chico's in a Tahoe and another in Tacoma."

"Ima send my two young-ins out there. They are certified with their murder game."

"Aight, Bet."

"Yea I need some wild niggas to set the law out there."

Mike-O said,

"Look you need to let your nuts hang and body two or three niggas just for the hell of it so you can make a nigga think twice about sizing you or anyone in your organization."

"Yea, you're right, big homie. Ima put together a Team of Hitters. What's up with them Flat Line Niggas?"

"To be honest, them niggas are way too high risk. They all young and don't give a fuck about anyone."

"That's Perfect, give them a position in your organization and let them eat. They will feel like they are a part of something and give you their loyalty."

"Bruh, Ima get on that as soon as I get back."

"Mike-O! How shit going out there on Canal Road, niggas ain't in their feelings"

"Yea but what can they really do about it?"

"I know that's right, we'll just holla at us if you need us."

Everyone went their separate ways. I went into Ling-Ling's apartment and grabbed all the rest of the dope and put it in the trunk of the BMW and told Julissa to get in it and go get me a room on Siesta Key Beach.

"Okay Papi, I'll text you later on with the room number."

"Do me a big favor, get three rooms on three different floors. I'll give you the money soon as I get there."

She pulled off looking so sexy. I called Keybo.

"Where you at bruh? I got Julissa on her way to Siesta Key to get three rooms, so we can find out what's going on over at the spot. I lost one of my phones over there, when I started shooting at the nigga who came out the back seat with the Chopper in his hand."

"Bruh, that ain't a good look for a real nigga. That's a lot of heat, we can't even go back to that spot anymore."

"I know bruh, Ima have one of the girls get a new spot but for now, I got Julissa getting us three rooms and Ima just play it by ear."

"You need to retain a lawyer just in case things get crazy.

"Yea Ima handle that bruh."

I called Carl a few times and he just been letting my calls go to voicemail. I truly hope he didn't get jammed up and that he just been busy. I left from down east and went over to see Nando in Oneco.

"What's good bruh?"

"Shit my nigga, everything been good."

Bullet came out of the back room.

"What it do bruh? I see y'all riding nice."

"Yea, me and Nando wanted to treat ourselves so we can have something to drive to the Parade."

"I just bought me a BMW 645 and dropped rims and music on the Charger and tricked out the Box.

"That's what's up, Nando wants me to slide with him down South to drop some rims but I wanna grab another car first, so I can have something to slide around in."

Julissa sent me a text.

"Hilton on Siesta, Rooms #310, 404, and 506."

"Aight Mami, go to room 506 and I'll meet you there."

"I'm already in that room, I knew you was going to want to be in the highest room."

"Text the girls and I'll call Keybo so we can all meet up out there in a few."

"I'm on it Papi."

I served Nando and headed to Big-B. He was inside with Nelly.

"Bruh, have you heard or seen anything crazy around here?"

"Just a lot of Police and Helicopters."

"Yea shit went crazy on the back road and we had to kill three Dominicans."

"I hit the cut and saw the Celtics shot the fuck up, but when I ain't see any cars, then I knew y'all was good, until I called your phone and the police answered."

"Damn, they got my phone. I dropped it in the shootout."

"Well, let's handle this business so I can duck off until I speak to a lawyer."

"Yea, you need to get low, at-least until we can figure out what's good."

I took care of everyone and headed to the Hilton. As I was driving I texted Keybo the hotel and the room number. At the room, I counted up all my loot and I had $271,500(two hundred seventy one thousand, five hundred) I called my mom and checked up on everyone. They was extremely happy to hear from me. Amanda was doing good and will be making a full recovery. Three days later she was released from the hospital.

I got in contact with my lawyer and dropped him $50,000(Fifty thousand) on a retainer fee, which can be used by any member of Tha Fam or Tha Hyena's.

## CHAPTER 14

# EASTER WEEKEND 2005

I went to 941 Kustumz because Abe called me to let me know my Box Chevy was ready to get picked up. It was Friday and my Easter Party at club Heat was already sold out.

I pulled up in my Charger with Keybo. The girls stayed in the room, nursing Amanda back to health. My Box Chevy was sitting out front looking Pretty and Wet! There were a few people around it taking pictures. Abe pointed at me and said

"He's the owner of the car."

One of the guy from Orlando said, "Yoo bro, I'm shooting a music video next week at the Citrus Bowl and I would love to have this car in the video, you is killing the Box Chevy Game."

"Yea, I'll slide out there."

We exchanged numbers and I walked in the shop so I could pay Abe the rest of his loot.

I got in and put on "Plies-Choppa Zone." I turned up the music and it was so loud that I couldn't even breathe.

"Damn bruh, you got a big ass smile on your face."

"Yea, I'm ready to hang out tonight. Follow me to my house out West so I can put the Chevy up and we can go shopping."

Keybo followed me out to my house.I parked my car in the garage and added another $200,000(Two hundred thousand) to the safe bringing the total to $600,000(Six hundred thousand). I was over half a million strong and I still had the entire shipment still to cut and move, plus the three Bricks I had got from the one Lick we hit on the Dominicans.

It's time to find me a New Plug, this money is way too easy to be made. Chewito needs to come on, time is money. I locked up the house and we rode to Tampa to get fly for the night, then on the way back, we stopped by Ling-Ling's house and Purp and J. Gangsta was both there.

"What's good with y'all niggas, how is everything going?"

We all dapped up, then J. Gangsta spoke up.

"The Gray Dope was Fire, our phones been jumping out the gym."

"I still have some if y'all wanna buy it, I'll give it to you at wholesale price for $50,000(fifty thousand) per brick and I have Six of them. I just flipped the Three Bricks into Six. Only people Ima move it to that cheap is Tha Fam. I wanna see all my brothers eating."

"Okay bet, Ima be ready in the morning to grab."

"What you and Keybo getting into?" Purp said.

"Shit tonight, we at Club Heat."

"Yea we already went shopping and we met some Hoes at the Mall from Tampa and they pulling up tonight."

"How many Hoes are coming out?"

"At least Ten of them."

"I know y'all better not bring any Foot Draggers."

"Nigga, we only fuck bad Hoes, Thick and Pretty Bitches."

Moon hit me on the Churp.

"Yoo, Yoo, Yoo!"

"Churp!"

"What it do bruh?"

"Churp!"

"I was just checking on you. I saw what went down in-front of the spot and I'm just making sure you was good."

"Churp!"

"Yea I'm in Wood Winds right now."

"Churp!"

"So you holding, I need to link with you. Are we still going out tonight?"

"Churp!"

"Yea, I have 40 Zips left and you know the party is still on for the night."

"Churp!"

"Okay I'll be there in Thirty minutes."

"Churp!"

"Bruh, load those two duffle bags into the trunk so we can take them out West to my house and then get ready."

"You want me to do all of it, or do you want me to take some out for later?"

"Ling-Ling has Three Bricks of that Gray, I still have to Cut and Flip that. So just pull Ten Bricks of the Sand and give it to Ling-Ling so she can put it up with the rest of the work."

"Purp you ever got the safe open from that one Demo?"

"Nah, Joey ain't been around."

"Let Keybo look at it."

Not even twenty minutes later and the safe was wide open. There was $90,000(ninety thousand) in all $50's. Purp and I split $40,000(forty thousand)for me and $40,000(forty thousand)for him and $10,000(ten thousand)for Keybo, just for getting the safe open for us.

When Moon got there, I served him and he went about his business, while I checked to make sure all my loot was here with me. I had Five Bricks of Heroin, Ten Bricks of Coke, $100,000(One hundred thousand) Moon just brought me plus $46,500(forty six thousand, five hundred). Keybo and I rode to my house so I could put up all the dope and cash. We got ready and headed to the Club. I pulled up in my Chevy and shut shit down. Keybo was in my Charger. Purp, J. Gangsta, Nando, Bullet, Moon, Rue, Big-B, Madd-Ball, Poe-Poe, Turd

Mike-O, Mike-E and Uzi all pulled up at the same time. I paid extra so we can all have our cars parked out front side to side.

We partied in the V.I.P. Section all night, popping bottles and throwing Bands. The vibe in the club was all love. Niggas and Hoes from all over came over wanting to hang out and link up with us.

I ended up exchanging contacts with a guy named Zye outta East Tampa. He seemed like he was about his business by the way he hung out with his Team. I also invited him and his Crew to come out the following night to a party hosted by Tha Fam and he agreed.

The night ended and everyone went their separate ways. I drove to Siesta Key to our room and Keybo followed me. I paid to have my car parked by Valet at the indoor parking garage and we went up to our rooms. I was so tired and drunk that I went straight to my room in hopes that Julissa would still be awake so I can get some pussy. When I opened the door, all the lights were on, so I got a lil excited with thoughts of getting some of that silky soft, wet pussy. I walked around the entire suite and found no signs of Julissa, only her purse and my keys to the BMW. She must be in another room with Amanda and the rest of the crew.

I took me a shower and got in bed naked. The room was spinning on me so I closed my eyes in hope that it will stop, but I must have dozed off because next thing I remembered, I woke up and it was daylight and Julissa still ain't made it back. I got myself ready and went to Keybo's room. He had a girl named Kandi in the room with him that he had in our VIP Section all night long.

"Get ready bruh, we have to slide and meet up with Turd and Madd-Ball."

"Aight, give me a couple minutes to get ready, then I'll meet you downstairs."

"Aight Ima go check on the girls and make sure Amanda is healing up well."

I went downstairs to the girls room and they was all awake. Nadeen was butt naked and looking so right walking through the suite.

"Come here Mami and give me a hug"

"Papi, Tu Me Quieres?"

"Hell yea lil mama."

"You better be careful with what you want, I know you and Julissa are fucking and about my feelings someone will die so be sure of what you asking for because I'm a whole problem."

"Julissa is my friend just like you are. Nothing more, nothing less."

"That's what you say but her feelings tell a different story."

"If you say so"

Then I walked off and went to see how Amanda was doing. To my surprise she was up and moving around, on crutches but she was moving. I walked up to her while she was chilling on the balcony and gave her a hug. We chopped it up a lil, then I got a text from Keybo letting me know he was on his way down the lobby.

"Ladies I have some things I need to handle but tonight Ima need at least Three of y'all with me. I have a Pre-Easter Party and it's hosted by Tha Fam, so by Amanda being out of commission, I want two of y'all to stay behind and look after her and the other Three to come out and represent Tha Hyena's."

Nadeen spoke up first.

"Okay Papi, I'll go with Scarlet and Desiree and Julissa and Berlin can stay back and look after Amanda."

"That's perfect, I need y'all to go shopping and make sure y'all three dress to impress. Go get your hair, nails and makeup done. I wanna pull up around 11:30 PM to the Club."

"Okay we'll get on that now and see you later."

I went out and got the Box Chevy and Keybo got in his Excursion. We drove to the Seminole car wash down East so Ray-Ray can wash my car. While he was busy getting it ready for the night. I placed a few calls to see what's going on with the Sarasota movement. Madd-Ball told me that everything was going well and that he ain't been seeing any signs of the Kings.

"Bruh, I want y'all to step out tonight with me. Tha Fam is hosting the Pre-Easter Party at Club Nitro."

"Nigga you know Ima be there, I'll let Turd and Poe-Poe know as well."

"What time are you trying to pull up?"

"Early, like 11:30PM so I can get a parking spot under the light at the bank."

I got in the Excursion with Keybo.

"Bruh, let's go by Richard's Chicken, I'm hungry then I wanna go on 33rd."

"Aight, but what's on 33rd?"

"I want to see Eric and Nino. You know they have a nice movement going on over there and I want in on it."

We left Ray-Ray washing my car and went to get some chicken wings and gars, then we went to 33rd. Soon as we pulled up on the block, I saw Eric doing a Wheely on his dirt bike. I told Keybo to honk his horn so we can get his attention and I stood up and hung out the sunroof. Eric zoomed by us, but when he saw us he turned around and pulled his bike up on the driver's side.

"What's good with y'all niggas, what brings y'all on my block. I know y'all wasn't just passing through!"

"Nah, we actually came looking for you and your brother."

Eric reached for his pistol, but Keybo upped his first and pressed it right at his temple,

"Don't move your hand so fast or you will turn a friendly conversation into a murder scene. Now, move your hands real slow and place them on the handle bar of your dirt bike before I splash your brains all over the middle of this street."

"Man, y'all are mighty aggressive for just a friendly conversation."

"You made it this way nigga. Keybo put your gun down, so he can see that we came in peace."

Keybo pulled the gun from his head and sat it on his lap but kept it pointed at Eric from behind the car door with his finger on the trigger ready for whatever.

"Look, let's get out of the middle of the road and go somewhere we can talk. Trust me, what I have to offer will change your life for the better, but not only yours, everyone around you."

"Okay pull up to the Pink house on the corner."

Eric pulled into the driveway and we pulled up right behind him. I got out and Keybo was right behind me. We followed Eric into the backyard and took a seat at the Picnic Table under the tree.

"So, talk to me, I'm all ears."

"Where is Nino, I would like him to be a part of this meeting"

"That nigga doing ninety days for driving without a license, but he been down like sixty days already. I'm holding down everything while he is gone."

"I want y'all to be a part of our movement. You are still your own Boss but I'm your Supplier. I can get you the Coke for a cheaper price, that's better than what y'all got on this block now and I can assure you that if there is ever a problem you can always count on Tha Fam to back you up. In return for you building your Empire up and taking your team to the next level, I wanna open a Heroin Trap on this block. You can have your peoples working it and you just get work from me or I can put my people in it. It's more than enough loot for us all to eat."

"It sounds good but can you really beat the Trinitarios Coke prices? I get Bricks for $22,500-$23,000(Twenty two thousand, five hundred- Twenty three thousand)."

"Fuck The Trinitarios, I got them going for $20,000(Twenty thousand) and it's damn near 100% pure."

Eric stood up and shook my hand

"Let's get this money then."

"No problem, I want to invite you to my party tonight so you can meet the rest of Tha Fam."

"Where is it going to be at? I'll pull up!"

"Nitro on Palmetto."

"Aight, I'll be there around 12:30-1AM after I shut the trap down and get ready."

"We going to start fresh on Monday."

"Oyah, I wanna be in control of the Heroin Trap. I already have a spot on this block that we can use."

"It doesn't matter to me who runs it. If you wanna do it, then that's better for me. Well let us slide and I'm sorry if we came at you aggressively, see you tonight."

"Aight bet, I'll catch y'all later."

We got in the Excursion and headed back to the car wash. I picked my car up and drove over to Villa Park and parked it out in front of Madd-Ball's mom's house. I didn't want to take it all the way over to Siesta Key and get those damn Love Bugs all over the front of my Box.

I got in the Excursion and we pulled off headed to the Mall in Tampa, so I decided to hit Zye up.... He picked up on the second ring,

"Hello!"

"Yoo Zye, this Oyah from the club!"

"What's good Boss?"

"Shit my nigga, I'm coming to your city so I can find something to wear out tonight, you still pulling up?"

"Yea, I'm on my way back from Orlando. I shot out there real fast so I can go to the Versace Store."

"Aight then, I'll just see you tonight."

"The club is called Nitro, it's in Palmetto."

"Yea, I saw the flyers. Ima get me a room out there because I wanna go to the Easter Parade tomorrow."

"That bih is going to be swole, but I'll just link up with you later at the club."

We rode to Tampa, I got me an all Black Polo Shirt with black Levi 501 Jeans, a black and gray Louis Vuitton belt. On my feet, I had on some OG Retro Jordan's 5's. Keybo went with all white. We stopped by the Jerk Hut for some Jamaican food, then we rode back to our hotel. Right when I got to the suite with our girls, my phone rang and

It was Tee-Baby,

"What's up babe, how is everything in Puerto Rico?"

"We had a blast, our plane landed at 10PM. tonight then by the time we drive back to Bradenton and drop your mom and Anet off, it will be after 5:00A.M."

"Okay just drive safe and call me after you drop her off so I can tell you where to come at. I've been staying at a hotel, it's a long story but I'll fill you in when we link."

"Okay, see you later daddy, I love you!"

"I love you as well."

We chilled and smoked and ate the food I had bought until about 9:30P.M.

"Bruh Ima go up to my room so I can shower and get ready."

"Okay then, Ima go do the same."

"Are you going to wear all your Jewelry?"

"Yea, how you figured that?"

"Because you going out in all black, so I figured you was doing that so all your jewelry can stand out."

"Nigga stop watching me! L.O.L!"

I left the suite and got on the elevator and went to my room. Before I could even get my clothes off, so I could shower, there was a knock on the door. I went over and looked out the peephole, it was Nadeen, Desiree and Scarlet. I was naked so I opened the door and stood behind it so the girls could come in. Desiree noticed first that I was all the way naked.

"What are you doing answering the door naked, you could wrap yourself in a towel."

"Um, I believe I'm in my room and y'all came up here, so I do what I want, plus I was about to get in the shower. The big question is, why y'all came to my room?"

"We had to get ready and didn't want to do it in front of the other girls."

"Well go ahead and handle whatever it is, Ima shower and be out y'all way."

I showered and when I got out so I could get dressed, Scarlet was naked and still wet like she had just got out of the shower.

"So why is you naked and wet in my room?"

"I just got out the shower and I like to air dry, it's better for your skin."

"Where is Nadeen and Desiree?"

"They are showering together."

Scarlet was nonchalant when she said that. I didn't even comment on it anymore either. I just got dressed and ready.I can't lie, it was hard for me to contain myself in a room with three beautiful and naked women, but I managed. We all was ready and looking good. I sent Keybo a text so he can meet us in the lobby. Nadeen was about to have the Valet bring her Excursion but I gave her the ticket to get the BMW. We had Valet park, the Charger and BMW. Keybo got in the driver seat of the Charger and I the passenger, while the girls got in the BMW. We was all heavily armed. Tha Hyena's had a Glock .40 in the car and a Kel.Tec.25 strapped to their Garter belts in between their thighs. Keybo had two LLAMA.45's and I had two baby Glock.40's.

We rode to Villa Park so I could get my Box Chevy and link with the rest of Tha Fam, then we all headed to Nitro. I pulled up to the Club Nitro jamming to Plies-I am the Club. We blocked traffic. I had the Box Chevy parked sideways with all four windows down in the middle of the street in front of the Club.

Everyone in line started pointing and taking pictures of my car. A Yella thick bih got out of line and came over to the driver side of my car, opened my door, grabbed my dick and leaned into the car so she could talk into my ear.

"I wanna suck this dick and for you to beat this pussy up from the back while you got the music jamming."

"Chill lil mama, I don't even know you."

"I'm Shambria, and how you don't know me? Everyone knows who I am!"

"Well back your ass up and you can't say everyone, because I damn sure don't know you."

I moved her hand off my dick, put my car in Drive and pulled off with my door still wide open with my music playing.

We all parked by the bank under the bright lights, then walked over to the Club bypassing the V.I.P. line and the General Admission Line. I had a few words with the Bouncer, slipped him $500 and he let us in the Club. We didn't have to wait in line, show identification or get searched. Then I paid for the Entire Exclusive V.I.P. section on the 2nd floor for the team. It was enclosed with two way mirrors so we could see out but no one could see in.

On our way to the V.I.P Section, the DJ cut the music off and put the spotlight on us. He announced that Tha Fam was in the building and put on "Young Jeezy's -Sky Is The Limit." The club went into an uproar. I opened the sliding glass window so everyone could see me Shining. I rapped along with Jeezy, The World is yours and everything in it, that's out there get on your grind and get it, Yeaaaah!

Some niggas was mean mugging me and some saluting me and I salute back. I could see the Strippers making their way to the V.I.P. with the bottle girls behind them holding trays with buckets of Ice and bottles of Remy and Grey Goose. The owner came in with a Bouncer holding a Gucci backpack full of Stacks of $1 bills.

"How much you got in the backpack?"

"Thirty thousand($30,000) the owner replied."

I looked over towards Nadeen and motioned for her to come over.

"Yes Papi"

"Give him Thirty Thousand out my Louis Vuitton backpack."

I grabbed the Gucci bag from him, unzipped it and dumped all the Stacks onto the little table, then handed the bag to Nadeen so she could fill it up with the bigger bills.

I bust a Stack and threw it out the window making it rain on everyone then I turned around and turned up with the Strippers and My Team. The vibe was nothing but Love. Everyone was having a good time, even Tha Hyena's was having a blast with the Strippers. Desiree had ass and Tities all in her face.

"Yoo Scarlet, come here."

I pointed through the closed mirror so the partiers couldn't see me.

"You see that Spanish guy with the dreads out there."

"Yea, in the Pirates Jersey!"

"Yea that's him, I want you to go out there and do whatever you need to do so you can get close to him."

"Okay Papi."

Scarlet walked out the V.I.P. and walked over in front of the dude, bent over and started to bounce one ass cheek and then the other. Buddy in the Pirates Jersey walked up behind her and started dancing on her. Damn she was good. I would have grabbed on that ass too, if she had just come up on me shaking her ass like that.

The Club was over and we all drove to IHOP on US 41. Scarlet left the club with the dude. These niggas think they can out smart me, but I'm ten step ahead of them. Niggas be weak for some pussy.

I sent Scarlet a text telling her to let me know where dude took her and to try and leave the room door open. I rode back to the room in Siesta Key. I was tired and Tee-Baby had not called me yet, so she must still be on the highway. I ended up going to sleep alone trying to wait on Tee-Bae to call me, so I could have told her where to come but I smoked a Gar to the head and tapped out.

The next morning, I woke up to missed calls from Keybo, Moon, J. Gangsta, Tee-Bae, Paradise, Anet and my Mom. I even had text messages from them wanting to know where I was at and if I was okay.

It was Easter morning. I called everyone back and told them to get ready, I wanted to go to the beach and Stunt a lil before the Parade started. I rode to my house so I could pick up Tee-Bae and Paradise. I let them sit up front while I got in the back seat twisting up a gar for us.

"Daddy, this car is clean as fuck. To be honest, I thought no matter what you did, that this car will always be ugly, but you showed me different. By the way, who is in that BMW and those Excursions?"

"Those are Tha Hyena's and Tha Fam"

"What the fuck you mean by Hyena's?"

"Tha Hyena's are Females Hitters. It's Six of them, but one of them got hit up when I got shot at in front of the Spot."

"Is you fucking any of them?"

"Hell nah, I just told you that they are part of my team and since when have you questioned me?"

"I'm not, but I just wanted to know what's around me."

"My family is around you. They are a sister branch under Tha Fam, so when I have a Target that's hard for me to catch-up with, I just expose him to his weakness and let them handle it for me."

"Okay daddy, I understand 100%. I'm sorry for making you feel some type of way, I won't let it happen again."

We rode to the beach and I swerved on a few Box Chevy's, Cutlass and Regals. I had Triller playing slow down out my car. It had so much bass and was so loud that Bradenton Beach Police came over and made me turn down my music. That was my sign to leave.

My Entire Team was with me. We left headed for Sarasota so I could find a good spot where we can all post up at without missing anything. We was twelve cars deep. Everything had either Paint, Rims, Music or all of it. Tha Fam was Shining hard, putting on for the city.

We was hanging out. We had the cars parked on the grass at the REC CENTER. Moon brought his Dirt Bike out and we was riding up and down U.S.301, having a Wheely contest to see who Wheely the longest.

The Box Chevy had its doors open and the music playing loud but not too loud so that Sarasota Police would come fucking with us. I saw dude from last night and Scarlet at the light, just the thought of it got me excited. Fool truly thinks he got him a bad bitch out the club last night. Stupid nigga, only if you knew what you have got yourself into!

"Tee-Bae, you see dude in that White Benz with bitch sitting in his passenger seat!"

"Yea bae, what's up with that?"

"He is a Target and the bitch name is Scarlet. She is Tha Fam, one outta Six of the Hyenas."

"Ohhh! Okay! I see what you're getting at now."

Zye, from Tampa showed up to the Parade in a truck with Four Bikes on the back. He had all the Banshee's on the back.

"Bruh, where was you last night? I was looking for you all night!"

"Man my crazy ass Baby-mama went to acting up right when I was about to leave so you know how that turned out."

"Let these Bikes down, I'm ready to hit doughnuts and turn up on one of these."

I got on the Banshee and Tee-Bae got on behind me so I could take her for a ride. We bent a few corners, then went back by the cars because the Parade started and the Floats started to come down the street. I walked over to the BBQ stand and got myself a Pulled Pork sandwich and some baked beans with an Iced Tea. Then as I was walking back to my car so I can eat, I saw Desiree running and pushing people out her way. When I looked real good, she had her Gun out.

"What the Fuck!"

I ran behind her but I couldn't get to her fast enough because it was so many people in my way. Desiree pointed her Glock.40 and squeezed.

Bang! Bang! Bang! Bang! Bang! Bang! Bang! Bang! Bang! Bang! Bang!

By the time I got up on her, she was still pulling the trigger, but was out of bullets. The crowd went to shifting and screaming. Desiree was standing over dudes dead body. I snatched her gun from her and pushed her towards the cars.

"Get in and go, get the fuck from around here before the police come."

Desiree got in the Excursion and Tha Hyena's was about to get in with her when Moon and Big-B stopped them. Big-B told Desiree she had to leave on her own, just in case she gets jammed up, that no one else gets fucked up because of her.

"Just leave, Ima have Scarlet call your phone in thirty minutes but I need you to get out of Sarasota now."

Desiree pulls off the grass and hops the curb headed to the back roads to Bradenton, while we all got in our cars and took either U.S. 301 or U.S. 41 back to Bradenton. I drove down U.S. 41 and there was two helicopters flying around. A Manatee Sheriff and A Bay News9 helicopter. I hope she makes it out of here. I drove to the bay behind The Banana Factory and dumped her gun into the water, then drove to my house so I can get out of this bright red Box Chevy that calls for attention everywhere it goes. I hit Keybo up on my Churp phone so he can meet me at my spot. Tee-Bae and Paradise was both quiet the entire ride.

"Are y'all ladies good?"

They both said yes simultaneously.

"Is that man dead, babe?"

I got pissed off instantly.

"What the Fuck do you think, she hit that nigga all in his chest area, then stood over him and emptied the entire clip into him. But Ima tell both of y'all this just one time. I better not ever hear y'all speak about this day to anyone, not even between y'all's self."

"Daddy I don't even know what you are talking about."

At the house, I gave Tee-Bae specific instructions to find me a Six bedroom house that ducked off for Tha Hyena's.

"It's Easter Sunday ain't shit going on until tomorrow."

"Okay just make sure you handle it."

I parked the Box Chevy in the garage, then I went inside with the girls so we could talk a lil more about their trip. Once Keybo got to my house, I gave both my ladies a kiss then told them both to find the cars that they wanted, only after y'all find a Six bedroom.

"Okay babe, we got you."

Keybo and I got in the Excursion and rode to Wood Winds. It looked like the Easter Parade came out here. All the trick outs was parked out here. People was vibed out and just enjoying the rest of the day. I stopped in the middle of the Alley and just had to laugh at how my peoples didn't seem to mind that a murder was just committed right in front of them. The party was just moved from one spot to another.

I called Julissa

"Where are y'all at? Come down East To Wood Winds."

"We're back at the beach just trying to blend in with everyone."

"Where is Desiree?"

"We don't know, she cut her phone off, so we are just waiting for her to call."

Tha Fam was all at WoodWinds, everyone but Desiree. Nando was nervous.

"Bruh, that ain't good, that crazy bitch killed that nigga in front of hundreds of people, we don't move like that."

"Remember our main rule, leave no witnesses behind."

Nadeen snapped when she heard Nando call her friend a bitch.

"Bruh, if you ever fix your mouth to say something disrespectful about Tha Hyena's or Oyah and Keybo, I will show you how we got the name, Tha Hyenas and if you think it's a game, try me.

# CHAPTER 15

# NAH IT CAN'T BE HIM

"Hey babe, how are you doing?"

"I'm good just a lil shaken up from that day, but I'll survive. I've been missing you a lot."

"I miss you too Mami."

"Have you heard from Oyah since the day of the attack?"

"Yes but I don't really think he believes me because he said if I really got home invaded and they came looking for him, then I would be dead."

"What an asshole, because it's his fault that all this happened in the first place. My face is all fucked up. I have a loose tooth in my mouth and my head is split in three different places, not to mention I'm out of a half a million dollars."

"Why would you be riding around with so much money for, that was just stupid of you to be honest."

"How? I came to see your man and dropped off some more work and wanted to see you as well, because I feel like I don't see you as much as I should."

"Well Piloto, you know I have a life out here in Manatee County, I just can't get up and leave because you want me to."

"Yes you can, you are just in love with that Thug, but I don't know why because he doesn't really love you. He told me you was just his girl and that you are expendable. A man who loves you will never let any harm come your way. He will treat you like a queen. Roxanna you deserve so much better."

"Piloto, I'm stuck between a rock and a hard place. I love that man because he was my first everything, but it seems like the more power he gets, the more money he is worth, the more evil he gets. Oyah is not the same anymore, all he cares about is that stupid family he is putting together."

"That's why you need me baby, I'll love you the way that he can't. All you have to say is that you will be mine and I promise you that you won't ever have to worry about anything ever again. I will care for you and love you babe."

"Look Im not ready to be in another relationship, can you just give me some time to get my mind right, I'm pregnant with this mans child and don't know what to do with it."

"Hold up, how you know it's his and not mine? We've been making love without protection."

"First of all Piloto, we have not made love, we been fucking so please cut that shit out. Look I just need some space, okay! Ima get off this phone, I'll talk to you later."

"Roxanna, wait! Who do you think could have been coming to rob or kill Oyah."

"I don't know, that man probably has the entire city gunning for his head."

"But it was all women who came into the house. Do you know of any women organizations around your way?"

"No but why don't you just ask him and see what he says. Maybe he knows who it could have been."

"Hell no! If I ask him that, he will want to know why I'm asking him all those questions and do his own investigation and find out me and you are fucking, ain't that what you call it."

"It's not like that Piloto. I just don't wanna rush from one relationship into another, plus you acting like you are afraid of Oyah. Ain't you his Boss, he should be afraid of you not the other way around."

"It has nothing to do with me being afraid of him. We just making a lot of money together and I don't wanna fuck that relationship up unless I know for sure that you and I will be together, then and only then will I expose to him that we are just fucking."

"You trying to save y'all relationship but to be honest I feel like he was behind what happened at the house the other night"

"Nah it can't be him, Oyah would have killed us himself plus I don't think he has females on his payroll."

"I don't know what to expect but one thing for sure, I need to get out of this house, I don't feel safe here anymore."

"Come to Orlando and I'll let you stay at my Westgate Timeshare until we figure out what's next. If you want, you can pick anywhere you wanna live and I'll pay for everything. I just want you to know I love you and want the best for you."

"Thank you, I'll call you when I get up that way so you can tell me where to go."

"Okay Mami, I'll be waiting on you."

Damn, Roxanna got me thinking about Oyah, could it really have been him behind everything! He probably came by her house and seen my truck, but if it was him, I believe he would have took matters into his own hands. Those women was like a Hit Squad, someone wants Oyah dead.

One thing about it, Ima get to the bottom of this because not only did I get fucked up and $500,000(five hundred thousand) was taken from me, but they also got the love of my life all shook up. Ima place a call back to Puerto Rico so my cousin Julio and his Goons can find the person. Ima kill them a very slow death. I'm going to make them beg me to hurry and kill them.

Ima call Oyah and just see how he acts when he hears my voice. Ring! Ring! Ring! You have reached the voicemail box of 941-250-3040. I hung up then hit him on his Nextel.

"YooOoo!"

"Churp!"

"What's good big bruh?"

"Churp!"

"Shit, I'm just checking on you."

"Churp!"

"I'm good, Yoo that Sand is good, Ima need to link with you here in a couple of days."

"Churp!"

"Aight bet!"

"Churp!"

Oyah can't have anything to do with the home invasion, he is way too nonchalant.

Ring! Ring! Ring!

"Hello, who is this?"

"Fool this is your cousin Piloto, get on the next flight to Orlando and bring some of your best men."

"I'll be there soon, just have me some wheels to move around with some artillery."

"Come on, you know all that is taken care of."

This nigga Piloto gots to know something for him to be reaching out to me. He usually just waits on me. I know he is going to be a problem. I need Chewito to hit me back as soon as possible so I can take care of this before it gets outta control.

Churp! Churp!

"Yooo what's good, I need you!"

"Churp!"

"Yoo, how soon can you get up here?"

"I can come up that way by tonight if you need me to."

"Nah come over in a few days, Ima hit you back and let you know what's going on. I just need you to be ready when I call."

"Just call me when you ready, I'll stop whatever I'm doing to come up that way"

"Aight and let me know how much you trying to spend."

"Ima grab small just to check shit out but as long as everything is pressure then Ima spend at least a half of Mil."

"Damn lil Cuz, you down there eating good in Florida, I see!"

"All bullshit aside, this is just the beginning, with the right plug, I can expand and take over all the surrounding Cities."

"Let me get down with your team if there is any room for me to eat!"

"Look, make this deal come through and I promise to give you a Spot on Tha Fam."

"Bet, Ima get in dudes chest."

"Aight just holla at me, One!"

Ring! Roxanna answered on the first ring.

"Yes!"

"That's how you answer your phone?"

"Only when you call, so what do you want?"

"I was just checking on your big head ass. Last time we spoke you was saying that you are pregnant and some shit about a bih coming to your Spot looking for me"

"Oyah, I never lied to you before so I'm not going to start now, I am pregnant, I've been for almost four months now. I just ain't say shit to you because I'm not sure if Ima keep the child."

"Hold up Roxanna, if what you saying is true, shouldn't I have a say so in all this"

"Look, you made your choice Loud and Clear, now you wanna act like you are concerned about me or what I got going on."

"Ima tell you this one time only, so make sure you understand what I'm saying. If you are carrying my child and you are sure that's my child and you kill it, then you killed our relationship. I won't ever fuck with you."

"Oyah, you really confusing me, like I don't know how to talk to you anymore."

"Play with me and see. If you kill that baby then you are dead to me and if you have that child and it ain't mine, you are dead to me as well."

"Oyah, this is your fucking baby. If it wasn't then who could it be."

"So you're going to play me like Ima fool? I don't wanna have this conversation over the phone, so let me handle a few things then I'll come over."

"Are you sure, you 're coming because I was about to head to Orlando with my home girl Kendra."

"L.O.L! You is so fucking funny, your ass better not go any fucking where."

Then I hung up, she really think a nigga stupid.

"Nadeen! Have you heard anything from Desiree yet because it's been going on seven hours and we still haven't heard anything from her."

"No, her phone is going to voicemail. I've called a few times and even sent her a text message."

"Turn on the News, I know what happened has to be on there now."

Breaking News Coming Up Next. We are right on time.

"Does anyone know who the dude was that she shot like that? It seemed more personal than anything. She ain't try to be discreet about it or anything."

"We don't know who that was. Everything happened so fast that none of us got to see who it was, but it had to be someone who harmed her."

I'm Georgia Wagner reporting live from Sarasota, Florida where there has been another senseless murder. Today at the Sarasota Easter Parade, this woman, Desiree Perez, Twenty years old from the Dominican Republic.

"My stomach felt fucked up, clear as day was a Mugshot of Desiree with a Sly Smirk on her face."

Murdered Benitez Ramos in cold blood, shooting him Ten times all in his upper Torso in front of hundreds of kids, women, men and Families out enjoying what started out as a beautiful Easter Sunday and ended in pure core. The County commissioner is pushing to ban the Easter Parade from Sarasota.

We all looked at each other with silence.

"Damn it's fucking crazy, here we are waiting on her to call us when she get somewhere safe and the whole time, she is in jail."

"What are we going to do, we need to get her out of jail, she can't stay there."

"Julissa just calm down, let me holla at my lawyer and see what we can do to get her out of there, but right now I need y'all to go to my house and help Tee-Baby with finding a place for y'all and I'll get on the phone with my lawyer."

Amanda spoke up. "That guy's street name is Pistoleto. He raped every single one of us at gunpoint and we made a promise to kill him on sight. Desiree kept to the promise. That smirk on her mugshot was a sign of accomplishment."

"How did y'all come in contact with that piece of shit?"

"He is Chocolate's lil brother."

"Oh Wow! Is that right, so now he has to attend his lil brothers funeral and that's where we are going to catch him and kill him."

The Girls rode to my house, while I got on the phone with my lawyer. He recommended me to another lawyer named Reinhart. He specializes in Murder Trials.

Everyone was still hanging out in Wood Winds when I walked outside to get in my car. Ling-Ling was on the grill and walked up to me.

"Where are you going, you ain't hungry or thirsty?"

"Not right now, I lost my appetite after the news I just got.

"Yeah I feel you babe, well I will just save you a plate with a little of everything."

"Do that, I'll see you later."

I rode over to Roxanna house so we can try to figure some things out with this baby. She thinks I'm really stupid but little do she know. I meant everything I said, only thing that will save her is a child that's mine, anything short from that and she will be taking a one way trip to

Lake Maggiore.

"Papi, I just saw the news and one of the girls who came into my house that night , just shot and killed a guy at our Easter Day Parade in Sarasota. She is in Sarasota County Jail right now as we speak for the murder of a man named Benitez Ramos.

Her name is Desiree Perez, she's twenty years old and from the Dominican Republic."

"Great news Roxanna, does she have a Bond?"

"I'm not sure, but I can find out."

"No it's okay, I'll have my lawyer on it and if she does then I will post her bond."

"Why the fuck would you do that for, who side are you on?"

"I'm on my side and the less you know the better, just know I only want to get to the bottom of what's going on. I need answers."

"Okay well I'll call you a little later when I'm close to Orlando. I'll be waiting but in between time I'll be working on getting Desiree out on bond."

I pulled up to Roxanna house and her ass was still here. I still got that ass in check. I walked into the house using my key. That's a good sign, the locks are still the same. She had bags packed up like she was ready to go on a long trip.

"Where do you plan to go and for how long? If I wasn't as smart as I am. I would have thought you was running away with another nigga, but not my girl, Nah she won't ever do that."

"Oyah! I'm not you, and you know that shit. You is the only one that's out here fucking everything with a pussy. I don't even know why I put up with your no good ass."

"So you're telling me that you have been completely faithful this whole time we've been together."

"Yea I have!"

"Shut the fuck up bitch and listen."

Roxanna started to cry, because I've never used this tone of voice with her before.

"Look me in my eyes Roxanna and tell me that I'm the only man you been fucking with."

"Why do you need me to look you in your eyes for? Either you're going to believe me or not."

"You can't look me in my eyes and lie to me Roxanna so tell me that I'm the only man you been fucking."

"Fuck you Oyah! Get the fuck out my house before I call the police."

"WOW! I can't believe you threaten me just now, you ain't shit but a Police ass bitch. If you wasn't pregnant right now, I would have given you a real reason to call the police, but I'm out of here."

"Oyah! Wait! I'm sorry for saying anything about the police. I love you but you just make me feel like I'm nothing to you."

"Because you take me for a fool. When you are truly ready for a heart to heart, so we can put everything on the table, just hit my line."

# CHAPTER 16

# *IN THA FAM WE TRUST*

"Lil Mama, please warm me up that plate you put up for me."

"Bruh, I spoke with my lawyer and Desiree in a real fucked up situation. They found Gunpowder on her right hand and some of the dude's blood on her face and shirt. He got her going for a bond reduction tomorrow so I just hope I can get her out because they are going to try and make an example out of her because of all the kids that had to witness the murder."

All J.Gangsta could do was shake his head from side to side.

"Oyah, she got shit hot right now, that type of shit will bring the Feds to the city. You don't think Shawty is going to take the pussy way out, do you?"

"Rienhart said she has refused to speak with anyone. I told him to tell her to chill and that we are working on getting her out."

"Let's cut this dope and get it ready for the streets. I called everyone up and they should all be here around 12:30A.M."

"Bruh what you got up your sleeves, you don't ever serve anyone at this time of night."

"Ima be getting ready to leave for New York for a few days and I just want to make sure everyone is good, because I don't know when Ima get the call to slide. But Ima need you and Purp on standby because I want y'all to fly out with me."

"Oyah, I don't think I need to go to New York with you, just take Purp and Keybo."

"They are already coming, I need you as well."

"Bruh, I have a few things to take care of down here."

"Nigga you must be scared to fly."

"I ain't never got on a plane before, we ain't meant to be flying, if so, God would have gave us wings."

"Nigga, your tough ass getting on that plane with me."

We got done cutting up all the Heroin just as Tha Fam was pulling up. I served everyone and then put the entire team up on game about what happened with Desiree and to be expecting a lil more Heat around the streets because this murder is on the World News, CNN and Head Line News!

I counted up $389,500(Three hundred eighty nine thousand, five hundred). All this is really profit for me. I still have Five Bricks of Uncut dope put up. Every member of Tha Fam except for Tha Hyena's are worth a minimum Quarter Mill. I guarantee everyone on my Team eats. I text Zye to see what he is doing.

"I'm getting ready to head back to Tampa, after the shooting we went to Whitfield so we can ride."

"Pull up on me down East to Wood Winds"

"Aight, let me finish loading up my bikes and I'll be there."

Chewito called me to let me know everything was a Go for next Monday. Damn he is right on time. I hate when I have to bite my tongue. Now, Ima send some Goons to go see Piloto at his main house. He wanted to disrespect me with my bitch, so Ima do the same to him with his bitch. J.Gangsta was ready to move at my Command.

"Call up some Hitters and get them ready for a trip to Orlando. I want you to lead this mission since you don't wanna catch a flight to New York with me. I'll just take Keybo, Purp and Madd-Ball. So don't even try to take any of them on this mission with you. Here is the address to his warehouse in Kissimmee. This is where all the Heroin, Coke and Weed is stored at, and on this paper is his main house with his safe and Jewelry. He talks about arsenal so it should be at his main spot as well, and this address to where he works out of, it's a mechanic shop. So make sure you check everything good because y'all should come back with a few mill in cash and like Two hundred Bricks of Coke and Fifty of Heroin. I'm not sure about the Weed because I never fucked with him on that. I saw it once and he had some low grade level Weed, but it's all money, we can find someone to buy it."

"Okay bruh, Ima get on that now and start putting me a team together. When do you want this to happen?"

"I need it done before Friday morning."

"Oh that's good, I have time to assemble a nice Hit Squad. Ima have Four Teams for this. One Team for each location and a van with Four guys in it ready to pickup whatever we hit for."

"Okay handle that and I have to go holla at Tee-Bae and Paradise to make sure they found a Spot for Tha Hyena's."

"Talking about the girls, I could use Tha Hyenas on this mission."

"Yea, they will take care of business. I'll send them over, so you can holla at them."

"Aight, I'll be here making calls and lining shit up."

I rode to my house and told the girls to go holla at J. Gangsta.

"Is everything okay?"

"Yea, I just got a mission for y'all in Orlando and he's going to put y'all on game. So leave Amanda here, I'll watch over her while the rest of y'all go take care of business."

Zye called my phone.

"Bruh, where you at? I'm out here."

"I had to bend a few corners but go to the house, Ima have one of my niggas give you a package, just get back at me when you find out if you can move it or not."

"Aight bet bruh, I got you my nigga."

"Babes, did you find anything?"

"Yes we have a few listings and they are all in the same range as in price."

"Okay that's good. I need two places babe, one for Tha Hyenas and the other for Tha Fam. I need y'all to buy some more cars for the three of us. I want an Infiniti and I want y'all in SUV'S so please get on this, I want both properties and all three vehicles in the next 48hours. Then I need a low key rental so y'all can drive some money to New York for me on Friday."

"Okay babe, we got the properties on standby. I'll have the Real Estate agent draw up the paperwork on both of the properties. Me and Paradise will go online looking for new vehicles."

She handed Paradise the laptop. I went to my Storage Room and opened my safe and added the money I just made to the $700,000(seven hundred thousand)I already had put up making the total in the safe $1,000,000(One Million). I took $89,500(Eighty Nine thousand, five hundred) out so I can get what I need before it was time for me to leave for New York.

While the ladies handled that for me, I went and took a shower and laid down so I could rest up a lil. I woke up to hearing two guys' voices but then realized it was Moon and Big-B. Their voices kept getting louder the closer they got. Then Big-B came in the room and snatched the covers off me.

"Wake your ass up nigga! Do you know what time it is?"

"Nah, I just took a nap."

"Nigga, look at your phones. Me and Moon have been calling you since yesterday."

"What the fuck, it's 3 o'clock on Tuesday, I thought I was just sleeping for two or three hours, not a whole fucking day."

I got up, took care of my hygiene and walked out to the garage where Big-B, Moon, Lala and Paradise was posted up smoking.

"Where is Tee-Bae?"

"She went out to get one of the new cars for an oil change, the other two cars are already done."

"So you mean to tell me I slept through all that. Damn I must have been really tired."

"Babe I sucked your dick trying to wake you up last night because Tee-Bae and I was horny, but you just didn't budge, so we just ended up in the Sixty Nine(69)position in hopes to wake you with our Moans but still nothing."

"Damn that's crazy, I know I was tired if I ain't wake up to you giving me head."

"Then this morning we had to go to Tampa to get your car and the other two got dropped off by a flatbed tow truck."

"What all did y'all ended up buying?"

"I picked you out a Infiniti G35. It's Black on Black, 2004 with 18,000 miles. I got a Lincoln Navigator, it has a Dark Brown Exterior with a Peanut Butter interior. It's a 2003 with 63,700 miles. They are both sitting outside."

"What did Tee-Bae end up getting?"

"She got a 2003 Cadillac Escalade with like 50,000 miles and it's Pearl White with Peanut Butter interior."

Soon as we walked out the garage, Tee-Bae was pulling up in her Escalade jamming to PaPa Duck-Dope Boy. She hopped out and left her SUV running.

"Baby, Paradise and I took care of everything. We took Amanda to Tha Hyena's house, she wanted to get it cleaned up before the other girls got back from Orlando."

"How the fuck is she cleaning up? when she can't really get around."

"I said the same thing and she said that she refuses to be treated like a handicap."

"Yea, I feel her, so did y'all get a rental?"

"Not yet babe, that's all that we have to do. I have a reservation for a minivan, I have to go pick it up at 8A.M."

"Okay then, I see y'all are on y'all shit. Ima keep that in mind for when this next mission is over. Ima treat y'all to something special, don't ask me what Ima do, just wait and see."

I had the Charger, Box Chevy and My 645 in the garage.

"Ima leave y'all with a space to park y'all truck. The Infiniti will be a Slider so it will be used the most. But go grab the Van and I'll see y'all later on tonight."

"What's good with y'all?"

"Shit, I need work."

"You moving all that work fast, I just served you yesterday."

"I know you ain't complaining about making money. I got $96,000(Ninety six thousand) in my Wal-Mart bag in the car."

"Give it here but you going to have to go down East to Ling-Ling's crib and get it"

"Shit that's where I pulled up first and asked her where you was and she acted like she ain't know. Then I saw Keybo, so we rode over here."

"Well now go back, because I have to slide by there anyways then to Tampa to holla at one of my dawgs over that way."

"Aight, Ima head that way now."

I took the $96,000(ninety six thousand) and added an extra $4,000(four thousand) so I can put up a even $100,000(ten thousand) in the safe. I went to sleep with $89,500(eighty nine thousand)and woke up to $39,500(thirty nine thousand, five hundred)because my ladies went and spent all the rest on down payments for our three new vehicles and so I can get Tha Fam and Tha Hyenas houses to stay in.

I drove to Wood Winds with Keybo, while Moon followed us. I served him a Brick and took another to Tampa for my Dawg Zye. He paid me $27,000(Twenty seven thousand) for Nine Zips of Heroin that I fronted him yesterday.

"Yoo Oyah! This the type of work you fucking with my nigga?"

"Yea, I told you Tha Fam represents Pressure."

"Well this is about to be an EPIDEMIC in Tampa."

"That's what I wanna hear so Ima slide to New York. I'll just link with you when I get back. That's a whole Brick, I want $108,000(one hundred, eight thousand) for that."

"Okay bet, I'll have that for you in a day or two."

"If that's the case, as soon as you get the loot then slide to my hood and I'll get you right before I go outta town. Ima be gone from Friday morning to Thursday evening. So Ima give you enough work to hold you over for a week or so."

"I got you my nigga, see you in a day or so."

"Aight bet, Ima get back on the other side of the bridge."

On my way South bound over the Skyway, I called my mom to make sure she was home. I haven't seen her since Puerto Rico. When I pulled up in front of her house, there were a few cars in her driveway. So we parked and got out the car. My lil brother pulled up on me on his bike.

"Oyah, can you buy me a Dirt Bike or a Four Wheeler?"

"Yea, I got you when I get back from outta town."

"Okay Thank You."

Then he rode off with one of his friends on their bike. Me and Keybo walked into my moms house and my mom, Anet and Millie Milz was chilling, taking shots of Patron and listening to music. Soon as Anet saw me, she ran up on me and gave me a hug and kiss on my lips. Anet even pushed her tongue into my mouth, so we made out while I gripped her ass. Keybo gave my mom a hug and kiss on the cheek and did the same to Millie Millz. Then I came behind him and did the same.

"How are you son, I haven't seen you in over a month!"

"I'm good mom, I came over to give you some money before I slide to New York for a few days."

I unzipped the backpack and pulled out $10,000(ten thousand) Stack, then another one, then one more.

"Here mom, this is for you."

Then I pulled out another $10,000(ten thousand)Stack and split it. I gave half to Anet and the other half for Millie Millz.

"Son, why did you just give away $40,000 for, Are you ok?"

"Yes mom, I just want to make sure you are good. Ima buy Joe a Dirt Bike so he can ride with me when I get back from outta town. But I have to go, I love you Mom."

"I love you too Oyah."

Anet looked my way and asked when Ima see her again.

"I'll link with you when I get back, I promise!"

I kept $22,500(twenty two thousand, five hundred)out of the $62,500(sixty two thousand, five hundred). I jumped in my G35 and drove to Sha-Sha and picked up Five pounds of weed, then drove to my house to put them in my freezer so they can stay fresh, until it's time for me to smoke.

"Julissa, you coming with me to Piloto's main house. Poe-Poe and Romeo can take any two Hyenas they want. Tang and Suave can take the other one. Then I want Moody and Boo with their Hitters in the van making rounds. Once y'all hit all three spots then Moody, you just head back to the hood."

Everyone had their orders and went their separate ways to carry out their mission. They all had Walkie Talkies so they could stay in communication with each other.

J.Gangsta and the other two Teams hit their marks at the same time. Inside Piloto's main house was his two daughters and wife. It was a nice two story home in a residential neighborhood.

Julissa ran down on his wife and slapped her so hard on the head with her gun that the blood misted the air and her body went crashing to the ground with a lifeless thump. J.Gangsta's two other goons ran through the house looking for Piloto, but turned up empty handed.

Poe-Poe hit the other spot where Piloto moved all his dope from, and all his team found was three guys playing PS2. When the front door went crashing in, they must have thought the Swat Team was raiding them because they froze up and had their hands up in the air.

Poe-Poe hit one dude on his head and shot the next when he saw him reach for his pistol on the coffee table. Tang and Suave pulled up to the Mechanic Shop like they was trying to get their car worked on. Once they peeped the scene and saw that everyone had their guard down, Tang upped his AK-15 and Suave pulled out his 12 Gage Street Sweeper and they made everyone lay faced down on the ground. Tha

Hyena's Zip Tied all of their hands and feet. Berlin pulled down the garage door so can't nobody see what's taking place inside.

While Suave and Tha Hyena flipped the mechanic shop upside down, Tang was trying to get the guys from the shop to tell them where to find Piloto.

Berlin came out the back office with a box piled high with stacks of cash in a vacuum sealed bag.

"What do you have there Berlin?"

"A box full of money and there is nine more boxes just like this."

Suave let the cars down that was on the lifts so he can search them. All the cars looked like they was about to get loaded up with all the vacuum sealed loot.

"So this is how he gets his loot back to the island. Oyah is going to be happy when he finds out we just hit him for the Re-up money."

Tang hit Moody up, so he can pull up and get some boxes. Once they got all the boxes out he told Berlin to search them and take anything worth money. Soon as she was done, Suave hit the first guy with a slug to the back of his neck, knocking his entire head smooth off. Before the rest of the guys even got the chance to react, Tang hit them all with the AK-15. so much blood was flying in the air.

Julissa took the girls into the Foyer with their mom.

"What's your name lady?"

"Mary!"

"So, Mary, where is Piloto?"

"I'm not sure where he at, to be honest he just left here right before 12PM and there is no telling when he will be back."

"Mary, I need you to be smart and think about yourself and your beautiful daughters. I'm here because I do good business with Piloto, always straight business. I was loyal to him but he betrayed me. Piloto has a beautiful family but yet he wants to fuck my bruh girl and fell in love with her. I came with instructions to kill you but I have a change of heart. Ima leave you a line so you can tell him why we are doing what we are doing to him. He will pay with his life!

Now, tell me where is the safe or you will watch these two beautiful lil girls die a horrible death."

"No please I'll show you where the safe is and I'll even open it for you just don't harm my kids. My oldest daughter is the only person that can get the safe open. It's her hand print that registers to unlock it. He has Four and a half million dollars put away in that safe, please just take it, I just want my kids to be safe."

We got the safe open and I called Moody and Boo to pull up and get all the loot. They will have to make few trips to the van.

"Thank you Mary for being so truthful with us and for that, Ima keep my word and leave you and your girls unharmed, well other than that big split on your head but that's better than losing your life."

"Mary, I need you to deliver a message for me. Tell Piloto that he has to pay for falling in love with Roxanna. He had a Loyal nigga on his team who would have went against the United States Army for him but now we are against him and everything he stands for. When the smoke clears up only the Strongest will still be standing. In Tha Fam We Trust"

Poe-Poe and Romeo got the entire house under control while Tha Hyenas flipped everything. They had the three guys Zip Tied with their mouth's Duct Taped, so they wouldn't be able to scream. Dude on the ground was bleeding out.

"Ladies hurry up, we already fired shots. I don't wanna be here if someone heard them and called the police."

"We got it lil daddy, go on and call the pickup crew, so they can come get all this."

Right as the pickup crew was loading the van with all Fifty Five Gallon Ice Coolers full of Bricks, a white S500 Benz pulled up blocking the van. Piloto was driving and there were three other passengers. All four doors opened. The passenger hopped out with a Military Grade Assault Rifle and pointed it towards the van, while the two guys in the back seat hopped out and tried to creep up on the side of the van.

Boo was already on point and soon as he saw the guys trying to get the upper hand, he let his gun do all the talking.

Rrrr-A! Rrrrr-A! Rrrrr-A!

Hitting the first dude all in his face and chest dropping him dead. The passenger let his Rifle rocking the van with every bullet that crashed into it.

Boom! Boom! Boom! Boom! Boom! Boom!

Then Nadeen came out the house with her Mini AK-15 spitting

Rrrr-A! Rrrrr-A! Rrrr-A! Rrrrr-A! Rrrrr-A!

She was shooting at the Benz. Piloto ducked down behind the Benz.

Romeo killed all three of the guys in the house and ran out the house to help with the gun battle. Boo, Romeo, Nadeen and Scarlet was busting at the Benz buying enough time for Moody to pull the van through the yard, giving the Goons in the back of the van enough space to shoot back. Piloto dropped to his knees and shot towards the van with a Marksman aim hitting one of the Goons with Moody dead center of his eyes knocking him backwards dead. The van ran over the fence into the next yard and made a clean getaway. A Ford Explorer pulled up in the middle of the street, but before any doors could even open up Poe-Poe was already on the other side of the block. He ran up and started shooting into the windshield hitting the driver and passenger.

Bang! Bang! Bang! Bang! Bang! Bang!

Painting the whole inside red with blood and brains.

Piloto took off running and hit a gate and got missing leaving two of his men behind. The passenger of the Benz took Six shots to the chest but not before taking Boo with him. Boo got hit with three bullets splitting his chest wide open down the center. The last man took off running and hit the same gate as Piloto.

Tha Fam got in their truck and took off. You could hear the police siren in the distance getting closer. Poe-Poe was trying to blend into traffic but Romeo was in the passenger seat tripping hard.

Nadeen spoke up,

"Dude if you don't let him drive us away from here, Ima spill your brains all over the front seat of this truck, you are doing way too much bitching for me."

"Bitch, Ima Gangsta. I kill for fun, but that don't mean I wanna go to jail."

"So shut your Dick suckers up and let Poe-Poe drive us to Safety. Oh and call me a bitch one more time and it will be your last time you will ever disrespect anyone again."

Poe-Poe told them both to chill the fuck out so he can concentrate on the road and they both got quiet. He was in and out of traffic. Scarlet hit the rest of the team on the Walkie Talkies and the other Squads making sure the van with all the dope and cash in it made it back to Bradenton safe.

I got a call from J.Gangsta.

"Oyah, I'm on my way back to Bradenton, we need to go somewhere low key. We ain't get a chance to kill Piloto but we did hit him for a lot of Dope and cash. He knows it was us because I left a message for him through his girl and Poe-Poe and his team got into a huge shootout in front of Piloto's Distribution House. We even lost a man."

"Damn okay, Ima text you the address to a new spot I got Tha Fam. Bring everyone here and I'll pay for our fallen brother's Funeral."

Tha Fam pulled up three cars and a van deep not even two hours later to the new spot. We pulled the van into the garage and emptied everything out into the living room. Keybo came with a duffle bag. He had two money counters, two scales and a few bags of rubber bands, a brand new vacuum sealer.

They hit for a total of $9.5(Nine and a half million.)I couldn't get my smile off my face for nothing in this world. There was also a total of Forty three Bricks of Heroin, Two hundred seventeen bricks of Sand and twenty one Bales of Weed.

I took my cut off top. $5,000,000(Five Million), twenty Bricks of Heroin, and Seventy Bricks of Sand and let the rest of the team split the rest.

"Make sure y'all bless Tha Hyena's with all cash because they have no way of moving any dope."

Poe-Poe gave Tha Hyena's $2,000,000(Two Million) for them to split between the four of them and just split the other $2.5(Two and a half million), Twenty three Bricks of Heroin and One hundred forty two Bricks of Sand between the rest of Tha Fam who went on this mission.

"Well this is y'all place. We are making this Head Quarters for Tha Fam. Ladies, call Amanda, I got her setup in a spot for Tha Hyena's as well. I need y'all to go and set those vehicles on fire, over at the Waste Management Field."

"We got you bruh. Let us know if you need us for anything." J. Gangsta said.

I got in my G-35 and drove towards my house but I took all back roads making sure I wasn't followed. I pulled into my driveway and called Tee-Bae to open the door. I walked in the house toting three heavy duffle bags. Soon as I sat the bags down, my phone started to ring. It was Piloto. He must want to talk shit. I answered the phone just to see what he had to say, not that it mattered anyways. What's done is done and there is lines that have been crossed and there is no coming back.

"Yoo! What's good with you?"

"Don't answer your phone trying to pretend that everything is good between us. You have gone too far, you send your nasty black friends to my house and disrespect my family, then you steal from me and kill my men and cousins."

"First off, watch your fucking mouth when you talk to a real Gangsta, second, I ain't steal shit from you, that's what Pussies will do. I came and took what I wanted, but what I wanted the most I still haven't got!"

"And what is that Oyah?"

"Your Soul, you pussy and third, but not last, would it have made it okay if I sent Puerto Ricans to do the job? Tha Fam sees no Race, everyone is equal."

"I will kill everyone related to Tha Fam."

"Not if I kill you first. Piloto, you ain't built like that. I spared your family but Roxanna won't be as lucky. She will pay for her betrayal."

"Fuck you! You Ghetto Mother!"

I hung up before he got to finish what he was saying. I put all my loot up in the safe and dope, then took a shower and went to sleep...

# CHAPTER 17

## PAID IN FULL

Tee-Bae parked the van in the garage so I could load it up while Paradise got ready.

"I need y'all on the road by noon."

"Okay bae, and the van is already in there."

Keybo and Purp pulled up at the same time. I put up a Million Dollars in the van. Keybo brought me two cups of coffee from seven eleven and I placed them in the cup holders. Both ladies have been schooled to spill the cups if they ever get pulled, so it can throw the K-9's off when they search.

Once the van was ready to go, I put the address to my grandma's house in the Tom-Tom Navigation and gave them $15,000(Fifteen thousand) to use for traveling and do a lil shopping.

I texted my cousin, Chewito and told him that I sent the whole ticket.

"What do you mean?"

"I sent the $1,000,000(One Million) in cash."

"Yea, In cash! I didn't write a check for that much."

"If you sent it, then when are you coming because Loso wants to meet the man, not the workers. You need to be here at least for the first round."

"Just chill, I'll be there on Sunday, I'm flying into JFK Airport."

"Ohhh! Okay bet! I'll just see you then, at grandma's house."

I drove to Oneco with both my niggas so I can warn the rest of Tha Fam about Piloto. Then, I called City.

"Bruh, I need more guns than the Army, also get me some bulletproof vest."

"I got you but what all do you want?"

"I want Big Shit, Automatic Shit, Shit that will explode. I need shit that uses silencers so I can roll up on a bih and pop them without anyone hearing.

"Okay, so you're getting ready for a war, I see!"

"Yea, I got $100,000(One hundred thousand) for you, just let me know when you ready and Ima have my nigga Big-B bring you the loot.

"Aight, I got you! Ima get on that now"

When I drove to Oneco, I got Big-B and Nando on point, then told them to meet me down East in Wood Winds, so I can get them right.

I had to go cut and Re-Rock some work so I could get it ready for the streets, but first I had to go back to the house to get some more work. On my way back, Roxanna started to call, so I answered the phone.

"Yoo! What you want hoe?"

She burst out crying.

"Why are you treating me like that, first you Home Invade me, beat me up, now you calling me out my name."

"Calling you out your name, bitch, you know what it is hoe, I don't even know why you calling me for. We have nothing to talk about, you are dead in my eyes."

I banged on her, got to the house and picked up Ten Bricks of Heroin and Twenty of Sand. Then we went straight to Wood Winds so we can get it ready.

Seven hours later, my team came by and got broke off with enough dope to last a week. I put everyone on game so they could be on alert.I had to make one last drop in Tampa to Zye and then we was going to the airport. Zye had the entire projects on lock. No one couldn't come in or out without being seen by someone on his team. These projects remind me of a Smaller version of The Carter. I love this Setup. When we pulled into the project, we was stopped at the front gate and asked who was we there to see.

"I'm here to see Zye!"

Soon as Zye name rolled off my tongue, the guy at my driver's side window upped fire at me, then hit someone on his Churp phone and gave a description of my G-35.

"Look homeboy, lower your fucking gun before you piss me or one of my brothers off and tell Zye, Oyah is here to see him."

Whoever was on the other end of that Churp told dude to let us through and to apologize. Buddy looked at me with a confused look on his face. I guess he was trying to figure out who the fuck I could be. The man lowered his gun and apologized to me, Keybo and Purp. I drove off and Keybo and Purp said it simultaneously.

"Dude was five seconds away from meeting his maker."

When we pulled up to the park, where Zye was at and he was around a bunch of goons. The projects was on full swing, kids was at the basketball court, pool and the playground. Some old guys had the big grill out and had the entire projects smelling so good with whatever they was cooking.I beeped the horn and Zye walked over to the car followed by two other guys. He got into the back seat with Purp and dapped us all up and apologized again for his man's action.

"It's all good but we have a flight to catch so let's make this fast."

Zye hit someone on his Churp and told them to bring his backpack. A guy pulled up on a Banshee with a JanSport backpack. Zye opened the door and the dude pulled up on him and passed it to him, then he pulled off. Zye handed me the backpack and I opened it and pulled out stacks and stacks.

"Bruh, that's the entire $108,000(One hundred, eight thousand) that I owe."

"Okay bet"

Purp handed him the work and I handed him the backpack so he could put the bricks in it.

"That's Five Bricks bruh and I want $400,000(Four hundred thousand) for all of them."

"How much is that for each?"

"$80,000(Eighty thousand) a piece and its pressure. I just want my team to Power all the way up and be able to serve the other niggas who call their selves the Plug."

"That's what's up bruh, we about to take over this city. I want to bring Tha Fam movement to Tampa if that's cool with you."

"Bruh you have my blessings to do it, just don't bring anyone here who will make us look bad."

"Tha Fam is a family and I stand behind it fully."

"I got you my nigga, I don't keep fuck boys around me. Everyone you see in these projects are my family and now they are your family."

"Okay when I get back, Ima throw us a party so everyone in Tha Fam gets a chance to meet each other, but I have to go, I'll holla at you when I get back."

"Aight bet and be safe, call me if you need me."

We shot over to Tampa international airport, parked the car in the indoor parking lot, Stashed $78,000(Seventy eight thousand) in the trunk and we took $10,000(Ten thousand) each, just to have spending money when we get to New York City. We got there right on time. JetBlue had a flight leaving in Forty five minutes for JFK airport in New York. We boarded our plane and three hours later, we were landing in New York City.

I love my City, the culture, the food, women and clothing stores.I called my cousin Chewito and told him I flew in early and that I was about to take a taxi to my grandma's house and for him to meet me there.

"I'm already here, I'll be waiting for you."

We pulled up to my grandma's apartment in the Bronx. I saw friends I ain't seen in forever. I introduced Keybo and Purp to my New York family.

"Yoo Cuz, I'm hungry and I want to take my brothers to get some good food."

"Let's go to the Cuchifritos on Burnside and Davidson Avenue."

"Let's go, that's one of my favorite Cuchefrito's around."

"Okay let me get my car from the garage."

"Hell nah cuz, we in New York, I wanna walk and take the subway everywhere."

We walked to the Cuchefrito's and Keybo was trying to holla at every bih we walked passed. Purp was amazed at how many beautiful women was walking the streets. By the time we made it to the Cuchifrito, Keybo and Purp had two sexy Puerto Rican hoes with them. I was dying laughing at these niggas. I ordered a plate of Arroz con pollo frito y tostones, my cousin got the same. Keybo and Purp ordered with the hoes. We ate then went to the Liquor store and got a bottle of Remy and Grey Goose. Then we stopped by the bodega and got some Gars, soda and plastic cups and ice.

In front of my grandma's building, we was chilling and just enjoying the New York Summer life and watching everyone playing in the water coming from the fire hydrant.

Chewito called Loso to let him know I flew in early but the money is not scheduled to be here until tomorrow evening.

"Yoo cuz, Loso wants us to meet him at Sin City tonight so he can meet you."

"Okay let's hangout then, but I wanna do a lil shopping because as you see, we ain't bring no luggage with us."

"Let's go to Harlem to Dopper Don, that's where niggas with money shop."

"Yea, I heard about that spot growing up. I want to go to Sneaker Stadium and get me some Retro's or some Foams."

We went shopping and I got Louis Vuitton, Keybo got Gucci and Purp got MCM. We hit the Strip Club that night and got us a V.I.P. section. All the women either knew we had money by what we had on or they was just fucking with us because they knew we was from out of town by our Swagger. Keybo had the bottle girl go get us two bottles of Remy and two bottles of Grey Goose and we each ordered a stack of $1. Fifty Cents In The Club played on the speakers. The whole club viben out and the stripper was showing their ass literally. The music stopped and the spot light shined on one of the V.I.P. 's right beside our section. The D.J. got on the mic and announced that the KING OF NEW YORK CITY was in the building and the Strobe lights went crazy and like Fifty more girls came out the back.

Chewito leaned over and said into my ear,

"That older guy in the middle with all the white on is Loso. He only wears white. Loso once went to an all black day party wearing all white."

Loso came directly over to our section and introduced himself to me. We shook hands then his men moved the Velvet ropes out the way so we can have one big V.I.P. Section. All eyes in this club on us, like trying to figure out who we were. These Dominicans know how to hangout, we had the baddest of the bad bitches in our section. Loso ordered $1,000 in all $5 bills. This nigga is really showing out, then he bought out the Bar and let everyone drink for free.

We each had two strippers at all times. Keybo looked over at me and said, "We need to come up this way more often"

and I agreed.

"I will have Tee-Bae look into getting us a Penthouse in the City, by Central Park somewhere."

Loso cleared a corner section of the V.I.P. and sent for me. We sat in the chairs around the tables and took shots of a very expensive drink named Louis XIII.

"So Oyah, tell me a lil about yourself, you seem very young to be in this game."

"Well as you know, my name is Oyah. I'm about to turn Eighteen but I have been raised around grown people. I have my own. I guess these Pigs will call us an Organization, but to me, we are a Family. I represent Tha Fam and I stand behind it 100%. We are controlling about 70% of the Drug Market in my city but looking into expanding into cities nearby and then maybe even States."

"Oyah, to be as big as you say you want to be, you have to be ruthless and rude with an Iron Fist. This game is really dangerous and there is always someone trying to take your place."

"Loso, with all due respect, I know how to run my Family. I'm not Seventeen years old and a Millionaire because I'm soft or because I don't know what I'm doing. I have a Million dollars on the way up here as we speak"

"Oyah, I was just making sure you was on point and understood what you was getting yourself into. I can fill your order and for a small fee, I can get it to you in your City in Florida. How close are you to Sarasota, Florida?"

"What you mean? I'm from Bradenton, that's the city right next door, almost like Queens and the Bronx. Why, What's up?"

"I have a small problem out there. I'm the Head of the Trinitarios and I have a Chapter down in Sarasota but the person who is over that Chapter ain't no good. I've been trying to get him exed out of the

Organization but there are certain protocols we have to follow and if we don't, I can be voted out my seat by other members."

"Okay and what is it you want from me?"

"I want him dead. If you can do that then I can put someone else into Power and will guarantee that I'll make the entire Trinitarios get their product from you."

"Sounds good but wouldn't Tha Fam be at war with the Dominicans?"

"Oyah, it's not what you do but how you do it. You will make them believe it's someone else, preferably an enemy or competition."

"Okay and what's this guys name and do you have an address for him?"

"Yea, his name is Chocolate, well that's what he goes by in the streets."

"You have to be fucking with me right? I must be some type of joke to you Dominican bitches."

When I was getting up, Loso put his hand on my shoulder, sit down Youngster and listen up.

"Make this your last time you disrespect me in my club. I play no games. I have kids older than you. If I want to play games, I will go play XBox with my grandchildren."

"My bad, I ain't mean no disrespect but I know that dude and I've been beefing with him. I just can't ever catch him slipping."

"Oh, so you the guy that we are spending so much money on trying to get killed. I've been praying for you to put an end to this already because it's costing me some unnecessary money that I could be using for my end of the Summer Yacht Bash, I throw every year."

"So can you make this any more easier for me to touch him, like give me a location he will be at, that I can bump into him at."

"He owns Latin Quarter's, have you heard about that Club before, they say it's one of the hot spots on a Saturday night."

"Yea, I know where that's at, but I thought Rafy owned that place!"

"He is just the face, because he is a Straight Arrow."

"Loso, consider this problem taken care of. Give me your number and I'll text you and let you know when the job is done."

My phone buzzed, it was a text from Turd. I'll just holla at him later on.

"Let's enjoy the night. Oyah, you and your brothers can have any of these women you see. Y'all are a part of the Team now so Ima let my Bouncers know to give y'all access to the Champagne Room."

"Enjoy the night because I sure am. Hold up, what are your numbers for each unit?"

"Since you coming with cash, Ima give you the Monteca for $50,000(fifty thousand)and the Cochins for $15,000(fifteen thousand)"

"That's what's up, I'll just text you when the money gets here."

We hung out that night. I even popped me Two Triple Stacks and was rolling harder than I ever had. Keybo took two Puerto Rican hoes to the Champagne room, Purp was getting his Dick sucked by one stripper while another was dancing and shaking her naked ass on his face in our V.I.P section. Loso even had a stripper sucking his old ass up in the corner where we was just at.

I grabbed this Puerto Rican and Asian stripper, her body was flawless and put her to dance in front of me. Then the Triple Stack kicked in and my dick got hard. The dancer felt it every time she grinned her ass on my lap, poking up on her ass and pussy. She undid my belt, then I closed my eyes because the weed, and those two triple stacks had me on cloud nine. She unbuttoned my jeans and unzipped them. Then she pulled my Dick out through my boxers hole and kissed the head with so much passion.

"What's your name lil Mama?"

"My stage name is Passion."

"So you live up to your name because you kissed the head with so much passion, almost like you was in love with the Dick already."

"That's why I got that name, everything I do, I love."

"Ohhh Damn! Mmmmmmm-a!"

She sucked me whole and was sucking loud and getting real nasty and sloppy with it. Passion was moaning all around the head. The heat from her mouth was causing my toes to curl up. I started making it rain on her because she was really putting on a show. I cupped her huge ass, it was soft and fluffy. As I squeezed it, I pulled her panties to the side so Loso and Purp can see her pussy. Chewito came outta nowhere with a dark skinned Dominican or black stripper. She was so fucking thick that I just locked eyes with her because she was so beautiful and thick in all the right places. She blew me a kiss and kept it moving with Chewito.

Passion must have sensed I wasn't paying her any mind because she sucked me faster and faster. She was sucking so hard and fast that her ass cheeks was shaking. The sight of that made me even more riled up, that I started fucking her throat. Then she pulled me out of her mouth, stood up and turned around and took her stripper clothes off, grabbed my dick lined it up with her tight lil hole and slid down on it.

"Mmmmmmmm-a! Shit! That pussy is good ma"

She went to riding me up and down, then asked me my name and spelled my name with her pussy as she rode me. I couldn't take it anymore. My abs started to tighten up.

"Huh. Huh. Huh. Uhhh-Shiit!"

I came deep in her and she started to cum as well. I could feel her shaking and her pussy tighten and loosen. She screamed at the top of her lungs.

"Yes Papi! Yes!"

I grabbed her tits from the side and played with her nipples. Passion was bouncing her ass into my lap over and over taking all of my dick, milking me dry. The way her ass was waving up from her slamming her ass into my lap, drove me crazy. Before I knew it, we was both cumming again. Then she got a baby wipe and cleaned me up. Passion took my phone and locked her number in.

"Call me next time you are in the City Papi."

"Aight, I got you ma."

I got up and Spinned the club a few times. By the time I was done, Keybo and Purp was back in our section waiting for me.

"Y'all niggas ready to get up out of here"

"Yeah, your cousin is already out the door with some thick bitch" Keybo said."

I dapped up Loso and told him we will be linking up in the afternoon, then we walked out the club. First thing I saw parked in the owner's parking spot was a two tone Gray and Black "62 MAYBACH." This nigga Loso sliding like a real celebrity.

I got us a room at the DoubleTree by Hilton In SOHO, New York. We all crashed. I woke up to my phones ringing. My stomach twisted into a knot. I answer both phones at the same time,

"Hello!"

"We here at the address you put into the GPS. We been here for almost two hours now and have been blowing your ass up."

"My bad, I was asleep but Ima get up now and be over there, give me like thirty minutes."

I woke up the rest of the guys, we got ready and caught a taxi over to the Bronx.

On my way over to my grandmother's block, I texted Turd back.

"What's good bruh, my bad for not getting back to you yesterday. I was a little tied up."

My phone started to ring, it was Turd, so I answered.

"What it do bruh?"

"Shit crazy bruh, those Latin Kings ran off in my spot, killed my dawg and got me for $273,000(Two hundred, seventy three thousand) and two bricks uncut and four bricks cut."

"What the fuck, how you know it was them?"

"Because they tagged the front of the house with a huge Five Point Star. Those bitches cut my dawgs hands off before killing him."

"Ima be back late tonight, we will take care of it. Better yet, Ima send my Hitters to go check Tito out, he is their leader."

"I can't even go back to my spot because the pigs got it roped off."

"Go to one of the other spots on Osprey until I get back , then we will figure everything out."

"Aight, bruh, I'm sorry but I wasn't there when it all went down."

"Look, we will just handle all that when I get back down there."

Keybo and Purp was both staring at me waiting for me to tell them what was going on.

"I'll tell you niggas later and I pointed at the cab driver."

At the parking garage where my grandmother lives, we pulled up and I got all the money out the van.

"Okay ladies, go get a room so y'all can rest up or go shopping. Ima handle a few things then, we will link up later."

The ladies left and we took all the Loot upstairs to my grandma's house. I placed the call and Loso said he was sending a driver to come get us. Inside the duffle bags was two hand guns for each of us and a mini AR-15 sports for each of us.

Not even an hour later, Loso called to let me know that his driver was outside in a Blue Chevy Astro Van. We loaded all the cash into the van and halfway down the street, part of the floor popped open and the driver told me to put the duffle bags in there and to slide them all the way to the back. I did as I was told and closed the latched door, then I heard a vacuum sucking all the air out.

We rode to Brooklyn to this small cleaners. The street was pretty much dead, other than a bum pushing a shopping cart full of cans. Keybo and Purp hopped out clutching onto their mini AR-15 and under their button up Polo shirts. The driver then got out and opened the back hatch door and pulled on both the seat belts at the same time opening another trap door on the back floor board.

I grabbed a duffle bag and the driver got the other. We locked up the van and went inside of the business. I followed the driver with my brothers behind me, ready for whatever. Behind the counter was a rack of hanging clothes in plastic bags. One of the workers moved it out the way and behind it was a big steel door. The man did some special knock and the door slid open. We walked through the door and down some stairs to the basement.

I can't believe it. If I ain't know any better, I would have thought we was in two different establishments. It was a Cleaners upstairs and a Casino and a Drug Warehouse and Strip Club. I saw Loso way in the back at a table with boxes of cash filled to the top. I also noticed that all the women here now are the same ones from the strip club last night. They must be his personal girls.

Loso was dressed in all white linen with open toe leather sandals and a cohiba in his mouth. This man is worth millions and don't even have on a watch. We walked up to his table and the driver sat my duffle bag on top of the table and walked away. I reached my hand out and shook Loso's hand. He offered us all a seat and pulled out a Money Counter, then snapped his fingers and the chick I fucked last night came out from behind a beaded curtain with a cart full of Silver and Black Bricks. I got up and looked at all the Bricks. The Coke had a BMW Stamp in the middle of it and all the Heroin was in waxed paper, dipped in Pink Candies.

"You can go over to that kitchen on your left and test your product. I just want you to know I do good business. If there is ever a time that my product is not A-1 then I'll swap it out for you and even go as far as paying one of my men to drive all the way to Florida. I'm in this business to make lots of money. One Million Dollars ain't shit to me and to prove it to you, Ima give you 200 Keys of Cocaine and 50

Keys of Manteca, so I'm trusting you to pay me back $1,000,000(One Million) on the next Re-Up."

"Loso, I don't like to get anything fronted to me, because I don't want pressure on when Ima have your money."

"I can respect that but you have two ears and one mouth. Meaning, you should be doing more listening than you do talking. I never said shit about a deadline. I said on the next Re-up."

"Oh okay then, bet that up. I do good business as well, but I'll show you better than I can tell you."

Everything checked out. We packed the dope up and loaded all of it into the stash spots in the Astro Van.

"Oyah, your stash box can hold all that dope. I-95 is a real dangerous interstate and those State troopers be looking for out of town plates on vehicles. They automatically feel like there is dope in out of town vehicles and even more with Florida plates."

"I don't have a stash spot, to be honest, I was just going to put it in a suitcase and slide it under the seats and put some in the luggage. I have two chicks driving for me."

"Nah Oyah! I can't let you go out like that. What Ima do is give you the Astro and you can use that to traffic shit back and forth. You need to put stash spots in all your vehicles and get your people to do the same, even if it's just a small one for a few keys and a gun."

"There is no place that I know of who puts Stashes into cars. But I can use them for real, because I'm not trying to get jammed up on some bullshit."

"Ship your cars to me and I'll get my guy to put it in. But they are not cheap, he does it for me and only charges $20,000(twenty thousand), vacuum and hydraulic pump is included."

"Okay bet, I'll let you know when I'm about to ship them off."

We drove the van back to my grandmother's house.

"This van is old as fuck, it looks like something old people should be driving."

"That's the whole point Keybo. We want it to blend in with traffic and for the police to look right past it. Ima send my BMW and my G-35 up here to get done and I feel like the whole team should get at least one car done."

"Well shit, we all going to get a Slider done" Purp said.

I texted Tee-Bae and told her to come back to my grandmother's house.

When my ladies came over, I ran down the game plan to them and we all got some rest. I woke up the next morning and my cousin took the rental back to Enterprise for me and the ladies took the Astro Van on the road back to Florida.

Me, Keybo and Purp invited my cousin to Florida but he a real New York nigga, he ain't trying to ever leave the city. We took a taxi to the airport and got on our flight. There was a beautiful Stewardess on the plane who kept flirting with me. We exchanged numbers and made a promise to meet up one day when she has an overnight stay in the Central Florida area.

We went to the parking lot and got in my G-35 and headed back to the hood, so I can put my plan into motion with Chocolate and Tito.

## CHAPTER 18

# WAR READY

"Yoo Turd, tell me what have you done to try and resolve this situation!"

"I haven't done anything, I was waiting on you to get back and let me know what was up. I ain't know how you wanted to handle the situation."

"Hold up! What the fuck do you mean by you don't know how I wanted to handle the situation. There's only one correct way to handle it and that's with a murder. They killed one of ours, so we try to kill all of them. My nigga, you really got me thinking you soft. I shouldn't have to tell you how to handle your business."

"I'm not soft at all, I just ain't want to do shit that will get you mad."

"So much for that because I'm pissed right now. I'm out of $400,000(four hundred thousand) one of our men is about to be put in the dirt and people behind it are still living life like everything is Okay. Purp, Keybo! Do y'all see anything wrong with this picture or am I wrong?"

"Bruh you know my Moto, shoot instead then ask questions later. If he was a real Goon like how he claims to be, the murder count would have went up around this bitch."

"Keybo, you're dead right, now I feel like he was either in on the lick or he just pussy but either way, I can't have him representing Tha Fam."

Purp stepped in front of Turd.

"What you wanna do bruh, because if he ain't one of us then he shouldn't be able to walk this earth. This nigga knows way too much about us for him not to be on the team anymore."

"Oyah, I swear I ain't have shit to do with the robbery. I wouldn't do that to Tha Fam."

"Oyah! That was my mother's oldest sister's child who got killed. Brand was my first cousin."

"I don't believe a hundred percent that you was in on the robbery but you too pussy to have on Tha Fam. What we are building is way too Powerful to have a weak link, and like Purp said, you are way too deep for me to just let you walk away."

Turd pulled his gun and pointed it at my face.

"Oyah! I'm not going to let you just kill me!"

He screamed at the top of his lungs as he gripped his Glock.45. When Keybo and Purp saw him pull his fire, they both upped theirs. Turd swung his gun towards Purp and pulled the trigger. I looked him dead in the eyes as he was doing it, then he closed them right as he squeezed. BANG! He shot Purp in the shoulder.

Boom! Boom! Boom!

Keybo squeezed off three rounds into Turd's chest knocking him off his feet. He laid on the ground of his front room with blood just pouring out the three quarter size holes in his chest. Turd was gasping for air, and his eyes kept shutting as his life slipped away from him. I walked over him and told him

"You was never cut out to be part of Tha Fam. You over here pulling the trigger with your eyes closed like a real bitch."

Then I pulled my pistol out and popped him four times in the face.

"Purp, we need to get you checked out by our street doctor."

"Keybo, find his phones. I don't want to leave it behind so they can get found by the police."

Keybo found the phones. One in his pocket and the other two on the dining room table. We left him there dead so one of his people could find him. We drove past Tito's Spot and he keeps a bunch of Goons around him. Then we shot straight down East to Matlean's house in Kingston Estates, so she can pull the bullet and patch Purp up. I left him at her place then drove over to Wood Winds. J. Gangsta, Poe-Poe, Madd-Ball and Tang was all chilling at the park with some Pit Bull puppies. I pulled up and put them on game as to what I want them to do. Madd-Ball and Poe-Poe drove up to Joy Land and bought a case of Yellow Bandanas, then came back over to Wood Winds.

"Let's put together some Teams because I want to start a War between the Latin Kings and the Trinitarios. I want a team to go by the baseball park on FruitVille and just hop out and kill as many Trinitarios as possible, but do it with Yellow Bandanas tied around y'all guns and around y'all faces as a mask. Then before y'all leave, pull the bandanas off the guns and throw them on the ground so they can be found"

The Trinitarios and the police are going to think it was a Gang related hit.

"Then I want y'all to go by their trap and shoot it up and drop a yellow bandana on the ground in the middle of the street. I want them to think it's the Latin Kings doing all of the killings, that way the heat is off us."

"Fuck a Team, we can go handle this mission on our own. That way we can make sure it get done the right way."

"Yea, I like that Poe-Poe! So you, J. Gangsta and Madd-Ball go take care of that and then if everything goes well, go hit the spot on 21st and Maples Avenue. I want that one to just be a drive by and leave a bandana behind to be found."

They hopped in a bucket and pulled off. Keybo looked at me and said, "that young nigga Poe-Poe gets off on killing."

"I like him for real. Let's swing by Tha Hyena's house, I want them to take over Turd's operation in Sarasota."

"Bruh, you think it's smart to put females in a trap?"

"Shit, they are not regular females, we are talking about Tha Hyena's. These females are more gangsta than half these soft niggas. I'm going to spend lots of time in the trap with them so I can make sure a nigga don't get bold and try them."

"Yea, okay! I know what it is, you fucked up by either Amanda or Scarlet, maybe even both."

Madd-Ball pulled up to the park, with Poe-Poe and J. Gangsta. They all had their guns and faces tied up with the yellow bandanas. All three of them exited with their bucket and walked up on the field. When everyone started to notice what was going on, they went to shifting and running, but for some, it was too late. Mad-Ball had a Tec-Nine, he let it spit first then Poe-Poe and J. Gangsta opened fire with their AK-47. It sounded like a Thunderstorm in the middle of a beautiful clear sunny sky day.

Rrrr-A! Rrrr-A! Rrrr-A! Rrrr-A! Boom! Boom! Boom! Boom! Boom! Boom! Boom! Rrrr-A!

Men and women screamed at the top of their lungs. Blood splashed everywhere. People was trying to take cover but got shot in the back before they could make it to safety. Madd-Ball walked up on the Dominican men that had been shot trying to get away and put two bullets in each of their heads. Once the field was cleared of Trinitarios that was able to walk, all three of them, Madd-Ball, J. Gangsta and Poe-Poe made sure there were no survivors. Then they snatched their bandana's from around the guns and threw them on the dead Trinitarios. They jogged back to the bucket and made a clean getaway.

"Damn, that shit felt better than getting some pussy, Madd-Ball said."

"Nigga you is wild as fuck."

They then went over to the Trinitarios trap and did a pull up drive by. Madd-Ball had the wheel and can get them out of a crazy situation if needed, so he was the driver. He pulled right up in front of the driveway and honked the horn a bunch of times. A guy opened the door, he started for the bucket with an attitude. He must have thought it was a Junky, because right when he got within hearing range, he started to talk shit and that's when Madd-Ball let down the passenger and back window. J. Gangsta came up out the window and let dude have it.

Rrrr-A! Rrrr-A! Rrrr-A! Rrrr-A!

While Poe-Poe Swiss cheesed the house up. Then they pulled off burning rubber and J. Gangsta pulled his bandana off and tossed it into the middle of the road.

My phone rang and it was J. Gangsta, I answered,

"Hello!"

"Bruh mission complete, send us a ride to get us from the field behind Waste Management."

"Aight Ima have Julissa go get y'all then we will link at Tha Fam Headquarters."

I hung up and sent Julissa a text telling her what I need for her to do. When I got to the store, I found a Baser to go inside and find me a case of Dominican flags bandana's. I gave him $100. Keybo asked me why I didn't go in myself and I just pointed at the camera that was at the front door.

"I don't need shit linking back to me or any of us."

"I feel you bruh."

The Baser walked over towards our car. I peeled off my loose change, like all my $5 and $1 bills and gave them to him then drove to Tha Hyena's crib.

Julissa had pulled in right before me with the guys. Poe-Poe was hyped like he just got off a roller coaster.

"Bruh, we put that work in for real. I shot at least Ten people."

"Y'all chill because I have another mission for today. I want to set a record for dead bodies in less than twenty four hours. The homie, City is on his way over here with some new artillery."

I sent a few texts out to see if anyone needed to Re-Up, then I called Ling-Ling so she can meet me at Checkers on Cortez Road with my duffle bag. Two hours later, I had served my Team and bought $100,000(One hundred thousand) worth of artillery. We had plenty of assault rifles, hand guns, bulletproof vest, Silencers and even a R.P.G. This nigga City showed his ass with this order. Poe-Poe grabbed the R.P.G.

"Look, we need a bucket for this mission."

"I have some young nigga's who keep Stole-lo's on deck. I'll just shoot him a stack for whatever they got."

"Yea! Get on that Madd-Ball and I'll give you the stack for the car now."

"Aight, I just sent him a text to pull up to the Checkers."

We rode to the Latin Kings hood. These fools out here playing their Spanish music, tinting cars and doing mechanical work to Honda's and Acura's. We spinned the block one more time, then tied the Dominican flag around our faces. Madd-Ball pulled up on their block

"Bruh pulled up into that driveway next door to where all them niggas were and parked. We about to walk up and hit these niggas close range."

We hopped out the Stole-lo and ran down on the Latin Kings like we was Swat doing a raid. One of them tried to make a run for it and I let him have it.

Rrrr-A! Rrrr-A! Rrrr-A!

Shooting him three times in the back, sending him crashing down face first. Poe-Poe, Madd-Ball and Keybo cleaned up behind me. Then the house door swung open and gun shots came our way out the front door and windows. I took cover behind a tree but could see more Kings coming out of other houses, so I sent shots their way to hold them back while me and my brothers could figure a way out this situation. I placed a call to Tha Hyena's but couldn't really hear anything, so I just gave them the location to where we was at and hung up.

The gun fire continued, we had good positions. I was watching Keybo and Madd-Ball's back while Madd-Ball was watching mine and Poe-Poe's back and he was watching Keybo and my back. Then Keybo made a run towards the house that the Latin Kings was shooting at us from. He caught them by surprise when he stepped through the front door letting his Choppa Spit. I ran in behind him. There were two dead Spanish guys in the front room, so I made my way to the back of the house and kicked in a bedroom door.

Boom! Boom! Boom!

"Ahhhh! Shit! Bitch! I got shot in the chest through the wall."

Keybo came from way in the back and saw me on the ground.

"Damn bruh, I ain't know anyone was in that room."

I could hear gun fire nonstop out that door. I grabbed my AK from off the ground and stood up. I let go about ten rounds into that room through the wall.

Rrrr-A! Rrrr-A! Rrrr-A! Rrrr-A! Rrrr-A! Rrrr-A! Rrrr-A! Rrrr-A! Rrrr-A! Rrrr-A!

I couldn't hear any sign of life in the room, so I got low and eased my way into the room. The bedroom window was wide open and the room was empty. My chest felt like it was on fire. I hopped out the window and found a Puerto Rican lady dead with a Mac.90 in her hands. I crept around the house to see dead Latin Kings everywhere. Keybo met me in the front yard. I pulled my Dominican flag out of my pocket and threw it on one of the dead guys on the ground.

I heard a few more gunshots then saw Berlin run from between two houses with Madd-Ball and Scarlet right behind her.

"Yooo where is Poe-Poe and the rest of Tha Hyena's?"

"They in the Excursion spinning the block."

Some Chico hopped out the window of the house and hit the gate. I called Julissa,

"Stop chasing whoever that is and come pick us up. We have to get out of here before the police pop up or more kings come around. I'm almost out of bullets."

Before I could hang up and put my phone into my pocket, I saw the black SUV coming down the block.

"Y'all, let's go, our ride is here."

Madd-Ball pulled his flag out and threw it on the ground then we drove off. The 11 O'clock news was coming on. I wanted to see what was being said about all the murders from earlier today.

"Breaking News Today in Sarasota, Florida, a one sided gun battle erupted where over two dozen people have been hospitalized and at least another twelve was dead on arrival. Investigators say it was a direct result over territory between two gangs emerging out of the 941 area. Then the other one came on from Bradenton.

Reporting Live from Bradenton Gardens in Bradenton, Florida, where Investigators believe a retaliation from a shooting which injured over two dozen people and killed at least another dozen at a baseball field in Sarasota, Florida. Detectives believe the increase rate of violence is a war over territory between two Latin gangs, The Trinitarios and Latin Kings. If you have any information on any of these two gangs that can lead to an arrest for the crimes that have occurred today, please call Crime Stoppers at 1-800-999-2992."

Phase one has been completed. My Ringtone went off and I answered without even looking at my caller ID.

"Yooo! What's good"

"Who this is?"

"Damn bruh, I got shot and you forget who I am that fast. I'm not even dead."

"Ohhh! My bad bruh. I just answered my phone without even looking to see who was calling. What's good, you ready for me to come get you?"

"Yea bruh, she did her thang on me too. Ohhh! Bring me two stacks so I can bless her for looking out for me."

"I got you bruh. Ima send Julissa to come get you , but look at Bay News 9 and see what we been up to while you was laid up crying like a lil bih."

"Fuck you, that shit hurt."

"I know! I got shot today in the chest but I had just got some vest, so it didn't penetrate the skin, but she on her way."

I called my ladies to see how everything was going with the trip.

"Everything is good Daddy, we already about to cross the Florida State Line, the police don't even look our way in this ugly ass van."

"That's the point lil mama. I left the garage empty, so pull the van in there and close the door.

"Okay babe, I'll call when I get back."

Four days later, it was Friday and Tha Fam was War Ready. All my Hitters was at Headquarters waiting on my instructions. Me, Keybo and Purp was in the room putting together a master plan for the night. Then we walked out the room and into the Game room.

"Okay Fam, y'all listen up, Oyah has some instructions for tonight's mission."

"First and foremost, how is everyone doing?"

Everyone put their cups in the air and nodded their head.

"Tonight we have one of the most important mission we have ever done. I need the Dominican Chocolate dead tonight, but I want the hit to be done by the Latin Kings in everyone's eyes. We will be killing three birds with one stone. Killing Chocolate and then creating a war between the Kings and the Trinitarios"

"Why, you want them to war for?"

"Dre, I want you to really think about everything I just said and tell me what you get out of it. You are smart enough to figure out what I'm trying to do."

"I could be wrong, but what I got out of it, you want Chocolate dead and you want us to make it look like it was someone else so the police won't come looking at Tha Fam like we had something to do with it."

"Dre, you are right in a way, but there is much more to my plan. My job as a Boss is to guarantee we all eat by any means. I want to kill the head of the Trinitarios and make it look like the Kings did it. That will make both gangs beef with each other. Tha Fam will just sit back and make money while their asses are at war and killing each other off. That's gonna make our jobs easier without anyone of us having to get our hands dirty. So we won't have to worry about the cops fucking with us or the Kings and Trinitario's."

"Now that's fucking smart, so we create a war between the two gangs and watch them kill each other off. Eliminate the competition and leave the dope market open for us. So, how you want us to go about this?"

"I bought Six Power Drills and Ten Quarter Sticks of dynamite. I want us to screw every window and door up except the side emergency exit.

Then I need two men inside posted by the emergency exit so y'all can open the door. The crowd is automatically going to make a run for the first exit they see. The reason why I want two men inside by the door is just in case y'all see Chocolate, I need y'all to splash his brains on site."

"Big Bruh, what are the quarter sticks for?"

"We are going to smash the front window with a rock, then throw a stick through every window and blow the entire front part of the club up. That will make everyone in the club run away from the explosion and once they see all the exit are locked in, they will all funnel out the only exit that's open. If Chocolate makes it past the men inside then one of us outside will catch him slipping. I need everyone to strap up. I want the ladies to post up across the street just in case things do get out of hand, y'all can slide in and help us out with the situation. Poe-Poe and Madd-Ball, I want y'all inside the club so grab a hand gun with a silencer on it. The rest of y'all grab whatever y'all feel comfortable using and let's roll. The club should be letting out in another hour."

We jumped in different vehicles and drove U.S. 41 to Latin Quarters. I had Keybo, Madd-Ball and Poe-Poe with me. Purp, Dre and J. Gangsta was in a car behind us. Tha Hyena's was behind them and Tang, Ced and Mario was in the last car. All four vehicles pulled into the parking lot but went their own separate ways. I pulled up and parked on the side facing the side of the club, but was able to see the front of the club as well. The rest of my team got into position. Madd-Ball paid his way into the club and five minutes later the emergency exit popped open and Poe-Poe made his way inside with both of their silenced guns.

Tang and his crew went around the building screwing the doors and windows shut. Mario gave us the thumbs up and we got out with our yellow bandanas around our faces. Once Tang saw me and Keybo get out the car, he busted out the first window. Then Dre, Mario and Ced followed right behind them and they all lit the dynamite and tossed it into the broken windows. Outside by the door, Keybo and I was waiting on the crowd to come running out. We had men posted in between cars and Tha Hyena's was at the end of the parking lot. They posted just waiting to see if things got out of control.I was ducked off behind the pillar when the explosion happened, then the crowd came pouring out. Dominican men wearing suits came out with guns drawn, then Chocolate came out wet and covered in white powder.

Change of plans, I hit Nadeen on her Nextel.

"Change of plan, kill anyone that gets in our way, but Chocolate is to come with us."

Not even a second goes by and the Excursion pulls up slamming on the brakes, coming to a screeching stop right in front of the Trinitarios. The Dominicans was so off guard they walked right past us, but kept their eyes on Tha Hyena's. Chocolate had a look of surprise when he seen them. I shot one of the goons in the back of the head. No one heard the gunshot, not even me. After I squeezed the trigger and watched the dudes head explode, I had to stop and look around to see if there was someone else around me shooting because I ain't hear a gunshot or felt the recoil of the gun.

The guy I shot, head exploded like a watermelon and blood went all over the other Trinitario. Keybo went to busting his guns picking off his targets like sitting ducks. Tha Hyena's hopped out and went to busting theirs. The Trinitarios all started to bust back. We was outgunned because it was more of them but we had the upper hand and better position.

It was like World War II in the parking lot of the club. People that had nothing to do with what was going on was getting shot. Cars was running people in the crowd over trying to make it out of harms way. My team was getting busy, putting in work. I could see Chocolate and his men trying to take cover but we was everywhere.

Tang and Dre was making their way towards the Trinitarios when an unexpected turn took place. Four Hayabusa 1200 street bikes pulled up with two guys on each bike. The ones on the back of the bikes had Uzies and Tec Nines.

"Yo Manito, is everything good with y'all?"

I was confused, this nigga called me Manito. He must really think I'm Latin King because of the bandana's. I ignored his question and kept my eye on Chocolate. Tha Fam and Tha Hyena's was on their asses. The Latin Kings sprayed their guns recklessly towards the Trinitarios.

Fuck, we have to get this nigga before the real Kings end up killing him. I want him alive. Keybo and Madd-Ball was knocking their asses off. Poe-Poe and Purp snatched Chocolate up, his pussy ass started crying,

"Please don't kill me, I'll give you everything I own. I have $500,000(five hundred thousand) at my house right now, I'll give it to y'all just don't kill me."

Amanda pulled the Excursion up and Purp put Chocolate in the truck then slapped him so hard that it sounded like his skull cracked, knocking him out cold.

"Y'all take him to Headquarters, the police will be here any second."

The rest of Tha Fam ran back towards our buckets and one of the Hayabusa's pulled up on us.

"Manito, where y'all going? Y'all not going to get the money out of the office?"

"Nah we came for what we wanted, but y'all can go in there"

And with that being said, we got in our cars and drove off. I tossed my bandana on the ground right as I pulled out of the parking lot. Shots could be heard in the distance but I couldn't see who it was. Then the back window to the car I was in got hit by a bullet but it didn't shatter. It just knocked a hole in it. I mashed the gas trying to get as far as I could.

Back at Tha Fam Headquarters, we had Chocolate upstairs tied to a chair inside a walk-in closet.

"Oyah you or the Kings won't get away with this, my men will kill everything you have ever loved. Even your ex-girlfriend."

"You so funny Chocolate, how are you talking shit right now but just an hour ago you was pleading and crying like a lil bitch."

I slapped him again with my 44Magnum revolver. This time splitting him open to the white meat on his head.

"The people you are talking about authorized this hit and the Latin Kings ain't have shit to do with it. I started this war between the Trinitarios and the Kings so that way y'all can kill each other off and Tha Fam can take over the Drug Market."

"My people would never authorize a hit on one of their own."

"Keybo grab my phone and dial Loso number and put it on speaker so this fool can hear that it's really him."

Bring! Bring! Bring! Bring! Bring!

You have reached the voicemail box of 941. I hung up and Chocolate started talking shit even more. This nigga really thinks I'm full of shit.

The ring tone on my phone started to sound and I knew it was Loso because Rick Ross "Push It" was playing. I answered and put it on speaker.

"Loso my guy, how is everything going? I handled that for you."

"So Chocolate is dead right now?"

"No sir, he is still alive."

"So, what did you handle Oyah?"

"We kidnapped him, but made it seem like the Kings was behind it. I wanted to know if you had any last words for this bitch."

"Yea, put me on speaker, so he can hear me."

"Go ahead, he can hear you."

"Chocolate! You thought all that bullshit you was doing wouldn't catch up to you, but you should have been war ready, but your time on this earth has expired. See you in Hell Bitch.!"

"Okay I have some Gators that are starving and it's almost feeding time. I'll call you in a few weeks when I need to see you again, but if it's good with you, Ima send one of my brothers you met and my drivers so I don't have to come back out there."

"That's cool with me as long as it's one of the guys who I already met."

"Oh no doubt about that, I won't ever send someone you have never met before."

"Purp! I need you and Keybo to take dude to Lake Maggiore, y'all know what to do with him."

"We got you bruh, the Gators gotta be hungry. We ain't fed them in a minute."

I texted Paradise.

"Lil Mama make sure y'all have sandwich bags, zip lock bags and go by Cool Gators, I need you to put me an order in for 100 kilos of Mannitol and 100 kilos of Quinine, but buy however much cuts he got on hand. It's time to put that New York on the streets, we had it for going on a week already."

# CHAPTER 19

# NOT GUILTY

Two weeks later everything was moving smoothly, like they say, a well oiled machine. I had close to $8,000,000(Eight Million) put up in cash. I was moving slowly but surely into safe deposit boxes in different banks throughout the state of Florida. Each box was in a different name of close people I trusted that weren't in the streets like me. I drove to my mom's house one morning before the sun came out. I was feeling good today for some reason. I was in my BMW 645 with the AC on low but as cold as it can get. I was puffing on a 3.5gram blunt of some Mango Kush that my dawg brought me from Cali. Listening to "Lil Boosie, Smokin on Purp" I pulled into my mom's driveway, parked then went inside.

"Hey mom, I want some of whatever it is you cooking."

"This is something fast for Joe before he gets on the bus for summer camp."

"Okay, but I'm hungry as well."

"I'll cook you something to eat, Oyah."

"Thank you and I love you mom, but I came over to speak with you."

I placed a Foot Locker bag with $500,000(Five hundred thousand) in it on her dining room table.

"What's in the bag, it sounds heavy?"

"It's half a million dollars. I want you to get with Tee-Bae so y'all can link with my Realtor and find you a nice house, that's ducked off to buy for yourself.

"You must want me to move into a huge house?"

"Yes mom, I want you to live well and to be safe. Leave this house here to me"

"Okay baby, I can pick anywhere I want to live?"

"Yes ma'am, it's your place."

"I want to live in the county on some land."

"That's a very nice idea.

I'm out of here mom, make that happen ASAP and in between time, I want you to go stay at my house, it's ducked off. I don't want you here anymore. Call Tee-Bae and Paradise so they can come and help you with the things you want, but don't worry about furniture. Ima give you $20,000(Twenty thousand) for new furniture."

"Okay, I'll text them when I get done here and be safe out there."

"I will mom, I love you and I'll see you later at my place."

I left and went to Moon's house. I ain't see his car so I hit him on the Nextel.

"Where you at bruh? I'm in front of your condo."

"Churp!"

"I'm making a few sales, go knock on the door, Lala is in there."

"Nah Ima just go, I'll link with you later. I'm not trying to wait on you all damn day."

"Ima be there no more than twenty minutes. Play my Call of Duty for me, so I can level up!"

"Aight but if you ain't here in twenty minutes then I'm gone."

"I'll be there bruh, for real."

"Churp!"

I got out my BMW and knocked on the door. Lala asked, who is it and I told her it was me, then I heard her taking off the chain and unlocking all three locks on the door. Then the door opened and I walked in. Lala shut the door behind me and locked all three locks and the chain. I never looked behind me, I just went in and sat down on the sofa.

"Moon ain't here, he just left like ten minutes ago."

When I looked her way, I thought my eyes was going to pop out my head.

"Lala, go put some clothes on, why would you answer the door in just your bra and thongs?"

"Nigga, this my house and I do what I want. If you don't like it, don't come here. But I don't think that's the case because you ain't taking your eyes off my body or closing your mouth since you laid eyes on all this pussy."

She patted her pussy.

"Nah, you a real trip, why would you size me like that when you know your man and I are like brothers."

"So fucking what, he don't even know what he got. He's always out there chasing behind those foot dragging hoes and basers."

"Wow, you really wildin right now. My nigga ain't fucking no baser."

He really was, but I'll never admit that to her. Every nigga in the dope game has fucked a baser or two.

"Nah, Oyah, he really is and I saw him. The other night he went to catch a sale and was taking forever to come back. So, I put on my robe then went out to make sure he was okay, but didn't see him so when I walked to his car, I heard moaning and looked into a old beat up car beside his and there he was, balls deep fucking a white hoe, who looked like she was dying."

"Damn sis I'm sorry to hear that. Did he see you?"

"No, because I felt so sick and embarrassed that I just ran back in here crying. Do you know how that makes me feel as a Black woman? He ain't only cheating on me with a white hoe, but a baser white hoe. So please don't be sorry, he's the sorry one!"

Then she walked over towards me.

"I don't let him touch me anymore. I ain't had no Dick going on a month and right now my pussy sopping wet."

Lala straddled my legs and grind her hot, wet pussy into my semi hard dick.

"Oyah please just fuck me, make me feel like a beautiful black woman again because he got me feeling so ugly with myself."

My natural instinct made me grip that fat ass of hers and we started kissing.

"Damn Lala, we are really tripping."

I pushed her off me and stood up.

"It's not that you're not attractive because you are, but you is Moon's bitch, I can't fuck you because I'm a solid and loyal nigga."

Lala stood up without saying anything and took off her thongs, then reached behind her and unsnapped her bra.

"So you just going to resist all this?"

And she squeezed her tits together and licked her nipples. Then she got on her knees on the sofa and placed her hands on the wall, looked back at me and made her soft big and fluffy ass clap.

"Come get this pussy Daddy, you know you want it."

I had to bite down on my knuckle so I could take my mind off what she was doing. Lala was a beautiful Haitian and Dominican woman. Brown skinned, 5'6 and had to weigh about 160 pounds. She was far from fat. Lala had a flat stomach with a fat ass that made me want to just sync my face in between them cheeks. She had a real exotic look to her. In other terms, Lala would have been nailed to the cross, but I just can't bring myself to betray my brother like that. So I just walked out the house and sat in the car and rolled up a gar then I hit Moon up on my Nextel.

"Where you at nigga?"

"Churp!"

"I'm pulling into the apartments now."

"Churp!"

Moon and I walked into the apartment Lala was in the room, Thank God.

"What's good my nigga, everything good?"

"Yea! Yea! Yea! I was just trying to put together a show and a trip, but I want to do a trip on a yacht for like a week. So your job is to make a guest list because it's an invite only event. I want all the Top Dawgs to be there. The rest of Tha Fam have to put in more work to prove themselves."

"What type of show are you trying to do and where at, so I can have an idea."

"I want to have all Florida rappers and something like the Sarasota FairGrounds, Robert Arena or the Van Wezel Performance Theater."

"I think we should do the Roberts Arena because they serve liquor."

"Okay find out about the guest list so I can rent the yacht. But lock your door, I'm about to go make a few sales and some phone calls, I'll get back up with you later."

I know Lala had her ears glued to the door to see if I was going to snitch on her, but all that's going to do is make Moon and I argue and fall out with each other. I'm not about to fall out with my nigga over a hoe when there is plenty of hoes out here that I can fuck with.

I went by all my traps to see how things were going and to my surprise, from Palmetto to Sarasota every single trap was doing good. Tha Hyena's are even doing good at Turds traps that they took over. I feel damn good because my dream is all coming together just like how I've been picturing it. I'm Boss Status. I'm like a God in my hood, I give everyone hope. Once I got back to my house, I placed a call to my booking agent so we could work on getting a date for Labor Day Weekend at Roberts Arena. Then I told him, I want to bring Rick Ross, Plies, Trick and Trina, Frank Lini, Papa Duck, Ace Hood, Flo Rida,

Haitian Fresh, Chill The Million Dollar Man and Triple J. Not even four hours later, the booking agent hit my line with some numbers for me.

"Oyah, we can have Labor Day Weekend but they want $50,000(fifty thousand) half upfront and the rest at the end of the event, but they want all the liquor sales from the bar. You can have all the sales from the Sections and Bottles and of course the entrance fee."

"Damn that's a lot of money, don't you think?"

"Not for what you are trying to do. If you get the Venue, you can rent out sections to vendors so they can sell food, drinks and T-shirt's. Make it like a Festival. Then you can do different acts everyday so the whole weekend can be something new."

"Okay let's do it then, now what's up with the artist?"

"I got you a deal. To get all them plus Uncle Luke and Tampa Tony with Jam Pony and D.J. Pro Styles on the Ones and Twos, all for a half a Million. Then with an extra $50,000(Fifty thousand) I can get you a street Promotion Team and Four Billboard's and Advertisement on 94.1 and 95.7."

"Fuck it let's do it. Come pickup $300,000(Three hundred thousand) from me right now and I'll give you the rest as the Artists perform."

"That sounds great, I'll be there after 6PM. Today."

"Aight bet!

I got all his money right in the trunk of my BMW plus I'm waiting on Zye to pull up with another $400,000.(Four hundred thousand) Today has been a good day so far. I had my booking agent and Zye pull up to Wood Winds so we can take care of business. As soon as I walked into Ling-Ling's house, she had an attitude for no reason whatsoever. I haven't heard from her or seen her in some time.

"Lil Mama, what's your problem? You over here in your room with an attitude like we beefin, whatever you got going on with anyone else leave that between y'all please. I have enough shit on my plate that I have to deal with."

"Nigga my attitude is with you. You beat me out some head, then you ain't give me the dick. I feel like I'm ugly around you or something. Oyah! I never and I mean never had a nigga just beat me out some head. Nigga you sized me!"

She screamed out loud and had tears running out of her eyes.

"Lil Mama, don't do that. First of all, you know a nigga ain't beat you outta shit. Look around you, this whole apartment has been furnished since I've been around. I was going to give you the dick but something came up and I had to go handle it and you know that. Secondly, all that emotional shit ain't for you and I, so cut that shit out and come give me a hug."

Ling-Ling smiled and got up to give me a hug, as we was embracing a knock on the door broke us apart. I walked out the room to go answer the door. It was Zye and a cute Asian bitch. I let them both in and he introduced her as his driver.

"Bruh, why do you have a driver?"

"Please don't say because your driver's license ain't good!"

"If you don't want me to say that, then what should I say?"

"Zye, you a Boss nigga, there should be no reason why your License ain't good. But what's up, how are things going out there in Tampa?"

"Supply and Demand, that's my movement. I'm creating in the 813 area. I also have family in Polk County, I was just waiting on the

Re-up so I can bring some that way because they only got that Tar bullshit in Mexico."

"Well I just got some new dope, it's going to come out after this last batch. It has to be good because I got the Puerto Ricans from Town N Country shopping with me. Those Chico's are moving shit all over the East Coast. I also got one set of projects "Ponce De Leon" on smash, but I'm trying to get the other projects across the street."

"So what's stopping you from doing what you want?"

"I need to find more guns for my Team, because to take over those projects we are going to have to apply pressure."

"I can get you some guns, what's your budget you trying to spend?"

"No more than $30,000."(Thirty thousand)

"Aight, Ima holla at my dude and give him your number. He got a (917) area code number."

Zye handed me a Nike duffle bag. I walked over to the dining room table and dumped all the bundles of cash on it. I ran each stack through the money counter, the total came out to $600,000.(Six hundred thousand)

"Bruh that's the $400,000(Four hundred thousand)I owed you plus an extra $200,000(Two hundred thousand)towards the Re-up."

"Oh, I like that bruh, on some real nigga shit. Ima bless you for that one."

"Yoo, lil Mama, bring me my Dolce and Gabbana duffle bag out the room for me."

I couldn't help but laugh at her. She was struggling with the bag. I had Seven Kilos of Heroin and Ten Kilos of Sand.

"Give it to him and thank you, with your weak self."

She flicked me off and mouthed the words, "fuck you" before going back to the room.

"Bruh, just bring me $500,000(Five hundred thousand) for everything in that bag. I want you to have Tampa on lock."

"My dude will be calling you about them guns, so you can put your plans into motion."

"Yoo babe, grab that bag and let's slide while it's still rush hour and we can blend in with traffic."

Bzzz, Bzzz, Bzzz! My phone was vibrating. It was Paradise.

"Yoo, what's good bae?"

"Nothing daddy, at the house, your mom is here. Tee-Bae found her three different houses and they are all nice. Tomorrow, they are going to let us do a walk through, so your mom can pick out the one she likes most."

"Oh and Tee-Bae said she got a email from Cool Gator saying your order is ready for pickup and the ticket is $50,000(fifty thousand), but he wants to meet at a Hotel off of Busch."

"Aight, Ima go handle that but first come to Wood Winds so I can give you some money to hold for me until I get home later on tonight."

"I'm on my way to you now."

The booking agent and Paradise pulled up at the same exact time. They both parked. I popped the trunk to my BMW and pulled out a Army Issued backpack and slammed it shut. Right as I was on my way to his car, I saw a Buick Park Avenue slide through Wood Winds with 5% tint on it because I couldn't see shit inside. Frank, the booking agent seemed a lil shook up when I got in his Escalade. I sat the bag in between my legs.

"Yoo, Frank, don't size my shit. This is a lot of loot I'm putting into your hands. I'm telling you now, if something was to go wrong, you better kill yourself before you end up in deep water surrounded by some hungry Gators and not only you but your wife Sarah, your oldest son Frank Jr, lil Mark and Emily."

Frank's mouth hung open,

"How do you know the names of the people in my family?"

"It's my job to know who I'm doing business with and even more if Ima put $300,000(Three hundred thousand) in your hands."

"Oyah, I do good business, $300,000(Three hundred thousand) ain't no real money. I just had someone give me $2,000,000(Two million) to have a Three day event on a Yacht. I like to make money, fucking you over, would be me fucking up my face."

"That's real, so give me a receipt so we can move forward with the rest of Our day."

He wrote out my receipt.

"Oyah, I will give you a call soon as I make all the deposits and have a contract drawn up."

"Aight bet"

We dapped up, then I hopped out the truck and Frank pulled off. I went inside the house and called Paradise.

"Bae, go on the other side, Ima hit the cut and bring you that."

"Okay, but is everything okay?"

"Yeah, just meet me there, I'm coming now"

I hung up, then I hit the cut with a Nike duffle filled with $600,000(Six hundred thousand) in cash. I opened the back door to her Navigator and threw the bag on the back seat, then got into her passenger seat.

"Look, I think I'm under investigation. I keep seeing weird shit, if something happens to me, Ima need you to link with Keybo and hold the fort down."

"I got you babe."

I gave her Chewito and Loso's numbers. Then I gave her Frank's number just in case something was to happen. I gave her a very detailed outline about everything so she can be up on game.

"Bae, only deal with my brother Keybo."

I got out the truck, walked around to her window and gave her a kiss.

"Drive safe and text me when you get home."

"Okay babe, will do!"

I walked back through the cut and now I saw a Black Explorer and a Dark Gray Impala in a parking space across the field where I can see Lil Mama's apartment. I made it in the apartment and locked the door.

"Ling-Ling, call Purp and J. Gangsta, tell them not to come this way, I think the Feds are watching me. Tell them to give Tha Fam and Tha Hyenas a heads up."

"Okay, but you are scaring me."

"Don't be Lil Mama, Ima slide to see if they follow me."

I got in my BMW and let the top down. I put on "Plies-Bond Money," on full blast and reversed out the parking spot. I took the long way out of the projects and stopped right in front of the Impala. I pulled my blunt out without looking their way and lit it up, took a big pull then blew the smoke up into the air. I pulled out and headed towards SR 64. When I made the right off 15th on the 64, I saw the Impala then the Park Avenue turn out in the same direction. I got on the gas and my 645 quickly accelerated to 85 M.P.H. leaving the Impala and Park Avenue three light behind.

I got on I-75 headed towards I-4. My car had a full tank of gas. I would run these crackers way to Daytona Beach if I had to. Fuck, they have to be Feds because no lights or marked cars have came on the scene. I was swerving in and out of traffic, I had the car going 100 M.P.H. going North on I-75. At the Brandon exit, I pulled off the interstate, headed towards the Mall.

I noticed a State Trooper was speeding up behind me and a green helicopter was hovering above my car. I pulled over because I was clean and the lights never turned on, so technically I couldn't be charged with Fleeing to Elude.

When I pulled into the Walmart parking lot, the state trooper hit his Red and Blue light, but I was already planning on pulling over. I was just looking for a good place where I could have lots of witnesses. It seemed like every fucking car around me was the police. I got boxed in and was surrounded by a bunch of police wearing black ski masks, with bulletproof vests and assault rifles with red beams pointed all at my heart and face.

Everything seemed to slow down for me as I looked around. These weren't just State Troopers and regular police. On their vest and jackets was A.T.F. in big bold yellow letters, D.E.A. in bold white letters, Manatee County Sheriff and Brandon Police Department.

"Get out with your hands up!"

They kept shouting over and over. I did not move an inch. I just kept my hands in the air because I ain't wanna get shot. One of the sheriffs from Manatee crept up on the car, snatched my door open and pulled me out by my collar. He slammed me on the ground and shoved his knee into my back all the while yelling,

"Don't fucking resist bastard or I'll break your fucking neck."

"Sir, I'm not moving, my hands are still up."

The police slammed my head on the ground and made me bust my lip, then he cuffed me up and searched me.

"Do you have any weapons in the car?"

"No sir I don't, why would I be driving around with a gun?"

"Oyah is what everyone calls you, right? Well Oyah I know just who the fuck you are, so please cut the bullshit out."

"I'm telling you the truth. I don't have any weapon in the car and other than a baseball bat at my house, I don't really mess with guns and knives."

"Oyah, you are under arrest for the murders of Alonzo Perez 24, Jose Rivera 26 and Carlos Cruz 31!"

"Hold the fuck up, y'all got to be mistaken me for someone else."

"You have the right to remain silent, anything you say could be used against you in the court of law."

I could see his mouth moving but I didn't hear anything he was saying. I could just hear him over and over telling me I'm under arrest for murder. Right now ain't the time for me to get locked up, not saying that there is a right time, but I got a Festival I just made a deposit on. I owe Loso a Million and a half, Tha Fam, Tha Hyena's, Mom, Tee-Bae and Paradise and if Roxanna is telling the truth, I got a baby on the way.

I was transported to Falcon-burg Jail, booked in as a Federal inmate. Once I hit the dorm, I went directly to the phone and dialed my mom's phone number.

You have a collect call from "Oyah!" a inmate at the Falcon-burg Detention Center, press "O" to answer this free one minute call.

"Hello Oyah! What's going on?"

"Mom tell Tee-Bae to roundup Keybo and Moon, also y'all add money to the phone so I can call... Fucking Bitch"

That was a fast minute call. I couldn't even finish talking to my mom before the phone got cut off. I went and put my bedroll up in my cell then went back to the phone but I couldn't remember anyone's phone number to even call them. So I tried mom's phone and she answered on the first ring. A minute later, the operator gave us permission to speak.

"Oyah! What's going on? I had Tee-Bae look you up and it shows you have a U.S. Marshal hold for the A.T.F!"

"I know mom, call my lawyer, Paradise has his personal phone number."

"She is on the phone with him now, he is looking up your case now."

"Tell him to get me a bond, Paradise has enough cash on her to move me."

"Okay baby, we are working on it. I have to go get your BMW, from the Federal impound yard in Tampa."

"Okay mom, thank you, tell my ladies I love Em. We going on lockdown so I'll call you in the morning."

"Okay baby please be safe in there."

"I'm good,ma, but please find you a house and take the girls with you and my Safes"

"We already spoke about that."

"I love you and good night."

The next morning at breakfast, the court list went out and my name was on there for 5:00 A.M.

"Damn, why the fuck they got me going to court so early!"

Inside the Federal Court Room, it looked really scary. The Magistrate Judge sat in the middle of the courtroom, but it seemed like she was sitting 20 feet in the air. I looked around and I saw the U.S. Attorney and Four Marshals dressed in all black suits. Behind me was my Mom, Lil Brother and sister, Tha Fam, Tha Hyena's, Keybo, Madd-Ball and Big-B. Seeing my Team made me happy, but I grew mad when I didn't see Tee-Bae or Paradise.

Some guy in a cheap brown suit came my way.

"Hello! I'm Ray Lopez and I'm with the Federal Public Defender's Office. I am assigned to your case."

"Hold the fuck up, I have a paid lawyer, I don't need a Public Pretender."

"As of right now, you have me as a lawyer, and I've had time to go over your case and from the evidence they have you charged with, you are facing the death penalty if convicted."

"Hold up, are you here to defend me or prosecute me, because right now, you talking crazy for one and for two, I have a paid lawyer so you can kiss my ass because I'm not guilty."

The doors to the courtroom burst open and in came my ladies and Richard Reinhart. Tee-Bae and Paradise went and sat with my mom while Reinhart walked up to the table beside me and sat his briefcase on the table and opened it.

I leaned over, "they already trying to talk about the death penalty, I whispered into his ear."

Reinhart smiled at me and that made me mad instantly. I know this nigga don't think it's funny that these crackers are talking about me and I haven't even seen my discovery yet. Rienhart pulled out three big yellow envelopes, then handed one to the Public Pretender, and one to the U.S. Attorney. Then he turned on his heels.

"Excuse me, Magistrate Sansony, may I please approach the bench?"

The Magistrate nodded her head and my lawyer took her the last envelope. Then came and stood beside me.

"What was that you handed them?"

"Well Mr. Sanchez, I gave your Public Defender a Notice letting him know that he no longer represents you, then I gave the Judge and Prosecutor a few motions. A motion to Suppress Evidence, A motion for speedy trial and a motion to dismiss all charges."

"So what happens now?"

"We wait for them to grant all our motions, then come back to court and argue with them. We win and you walk out a free man."

"That's what's up, please let my family know what's going on."

"I already informed your child's mother and your girlfriend. I'm going to be straight up with you. I don't know how you do it, but it's every man's dream to have his current girlfriend be friends with the mother of his child."

I was confused, why he kept referring to Tee-Bae as my baby mama, when she wasn't. I never said anything. I guess that was her way of letting him know she was an important factor in my life. The Bailiff came and escorted me to the back then I was transferred back to the jail. On my way back to the dorm, a short black woman deputy was walking me back. I looked at her from head to toe. She ain't had no confidence in herself whatsoever. Her hair was in an old nappy ponytail, her uniform looked real dingy and she had seven out of ten nails broken on her hands and she didn't believe in body spray or perfume because she smelled like shit not even fresh clean clothes.

I jumped out there with her and asked her to bring me a cellphone that I will give her $5,000(Five thousand). She looked at me like I was out of my mind. I waited for her to scream at me but she never did.

"Lil Boy, don't even try me, $5,000(Five thousand) ain't shit, if you want me to do that, Ima need at least $10,000(Ten thousand) and you have to buy your own phone."

"You ain't saying shit. Bring me some weed and I'll give you an extra stack."

"Your parents got money like that, for you to just blow $11,000(Eleven thousand) on some weed and phone.?"

"First off, I spend my own money, don't let my age and this baby face fool you. Boys do what they can, I do what I want. I'm a grown ass man. Get my ladies number, one of them will take care of it. Ima call them and tell them to be expecting a call from Rose and to handle whatever you ask them to."

"Who the fuck is Rose?"

"Your little nappy head ass. That's a code name."

"Oh okay then, what's the number?"

I gave her both numbers to Tee-Bae and Paradise, then walked in the dorm and got straight on the phone with my ladies. I told them to be expecting a call and to do as the person says. Then Tee-Bae told me that my mom is doing all the paperwork for a two story house on Anna Maria Island as we speak. I told her aight, bet and don't miss that call. It's really important.

"Babe, y'all get with Keybo and hold shit down until I get home."

"We got you, just relax and be safe in there."

"Aight I love you."

Two weeks went by and we had a shake down in our dorm. Miss. McDaniel went into my room and fucked it up. She flipped my shit thoroughly, even looking through my mail like she was reading my letters and looking at my pictures.

My bunky was mad.

"What's wrong nigga?"

"I hate that bitch, she is always doing the most. She flipped this bitch like she was looking for a tattoo gun or some weed. This jail is weak and petty as fuck. Where I'm from, we had phones, weed and the female cops be fucking."

"Where is you from anyways? I've been wondering but never wanted to ask you, because I didn't want you to feel like I was all in your business."

"I'm from Baltimore, I'm doing Fed time at Coleman USP and caught another charge for Heroin."

"What do you go by? I have people at that prison. They at USP Coleman 1!"

"Everyone knows me by the name, The Mayor. I ran Baltimore when I was out and I still do."

"How much time are you looking at now with this new charge?"

"Nothing really, I already have life in the Feds."

"Damn man, sorry to hear that, but I got something for us."

"I'm good right now bro, I got my locker full plus shit in other cells, because this shit so petty. If you have a lot of food, they will take some and leave it in your property."

"L.O.L. now why the fuck would I offer you food when I can clearly see your locker is filled up to the max."

"Well what else you got?"

"Just chill, Ima holla at you when the time is right."

The Mayor walked out the cell to get on the phone while I got my shit back in order. I was making my bunk and as I flipped my mattress, I found a Motorola Razor with the Charger sitting underneath.

I powered the phone on and Deputy McDaniel was on the screen saver in a yellow bikini looking so right out of her uniform. Two text messages came through

"Hey Sweetie, send me a text when you read this, I will bring you the smoke next time I come to work."

"I got you lil mama, there is plenty more cash that can be made."

The Mayor came into the cell and his eyes looked like they wanted to pop out his head, all I could do was smile. I passed him the phone.

"Here you go bruh, reach out to the real world, Ima go take me a shower."

Forty five minutes later I came back to the cell and the Mayor had all types of numbers written down on his pad, like he was adding up shit. I was being nosey so I looked at his pad and this nigga was adding up hundreds of thousands of dollars.

"Here you go bro, bet that up, I had to handle some business but just couldn't do it on these wall phones. How long are you keeping the cellphone for?"

"This is my phone, I just had it brought in."

"Nigga you is the man, I've been trying to get a phone up in here for the past two months now."

I got on the phone and gave Keybo instructions on what I need for him to do, he said he understood it all, then I three way Tee-Bae and put her up on game as well. I know that I could depend on my ladies and Keybo to handle business for me until I get out. Then I called my cousin Chewito and put him on game, so he can handle shit with Keybo while I'm gone.

"I want everything to run smoothly while I'm gone or there will be some major changes made."

"We got you big bruh, yea bae, don't even stress that, we are going to hold you down."

"How are Tha Hyena's doing and The rest of Tha Fam?"

"Everyone is handling business bruh, I got this, trust me."

A week later, I got called out for a lawyer's visit but when I made it out of the dorm, it was Miss McDaniel waiting on me. She smiled at me so I smiled back. Nothing was said, because what was understood didn't have to be explained. When we got to the Lawyers room, she closed the door, pulled my blues down and dropped to her knees. In one swift motion, she grabbed a hold of my dick and sucked on the head with so much passion until she made me stand all the way up. Then she deep throated me. I had to bite down on my shirt so can't nobody walking the halls could hear me in there. Miss McDaniel sucked a mean dick for real. I felt my abs tighten up and then my seeds went flying into her mouth. She sucked up every drop making sure she milked me dry. Then she rubbed my meat on her face while she sucked my nuts one at a time. She stood up, wiped her mouth with the back of her hands and reached into her shirt and pulled a zip of weed out and a small BIC lighter.

"You got the number, that's a burner phone I bought just to talk to you on."

"Aight bet, just hit the line when you are off work."

Miss McDaniel walked me back to my unit and all I could do was picture her in her bikini. She has a nice body under her uniform.

When I got back, The Mayor and I smoked some fat Gars and handled business on the phone. Everything was going well, my team was really handling business in the streets. The Mayor and I started to even put together a Master Plan because he had the Bloods behind the wall who was working for him, but his big brother wasn't dropping off the package. So the Bloods were starting to get hungry and doing shit in prison to catch new charges. The Mayor needed my help and the numbers he was talking about was unheard of. I put him in a position with a new plug for his operation. In and out the prison system. I was starting to feel like everything happens for a reason. Later on that night, I was talking to Tee-Bae and Paradise. They were at my mom's new house, helping with the decorations. They had me on speaker phone.

"Hey Baby! How you holding up?"

"I'm good Ma, have you heard from my lawyer?"

"Yes he said don't worry about anything, you will be out before your next court date. The Feds came at him with a plea deal but he never took the time to even look at it. He said that he didn't even accept the plea from the Prosecutor. He just let them know, they either drop charges or get ready to spend money on a trial that will be won by the Defense because you are NOT GUILTY."

"Now that's why I fuck with Reinhart. Ima holla at y'all tomorrow, Ima let my bunky use the phone while I get some rest."

Tee-Bae got on the phone.

"Daddy we have a surprise for you when you get home."

"I can't wait to see what it is. I love y'all."

I heard Paradise scream over everyone,

"I Love You Too Daddy"

"I love you too Lil Mama."

I hung up and passed the phone over to The Mayor. Four months later my name came over the loudspeaker at 5:30AM. telling me to roll it up "A.T.W all the way."

"What the fuck is really going on!"

The Mayor got up.

"You're out of here kid, it's all over with now."

"But my Lawyer ain't even come see me to tell me what's going on.

"Nigga, I know you ain't over there complaining about getting out. Get your mail and get the fuck up out of here. Stay in touch, we about to make more millions."

"Nigga you is Fam now. I got you and Ima put together a Dream Team so they can work with the Five lawyers you have. We need you out there with your Fam making moves."

"Ima be out when my higher power feels like it's time for me to be out."

"Bruh that's why I always fuck with you because you always positive, no matter the situation."

My cell door opened and I dapped The Mayor up and gave him a half hug, then walked out, and the door closed behind me.

## CHAPTER 20

# HAPPY HOLIDAYS AND
# CLASSIC WEEKEND 2005

was met at the gate by Keybo. I called him while I was in booking waiting on my finger prints. Soon as I seen my nigga, I looked him up and down, then we dapped each other up.

"It's good to have you home, bruh."

"Yea! It feels good to be home and I see you out here eating good. You ain't no lil nigga anymore."

"Yea, I don't even eat McDonalds anymore, Dine-In Only."

"That's real, well I tell you what, take me to McDonalds because I still eat it."

I got me a steak egg on a bagel, plain just cheese with large fries and sweet tea.

"Bruh, take me by my house so I can check on my loot then take me by my mom's new spot."

At the crib, everything was nice and clean, smelling fresh. I checked on my money, everything was just how I left it. My

$7,000,000(Seven million) was untouched. I showered and put on a brand new fit that I had in my closet.

"Bruh let's go by my mom's house."

"Aight let's roll, do they know you home?"

"Nobody but you. I ain't even know that I was getting out today."

"Damn so everyone is in for a surprise!"

"What is that supposed to mean, everyone?"

"Just chill, we going to be there in like fifteen to twenty minutes."

Pulling onto my mom's road, I knew she had a nice house because all the rest of the houses was nice and big. When we pulled into the driveway, I was really impressed. We parked and got out. When Keybo rang the doorbell, I hid behind the big bush so no one would see me. Tee-Bae answered the door looking so Fine. Keybo walked in and Tee-Bae walked back to the kitchen leaving Bruh to lock the door, but he never did. He just closed it and followed Tee-Bae. I waited a few minutes then walked in.

"Damn Ma, you're living better than me."

I could hear all their voices, so I just followed it until I popped up in the doorway of the kitchen. Tee-Bae was the first to see me, then my mom. They was both frozen, looking at me in shock. Then my mom screamed at the top of her lungs causing Paradise to look my way and screamed as well. Everyone was screaming as they all ran up to me so I could hug them. Then Joe and T.Jay came running around the corner with so much excitement. I talked to them and my little brother asked for the new PS3 and T.Jay wanted a Barbie House.

"Okay Ima do that for the both of y'all, now get out of here so us grown folks can talk."

They left and my attention went straight to Paradise. I walked up on them looking at every single one of them in the eyes.

I stopped on Paradise,

"Do you have something you want to explain to me?"

"Daddy we are having a lil girl, I'm six months pregnant. We was going to tell you but then you got locked up, so your mom said to hold off so you won't be in there stressing."

"Damn, so is this the surprise everyone keeps talking about? This calls for a Celebration."

I grabbed my Baby Momma and kissed her, then I grabbed Tee-Bae, kissed her and told her she is next. She just smiled, wrapped one of her legs around me and gave me a intimate kiss.

"We're going to be a family now daddy!"

"We been a family lil Mama."

"Let's talk business, where is all the Loot from the Show we did at Roberts Arena and the video I asked y'all to take for me of the entire event. I wanna watch it tonight while I lay in between both my ladies."

"All the money is in the safe, even the money for all the dope you left out here. We owe Loso $2.2 Million, but we almost got that up already."

"Who been handling all that?"

"Bruh I've been taking care of business and just having sis put up all the Loot."

"Okay bet, let's get the money counters out."

Two hours later and about fifteen gars, I had two piles of cash sitting on my moms kitchen Island. The stack from the show was $1.325 Million and I had $2.7 million from all the dope I left behind.

"Where is the money for Loso?"

"I got that stashed inside the Astro Van babe, in the garage."

"Oh okay! How much is in there?"

"It's $1.7 mill, and we still got 60 Keys of Sand and 22 keys of Heroin."

"Damn bae, you really holding shit down for me, huh?"

"Yea, bruh you got a solid one here!"

I put up $3 Million and bust Keybo down $500,000(five hundred thousand) out of the show money. Then I gave my mom $25,000(twenty five thousand).

"What's this for baby?"

"It's for you mom. Ladies I need y'all to see what's good with the Latin Quarters. If it's for sale after the shootings then I want to buy it. Tha Fam is starting to grow, our money is getting longer than train smoke."

"Okay babe, I'll get with the real estate agent and see what we can come up with."

"Paradise! When is your due date?"

"You won't believe it. Take a wild guess!"

"I don't know, just tell me, I hate playing the guessing game."

"You ain't no fun Oyah, she should be born on your birthday, Damn!"

"Oh shit! For real bae! Me and my lil mama are going to have big parties. I want to have an event in Orlando for Classic Weekend."

"Bruh, we are going to have to get on that ASAP because everyone is going to try to lock in on those dates for that weekend."

"Daddy, how you wanna do that when it falls on the same weekend after Thanksgiving."

"Well Thanksgiving is on that Thursday, so I feel like we can have a Thanksgiving dinner here, y'all can invite y'all's family, bruh you can bring yours. Then after dinner, to Orlando we go."

I got on the phone with my booking agent.

"What's good Fam, I'm trying to get Club Taboo on Church Street in Orlando for Classic weekend."

"That's going to be expensive."

"It's all good, I can afford it. I also want to bring Lil Wayne so get me the numbers on all that."

"Okay cool, I got you."

"Mom, buy all the food and the ladies are going to help you with the cooking."

"Ima get one of my Basers to get all the drinks."

"Mom, is your pool heated because if so we are going to have a pool party."

"Yes it is, but I don't want all them people running in and out of my house, all wet and shit."

"Well, Ima leave the $3,000,000(Three Million) here and just take a half Million with me."

"Yoo Keybo, call Chewito up for me so I can let him know I'm home. I also need to take my lawyer some more money and ask him about a business lawyer."

"Bruh, let's go handle that right now, I will drive us while you call your cousin and the plug because he wants to talk with you as well. Then after that, we going to swing by all the spots."

"Naw, give me your phone, Ima send everyone a text, we are going to have a dinner meeting at JOTO's in that back room. I only want to see Julissa after we get done at the lawyers office."

We rode around taking care of everything then ended up at my house. I had texted Julissa off Keybo phone telling her to pull up alone. Not even forty minutes later, Julissa pulled up into my yard in a White C300 AMG. She got out looking so fucking sexy.

"These your Wheels lil mama?"

"Yes Papi, all Tha Hyena's got one in a different color. I even got one for Desiree"

"Reinhart said he about to beat her case in trial next week."

"Say word lil mama, that's good news. I was calling you over to talk about that"

"When did you get out? We been holding shit down out here, but we been missing you, well at least I know I've been missing you."

"I've been missing you as well, I miss everyone and you looking real good"

"Thanks, you look good yourself."

Later that night, I paid the owner of JOTO's restaurant to lock the doors. I want only Tha Fam and Tha Hyena's to be here. Big-B arranged for the youngin's to post up in the traps from Sarasota to

Bradenton. I wanted everyone to be present at my meeting. By 10:00 P.M. Everyone except Uzi and Davi was present. I hit Uzi on the Nextel,

"Where y'all at Fam?"

"We pulling up now, order me a triple shot of Goose on the rocks."

"Aight!"

My whole Team was here. Keybo, Purp, J. Gangsta, Madd-Ball, Big-B, Nando, Poe-Poe, Rue, Bullet, Suave, Tang, Carl, Mike-O, Mike-E, Uzi, Davi, Julissa, Amanda, Berlin, Scarlet, Nadeen and I even had two representatives of the Trinitarios, Zye and two of his men was also present, Moon and we have Chewito on a burner phone only being used for this meeting. Keybo stood up with a cup and butter knife in his hand. Cling! Cling! Cling! He tapped the cup with the knife to get everyone's attention.

"Y'all listen up for a few minutes, Oyah want to have a few words with y'all."

I stood up and held my cup in the air.

"This is for Tha Fam."

Everyone held their cups in the air and screamed out Tha Fam!

"First and Foremost I want to Thank everyone for handling business in my absence and making sure what we have built didn't come down crumbling. Everyone in this room is a part of Tha Fam. We are all eating at an all time high. I'm looking into some businesses that I can start up, so we can make our money legit. I'm working on a Club, so Ima need three investors so we can build it into a super club. Then we only let Tha Fam promote and bring artists to the Club. I also want to send our ladies to Real Estate School, so we can have Tha

Fam Realty. We buying, selling and renting houses, Lofts, Apartments, Condos and Businesses. Ima start helping small businesses in our hood build up by investing money into them and paying for advertising."

We take care of our hood and our hood would take care of us.

"Ima spend $100,000(One hundred thousand) on Christmas gifts for the children, but I also want to raise some loot for our single mothers to get them gifts because taking care of these kids is hard and I just want them to know that Tha Fam appreciates them."

Keybo stood up, "bruh can I say something?"

"Go ahead bruh, anyone at this meeting can speak on what's on their mind."

"Thank everyone here for playing their part while bruh was gone those few months. Let's just keep up the good work and make 2006 a Epic year for Tha Fam and Manatee and Sarasota County. I will like to give all the seniors in our city $250(two hundred and fifty) and the single mothers, so they can cook a nice Thanksgiving meal for their families."

"So at every Re-up, if you trying to share your blessings, then you throw in your donations and once we reach our quota, I will handle the rest. But now to our current business at hand. We need to expand our business and take shit out the state and out of the County, so our net worth can triple. I want us to start traveling and hanging out. When people see you doing good and living, they want to get down. It's time we move around because staying here ain't going to do shit but get us a long prison bid."

Two weeks later, it was Thanksgiving morning. I had the whole Team at the park donating Food and Cash to help make the older people and single mothers in our hood have a Happy Thanksgiving. I was happy when I saw my girl.

"Damn! Lil Mama, it feels like forever since the last time I saw you."

"Yes it do bro, I heard you had a lil situation with the Feds. Are you good on that now or you still fighting the case?"

"I'm good, my lawyer or should I say, our lawyer got my shit dropped with a Motion to Suppress Evidence."

"Damn, he got my shit dropped with the same motion. Are you coming back to the house babe, Nadeen and Berlin cooking. The whole team is coming over?"

"I'll be over there when I leave my mom's house."

"Okay! You better come chill with me, shit, I ain't seen you in forever."

"Yea! Tell me about it, those seven months you been gone seems like years, but Tha Hyena's ain't tell you we all going to Orlando tonight!"

"Nah, but shit, I'm down for whatever and I mean whatever! We going to link later."

I shot over to my moms, it was dinner time. My aunty Millie Millz and her two kids. My other aunty Luz with three of her kids, both of my ladies, my grandma and grandpa, Anet, Tee-Bae's and Paradise parents came over. We had a big feast. The vibe was all love, even Anet was chill. I thought she was going to be sweating me but she proved me wrong.

"Ima slide to Orlando, it's Classic Weekend and I have one of the biggest events going on."

Friday, we are at Club Taboo with Lil Wayne and Plies, then Saturday we have Lil Boosie and Webbie at the same club. It's literally a sold out event on both nights, then I asked to Host the Car Show on Sunday.

"I would bring y'all but Orlando ain't a safe place to be. I'm at war with a Puerto Rican and I'm sure he knows we are going to be in town."

"If you know all that, then why are you going?"

"Because I stand to make a lot of money, plus I don't give a fuck about dude, I wanna run into him."

I had Dinky go pick my Box Chevy up and tow it to Orlando. We all pulled out at the same time. I rode in the passenger seat while Julissa drove all the way to Orlando. I had rented us a Fourteen bedroom mansion so we can all just hangout and have our own after party.

Friday night, I had every single piece of Jewelry that I owned on me. I had on a Coogi sweater and Red Monkey Jeans with some Dior Shoes that I flew all the way to Paris just to get them. My whole team was T.V. ready, dressed in Designer and Shining. Tha Hyena's all had Choker Chains with Iced out Hyena Medallions. We were like Gods in our hood, we gave everyone hope. Young Self Made Millionaires. We was living the American Dream.It was like a car show outside of Club Taboo and Church Street looked like there was a block party going on. Women and men from all over the United States was dressed to Impress. I had pulled up out front in my Box Chevy with all my windows down jamming to Plies, "Just hit me a lick finna blow a check, I got stacks on me, goons on deck." Everyone on the strip was looking and taking pictures of my Box Chevy. I had a real show stopper. Valet came to my driver's door and opened it for me. I gave the dude a crisp $100 bill.

"Park my shit right here in front of the club doors."

"I got you, Ima just put all the windows up and lock the doors."

It was a 941 takeover. We was deep, like a fleet of new cars and a few tricked out old schools. The photographer for Ozone Magazine was in front of the club, snapping pictures of my car and then of me when I stepped out with my Neck, Ears, Fingers and Wrist looking like a Chandelier. I was feeling like a Celebrity walking on the red carpet, as I made my way inside the club with Tha Fam and Tha Hyena's by my side. We was met by three bottle girls with sparkling fireworks who led us to the upper V.I.P. Section that I had reserved for Lil Wayne, Plies and Tha Fam. The vibe was all Love. I had ordered 100 hundred bottles of Moët Rose and 100 bottles of Remy. Our section was lit, we had people trying to sneak in but security was on point letting only selected few of the females. You had to be bad enough to be featured in a Straight Stuntin Magazine to come in our Section.

Keybo and Purp both ordered $20,000(Twenty thousand) in one dollar bills. Between all six of Tha Hyena's, they ordered another $20,000(Twenty thousand). The rest of Tha Fam all ordered a total of $60,000(Sixty thousand). The DJ announced that Tha Fam just bought $100,000(One hundred thousand) in ones. The club lights started flashing green then every bit of 100 Strippers came out.

Plies and Lil Wayne's crew had to order like another $100,000(One hundred thousand) in ones. Big-B was making it rain on two of the strippers and Scarlet. I nudged Keybo,

"Look at Big-B, he feeling himself."

I looked at my team, then at all the people partying and felt good that I was able to help everyone eat and create memories that will never be forgotten.

Both artists got on stage and put on the show of 2005. The entire club was Lit. All the women was twerking, even the ones who didn't know how to make their ass move, was out there on the dance floor shaking their bodies like fish outta water. The floor in the V.I.P. the area was filled with one dollar bills to the point everyone's shoes could not be seen. As the end of the night approached, my team made their way to their cars! The club handed me a suitcase with my money from the door. I had collected upfront all the Loot for the V.I.P. and Tables and Sections. I gave the Suitcase to Julissa and Tha Hyena's made a wall around her making sure that no one was able to get close. Then Purp, J. Gangsta, Madd-Ball and Poe-Poe surrounded them. Outside was all of our cars, we left early so Tha Hyena's could leave with all the cash before everyone got out the club. I hung out in my Box Chevy with all my brothers with me while Tha Hyena's went back to the Mansion. Tha Hyena's was hanging out in the swimming pool naked. Lala, her best friend Monica, DeDe, Delta and Mary was also naked in the swimming pool. Moon saw his girl and snatched her by her hair out the pool. The entire team was able to see her Flawless body for a split second until they went into the house. Nadeen and Julissa came over towards me and started to take off my Coogi Sweater and Red Monkey jeans. I helped them by kicking off my Dior shoes and stepping out my clothes just keeping on my Polo boxers and all my jewelry. The rest of the guys did the same. I swam and got my share of feels on the women that was in the pool with me. I was feeling horny, but I had to go count up and see how we did. So I got out the pool and grabbed my clothes then went to my room so I could shower and count up my loot. I made a nice profit tonight. I got my money back for Lil Wayne and Plies, The Club and All the money spent on promotion and $93,000(Ninety three thousand) all profit. The next night was a success as well. Every time we stepped out, it was a movie. I met Armstrong, the head of the infamous gang, "MoHawk Boyz" and we exchanged numbers. I like his movement and from what I could see, he was about his issue.

We headed back to Bradenton, a fleet of Luxury cars sliding down I-4, when two Dually trucks pulled alongside our cars and just Swiss cheesed a roll of cars making some cars swerved, Glass shattered and Slammed on breaks. Julissa was driving my BMW and I sat shotgun. When we noticed what was going on. No words had to be spoken. She smashed the gas making my engine roar like a Lion, RRRAAAA-H! I got pinned to my seat, when I looked over at the speedometer, she was doing 143 MPH and the speed kept increasing. My BMW caught up with the Dually truck with no problem. As we was pulling up, I let my window down.

"Pull up beside the driver, hurry up!"

I could see the lights of all the Benz getting closer.

"Baby, be careful, they have automatic weapons!"

"Fuck'Em! Pull up on the driver side, Ima let them have it."

Tha Hyena's about to pull up now, so the Dually trucks ain't have nowhere to run. I hung out the window letting my Colt.45 ride out into the driver's side door.

BANG! BANG! BANG! BANG! BANG! BANG! BANG! BANG!

I could see blood splatter everywhere inside of the truck and glass shattered. Then I saw one of Tha Hyena's Benz flew past us trying to catch up with the first Dually. When the second Benz went to pass us, the driver of the truck that I just shot up must've lost consciousness and swerved almost smashing into the Benz. Nadeen had the wheel, she gassed the Benz making the Dually miss her and running off I-4 and into a Wooded area.

We boxed in the other Dually. My BMW, Nadeen's Benz and J. Gangsta's Magnum. The truck couldn't do shit. Purp hung out the back window of J. Gangsta's Magnum with his Tec.9 while I hung out the passenger side of my BMW. We wet the Dually up. Some guy popped up out of the bed of the truck and shot the side of my BMW with a 12 Gage, rocking the entire 645. Julissa almost lost control of the car but she got it right. She slowed down a little and I could see Purp firing shots after shots flipping dude off the back of the Dually.

"Watch out bae!"

I yelled out loud, Julissa had to swerve to the far right lane to keep from running dude over, because that would have really fucked my car up, maybe even totaled my car. We all just let the Dually speed off Recklessly, while we all slowed down enough for everyone to catch up. Madd-Ball pulled up beside me with his Cadillac, looking like a block of Swiss cheese. I hit him on the Nextel.

"Bruh, is y'all alright over there?"

"Churp!"

"Nah, bruh, we have to get to the hospital fast. One of the Hitters took a few shells to the side, he keeps going in and out. Poe-Poe trying to keep him up now."

"Churp!"

"Fuck just drop him off at the next hospital."

"Churp!"

Right by exit 9 on I-4, I saw the Dually truck on its side in the middle of the interstate. We rode past them and I couldn't help myself but to smile.

"Stupid Bitches!"

We all got back to Tha Fam Headquarters and went inside trying to figure out how we got so relaxed and let two raggedy Dually trucks get the up's on us like that. Keybo was mad as fuck.

"Yoo bruh, we have to go to Orlando and apply pressure to Piloto and his Goons. That shit he just pulled could have caused any one of us our death."

Madd-Ball and Purp came storming into the house covered in blood.

"Yoo, please tell me y'all know who was behind all that, because my lil nigga died in my arms and someone has to pay for that."

"Poe-Poe! Just calm down, we know who it is and trust me, we about to put an end to this shit once and for all."

I called Armstrong and put him up on game as to what happened when we was leaving Orlando.

"Damn bro, that shit really got me mad, because this is my City and we trying to build a relationship. So if a nigga size you, then he sized me."

"Look, I could use some of your help. He knows me and he be real fidget when he see out of town niggas, but he won't ever suspect you or anyone in your crew to hit him."

"Bro, say less. Ima do my homework on dude because I want to hit Chico for some work before I just down him."

"Bruh, he got a Barbershop on Sand Lake and Orange Blossom Trail. It's the only Puerto Rican barbershop on that corner. He drives a Navy Blue Jeep Wrangler and a GLS 400 that's Money Green and has 20 inch chrome rims. He also has a mechanic shop on OBT and Americana."

"Okay bet, Ima lay on him and see what's good but his days are numbered."

"Bruh handle that for me and Ima throw you a Brick of Sand and give you the zips of Heroin for $2,500(Twenty Five hundred).

"Damn that's love bro, Ima start working on that today."

"Everyone, go check on y'all traps and make sure everything straight! Ima go put up the BMW and the Box Chevy."

"Aight bet bruh, we are on our way to handle that, but be safe out there."

"Yea Ima circle the block a few times before I pull up to my spot."

Everyone left their own separate ways. I pulled up and my Box Chevy was already sitting in front of my house, so I just pulled it into the Garage. I'm sure glad them niggas ain't fuck with my Box Chevy because I would really hate to have to re-do my car all over again. The next morning, I pulled up to 941 Kustumz with my BMW. Abe came out looking at my car.

"What the fuck happened here, it look like someone was gunning at you with something huge."

"Nah, someone was trying to carjack Moon but he opened this bitch up and let it do what it do. But today I want to paint it a Pearl White color with the black interior and sit it on some 22 inch chrome Lexani."

"I think you should take all the chrome off and do it black and white. Call this bih, Cookies and Cream."

"Yea, I like that, handle your business, here go $20,000(Twenty thousand dollars)."

"Oyah, your daughter is so cute, you should go and meet her. She even gave her your last name."

"What's the baby full name and birthday"

"Lahisa Sanchez and she was born November 16th, 2005."

"Damn that's my grandma, Celia's birthday."

"I guess that's more money Ima have to fork out if the baby is mine."

"Fool that baby is your twin."

"Ima go check on her sometime this week, but hold up, Ima go grab some cash out the car before I leave it and give you $10,000(Ten thousand) for Roxanna."

"Nah! You give her your money when you go and meet your daughter."

"Aight bet."

I went over to Headquarters and Moon and Nando was there just talking.

"What's good with y'all fools?"

"We just living life and getting rich my nigga. We was talking about this contribution that we want to do for all the kids in the hood."

"Yea, we going to do something, then I want us to take a vacation after my birthday, because Ima have a New Year's and Birthday Party."

"I know that bih is going to be on Swoll, but where you going to have it at?"

"Club Heat, Ima do it for the hood."

"We need to go shopping then!"

Moon said.

"I was thinking, we go shopping in Atlanta."

"I'm down for whatever, I just wanna be fresh when 12 o'clock hits, bring in the New Year the correct way."

## CHAPTER 21

# BIG BRUH, YOU GONE BUT NEVER FORGOTTEN.

Fuck, my alarm was sounding off. Beeep! Beeep! Beeep! I hit the snooze button and fell back to sleep. Five minutes later, Beeep! Beeep! Beeep! My alarm went to sounding off again. I just said fuck it and woke up. I looked at my phone and it was December 5th, 2005, 7:00 A.M. I got out of bed, Tee-Bae and Paradise didn't even flinch at the sound of my alarm. I went and took a shower, then got ready and hit the road. I shot over to Roxanna's house. Her car was parked out front and it seemed like she didn't have any company, so I put my key into the keyhole but it wouldn't turn.

"What the fuck!"

I got pissed, but I had to calm myself down because I know the only reason why she changed the locks was because I been ghost on her ass. I rang the doorbell. Ding Dong! Ding Dong!

"Who is it?"

"Your baby daddy!"

Roxanna unlocked the door and opened it just enough to poke her head out.

"Oyah, I hope you ain't come here to argue because I have enough stress on my plate without working and making sure "Our Daughter" is getting treated the right way."

"That's why I came over here for, to drop you off enough loot to hold you over for a few months. But you talking about stressing from working, what happened with your nigga?"

She tried to slam the door shut but I put my foot in the way and stopped her, then pushed the door open and stepped inside.

"Oyah, please get the fuck out of my house, you can be so stupid at times."

"Roxanna, I just want to see the baby and give you some loot."

Roxanna turned around and walked into the room. I locked the door and followed her. Soon, as I saw the baby, my heart softened. Lahisa was really my twin. I reached into her crib and pulled my daughter out and just held her in my arms. I couldn't stop smiling. When I looked at Roxanna, she had tears coming down her cheeks.

"Why are you crying for Roxanna?"

"Because, we should be a family, look at yourself in the mirror and see how good you look holding your daughter. Don't you want this, don't you want to be a family?"

"We don't have to be together in order for me to be a part of her life. Ima handle my business as a man and be a great father to her, you just have to let me."

"Oyah, I won't ever keep you from Lahisa no matter what we have going on, because it has nothing to do with us."

My Nextel sounded off, Churp! Churp!

"Yoo, Rue! What it do my nigga!"

"Shit bruh, I'm cooling but my cousin is down here from South Carolina and he's trying to get plugged in. Everyone he keeps running into don't be having pressure and there is a lot of competition in his hood."

"Churp!"

"Can y'all meet me over at the trap and I can show him what I got and we can figure out numbers."

"We over here now and bring some work for the trap."

"Aight bet, I'm on my way."

"Lil Mama, daddy has to go, but I will be seeing you again real soon."

I gave her a kiss on the forehead and laid her back inside the crib. My baby looked so sweet.

"Roxanna, here this for you and the baby."

I handed her the Crown Royal bag with $30,000(Thirty thousand) in all hundred dollar bills.

"Buy whatever you need and pay your bills, Ima bring you some more loot in a few days."

"Thank you, because I was stressing how Ima pay all these bills."

"Ima bring you some more so don't worry about running out of cash. Ima slide and go handle some business."

"Please be safe out there Oyah! You may not believe me but I do love you."

I shook my head from side to side and just walked out of her house. She's trying to play a dangerous game. I hopped in my Infiniti and slid to Oneco. My phone buzzed and it was Tee-Bae.

"Hello babe, what's going on?"

"Where you at? Why you ain't say where you was going? Why you ain't."

"Hold up Ma, I don't even know what question to answer first."

"I'm sorry bae!"

"I'm out taking care of business. I'm on my way to Oneco, but since I got you on the phone, grab me Ten keys of Sand and bring me Four keys of Heroin that's done up, then come to your old spot."

"I'll be there in like Forty Five minutes."

"Be safe on that road."

Three hours later, I served all my people who called my phone. Between everyone that was at the Trap, there was at least One Million dollars in cash, drugs and jewelry.

Rue introduced me to his cousin J.T!

"What's good with y'all"

I dapped them both up.

"Shit bruh, I'm just trying to expand like you said to do."

I shook my head up and down,

"That's what's up bruh."

Then I looked over to J.T

"So tell me, what's the numbers out there and what you can do."

"I got a Team that is ruthless, but supa Loyal to me. I can take over the entire South Carolina, all I need is a consistent connect and some pressure."

"I'm the man you've been looking for. So what are your numbers and what do you think you can move on a monthly basis?"

"I'm paying $120,000(One hundred twenty thousand) per key of Heroin and $24,500(Twenty four thousand five hundred) per key of soft."

"Damn that's expensive as fuck."

Keybo looked at me and said

"Bruh, South Carolina sounds sweet."

"Yea! It do, huh? J.T paying them numbers, how many times do you cut a brick, so you can make money?"

"I don't even know how to cut it, so I leave it just how I get it."

"I bust my shit down into $20 baggies and pump them in my hood. I got Five Blocks that fuck with me, but I know everyone who be hustling and we have the same problem. No consistent plug with gas."

"I can give you what you are looking for. We run like a real Family. Tha Fam lives up to their name and we stand behind our product because it's our brand. Ima put the dope on your front door step but Ima want $95,000(Ninety Five thousand) for a Brick of Heroin and $21,500(Twenty One thousand Five hundred) for a Brick of Sand. It's always going to be high grade and Ima show you how to break it down, cut it and put it all back together."

"Bro, if it's like that, Ima lock down South and North Carolina."

"That's what I want, you know that B.M.F. The Empire just got indicted on a big Conspiracy Drug case, so the market is open and up for the takes."

"Rue, if we going to be out here, we need to make money moves and make shit worth the Penitentiary chances we are taking."

"I'm down with it my nigga, I'm ready to get on some real Boss Shit."

"Aight bet, Ima need an address and Ima get shit ready."

"Rue, I want you to go out there so you can make sure everything is everything for at least two months."

I got the address and everyone left the trap leaving Nando, Bullet and Hustle behind. Hustle is one of our homeboy who came home from state prison and didn't have a pot to piss in or a window to throw it out of.

I Slid to my house, on my way out there, I texted Keybo.

"Bruh, when you get done with your rounds, pull up to my spot."

He texted back.

"Aight give me about an hour."

I was loading the Astro Van with all the Sand that we had from Piloto and Ten keys of Heroin. I also loaded up a small 9.oz re-rock machine, Fifteen keys of Mannitol and Quinine mixed together. Keybo hit me on my Nextel.

"Bruh, open the door, I'm pulling up"

I pressed the garage clicker so it could open up, then I pressed it again so it could stop with just enough space for him to slide under, then I closed it.

"What's good bruh, I'm really liking the sound of that outta town move. I was thinking about going to other states just so I can lay on a nigga and peep out what he's doing, then befriend him so I can make him a offer that he won't be able to refuse."

"So you saying, you want to basically go to different states and cities and just pull up on random niggas and put some work in their lives?"

"Nah big bruh, I want to hangout for like three to four weeks at all the hot spots so I can get familiar with the Ballers and vice versa. Then like most niggas do, we going to want to know what the next man is doing to make paper and just go from there."

"That's why I keep you as my Right Hand because two minds are better than one. I love that idea. Let's handle this South Carolina take over first, then after New Years, we move forward with your plan."

"Aight bet, so what Ima do is tighten things up around here so that while I'm gone, things can keep moving smoothly."

My phone started to vibrate. Bzzzz! Bzzzz! Bzzzz! My caller I.D. said it was Moon calling me, so I answered.

"Yooo! What's good bruh?"

"Nothing bruh, Nando just said some niggas in a Gold Impala been creeping on the block. He said he was getting bad vibes."

"He's just overreacting but Ima go out there once I get done taking care of some business."

"Yea, I thought the same shit."

I packed up $2,200,000(two million, two hundred thousand) so I can ship it to Loso, all at the same time, we drop the work off to Rue and J.T. in South Carolina. I called Berlin because now that

Paradise is pregnant, I don't want her on the road for all that time. Berlin answered the phone on the first ring.

"¡Dimelo Papi!"

"I need you to go on a trip, pack your bags and meet me at my house."

"Okay Papi, I will be there in one hour."

"That's perfect, hit my line when you are down the block."

I sent Tee-Bae a text telling her to get home and to leave Paradise with my mom.

Not even thirty minutes later, I could hear my ADT alarm sensor beep indicating someone just walked through my front door.

"Oyah, where you at bae?"

"In the garage."

She walked in and saw that I was all sweaty and Keybo was at my work table getting a batch ready for our Team.

"Bae, is everything okay, please tell me you are good!"

"Yea, I'm straight, why you asking me that for?"

"Because the text you sent me, seemed like it was really urgent, as if something was happening!"

"I'm sorry if I had you worried, it's nothing like that babe, I just need you to take the van to this address and unload it of everything but the duffle bag with all the cash. Then once you make that drop, get back on I-95 North and head to Loso."

"You want me to take that trip alone?"

"Absolutely not, I have one of Tha Hyena coming over so she can ride with you"

"Which one of Tha Hyena's, it's Six of them?"

"Berlin is going to ride with you."

"Good because I would hate to take that ride all alone. When do I leave?"

"Tonight at Midnight, so do what you need and get some rest, the van is already ready to go."

It was about 7:00 PM. When Nando was headed out of the trap on his way to go drop some loot up at his girl's house. When he opened the front door to the trap there was a guy standing there pulling his Ski Mask down. When he realized what was going on, he made an attempt to slam the door shut, but the robbers were a lil faster than he was, because he charged the door like a linebacker at the Super Bowl. Pushing Nando back into the house while three other men wearing masks rushed in behind him. The first man who came through the door, smacked Nando on the head with his pistol so hard that it split him open making his forehead look like a bloody pussy and knocking him down to the ground out cold. While the other three guys ransack the house. One of the guys pulled Bullet off the bed and made him walk into the living room with his hands in the air. One of the other guys found Hustle inside the closet hiding. He tried to pull him out but he was just too heavy to move. The third guy was flipping the trap looking for work and cash. When dude couldn't get Hustle to come out of the closet, he started to kick, punch and pistol whip him. The second guy kept asking Bullet where Oyah lives, where is the Stash house, where is all the dope and money being kept?

"Suck my dick, bitch ass nigga, I'll rather Die before I turn on my brother."

Bullet told the dude with a nonchalant attitude. The guy must've got furious because without giving it a second thought he squeezed the trigger on his gun twice. BOOM! BOOM! Sending two hollow tips smashing into the back of Bullets head, sending him to sleep forever. When the dude in the room heard the gunshot, he squeezed his trigger sending a bullet crashing into Hustle ass cheek and then running out the room with his eyes wide open, all scared and shit. Nando woke up when he heard the first gunshot but decided to lay there and play like he was still knocked out. The two men searching the house came out the back running at full speed when they heard the three gunshots. They both had pillow cases filled with dope, cash and guns. They both ran out the trap with the other two following close behind.

Berlin hit me on my Nextel,

"I'm pulling up so open the door."

"Churp!"

I didn't even answer her, I walked outside and fired up a gar. I got a real calm and warm sensation wash over my body, starting at my toes all the way to the top of my head. When Berlin pulled up and got out the car, I passed her my gar for her to smoke and we walked into my house and into my office so I could run down my game plan to her.

"I'm ready Oyah, trust me, I'll do everything you asked me to do and make it all the way to New York and back."

"Lil Mama I trust you, why do you think I called you and only you? But y'all about to leave here around midnight so go get some rest."

I got a call from Moon telling me someone just hit Nando's Spot and killed Bullet and shot Hustle in his ass.

"What the fuck man. Keybo let's roll, a bih just killed Bullet."

"Nah bruh, you playin!"

"You think that's something I will play about?"

I looked at him with a blank expression on my face.

"Ladies, some shit just went down at one of my Traps so I gots to leave but the van is gassed up, so please make sure y'all are on that road by Midnight. I programmed the GPS in the Van with the holiday Inn address in New York that's closest to the drop off location and the address to Loso's restaurant in Washington Heights. Call me when y'all check into the room in South Carolina."

"Okay daddy, we got you."

On my way to Nando's Spot, all six of my phones was blowing up nonstop. I ain't want to even speak with anyone. Keybo and I rode in silence. All that could be heard was the lines, cracks and holes on the road. I looked over to Keybo,

"bruh roll up. I need to calm my nerves. I'm 38 Hot right now."

He ain't even say anything, he just started rolling up. I rode past 12th Street because it was roped off with Marked and Unmarked cars. The Coroner's Unit and Bay News 9. I parked on the next Street over and we walked over. I saw Big-B and Nando standing by the Trap just staring like they was waiting on something. Then that's when I saw the Paramedics came out with a Gurney, it had a body covered from head to toe with a white sheet. I figured that was Bullet by the way Nando and Big-B held their heads down. It seemed like the Entire City was out there. Purp and Madd-Ball walked up on me with tears of anger in their eyes.

"Bruh, Poe-Poe snapping the fuck out. J. Gangsta just had to take him back down East before he did something to get us all fucked up."

"We are going to get to the bottom of this."

Later that night, we was all at Headquarters. All the Big Dawgs from Tha Fam and Tha Hyena's. We sat around the Den in Silence, no one speaking, no one moving. All you heard was the water pumps from my 250 Gallon Saltwater Fish Tank that sat in the middle of the Den.

I pulled my phone out and called Armstrong.

"Yoo bruh, I need you to find dude ASAP! He just had one of my Spot hit and one of my brothers killed. I can't keep letting this nigga breathe."

"Bro, I think I figured out his stash house. It's in some Condos off Curry Ford and Conway called Watauga Woods, we just going to follow him next time to his front door and walk in with him."

"Don't kill him, snatch him up for me and call me. I wanna kill his bitch ass myself."

"I got you, we are going to handle that tonight or no later than tomorrow."

"Bet that up, Ima have you something sitting to the side for handling that for me, for my brother, for Tha Fam."

"Keybo, tell his people's that Tha Fam will pay and plan his entire funeral and burial. All they have to do is show up to pay their respects."

"Will do bruh!"

"I'm outta here, Ima go to my moms house to get me some rest, but keep me posted on everything. Ima leave Julissa, Amanda and Desiree in charge of Bullets funeral. Make sure my nigga looks good and that his funeral be one to be talked about for years. Here go $100,000(One hundred thousand) make sure y'all go all out."

"Don't worry, you will be happy with the outcome."

"Aight, I'm outta here."

When I got to my moms house, everyone was still up, so we chopped it up a lil but I was exhausted so Paradise and I went to the room. I took a shower then got in bed with her, sliding in behind her. Paradise put her bare ass on my dick as I wrapped my arm around her and held her stomach. As soon as I touched her belly, I could feel my daughter moving. I couldn't help myself. I had one of the biggest smiles and I kissed her on the neck.

"I love you Lil Mama."

"I love you too Daddy, mom said she wants us to name her Miamor Sanchez and I really like that name."

"So that's her name because I love it."

Paradise reached back and grabbed my dick and slid it into her hot and wet pussy from the back. She felt so snug. I lifted her leg up and went to stroking that pussy, slow deep strokes.

"Damn bae, you've had some good pussy but this pussy gets better the further along you get in this pregnancy."

She reached her arm over her shoulder and gripped my neck, squeezing her nails into me. The harder Paradise squeezed, the harder I stroked that pussy. I could feel her sweet nectar oozing out her pussy.

"Mmmm-A! Daddy fuck this pussy."

"Baby I'm bout to nut in this pussy. Ohhh! Shiiit! Here it comes."

"I'm about to cum too daddy, let's do it at the same time. Dayyyum! Daddy!"

"Yeeeess-A!" Fuck babe"

I'm cumming and I spilled my seeds into her. Then I just held her rubbing on her big belly with my dick still inside her all limp. I ended up falling asleep. I woke up to Paradise getting outta bed to go take a shower the next morning.

I looked at my phone and saw that Tee-Bae called and texted me, so I returned her call.

"What's good babe, where you at?"

"I got a room at the Holiday Inn."

"Okay, get one of the prostitutes out there to get a room in that same hotel. Then have her sit in the room with y'all until everything goes down. Once you get the key to the room, set it in the closest fire extinguisher box, then have Berlin text Rue the room number and location to the key, also have her empty the stash spot and put it all in the room. Only thing that should be left behind in the van should be the duffle bag with the loot. After the drop is done and picked up, leave the hoe there and head to New York"

"Okay daddy, Ima keep you posted."

I got up, showered then got ready to leave when my mom stopped me.

"Baby, I made you breakfast. Me and Paradise have to go somewhere just lock up the house, Joe is out with his friends and T.Jay is coming with us."

"Okay mom, I love you and will see y'all later. Where is that crazy girl at anyways"

"She's putting your sister in her car seat."

My mom left and I took my plate out of the microwave. Mom had made me scrambled eggs and cheese, bacon, corn beef hash and toast. Yea mom hooked it up. I fixed myself a big cup of orange juice with crushed ice and sat at the dining room table and ate while I called everyone to make sure things was going as planned. I had to bring everyone their Re-up. When I got done eating I washed the dishes I used because my mom would cuss my ass out if I left dirty dishes in her sink. When I got done, I heard the doorbell ring.

Ding Dong!

"Who is it?"

"It's me baby, Anet!"

I opened the door and before I even told her to come in, she jumped into my arms and wrapped her legs around me as she kissed me with so much passion.

"I've been missing you so much!"

"I miss you as well babe, but my mom ain't here and I'm about to slide. I have some things I have to go handle."

"Can I ride with you, I promise to mind my business."

"Yea come on."

I headed to my house to get some work for my team. I fired up on the way over there, as I was driving, Anet reached over and pulled the front of my basketball shorts down and took my limp dick into her mouth. I put on "Young Jeezy Tear the Pussy Up" then turned up the volume. Anet was giving me some Porn Star head. This some Real Boss Shit here, on my way to the money with a Sexy Dick sucking older chick. I pulled up to my house before I was able to catch my nut. I was drained from the night before.

"Hold up babe, you can finish when I come back out."

I put my dick in my shorts then hurried on inside, then I came back out with a black Nike duffle bag with all the work for the day. I put it in the back seat then pulled my semi-hard dick and Anet wasted no time in getting back into the groove as we headed to Headquarters to catch all my people.

"Ahhh Fuck! Ma, you sucking the hell out of that dick."

It was hard to concentrate on the road but I had to because there was a life sentence in the back seat of my Infiniti. I hit all the back roads to Tha Fam's Headquarters. Anet was making loud slurping sounds and humming as she sucked fast and hard. She was experienced, I could feel my balls getting tight. Then I grabbed the back of her head and shoved my dick down her throat, letting my seeds fly as she swallowed every single drop.

When we pulled up to the house, Anet was looking so amazed.

"Is this another one of your houses?"

"Yea, something like that. I got this house for my brothers but I do have a room here"

We walked inside and all you could smell was some Purp in the air.

"Wow bae, someone is smoking some good ass fucking weed."

"Yea, Tha Fam always does, but let's go upstairs to my room."

Anet was looking like she ain't never seen anything so nice.

"Your room reminds me of the Tony Montana Office. Everything was Black, Gold and Red."

"Wait up here while I go handle my business then we can slide."

"Okay babe, Ima just lay in your bed until you are ready to leave."

I went downstairs and two hours later I had served all my people's even Zye came on by. When I got back up to my room, Anet was asleep and her dress rose up above her ass. I sat both my bags down and slid on to the bed beside her and moved her panties to the side and ate her pussy until she woke up and started grinding her pussy back and forth on my face, swiping my nose like a credit card.

"O.M.G. Papi, you eating this pussy? You can't be doing me like this. Fuck! You're going to make me fall in love with you."

I was spelling my name with my tongue.

"It's too late for that Anet and you know it.

"I'm cumming bae, please don't stoooooooop!"

She flooded my mouth with her sweet tasting nectar and I swallowed every bit of it. Then I got up to go wash my face and brush my teeth.

"Oyah, now where do all this leave us, because I'm really feeling you."

"We cool Anet, you got a man, husband or baby daddy, whatever he is to you and me, I'm just living life as best as I could. You know what it was before any lines got crossed. We are friends and if you need anything I got you, but other than that it ain't nothing."

"I'm okay with that, I just want sex, you make me feel beautiful and young again."

"You are beautiful but let's go, I have something to do."

Two weeks had gone by, and today was Bullet's funeral. I truly dreaded this moment and if he wasn't Tha Fam, I wouldn't have gone to his funeral, but I had to pay my respects to a fallen brother and say my goodbyes. I was dressed in Burberry from head to toe. Nadeen and

Amanda said it was a Designer Funeral. I was picked up in a White Lincoln Navigator Limo. When we pulled up at WestSide Funeral Home, there were Nine more Limo's. Amanda got them for Tha Fam, Tha Hyena's and Bruh's Family. Me, Keybo, Rue, Nando, Big-B, Madd-Ball and Tha Hyena's walked in, all dressed in Designer. I was amazed at how everything came together for my Dawg. Everyone looked good even though we were grieving. When they told me everything was designer, I didn't think they meant it literally but the entire room was Designer. The chairs were draped in White Gucci material, he was dressed in white Gucci with his Rolex and Cuban Link Chain with a Medallion that said Tha Fam in VVS Diamonds. There was a Gucci backdrop behind a Mahogany Wooden Coffin. Red and White flowers in the shape of the Double Gucci G's all over the room. It even smelled like Gucci Guilty Cologne. I was impressed, my brother was going out like his true self. The Entire City was in attendance showing Love. I placed a bottle of Louis VIII REMY, A Zip of Purp and a $10,000(ten thousand) Clip.

"Rest In Peace Homie!"

After the viewing, everyone went on 12th and it turned into a Block Party. I had a catering company bring out two dozen platters of Seafood. Shrimp, Snow and Blue Crabs, Scallops, Eggs, Corn on the cob, Sausages and Potatoes. There were multiple platters of chicken, hotdogs, hamburgers and drinks. Everything was free, paid for by Tha Fam. The next day at the church, it was really sad. Bruh had girls showing the fuck out about who was his main, his family sat front row crying. After the church service, we all rode to the Skyway Graveyard and said our last goodbyes. I had the undertaker open his coffin to make sure he was getting buried with everything that was inside the coffin the day before at his viewing. I made sure all the dirt was on top of the coffin before I left and headed back to Tha Fam Headquarters.

It's crazy that my brother has been dead for two weeks. Christmas is almost here and I still haven't heard anything from Armstrong about Piloto. I sat my main Hitters down Keybo, Madd-Ball, Purp, J. Gangsta and Poe-Poe.

"Look, I want dude from Orlando dead before the New Year, we have give or take two weeks. I've been thinking about playing up under Roxanna to get her to bring the nigga to us. He is weak for her so Ima use his weakness to get him where I want him. Ima slide to Palmetto and get in Roxanna's chest and give her an Ultimatum. If she wants me in her life then she has to fix what she has fucked up."

"Yea, bruh, make her bring the nigga to us and we just snatch his ass up."

"Aight Ima slide and put that in Motion, so we can get this shit over with and bring in the New Year the correct way."

I drove over to Roxanna's house and she was there with the baby. I got straight to the point,

"Roxanna I have some questions and the way you answer them will determine our future."

"Okay what it is?"

"Do you love me?"

"Oyah, you know I love you."

"Do you want to be with me?"

"Always have and I always will."

"Would you do anything I ask of you, so we can get back together?"

"Just name it Papi."

"Call Piloto and get him to meet you out here."

"WHAT? Why do I have to call him and meet up with him in order to prove my love to you?"

"Are you going to do it or not, because if not Ima leave now."

"I'll do it but I don't know how that will prove anything to you."

"It will show me that you choose me over him."

"Okay I'll do it because I truly love you and want to be with you and I don't give a fuck about him but it's going to have to be in a few days because Ima have to finesse his ass, because I ain't been fucking with him."

"Do whatever you have to do bae and just get at me and let me know what's up, so I can be in place."

"I got you, just give me some time."

"I want this before New Year's Eve to go down."

"Ima do it before that, it's going to be a Christmas gift from me to you."

I got up, gave her a hug and kiss then I left. She is a real silly bitch, I thought to myself as I drove back to Headquarters so I can put everyone up on game. The night before Christmas, I got a text from Roxanna telling me that she couldn't get him to come anywhere in Manatee or Sarasota County but he did agree on meeting her at a restaurant called "Ocean Flame" on Clearwater Beach for dinner. I told her to take him for a walk on the beach and we can run into each other behind The Hilton by the small pier. Keybo called Tha Hyena's and told them we were about to go on our last mission for the year.

"Aight bet, Ima handle that now."

I called Rue to see how things was going out there in South Carolina.

"What's good Bruh, how is life outside of Florida?"

"Bruh this shit easy out here. The type of money being made out here is unheard of."

"That's what I like to hear. We are having a huge New Year's party and my 18th birthday party at Tha Hyena's Spot, then after the Ball drops, we going to The Outer Limits Night Club to turn up with the hood."

"I'll be out there for that and Ima bring two niggas and a few hoes from out here just so they can see how we living."

"Bet that up and let me know ahead of time, when you trying to Re-up so I can have you ready and sitting aside."

"Well I got your money now but I was going to wait until I come out there."

"Nah, don't do that, Ima send my driver to get you right and pick that up from you"

"Bet, just let me know what's up then."

Me, Keybo, Julissa, Nadeen and Desiree rode to Clearwater beach so we could get into position and be ready for Roxanna to call or text and give us the heads up.

"Papi, what if he was to suspect her of betrayal and kill her before we get to him, then what?"

"Then we're back to Square one and he would be doing me a favor."

Bzzz! Bzzz!

"Babe we are leaving the restaurant now."

"We on go, I just got the text from Roxanna. Let's split up, just in case so we can be all over them like Stink on Shit."

I was posted behind some pillars under the Pier. I could see the rest of my team from where I was ducked off at. I could also see Roxanna and Piloto making their way towards us. Something just didn't sit well with me. Piloto was just too nonchalant. He either felt untouchable, had Hitters around watching over him or he was just stupid and felt like Roxanna was truly his bitch. They was almost under the bridge. Piloto must really think he is going to get some pussy. He couldn't keep his hands off her and he kept telling her "Te Amo Mami" as they kissed and continued making their way under the bridge where it was nice and dark. Tonight is a beautiful night. The sky was clear, all the stars was shining bright and it was in the upper 60's. That was rare for December weather. The moon was a bright orange and it reflected off the Gulf of Mexico. Tonight was a perfect night to die. Under the Pier, they were kissing and feeling up on each other while Piloto had Roxanna pinned to one of the pillars. She had one leg around him making her Dior skirt rise showing off her bare ass cheeks. Piloto was kissing her on the neck and rubbing her ass, while she was struggling to take his belt loose and pull his pants down. I looked around the beach looking for any signs of his goons, but I couldn't see or hear anyone. It was like we were the only ones on the beach at this time of night. This made the night even better. My dick got on hard instantly. I'm not sure if it was from the excitement of knowing Piloto was about to meet his maker on this Beautiful night or because Roxanna was moaning from Piloto fucking her against the pillar. When I saw her enjoying herself, I snapped and said fuck it. I came out from behind the pillar across from where they was fucking.

"That pussy must be fire, is it worth dying over?"

Piloto froze in mid stroke and looked over his shoulders at me.

"Merry Christmas fool!"

"Oyah! What the fuck, You Set me up, You Trifling Hoe!"

Piloto said looking back at Roxanna...

**To Be Continued**
*Been Had Paper 2*
**Coming Soon**